ODELL'S FALL

D1509527

ALSO BY NORMAN BACAL

BREAKDOWN: THE INSIDE STORY OF THE
RISE AND FALL OF HEENAN BLAIKIE

(NON-FICTION: *A GLOBE AND MAIL* BESTSELLER)

ODELL'S FALL

A NOVEL

BY
NORMAN BACAL

BARLOW BOOKS
fine books for enterprising authors

Library and Archives Canada Cataloguing in Publication data available upon request.

978-1-988025-43-8 (paperback)

Printed in Canada

TO ORDER IN CANADA:
  Georgetown Publications
  34 Armstrong Avenue, Georgetown, ON L7G 4R9

TO ORDER IN THE U.S.A.:
  Midpoint Book Sales & Distribution
  27 West 20th Street, Suite 1102, New York, NY 10011

Publisher: Sarah Scott
Book producer: Tracy Bordian/At Large Editorial Services
Cover design: Lena Yang
Cover art: Sharon Bacal
Interior art and layout: Liz Harasymczuk
Copy editing: Wendy Thomas
Proofreading: Eleanor Gasparik

For more information, visit **www.barlowbooks.com**

Barlow Book Publishing Inc.
96 Elm Avenue, Toronto, ON
Canada M4W 1P2

For my wife, Sharon, who created the artwork
for the magnificent cover of this book.
She is where she belongs—front and centre in my life.

For my mother.

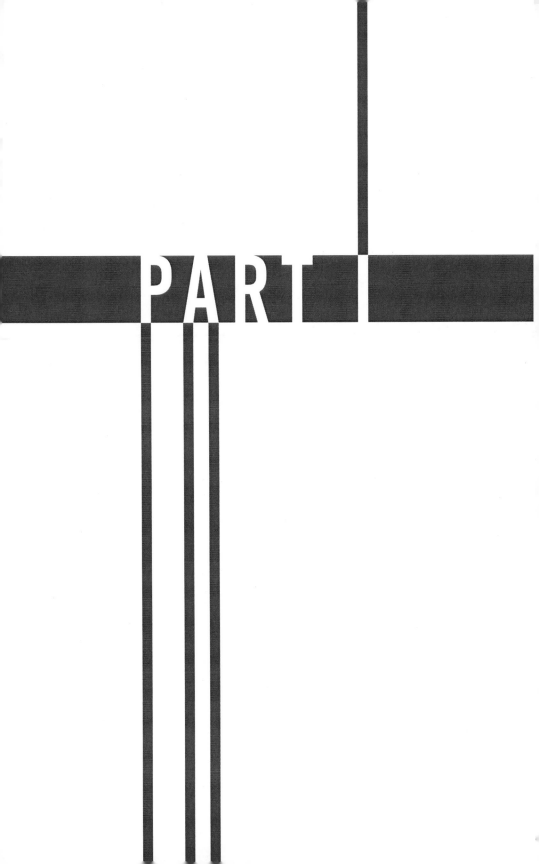

PART I

CHAPTER 1

Odell Moore stood alone, back against the wall. His broad shoulders sagged, his eyelids drooped, and the champagne glass slipped out of his grip, triggering an electric shock. His long fingers grasped for the stem just before disaster struck, spilling a few drops on the beige boardroom carpet. He was not in much of a party mood.

He studied the busy movements all around him. No one seemed to notice. Men and women of all sizes, ages, and colours, his army, reached for hors d'oeuvres from the floating silver trays offered by the wait staff. Some of the lawyers smiled on the way by, careful not to make too much direct eye contact. Odell nodded and tipped his flute. That was the Odell they'd come to expect. Alert to all contingencies. In control.

This was home base—central command—the offices of TGO, on Sixth Avenue, the focal point of the business universe. A hundred-hour-plus workweek, minimum. No complaints. TGO fed you and, if necessary, seduced and bedded you in order to service the clients and their enormous deals. No question this was home, though this was not family. This was better than family. And Odell was their leader.

The secret to leading an army, he thought, is not getting too close—too personal. The key to command is learning who you can trust and, more important, who you can't, an instinct developed early in life. His trust had to be earned.

Jackson Sherman had earned that trust. Busted his rear end on the last few deals for it. A solid associate. And the man could work a room. Waltzing across the boardroom floor, making small talk with the key senior lawyers. Could Odell call Jackson a protégé? Probably by now he could. He just needed to put some time into rounding out the younger man's potential.

There had to be at least forty lawyers milling around, congratulating each other on their successes, their voices growing louder as the bottles of champagne popped, fizzed, and emptied. The men had loosened their neckties and some had abandoned them altogether, though none would dare to attend a boardroom celebration, hosted by Drew Torrance, the firm's chair, without the unofficial firm uniform: the navy or black suit, white dress shirt (though the truly daring wore powder blue), and gleaming shoes. The women wore their skirts or dresses two inches above the knee—no higher, their heels sensible and their toes anything but pointed.

The forty-foot walnut boardroom table in the centre of the room radiated distinction. At one end, copies of the *New York Times* and the *Wall Street Journal* had been opened to the business pages, praising Odell's efforts in putting together the transaction that was going to create hundreds of jobs in Mobile, Alabama. The veil of secrecy that had surrounded this legal transaction had finally been lifted. The troops no longer had to refer to the deal by its code name, though it was likely to be remembered as the "Bounty" deal whenever TGO lawyers got together to tell their war stories about how they had battled under Odell's leadership to get the deal closed against incredible odds and impossible stress.

Odell's team had been going hard for months and they deserved to celebrate. Let them have their moment, but right now he was exhausted. Immediately after closing the Bounty deal, he and Dee had rushed to Vegas to get married, followed by a weekend honeymoon in Paris. He had only ever been there on business and she had professed a love of the Louvre that she wanted to share. What better way to start the marriage? Then it was back to Manhattan to pitch the bankers on the next deal while she headed to Mobile. Tonight he would be off to Houston. There was hardly a moment to breathe much less spend time with his bride.

At least today he could devote himself totally to work without guilt. She had insisted on visiting her parents by herself and breaking the news.

Jackson Sherman approached with a short blond woman in tow. They were both holding half-empty flutes.

"General, I want to introduce Betty Carolli. She's one of our first-year associates. Did great work on Bounty."

Odell extended his hand and smiled warmly. "An honour to meet you, Betty."

"You too, sir—" Betty said.

"Call him General. We all do," Jackson interrupted.

"General," Betty corrected herself, "I just wanted to introduce myself and let you know how much it means to me to work on your deals."

"Betty, if you're working at TGO it's because we see potential in you," Jackson said.

The little fawn blushed. "Jackson's been a real mentor to me. Anyway, I don't want to take up any more of your time."

Odell wondered if anything was going on there. In his experience, office romances never worked out well—particularly if one of the parties was married. It showed a lack of judgment and discipline. It also spoke to a person's loyalty. Odell was probably reading way too much into a thirty-second encounter. In any event, Jackson seemed happily married. At least that's what Dee had been telling him. Jackson's wife, Emily, had befriended Dee just after she moved to New York. Strange how life coincidences worked.

Jackson desperately wanted to become a partner at TGO. It was obvious. His time would come. He had the tools: smart enough, trustworthy, great work ethic, and the ability to scheme. Odell made a mental note to speak to Jackson next week. He could even be given a lead role on this upcoming Houston deal.

The members of his team were a diverse group, but they had one thing in common: they put their personal lives on hold when they had to get a deal closed. When he took on the Bounty deal, Odell had budgeted five months. Instead, it had dragged on for almost a year. The last three had wreaked havoc on his personal life—not that it had stopped him from getting married.

Odell had to hand it to Drew Torrance, holding court at the other end of the room. The old man knew how to run a law firm. He had a sense for the exact moment to say thanks to the troops so that they wouldn't mutiny.

The celebratory toasts began with a short speech by Drew. Odell feigned interest but his mind was elsewhere. The courtship had been a whirlwind, squeezed in between meetings with Senator Brabant. Odell and Jackson had flown down to Mobile to lobby the senator. Jackson's family was well connected to the community, and he had set up the meeting. Odell's mission was to convince the senator to back his client's plan to invest in an Alabama infrastructure project—Bounty. Nothing ever distracted Odell from his mission. At least until the night of the fundraiser at the senator's mansion when Odell caught sight of a woman sweeping down the staircase toward the onyx and mother-of-pearl checkerboard floor that was packed with the cream of the Mobile social set, armed with mint juleps and chequebooks.

Odell had staked out the mystery woman, followed her out to the back lawn of the senator's estate, and struck up a conversation. There was a pace to cocktail party flirting that he had mastered. This time it had started well enough, but within a few moments she launched a counter-offensive to his charm. The usual weapons he utilized to advance were being neutralized by one sharp comment after another. Did she dislike him? He could usually decipher quickly and move on to the next. She was sending messages he was not able to decode. A first. But she was also not blowing him off. Her blue eyes measured every inch of him. Was he getting anywhere? The moment felt right to move into her space for the first kiss. She demurred, slipping just out of reach. Who was the cat and who was the mouse? He hadn't a clue. He was still suffering the bruise of the rejection, when she linked her arm in his and walked him around the estate and under the oak tree in the front yard.

"This is my favourite place in the world," she said. Perhaps he had misread her. This might be the moment. She moved toward him, stared into his eyes, teasing him, then stepped back. The moment passed. He'd completely lost his way emotionally while she guided him toward the senator. She called him Daddy. It took her no time to convince Daddy to invite Odell for dinner the next evening and only twenty-four hours to set the stage for their first embrace. The first of many.

Later, during his lobbying efforts to sway the senator to support the Bounty acquisition, there was hardly a moment when Odell was not daydreaming about his encounters with Dee. If the senator had had even an inkling of what had gone on between them, the Bounty deal would have been as good as sunk. Eight million in legal fees at risk. Humiliation in front of the client.

But neither that risk nor the knowledge that Senator Brabant would never accept his only child having an affair with the descendant of a slave kept them apart over the following months. And now that the deal was done, allowing them to step out of the shadows and get married, he planned to take on the senator the way he took on a deal: with careful planning and a directed approach. Confrontation never bothered Odell. Not after his childhood. But he didn't have time for that meeting yet, and Dee had said she would take care of it. She knew her daddy and was certain she could handle him. Odell had laid out a simple plan for her to follow.

He stepped out of the boardroom briefly and tried Dee's cellphone. No answer. The third time in the past hour.

Odell stepped back into the room and was handed another champagne glass. Torrance was about to make another toast.

"Bravo to all of you and to your teamwork," Torrance said, gesturing around the room with his flute of champagne. "The partners wanted to recognize the Herculean effort you all put in on Bounty."

There were loud cheers and clinking of glasses.

When the din died down and the celebrations continued, Torrance approached Odell in the corner of the boardroom and put his hand on his shoulder. "Your team has really performed."

"I appreciate the vote of confidence, Drew."

"I figure I owe you one. Bounty was our biggest deal of the year."

Odell smiled. "If I land the Houston deal, you won't be saying that for much longer. It also means you won't see me at all until the year-end holiday party."

"Not so fast. Bill Overton called me from the west coast this morning. There's a takeover battle looming at Cypress Entertainment. If the buyer succeeds, Bill will lose his biggest client. He wants you involved immediately."

A takeover battle for Cypress might go on for months. It would make handling the Houston deal simultaneously a real challenge, but not impossible, Odell thought. Dee was just going to have to understand that he might be tied up for a few months until the work flow ebbed.

"I can't get to it until Friday. I'm off to Texas tonight. I'll have Jackson organize the team to gather up all the materials and prepare a briefing memo."

"Which one is he?"

"Jackson Sherman. Navy blue suit and tan shoes standing beside the blonde. He was a real asset."

"Yeah, but I hear you're the one who came up with the genius tax angle to save the deal."

"It's just what I do."

"And the lobbying you did with Senator Brabant? You know damned well that the deal would never have been closed without his support at the Senate Appropriations Committee. That was all you."

"Jackson's connections helped set up my relationship with the senator. I think he has partnership potential."

"He's only been with us for two years. Besides, eight years in practice is a little early for partnership around here unless your son is Jesus." Torrance chuckled at his own joke. "Don't worry, Odell. You asked me to speak with him and I will. It's the least I can do for you." He patted Odell on the back and headed over to chat with the head of the tax group.

It had been nine months since the cocktail party he'd attended at the senator's estate. From the moment Dee glided down the staircase, his personal life had rocketed up and down like a roller coaster. Because of the Bounty deal, Odell had to keep his distance from Dee. He couldn't afford to have a relationship with the daughter of the politician he was lobbying. Far too risky—TGO would never have withstood the scandal if the story got out that he was dating the senator's daughter—but it was a risk they both took. They should never have ended up in bed together, but they did for four months, again and again, and again. That was his problem with Dee. Every moment with her was unplanned, uncharted, unbelievable. Ethically improper, yet the longing for her when he travelled ate him up every night, and when he returned to her after spending a day in Washington with her father, they devoured one another.

He'd put the deal at risk by dating her surreptitiously. He'd deceived the senator about his intentions outside the confines of the deal. Had he deceived Dee about his own intentions? He still had not come up with a strategy to deal with Dee—he was still just getting to know her.

"My body clock is ticking," she'd whispered anxiously between the satiny sheets of the suite at the Paris Ritz, only two nights ago. "We'll have them close together. I want four."

The recollection triggered the same bout of dizziness he'd experienced when she'd first uttered the words. One more issue he figured they would talk about eventually. First she had to face the consequence of their impulsive marriage. Alone. Still no news. She should have called by now. Maybe she hadn't followed the plan he'd laid out to her on the flight home. Maybe he should have trusted his own instincts and insisted on accompanying her. The train in his stomach was barrelling downward, out of control.

"To the General!" Jackson yelled from the other end of the table. "The paragon of thoughtful leadership."

Odell stood to acknowledge the toast and put on a smile. If they only knew.

CHAPTER 2

4:00 p.m., Monday, August 10, 2015
Suburban Mobile, Alabama

Dee Brabant stepped out of the taxi onto the country lane, then slung the strap of the overnight bag onto her shoulder. The afternoon humidity, perfumed faintly by the late-season magnolias, greeted her like a familiar friend, escorting her toward the knoll. Halfway up the knoll, the gnarly oak tree, stooped with the passage of time, cast its shadows over the upper storey of the whitewashed house behind it.

Everything in its place, exactly where it had always been. Everything except Dee. She began the slow climb along the winding grey flagstones that she had skipped along a thousand times as a child. She paused under the tree and leaned against the trunk. Here, her life had been forever altered nine months ago. She closed her eyes, reliving that first kiss with Odell at this very spot. A soft breeze shook droplets of water, the residue of an earlier flash rainstorm, from the leaves onto her shoulders.

She hoped the storm clouds hanging over her head would pass as quickly. Momma probably thought she was still in Paris. Maybe she ought to have brought Odell to properly introduce him rather than go this alone. It wasn't as if he was a complete stranger. Daddy had worked with him for a few months, and Momma had met him here at the dinner with the Canadian ambassador last November. Still, she figured it would be better to break the news without Odell around. "Just stick to the plan," Odell had told her on the flight back from Paris yesterday. "Take them on one at a time. Stay calm. Let them react. They love you. Eventually they'll accept this."

She steeled herself, then continued on her way, waving to Henri, who had just stepped outside with a glass of lemonade on a break from his daily routine.

"Miss Dee. What a wonderful surprise! May I help you with your bag?" he asked, reaching out toward Dee's shoulder.

"Thank you, Henri." The bag was featherweight, but she did not want to offend him.

"Your father was detained in Washington over the weekend, though we're expecting him to return home at any moment. Should I announce you to your mother?"

"Thanks, Henri, I'll see myself in. I still remember where to find Momma at this hour." Dee beamed at the man who had known her since the day she was born. His temples had greyed, but he and three generations before him had been in service to the Brabants since the estate was rebuilt in the late 1870s.

Dee made her way up the sweeping staircase, tracing the outline of the mahogany carvings with her fingertips. Reaching the landing, she stood for a moment and gazed out the picture window overlooking the front lawn. The thickened leaves of the oak tree below dominated the view. There was such a difference between what you could touch and smell outside and what you could see and feel inside, she thought. She shivered for a moment before turning to the left toward the alcove just outside the master bedroom. Momma was in her usual spot on the dark chocolate settee, facing the vanity mirror, proudly erect, combing her long blond hair. Dee remembered the days when the colour was natural.

Momma could have been a beauty queen contestant. Probably still could be if there were such a thing for mothers in their sixties, although Dee doubted that ever would have appealed to Momma. A woman must have a purpose in life beyond pleasing a man, the lesson she had drilled into Dee, with the same determination she brought to every task from tending to the gardens around the estate to supporting Daddy's career. She might have been a success in business had she been born a generation later. Instead she'd stuffed her college business degree in a drawer and played Sherpa on his climb from obscure small-town lawyer to the Senate.

Dee caught her mother's eye in the mirror. The same azure as her own. Same for the high cheekbones, the button nose, and the slight shoulders underneath her silk housedress, though Momma's lips were thinner. Dee's were a little plumper. Odell called them kissable.

"Darling, you're home. How was Paris?" Eleanor's reflection performed a motherly appraisal. "That's some bling on your finger! A new beau?"

Dee smiled. The next words stuck in her throat.

"Wait a minute.... That's not your right hand," Eleanor said, rotating on the settee to face Dee.

"I have something to tell you, Momma."

Eleanor jumped to her feet and came rushing over. "Oh, my stars, would you look at what is sitting on your finger." She hugged her daughter close, then stepped back and reached for Dee's left hand. "My goodness, that stone is dazzling!"

"Not just a diamond, Momma." Dee bent her finger to allow a better view of the two slim gold bands, side by side.

"M-married… You're m-married? Who, when, for goodness' sakes, why? How could I have no idea?"

Dee was holding her breath. Her face felt flushed. Her tongue thickened like molasses.

"Dee. How could I have *no idea*?" The final two words were spoken slowly. Painfully. *No idea* hung in the air. Dee could feel the words encircling her neck—choking her. Cutting off the lifeline to her explanation.

"I'm sorry, Momma," Dee blurted.

"I thought we were close. Best friends, you called us." Eleanor took a step backward.

"We are, Momma. You don't understand."

"The most important decision of your life. You made it on your own."

"Exactly like you!" The words erupted from Dee's mouth in a high-pitched explosion, reducing to ashes what was left of Odell's plan.

Eleanor dropped her head and nodded. "You're comparing me to Grandma?" She sighed, then lifted her head slowly and stared directly at Dee. "It wasn't at all the same. My mother was certain that Edward would follow in his father's footsteps. That he had already joined the Klan."

"I heard the rumours in school," Dee said. The girls in sixth grade could be cruel. Especially when you denied. They crushed your spirit once they sussed the bluff. "Did he?"

"How can you ask such a question?" Eleanor bristled and turned to look at the wedding picture on the vanity. "He was the love of my life. She forbade me from seeing him. We had no choice but to elope."

"And you think I had a choice?"

"Every choice comes at a price."

"What do you mean?"

"Grandma didn't talk to me again until you were born. Do you *know* how many days there are in seven years?"

The question cut through Dee's stomach like a knife. There was not a word to say.

"She finally called me up the day I brought you home from the hospital. 'I forgive you,' she said. Never asked whether *I* forgave *her*. Eventually I did, for your sake. Family is more important than principle. Sometimes you just need to swallow the pain."

Dee wasn't ready or able to swallow. She stepped forward and reached out, touching her mother's shoulder. "Can you forgive me, Momma?"

A single teardrop rolled down Momma's cheek. Dee could feel her own cheeks moistening. "I'm sure you didn't mean to hurt me," Momma said. "Neither did I all those years ago. It's just—look at us. Two crying foolish girls."

Dee reached into her purse for a couple of tissues and handed one to her mother.

"I always just assumed," Eleanor said, dabbing at the corner of her eyes. "Long engagement, showers, parties, proper church wedding. We thought you were close with that banker in Montgomery a few years ago."

Dee's eyes tightened. "Come on, Momma. By the second time I brought him for dinner Daddy had compiled a complete review of his finances. As if that was the only thing that should matter. He made it pretty clear that Maurice wasn't near good enough."

"Did you love Maurice?"

"I had just graduated college. I still had no idea what love was. I just knew I wanted children."

"And Maurice was divorced."

"What did that have to do with anything? It was supposed to be my choice in the end. My life. Not Daddy's."

"Your father knew what you couldn't see. Marriage is hard enough without beginning with a child from a previous marriage."

Dee dropped her head. "I was prepared to accept his daughter. She was only two at the time." Her eyes softened as she looked up into her mother's eyes. "Maybe I loved her more than I loved Maurice."

"So we weren't wrong."

Dee shook her head. "I should have known you were in on it. Right or wrong, I swore Daddy was not getting another chance to interfere in my life."

"I'm sorry, child. We have no right to interfere. If anyone should understand that, it's me." Eleanor lowered herself on the settee, pulling Dee down beside her.

"I'm so sorry I kept the courtship from you, Momma, but it was for your own sake."

Eleanor turned her head sideways, her mouth curling at the corner, as if she were evaluating how any secrecy could have been for her sake. "Does the man have a name?" Her eyes narrowed as the only plausible explanation hit her. The train of modern relationships had run off the tracks and into the bedroom. "I'm sorry. I shouldn't presuppose it's a man, should I?"

"No, no, no, Momma. Odell and I got married in Vegas, and then he insisted we fly to Paris for our honeymoon. He wanted us to experience *Mona Lisa* together. That's his nickname for me."

"Odell?"

"Remember Daddy's fundraiser last November? You held a dinner the next evening. I had Daddy invite a man I'd met the night before."

"Odell Moore? That handsome lawyer. You think just because of your father's attitudes you had to keep him a secret from me?"

"There's more to it than that."

"Tall, dark, and striking," Eleanor continued. "And those broad shoulders, just like your father's." Eleanor closed her eyes for a moment. "When I think back, that's the way I remember your daddy when we first met. Except for the skin colour, of course. And that sexy moustache. A man you can melt right into and who's built to protect you. Not that we Brabant women need protecting." Eleanor laughed. "I suspected something was going on at the time but you never brought him up."

Odell certainly knew how to fill out a dinner jacket. He had caught her eye the moment she came down the staircase that first evening. His dark skin separated him from virtually everyone else in the room who were not hired help. He didn't seem to care, elegantly sliding in and out of conversations in the grand hall as if he were born a Southern gentleman. She caught his gaze more than once before she slipped out the door into the back garden. She hoped he would follow. He didn't disappoint.

Five minutes later he'd approached. He said all the right words, asked all the right questions. Then he crossed into her space after the right amount of time and at just the right pace. Slow and easy. The experienced hunter. A specialist in catch and release. He smelled like intoxicating power, like a man used to having his way, from determining the moment for the first kiss to moving in for the kill. How best to handle him? She thought she knew the answer, keeping him off-balance when he made the first advance that first night and making him wait.

He admitted that he had come to enlist Daddy's help in the Senate on behalf of a client. But he had followed her outside for an entirely different reason. Every time he smiled at her, another one of her sharp edges melted. No man had ever done that to her. She planned her counterattack around Daddy's dinner with the Canadian ambassador the following evening.

She knew exactly when and where the first kiss would take place. She made Odell wait.

Odell came to dinner the next evening to woo the senator, but that was not the relationship Dee wanted Odell to nurture. The fireworks continued to explode between them. Right at the dinner table. Her hand rested on his knee under the table, and she leaned into him at every opportunity. There was nowhere for him to hide—that was part of the fun. She'd behaved like a teenager right under her father's nose.

"I recall that you were all over him during dinner," Eleanor said. "Did you think I hadn't noticed?" Dee shook her head sheepishly.

How much of what had followed could she reveal to Momma? She had never kept anything from her before, but the past months had been exceptional so that the confidentiality of Odell's business dealings could be protected. After months of a secretive long-distance courtship, Dee had given up her job at the art museum in Montgomery and moved to New York to live with Odell, telling her parents she was being sent to research the path blazed by Zelda Fitzgerald early in her marriage—the city was hoping to dedicate its own museum to her art. The story was almost true. Dee had intended to take advantage of her spare time in New York to research Zelda's life with Scottie in Manhattan and the landmarks she had painted in such surreal fashion in the early forties. It might make an interesting Ph.D. project. As it turned out, she'd spent more time researching her heroine than learning about Odell once there. He had been totally tied up with work, secretly shuttling between Daddy and his contacts in Washington by day and Dee for a late dinner and romantic interlude, when the deal permitted a night off.

"He's the one, Momma. But it didn't happen the way I always expected it would."

"It never does, except in the movies."

"Six weeks ago, he took a day off work and announced we were flying to Montreal to visit his mother. His momma is all he has. His sister, Sheneitha, died a couple of years ago, and Marisol lives in a nursing home up in Montreal."

"She's ill?"

"She's not all there. And she's a runner. Twice they found her wandering on the street last winter. The home is a spanking new tower in the centre of town, near a busy highway. She had no idea where she was. After the last episode, Odell hired attendants to be with her round the clock. He covers all the bills."

Dee continued to tell her mother about the visit. When they'd arrived at the nursing home, Marisol was dressed in a peach chiffon dress cut off at the knees, bobby socks, and slippers that glittered. Her thick white hair was braided in a long pony tail that ran halfway down her back in a style more suited to a teenager. Her face was deeply wrinkled, her complexion slightly darker than her son's, and her eyes sunk, but they brightened the moment Odell walked in the room. Odell brought a corsage to slip on her wrist. "That's what Mum loves," he told Dee.

Odell took a seat beside her on the love seat in the one-bedroom apartment and she took one of his hands in hers. There were moments when she knew who he was, and others when she called him by another name. Odell played along, smiling, telling her he loved her, over and over again, even in those moments when she called him Roy. He didn't want to confuse her.

She gave Odell a tender hug, then gently pushed him away and looked over at Dee. "Odell, it's not polite to ignore the young woman," she said. "Give her your seat. Come over here, sweetness, and let me get to know you." Odell stood up, facing the two women. Marisol put her arm around Dee and squeezed.

Dee said, "It was like she knew exactly why I was there. 'You know,' she said, 'he's the spitting image of his father.' She smiled but when I looked at Odell I saw his jaw clench and his eyes tighten. He marched out of the apartment and closed the door, leaving us alone."

"His father is a sensitive subject?" Eleanor asked.

"They've been estranged for over twenty years. He won't ever talk about him. Won't even call him father. All he'll tell me is that Isaiah is the reason why his sister Sheneitha is dead and his mother is like this."

"So you had a few minutes alone with his mother?" Eleanor asked.

"At first she was completely lucid. 'Take care of him, Dee,' she said. 'He spent his entire life protecting Sheneitha. And he always did as much as he could for me. Promise me you'll keep him safe.'

"I nodded and she kissed me on the cheek." That was just before Dee noticed the black amulet on Marisol's neck and commented on it. It had been passed along from generation to generation, going all the way back to Africa when Odell's ancestors were still free. Marisol promised to pass it on to her one day. Then she brought her wrist up to her nose and inhaled the corsage deeply. Her eyes hazed over and she smiled. "I hate to rush you, Sheneitha, but I can't keep my beau waiting any longer." Dee was still not certain who Marisol was talking to when she promised her the amulet.

Dee looked up at Eleanor. "Within a couple of minutes she was calling me Sheneitha. Marisol had run off again to some warm spot in her memories, where neither Odell nor I were going to reach her." Dee had taken Marisol's cold, frayed hands in hers and kissed her fingers. "I know that, Mum," she said.

Now, in the familiar comfort of her family home, Dee found the vivid recollection of that meeting just as upsetting as it had been at the time. "I could feel the tears burning my cheeks after I turned to leave. Odell was waiting for me outside. He wouldn't speak so I just walked over and hugged him. 'I did all I could,' he whispered, 'but it was never enough.'"

"Sounds like you've found the right man and he's found the right woman," Eleanor said, comforting her daughter.

Dee searched her mother's eyes. "We got married in a private ceremony last week. No guests."

"I wish I'd been there, if only to support you. How are you feeling?"

"My heart feels like a helium balloon that's about to burst."

Eleanor laughed. "You're bringing back some lovely memories for me. Right back to my first days of courtship with your daddy."

"I'm still floating."

Eleanor reached out to caress Dee's hand. "If y'all really love each other, you'll never crash. It may get more normal, but it'll only get better."

"Daddy will be good with this, won't he?" Dee asked.

Eleanor withdrew her hand and swept a few strands of hair behind her ears. "You're his daughter, aren't you?"

Dee nodded.

"And he always wants what's best for you, doesn't he?" Eleanor added. "Just be patient with him. You know your father."

They heard the front door shut downstairs and Edward's deep voice giving instructions to Henri about some service work that the Mercedes required. If he followed custom, he would appear in the sitting room in about five minutes armed with a couple of Absolut martinis, straight up, one with a twist and the other with three olives. Happy hour on the estate. Edward was back from Washington.

As he entered the room, he did a double take. "It seems I am short one drink. Dee, I can't tell you how happy I am to see my two favourite girls together again. It's been months. Did you just get back from Paris? Would you like a martini? Take this one. I can get myself another. It'll take but a couple of shakes."

"Daddy, slow down, I'm just fine." Dee rushed over, throwing her arms around his neck.

"Whoa, honey. Let me put these drinks down before your daddy gives you a proper hug hello. To what do we owe the surprise pleasure of a visit from our favourite daughter?"

"You mean your only child." She unlocked her embrace.

"The heir to the estate!" he trumpeted. They all laughed. "What are you two ladies cookin' up?" he asked, leaning over to give Eleanor a quick kiss on the lips.

"Daddy, I have some news."

"Good news, I hope." He took a small sip of the martini.

Dee decided to launch right in. "Daddy, I'm married."

Edward laughed. "Not to some Frenchman, I hope?" When he saw he was laughing alone, he cast a stern glance at Eleanor. She barely nodded at him. "Dee, stop toying with me. My heart's too old to take this. Why're you really here?"

She held out her left hand. The diamond sparkled and the wedding band sat quietly beside it.

"She's not kidding us, dear. Sit down," Eleanor finally said. "Take a deep breath. I know it doesn't feel like it, sugar, but your heart's still beatin'."

Edward dropped into place beside his wife. "I can't even begin to fathom who it is," he mused aloud. "Just tell me it's not that insipid Ferguson boy."

"Daddy, it's not Rodney. That was high school." The very mention of Rodney Ferguson caused her to bristle. The prom datemare from hell. How could Daddy forget that he practically forced me to go with Rodney? she thought. A favour for the Sherman family, who, in turn, were doing a favour for the Fergusons. That's the way it worked. And Dee was the victim. "Now *please* let me explain. I know it's a surprise, but I promise you this is a man you know and respect."

He stared dumbly at her. His full jaw slacked, and Dee could hear him breathing through his mouth. Long deep sighs.

"Daddy, you remember the fundraiser here last November. I met a man; you invited him for dinner with the ambassador the following night."

"Yes, that Moore fellow. Dinner was a pretense as far as he was concerned. He used it as a springboard to lobby me about his client's business issues. A snake charmer, that one, and a heck of a negotiator. He talked Congress into a two-hundred-million-dollar appropriation! What about him?"

"It's him, Daddy. We've fallen deeply in love with one another."

The senator's face turned ashen. "This can't be happenin'. You barely know him. He must be ten years older than you."

"Don't treat me like a child. I'm almost thirty-three."

"He lives in damned New York. Did he manipulate you too?" The words poured out of Edward's mouth like shotgun blasts. Sweat gathered on his brow.

Eleanor interrupted. "Easy, Edward, you're not in the Senate. Calm yourself."

"Don't be telling me to be calm, woman. Not at a moment like this. I'm perfectly calm. I'm the picture of calm. It's your daughter. She's the one in desperate need of our attention. She's gone crazy." He paused. "Wait a minute. Did you know about this, Eleanor?" His eyes had turned fierce.

"Do you think I would keep something like this from you?" Eleanor said with matching force. Her own eyes had narrowed in a manner that seemed unmistakable to Edward.

"Sorry," he mumbled.

Edward turned back to Dee. "I know Mr. Moore is an impressive lawyer, and I can appreciate that he has made himself a success." Edward sounded a little calmer, almost matter of fact. Eleanor's influence. Perhaps all was not lost. Edward took a long sip of the martini. Dee glanced over at her mother and caught the slightest nod of her head side to side.

"Edward, perhaps you and I can speak for a few minutes alone," Eleanor said.

"No need, darling." Edward was smiling, but his dismissive eyes were sending a different message. "There is no room for *that* man in *my* family."

"In *your* family?" Dee asked. She could feel her cheeks begin to burn.

"I do not consider myself a bigoted man but there's no way under heaven that you could possibly have evaluated this decision clearly, Dee. He's a bewitching man, interested in you only until he gets what he wants. Mark my words. He'll take advantage of your trustin' heart, and he'll surely break it."

"Daddy, you don't—"

"I cannot abide this." The train had left the station and Edward was rolling. "And I will do everything under my power to undo the egregious error you've made with your life. It's not too late."

Dee crossed her arms. It was pointless to speak. She had expected a thunderous response. He continued talking but she was no longer listening. Odell's plan: "Wait him out. Don't interrupt. He needs to emote. Only then will he listen. When you finally respond, keep control of your own emotions. Wait for silence before you speak."

She took a deep breath. "Daddy, it's done and there's no undoing it. This is my life. I know it's all happened very quickly." Dee glanced over at Eleanor. "But Momma told me that when the day came, I would know."

Edward's face was now a deep shade of plum. "Know what? Did you learn nothing living in this house?"

"You mean finding the right boy from the right family, so you could mate me with the right stud for the bloodline?"

Edward stepped forward into Dee's space. "Don't get cheeky with me. This is not a game, and we are not living a scene out of *Guess Who's Coming to Dinner*."

"Don't patronize me." Her fists clenched at her side.

"Patronize? This is the real world, not some fairy tale. In this world these types of marriages do not happen. You can't—"

"This marriage has already happened, Daddy," Dee interrupted, her voice a block of ice.

"This will never be accepted in our local circle. Oh yes, our friends and relatives will smile to our faces and tell us how fortunate we are to have our only child finally betrothed and isn't it just sooo wonderful. Then they'll return to their homes and wonder aloud to one another what you were thinking about, how you were planning to avoid the undercurrent of controversy that still underlies mixed marriages in our community. We're not like those fancy-pants Yankees who'll tolerate anything."

"Don't worry. I won't be around to embarrass you. I've already moved to New York where the 'fancy-pants Yankees' will accept me and my husband. And our children, whatever colour they happen to be." Dee rushed to cover her mouth. There was no putting the words back in.

"Enough." Eleanor's harsh tone silenced father and daughter immediately. "Too many words have been spoken already. You both need to take a break." Turning to Dee, she continued firmly, "Daddy's had a shock and needs some time for everything to sink in."

She glared at her husband as if daring him to open his mouth in response.

He turned on his heels heading toward the hallway with what was left of the martini. "I need to take a walk, if you'll excuse me."

Eleanor waited until she heard Edward's heavy footsteps making their way down the staircase. She reached over to Dee and wrapped her in motherly tenderness. "This project may take us considerably longer than I might have guessed. Give him time and I'm sure he'll come around."

"Momma, I'm headed back to New York."

"Weren't you planning to stay over?"

"My plans have changed. I can't stay here. Not now."

"I understand. Let me work on him."

"I had hoped to come back down with Odell next week."

"We may have to put a pin in that for now."

"Then let me know when you'd like to visit. I miss you."

Eleanor sighed. "I will, and hopefully your father will have recovered enough to accompany me. Give him some time. You know the family history on the subject of race relations. There may be some deep issues he needs to work through."

CHAPTER 3

6:00 p.m., Monday, August 10, 2015
Manhattan

Jackson Sherman slipped out of the party at around six p.m. Waves of heat bounced off his office window but he felt nothing but the processed air conditioning of the glass and steel office tower, a champagne buzz, and the taste of success. Bounty would never have gotten to the finish line without him. It had also cemented his relationship with the General. The red message light on his office phone was flickering, and he shut his door before settling in behind the desk.

The artificial female voice on the message machine told him he had one unheard message. It might be important. He had heard rumours about a deal brewing in Texas. There were no secrets at TGO. The General might have thought no one at the firm was aware of what was going on in his personal life, but Jackson had been following closely. Emily was his eyes and ears. He hit the play button.

The voice was old and familiar with the powerful Southern drawl that Jackson had worked so hard to eliminate:

"Jackson. Did you know about any of this? I can only assume you did not. Because I swear if you did and been keepin' it secret from me, I would find that un-for-giveable. Your father and I have been close friends forever, and I would hate to think his son could betray me like this. It's Edward Brabant. Please return the call as soon as you pick this up. I need your assistance. I am *beside* myself."

The senator had finally discovered what Jackson had known for months—that his precious daughter had been having an affair with the lawyer who had been lobbying him. And now they were married. Odell had been careful to keep their relationship under wraps, having dinners where no one could recognize them. It was all so cloak and dagger. At least that's the way Emily had been describing it to him.

He'd noticed them slip out of the senator's house the night of the fundraiser last November. First Dee, then a minute or two later Odell followed, then he'd spied them linking arms out on the front lawn an hour later. There'd obviously been something going on between them after that event. When he'd discovered Dee was visiting Odell in New York, he'd arranged for Emily to befriend her as a fellow Southerner lost in the big city. They had bonded immediately and Emily became the pipeline of information about the budding relationship between the two lovebirds.

What to do now about the senator? The Brabants and the Shermans had been friendly for a century, maybe longer. He and Dee had known each other casually through their high school years. His father and the senator were golfing buddies. Without that connection, Jackson could never have arranged for Odell to meet Senator Brabant last November. That meeting had propelled Jackson's career at TGO. The General was a key to Jackson's immediate future and the track to partnership. On the other hand, having a connection to one of the most powerful senators in D.C., the ranking Republican on a number of committees, and possible next vice-presidential running mate in 2016, was a trump card that Jackson did not want to give up.

"Determine the threat and eliminate it." Those were the General's words. Jackson may not have gotten it exactly but he understood the gist. But who was the threat here? Was the senator going to expect Jackson to do something that might jeopardize his relationship with the General? Could he say no to the senator without killing this golden career goose? If the shoe were on the other foot, Odell would know instinctively what to do. But that was no help to Jackson now. He was on his own.

"Rely on your developed instinct when going into battle." Another one of the General's sayings. Something Odell had picked up from his mentor Sun Tsu, the ancient Chinese general he was always quoting.

Jackson picked up the phone and dialled. He needed to buy himself a little time. Just a week.

CHAPTER 4

9:00 a.m., Tuesday, August 11, 2015
Los Angeles

Michael Cassidy reclined on a leather couch in the American Airlines lounge at LAX. Associates at TGO never flew business class, one of the unwritten rules, but Bill Overton had insisted. This was the biggest file of the year for his most important client, and he wanted Michael to arrive in New York ready to work his butt off. Bill was one of the three great ones, the founders of TGO. If Bill gave an order, it was the law in the L.A. office. Michael was not going to argue this decision. At six foot four, he barely fit in an economy seat. He was as big as any tight end in the NFL, though he had not caught a pass since his days at McGill University in Montreal. He'd come a long way from McGill, and he owed a great deal to Bill.

Michael had begun his career with the firm as the junior note-taker for the legend, but after seven years, he was running deals on his own and without much supervision. Partnership might even be offered one day, if he continued on this trajectory, particularly with Bill's support behind him.

Michael's seat in the lounge afforded a splendid view of the incoming flights rolling up to the gates, but that was not all he was observing. The young blond woman sitting across from him had given him the eye more than once in the past ten minutes. At least he thought she had. He raised his beer and gave her his most charming smile. It worked. With any luck she might be on his flight. Footballs were not the only thing Michael had caught in Montreal—twenty years had passed and he still had not lost his taste for younger women.

He had a half-hour wait to board the morning flight to New York, and there was one call he needed to make before heading to the gate. He put his half-finished pint aside, broke off eye contact, and hit the number recently stored in his phone.

"Am I talking to the world's most high-powered attorney?" he asked when the call went through.

The hesitation at the other end of the line was brief. "Cass? I'd recognize that voice anywhere. How are you? How's the kid doing?"

"Liz is not a baby anymore."

"Sorry, it's been so long."

It had been way too long. After Liz's christening, they had lost touch. Odell had moved off to Europe and then Asia chasing deals, while Michael had to focus on raising a daughter as a single parent and holding down a job. Their lives had tracked in such different directions. Ironic that fate was finally drawing them back together.

"Liz thinks she's a woman now. Wants to go to a school in the northeast so we've been doing the campus tours. I think it's time for me to start worrying."

"Don't ask me about teenage girls. I wouldn't have a clue."

"I can't believe we're playing on the same team again. I always had your back on the field."

"And I never left you alone in a bar. I was one hell of a wing man," Odell said. They both laughed.

"Listen, General. Nothing's changed. You call the plays and I'll execute. Wild Bill told me you've spoken already."

"Wild Bill?"

"Overton. That's what we call him out here," Michael said. "If you haven't worked with him yet, you'll eventually find out why. No way the local office can handle anything this big. That's why he's turned to the Big Gun in New York—at least that's how he refers to you. The only man in the firm who can take on the Turk."

"Sterling Yildirim and I have been studying each other for years. Battling as well. There've been at least half a dozen shareholder fights where we've been opposed."

"He can't go to the washroom without you following him in?"

"If he had the chance, he'd flush me down the drain."

"So you've been briefed. Bill wants me at your office assisting you at every turn. Cypress Entertainment is his biggest client. Anyway, I'm pumped to go to war. Just about to head your way."

"Great news, but I'm tied up in Houston for the next couple of days, so nothing is going live until I return. Get in touch with my associate, Jackson Sherman. I've asked him to prepare a dossier for you. He'll show you the ropes."

"And how about the rest of your life?"

"Shock alert. I finally did it."

"What you swore you'd never do?"

"Yup. She's the one, Cass. She's heard a little about you and our crazy college antics. I'm sure she'll love you as much as I do. I'll text Dee and let her know that she should be expecting to hear from you."

"Can't wait to meet the one who stole your heart."

"She doesn't have a lot of friends yet in Manhattan. I'm sure she'd love the company."

"All right, kemo sabe. My flight is about to depart and I want to be on it."

■ ■ ■

6:30 p.m., Wednesday, August 12, 2015

Jackson Sherman could feel the adrenalin building as he sorted through the Cypress file. Odell had sent an e-mail Monday night, asking him to put a Google Alert on the company. Jackson requested a student to catalogue and summarize every piece of information on the company for the past year: Securities Commission filings, press releases and media coverage both good and bad, as well as anything the media had to say about the senior executive and board members. One of the young associates did a memo on where Cypress Entertainment stood among the Hollywood studios. A second had researched every takeover bid Sterling Yildirim, also known as the Turk, had made in the last five years. Intelligence was the key to success on Moore's files.

The best way to understand what the Turk was likely to do in his attempt to get control of Cypress Entertainment was to study his tactics on the previous deals. How many board members did he insist on replacing? How many weeks or months did each campaign last? How many times had he sued management or the board over alleged improprieties? The list went on. There would be no stone unturned as far as Jackson was concerned. "Follow the teachings of Sun Tsu," Moore had kept advising him on the Bounty file. "Intelligence on the opponent is a key to victory." Intelligence had won Jackson's favour with the General on the Bounty file and made him practically a shoo-in to run the Cypress defence.

Yesterday he had received an e-mail from the General asking him to integrate Michael Cassidy into the file. He'd already checked out Cassidy's company CV. He had arranged lots of acquisitions in the music industry but he had no securities law experience and had never worked on a hostile bid. No doubt he was Overton's boy, sent to keep an eye on the New York team that would be moving out to L.A. as soon as the General gave the word. A team Jackson expected to be running.

This morning Jackson had called Michael and suggested that they meet at the end of the day to go over the material Jackson had pulled together for him.

Jackson heard the rap on the door. He swung his legs off the desk reflexively, returning from deep thoughts about partnership and coming back to reality.

"Is now a good time?" Michael asked from just outside the doorway.

"Please come in, Michael. I was just winding down and the work will still be here tomorrow."

Jackson stood up and shook Michael's hand. The grip was firm, though Jackson's hand had disappeared. "It's great to finally meet you," he said.

Michael did a quick scan of the bookshelves. "The associate offices here are about the same little cubicles as in L.A."

"It might be considered Spartan but over time it grows on you. Laminate desk, one guest chair, probably because there is only room for one guest, basic bookshelves. Uniform in every respect."

"Except for the photo."

Jackson reached up on the bookshelf and pulled down the wedding picture. "A handsome brunette, isn't she? My momma always told me to avoid the *thin cuties*, as she called them. 'Play around with 'em but promise me you'll never marry one,' she insisted. 'Marry a sensible woman with an ample bust and big hips, who can turn out lots of grandkids.'" Jackson laughed for a moment. "Emily's my rock. Always there for me. You married?"

"Divorced. Ancient history. I'm a free agent."

"We can head down to the bar on Forty-sixth or we can stick around here," Jackson said. "I'm on very good terms with the local bartender." He opened a cabinet drawer. Reaching behind the legal files lined up in meticulous order, he pulled out a bottle and a couple of glass tumblers. "Eighteen years. Can't do much better than that."

"I think that's reason enough to stick around here," Michael responded with a broad grin. He lowered himself into the visitor's chair.

"This bottle was a gift from the client on the Western Telecom deal that I worked on in second chair last year. I save it for special occasions."

"Not sure I'd call this a special occasion, but I never turn down a good single malt," Michael shot back, sliding lower in the chair.

"It's rare that I get to work with a senior associate from another TGO office, so that makes it special in my book. Make yourself at home. Something my momma always insisted from her guests. Relax." If they were going to drink seriously, he might as well get Michael comfortable. Who knew what intelligence he might be able to gather tonight.

Michael reclined, putting his feet up on Jackson's desk.

Jackson filled a couple of fingers of the honey gold liquid in each glass and handed one to Michael. "Do you take it neat?"

"Wouldn't ruin it with ice."

"Before you say another word, just inhale. You'll find that if you appreciate the nose of the Scotch for a moment, you can smell the peat all the way from Scotland."

Michael took a long haul on the glass. "This is a major league step up from Pabst." He boomed a hearty laugh.

"Here, let me top that up," Jackson said, reaching for the bottle. Michael certainly knew how to put it away. "Odell Moore suggested I pull some material together to get you better integrated. I've also begun to set up the organization of all the information we'll need on the Cypress file."

"Great. Bill Overton wants me involved in whatever way the General can use me. Cypress is one of his biggest clients."

"This your first hostile defence?"

"Yup. Since Bill took me under his wing, he's sent me all his music industry deals. They can get complicated and ugly but nothing like this. Have you worked with the General before?"

"We worked on a big deal together that closed a few weeks ago."

Michael swirled the Scotch in his glass and sniffed it once more. He tossed his head back and closed his eyes as if trying to capture a memory. "Last time I worked with Odell we were crushing another kind of opponent."

Jackson felt a tingle in his spine as he straightened in the chair. He sensed an unexpected threat. "You know him?"

"Yeah, we're old college buddies. We played football together up in Canada in a previous life. He tossed 'em and I caught 'em."

Jackson tapped his foot slowly. Not a good idea to show an obvious interest and risk showing weakness. More important to keep control over the direction of the conversation and get some personal information about Odell. A chance to discover what made the General tick.

"You knew the General before he was famous? Was he always so intense?"

"I can only talk about my football experience but there's no question the guy was scary focused on the gridiron. Always in control. No one questioned his command. That's how he got the nickname," Michael replied. "After that, we lost touch for many years. I went off to do a master's and doctorate in math at MIT, followed by a law degree at Stanford, and then I ran my own start-up for a few years before beginning to practise at the firm."

"I had no idea you were such an egghead. Why would you ever come back to law if you're that smart?"

"I needed to make money. Long story. Not for tonight."

"Sorry to interrupt."

"Odell headed straight to Harvard law. After that, we kind of slipped away from one another. We speak from time to time, but we haven't seen each other in years. I was happy to hear he got married. He'd always told me his career would come first until he made it as a lawyer, and he said he never wanted kids. I guess people change."

Jackson wasn't so sure. Maybe what people want could change, but they were stuck with who they were.

"It all happened suddenly," Jackson said, hesitating as he feigned a sip from his glass. "When we closed Bounty, Odell was single. America's most sought-after bachelor. Then he arrives in the office last week with a ring on his finger. Doesn't even tell his assistant. Lets her figure it out for herself. He's a very private man."

"Dee's a sweet girl. I had a drink with her last night. I'm glad she finally tamed the ladies' man. At least that's the way I remember him."

This was more serious than Jackson had thought. Until today, Emily was the only friend that Dee had in New York. If the General was encouraging a relationship between Dee and Cassidy, that meant he and Cassidy must be tighter than Cassidy was prepared to admit. What did it mean about the role Michael would play on the Cypress file? He'd need to rethink his approach to running Cypress.

"Do you know much about the General's background? Did he start rich?" Jackson took his second sip of the Scotch and topped up Michael's glass once more.

"I don't know much about his family, but he made sure the entire football team knew the story of his ancestor, Elijah the prophet. He was a slave, but the stories about his iron courage and emotional strength were the stuff of legends. It was inspirational."

"I never would have guessed."

"I got the sense that Odell himself came from a tough background. He was never afraid of anyone. Maybe it comes from his family heritage. Or his third-degree black belt in karate." Michael clasped his hands behind his head. "Or the scars on his back. He'd never talk about that in the locking … locker room." Michael's words had begun to slur. The big man was slowly cooking.

"I guess he's not the kind of guy you want to get into a fight with."

"No kidding," Michael said. "When his eyes go dark, you know he's about to launch lightning bolts. Like the Thunderbird. Whammo." Michael's palm slammed the desk. "We were behind in the final minute of the college championship game. The man never quit and we rallied behind him. No choice. He's a sore loser." Michael laughed.

It wasn't funny but Jackson joined in. A little male bonding. "I faced the wrath of Odell last year just before Christmas. Those eyes frightened the hell out of me. Sent me running out of the office and I didn't come back for a week until I had the answer to the question he asked. First time in my life I understood the words 'if looks could kill.'"

Michael pushed himself out of the chair with both arms and grunted. "Great getting to know you, Jackson. Any idea when Odell returns?"

"He told me to spend a few days integrating you. Friday, we'll begin the defence of Cypress."

"So I have some time to sober up." Michael was smiling broadly, though his knees wobbled.

"Need a hand?"

"Nah. I'm not driving tonight. Just a few brocks … blocks."

Five minutes after Michael left, Jackson stared out his office window overlooking Sixth Avenue. A man was zigging and zagging along the sidewalk across the street. Cassidy might represent a threat. Jackson knew how to deal with threats.

CHAPTER 5

Jackson paced nervously in his office, preparing himself for a meeting with Drew Torrance in the corner office. Why the sudden interest from the chair of the firm? He never met with associates. Maybe it had something to do with partnership.

Jackson knew the rules of the game here. Eight years as an associate before the first consideration for partnership. Almost no one was considered at this point for equity partnership. At eight years the best you could hope for was income partnership. An income partner was a glorified associate. You got a slightly larger office, a raise in your base pay, a small share of profits, but no say in the business decisions. It was a bone all the big firms threw out so that you could tell your clients and family that you were a partner. If you were lucky, it would be three to five more years before they promoted you to equity partnership.

The equity partners had made it to the penthouse of the legal profession. They all made a fortune. Everyone bowed down to them. Sixty per cent of the existing partners had to approve nominees, and only a select number of income partners ever made the jump. Odell had told him just last week that the partnership agreement had a "walk on water" provision dating back to the formation of TGO out of the three original offices in New York, L.A., and Washington. The provision stated that the three founders—Torrance, Gottlieb, and Overton—had the right each year to nominate one associate direct to equity partnership. One per year. The equivalent of winning the lottery. The nominated lawyer had to have special qualities. If more than one associate was nominated in any year, then the losers got stuck as income partners and waited in line with everyone else. Tough luck for them. Gottlieb was the only one to nominate last year, so the rumour mill said there would be no more than two nominees this year. One from Torrance and one from Overton. It had to be more than coincidence that the General had shared this with him.

According to the partners, Torrance was impossible to read. They called him the Buddha when he was not around. He also had a reputation for being a master strategist, building three unknown local firms into a national powerhouse. Until this morning Jackson would have bet that Torrance didn't even know his name. Unless word had got around of his success on the Bounty file. The General did say that he would put in a good word for him. Jackson really had walked on water, discovering critical information about the target company board that the General had asked him to investigate. Maybe this was it? The interview where Torrance would be evaluating him for equity partnership. This could be a lifetime moment.

Jackson's move to TGO had been the smartest of his life. In almost two years, there had been no need to climb over the bodies of any other lawyers to make his way toward the top at TGO. Not after Bounty. The path to partnership was opening wider, until Cassidy arrived yesterday from L.A. Cassidy was a distraction—but was he also a competitor? That was the trouble with New York law firms. There was no moving ahead unless it was at the expense of someone else. Partnership was a zero sum game.

The guardian of the Den, as the office was called by all the associates, was Torrance's executive assistant, Arlene Tousignant, the dean of all the assistants in the office. Wavy hair as silver as her boss, but the cruel lines of time and experience cut into her face. Jackson noticed a brief smirk as she sent him in. Another sheep to the slaughter, she was probably thinking.

He knocked and poked his head in the door.

"Come on in, Sherman." Torrance stood up to greet him. "We have a lot to talk about. Follow me."

Jackson was expecting a big corner office, but nothing had prepared him for this. They walked past Torrance's imposing oak desk and the two Louis XIV chairs. The floor was a red-stained hardwood, unlike the plain beige carpet that adorned the hallways and other offices.

Jackson noted the array of sports memorabilia on the matching credenza. "Nice trophy case, sir." Jackson couldn't help himself. It sounded so ingratiating, but there they were: an autographed basketball, a World Series baseball, a bat with a Jeter signature, and an NFL football inscribed by Manning. It was like the hall of fame. He passed by too fast to catch all the photos.

"Impressive, isn't it?" Torrance said it in a matter-of-fact way. Not bragging. "Come. Let's move to the sitting area."

He followed Torrance to the rear of the office where the two glass walls met, providing a spectacular view of New Jersey across the river. The sitting area, which was larger than Jackson's living room, was marked off by an ornate Persian rug. A solid beige couch faced a matching love seat and chair with an antique wood coffee table in the middle. A fourth dimension swallowed him, a place not of the real world. The climb to the pinnacle of the profession where the air was rarefied. Where he could not breathe. Where his heart pounded. Time speeding up, leaving him behind.

Jackson began to fight the flight reflex. He breathed deeply and tapped his foot. Gather control. Think. How would the General handle this? Maybe this was a game for Torrance? Or a test? Maybe he was trying to gauge whether Jackson was easily intimidated. Where to sit? They still had not shaken hands. The General would give the impression of being completely relaxed. Breathe, Jackson. Breathe. Take charge. Play the game.

Jackson extended his hand and matched Torrance's firm handshake. He held it for half a second too long. Deliberately. Caught himself staring at their interlocked hands. "Look up and take your measure of the man, Jackson. Hold the gaze but not too long. Make an impression." The quiet voice of the General in his ear, reminding him of the priorities. Guiding him for the moment. The General would be studying his subject at this stage of a first meeting. Cataloguing facial gestures, evaluating age and experience. Gathering intelligence on the adversary. Torrance had to be close to retirement, yet his face was smooth, his teeth bleached. No crow's feet around the eyes. An indication of vanity. He could obviously afford the best plastic surgeons in town. His face looked relaxed but something in his stare suggested otherwise. Was it smarter to remain passive and let Torrance call the shots?

"Why don't you take a seat on the couch?" Torrance said. At least that settled where to go from here.

Jackson sat down, sinking low into the plush couch, while Torrance took up the chair opposite, perched a little higher, straighter and taller. Strategic error. Disadvantaged by his lower body position. He shifted forward to the edge of the couch and arched his back uncomfortably, which allowed him to focus on Torrance, but he had lost the first point. That was not going to happen again.

"I don't believe we've spent much time talking to one another, Jackson. Before our young talent is considered for partnership, I like to get to know them personally, understand what motivates them."

Torrance was distracted by something outside the window over Jackson's shoulder. Jackson wondered whether a buzzard was circling, preparing to feast on his carcass. The silent seconds passed. Could Torrance hear the hammering of his pulse? Was the ball in his court? Time to learn the rules quickly in order to survive. He decided to wait it out, though his forehead flushed with heat.

"Is this what you aspire to, Jackson?"

"I'm sorry, sir, I'm not sure I understand the question."

"My office. In the bookcase behind my desk, I have a bottle of hundred-year-old Bordeaux. Beside it is a signed photograph of me and President Reagan taken in Berlin, just after the Wall came down."

"I noticed it on the way in," Jackson replied. Now it sounded like Torrance was bragging. Why? Think, Jackson. Get ahead of where this is heading. He tapped his foot. Pulled his upper body up as straight as it would go.

Torrance continued, "This office has entertained a countless array of stars and newsmakers over the years. Some might be humble about it, but I clawed and scratched for every advantage I've achieved for myself and for this firm. I'm asking you right here and right now, is this what you want for yourself?"

Jackson held the response for four more taps. Time for rhythmic responses. Short and purposeful. "I chose this firm because of your reputation. Please don't misunderstand. I'm not saying this because I care what you think of me." Jackson paused. Fixated on Torrance's grey eyes. Torrance would be grading him on eye contact. A sign of emotional intelligence.

"Go on, Jackson."

"I'm a hard-core deal junkie and I respect what you've achieved and created. I came here because I want to be part of this firm's future."

"And what exactly do you think that future is?"

"Eventually running important deals. Deals that I work on, learning from the best. I'm not the type that likes to sit on the bench. I came here for the action. All day and all night if necessary. I intend to earn a corner office here, sir."

Torrance's eyes gave away nothing. Cold and steely. He was probably mulling over the response. Jackson was not going to be intimidated. Not by Torrance. Not by anyone. He had recovered well from the first disadvantage and hoped he was projecting a certain confidence.

"Jackson," Torrance finally asked, "exactly how much are you prepared to sacrifice for this firm?"

Time to show Torrance how the lieutenant was on his way to becoming the next general. The game plan was set. All that was left was flawless execution. He sat there without responding, maintaining eye contact with Torrance the entire time. Imagining his own eyes turning coal black, like the General. Waiting. Luring Torrance. Teasing him with his own silence. Preparing, like the Thunderbird, to emit the lightning bolt that would scorch the earth, clearing the pathway to partnership.

After an eternity Torrance asked: "Jackson, did you hear my question?"

Moment of truth time. This was no game: it was the rest of his life ready for the taking. Jackson sat perched. Stiffened his neck. Summoned every drop of energy in his universe until the heat raged at the back of his eye sockets. Time stopped moving. The Thunderbird fired.

"I would *kill* to become a partner here, sir." Boom.

Torrance's lips puckered as if he'd just sucked on a lemon. His eyes widened. The Buddha had a reaction! Jackson's heart froze. Had he misplayed it? Almost immediately the old man's eyes retracted into their unreadable selves, but Jackson had seen it. They continued staring at one another.

Time stopped. Jackson's mouth was suddenly dry. His future at TGO hung in the balance. Had he gone too far? Torrance's lips began to move but Jackson could barely process the words. They finally registered in slow motion a moment after Torrance spoke.

"That's the spirit, Sherman. Wicked sense of humour. I like it."

Welcome back to reality, Jackson. The first moments of your new life. "I don't want to take up any more of your valuable time, sir, unless you have any more questions?" Jackson said. He stood up and extended his hand to Torrance. No need to worry about the strength of the grip this time.

Torrance smiled. "I want you to know that some of us see potential in you. It's time to put you to the test."

Jackson passed by Arlene's desk and winked at her. Who was smirking now? He headed down the hallway and pulled his phone out of his pocket to check messages. The first was a note from Odell Moore reminding him of a planning meeting at four this afternoon concerning Cypress. The meeting was intended to last a couple of hours. Everyone invited to the meeting was advised to clear their calendars for the next month. There was a second e-mail from Moore asking him to arrive fifteen minutes early.

Jackson tapped the "accept" tab on the meeting request. Torrance wasn't wasting any time. This meeting had obviously been orchestrated with Moore in advance. He hit the speed dial.

"Emily, my darling, I owe you a dinner and tonight we celebrate. I'm about to lead the biggest deal of my career. Get us a table at Le Bernardin at nine. I'll be tied up all day so text me to confirm and I'll meet you there."

■ ■ ■

Emily sat stunned as the phone disconnected. Dee was sitting on the other side of the small wooden table at Alice's Tea Cup, playing with her eggs Benedict, politely not making eye contact. Emily had opted for the carrot cake. She had taken only a few bites and now she would probably leave the rest. The place was still quiet, before the lunchtime rush.

"I cannot believe it, Dee. That was Jackson."

"I figured." Dee stirred her raspberry tea.

"Sorry to be so rude. I hear so rarely from Jackson at the office, I always take his calls."

She had been answering his calls since 2008. It all started over the summer of 2007. He'd taken a summer job in Kentucky working for the local Republican candidate for the House. She was the sixth of seven children who grew up on a farm in Adair County—she desperately needed to escape. She was the prodigy, the only sibling to attend university, financed by student loans, bussing tables in the cafeteria during the school year, and in the summers doing research for the Republican party. Anything to earn a buck, get her degree, and move to a real city. The first summer he didn't even notice her.

By the second summer, Jackson had developed a reputation. He was willing to do anything to advance the candidate's campaign. He had raised eyebrows in party headquarters. Even some senior people in Washington had taken notice. They were talking about recruiting him to work on a national campaign for the next election. Jackson had asked her to assist in researching the incumbent Democrat, Eddie Canton, digging for any dirt. There was always dirt if you shovelled deeply enough—a public statement that could be taken out of context to allow you to turn the voters at the end of a long campaign. Emily and Jackson spent two weeks cloistered doing nothing but research. Eating together, going through the clips, talking about their dreams.

She had often wondered what he might be like in bed. His blond hairline was full. He would not be losing it any time soon. That was important and compensated for his build, which was not athletic, though still better than average, and attractive enough. His toothy smile melted her. Jackson was a charming schemer and everyone in the party had figured it out. He might not be the most handsome, but he was smart as all hell, had a sense of how to advance himself, and was a couple of inches taller when she was wearing her sensible heels. Good enough to hope something might happen.

A few minutes before midnight on a Friday in late August, she found what they had been searching for. Two years earlier, Canton had made an offhand remark at a Democratic Party rally outside a local slaughterhouse. He said his Republican opponent would be like a "pig to the slaughter." Sixty seconds later, he held up a butcher knife over his head and brought it down forcefully on the butcher block, with great satisfaction. Jackson froze the video clip and spliced the piece together along with a clip of a decapitated baby piglet surrounded by pools of blood. They would run the ad in the ten days leading up to the election. By the time anyone figured out the tape had been doctored, Canton would be finished.

Jackson had been euphoric. He stood up, pulled her out of her chair, drew her toward him, and kissed her deeply. He tasted salty. Almost savoury. Perfect. Until he growled with anticipation. She pushed him away with both hands. "Not yet," she ordered. "You owe me dinner first."

They stood facing one another, neither moving until she began to open the buttons of her blouse. Slowly and with great care. Then she slipped her hand between her breasts and undid the front bra clasp, letting it slip down a few inches. She watched his eyes drop away from hers and kept reading them until they told her that her nipples were bared. Good. She stepped forward. "I want a rain check." He nodded and smiled. Then he led her to the couch in the office of the candidate. He was every bit as powerful as she imagined he would be. She knew at that moment that Jackson was her ticket out. He had superstar written all over him. It was only a matter of time.

And now, seven years later, Emily was at a café in New York and bubbling with excitement. "I'm finally collecting on my rain check."

Dee looked at her blankly.

"One of our in-jokes. My husband is taking me to dinner tonight," she said. "Completely unplanned. Must be his big break. Do you realize this is the first time in months I'll see him before eleven on a weeknight?"

Dee's set mouth suggested that she was keeping tears under control—just barely. "I know what you mean. I'm not adjusting well to this kind of existence. If it wasn't for you and Zelda, I'd be drowning in loneliness."

Dee was not the only one drowning in loneliness. Jackson had insisted that Emily quit her job in advertising three months ago. She was working too hard, getting nowhere, and he'd told her to find something part-time. Easier said than done. She was hoping it was a signal that he was ready to start a family. The first month out of work passed very slowly. All her work friends stopped calling, and nature was not cooperating. When Jackson asked her to get close to Dee, it was a relief. Their first few meetings quickly blossomed into a genuine friendship. "We may be alone out here, Dee. But thank goodness we have each other."

Dee pierced the remaining cold poached egg in front of her with the tip of her knife. The golden yolk flowed indiscriminately across the plate. She showed no interest in eating it. "At least when I was single, I felt more in control," she confessed. "I had a gang of girlfriends back home to rely on. Strange that not a single one of my pals from Mobile have even sent an e-mail congratulating me. Everyone back home knows about the marriage by now."

"Maybe it's the code?"

"What code?"

"The code you broke marrying Odell." Jackson's mother had told her all about it during the engagement, about that higher-society clique that had its unwritten set of rules and double standards to live by. Jackson's mother bragged that while they didn't have the wealth, Jackson's father, also a lawyer, was a member of the right clubs, got them invitations to the right parties, stayed out late with the right drinking buddies, and knew enough to shower before getting into bed at two in the morning. The men delivered the social status. The wives were supposed to shut up and keep the smile pasted on between affairs. Divorce led to excommunication. Showed a lack of backbone. You also didn't marry out of class; that's why Jackson's mother hated her. And you certainly didn't marry out of race. Not if you expected to keep those friends.

"You don't mean what I think you mean?" Dee asked.

Emily nodded. "Not a single recognition? As Jackson would say, *res ipsa loquitor*. The facts speak for themselves. That's why dinner tonight is a big achievement for me!"

"I have my own code," Dee said, cracking the knife back down on the plate. "I put my foot down a couple of days ago. Insisted that I was coming on the next business trip. Since I moved in with him he's been on the road for more than half the time and working late hours the rest."

"And you figured things would change after the honeymoon?"

Dee's shoulders sagged slightly. "Yeah. The last week has been the noneymoon. We barely see each other."

"It's the life we chose, dear."

Dee's phone pinged. "Sorry," she said, reaching into her purse and taking a quick look. Her eyes popped. Then she reached across the table to squeeze Emily's hand. "I can't believe it. We're going to Beverly Hills tonight." Dee's voice was brimming with excitement. She put the phone down. "It's a business trip but that's not the point, Em. He heard me. He was actually listening. How I love that man."

"So we're both going out on the town!"

"Time I headed home to pack," Dee said.

As they got into the taxi together, Dee leaned over and the necklace around her neck jingled.

"Dee, I've been meaning to ask you about that little jug on your necklace. Is it an antique?"

"Odell had to do a last-minute trip to Athens just after we visited his mother in Montreal. Marisol is in a nursing home and she's so young to be losing her memories, but she gave me her blessing and promised me that one day she would give me an amulet passed down from generation to generation in Africa and through Odell's ancestor, Elijah the slave."

"That's quite a blessing." Emily repressed a sigh. Jackson's mama was a mixed blessing. She had to keep reminding herself that his mama made Jackson who he was. Maybe she'd soften a little once Emily delivered a grandchild. "So she gave you the jug?"

"Sorry. The jug has nothing to do with the amulet. Except it does. Let me tell the story. Anyway Odell is away in Greece, something about a re-financing of the government debt. He got back and raced straight from the airport to the Bounty closing that Jackson handled for him. He finally walks in at seven in the morning, slides into bed beside me, and hands me a little black box. I was still half-asleep."

"Not *the* box?"

"'Open it,' he says. It sounds more like a command. I lift the lid and the jug is sitting there on a cotton square. 'I got this for you in Athens. There wasn't a moment that I wasn't thinking about you. Wishing I was with you. When I saw this jug, that's when I knew for sure. This is my way of saying I love you and I want you always. We can't wait for my mother to remember to give you the amulet, so for now this will be our amulet. Our new family tradition that you can keep with you always.'"

Emily was delighted. "That's the most romantic story I ever heard, though it doesn't look very expensive. Especially compared to that ring on your finger."

"That's the point, Em. I have no idea if he got it at an antique shop or from some street vendor. The chain is old and the clasp needs replacing, but it meant he was thinking about me. And he used the words '*our* new family tradition.'"

"I only wish my husband did things like that."

"And it's only half the story. I told him there was only one thing I desired. I meant him. Odell. At that point he didn't need to propose. I didn't need a ring. Except in his other hand, he had a second black box—*the* box, as you said. He didn't even have to ask."

"I swear I'm swooning, Dee."

"I'm calling it the fertility amulet. Four kids, I told him and I wasn't kidding."

"When are you going to use it?" Emily laughed.

Dee's eyes clouded over as if a sudden rainstorm was about to hit. "Not funny. It requires someone who's around to make it happen."

"You'll have a fancy hotel room in L.A. Seduce him there."

"You have no idea how much I need it." Now Dee was smiling.

Emily took her compact out of her purse and opened it. She focused on her image, in the mirror, knowing that makeup and lipstick could transform her from average to extraordinary. The magic of the cosmetic world. "You don't really believe that this is an amulet, do you?"

"Does it matter? I've promised him that I'll keep it with me at all times."

"Then remind him of his obligation to make its magic." Emily closed the compact with a firm click to underline the strength of her advice.

"He's been distracted—and distant. Every time I've raised the subject of his father, he shuts me down. He's very proud, and there's something he doesn't want me to know. He tries to hide it but I can tell when he gets upset. He strokes his moustache."

"Give him time and a little space to open up. You're still newlyweds. Jackson says Odell is a quiet leader but with great pools of passion right below the surface waiting to rise up."

Dee glanced out the window as the taxi made its slow way through the traffic. "When he gets passionate about an issue, his eyes glow. I've never seen it in my life. Well, that's not completely true. I've seen it in my father."

"So you married your father?" Emily wasn't entirely teasing.

"I know Daddy would never see it that way. Not yet anyway. Maybe not ever. Right now he can't stand the thought that Odell is black. It's completely impacting his judgment."

"Have they talked about it?"

"They haven't had the chance. Odell's been tied up with work since we eloped. He's still mostly a stranger for my mother too. I'm afraid that's my fault. We got married so impulsively."

"I know. It sounds so romantic. Like star-crossed lovers."

"Let's not go there. I know how that story ends."

The taxi pulled up in front of Dee's building.

"Here comes Giancarlo," Dee said, almost under her breath. Emily could see her jaw tighten.

"Sexy name for a concierge."

"Not now, Em. Every time I come or go, he gets a little too close. He's always offering to help me upstairs. And he never looks at my face. His breath always smells of mouthwash."

"You think he has a problem?"

Dee turned to face Emily to avoid having to look at Giancarlo. "Half the time he's in the storage room behind the desk. It's almost a relief when he doesn't come out. I rush through the lobby and use the keyless entry code to get in. I keep meaning to tell Odell he gives me the creeps."

"It sounds like you're worried."

"I watch his eyes. He knows I know. I had a boyfriend after university who was an alcoholic so I recognize all the signs. And he could get into the apartment whenever he wants. I imagine him going through my personal items."

Emily touched Dee's arm. "You have to tell your husband. Get the guy fired."

"When we get back."

Dee had begun to open the taxi door when Giancarlo bent over and leered into the rear seat. Dee tensed. "No need to help me, Giancarlo," she said curtly, as she stepped out of the car and pushed by him rudely.

■ ■ ■

Odell normally let his assistant Jocelyne take all his calls, but when the name Torrance flashed across his phone screen, he put down the Cypress briefing and clicked on his headset.

Torrance did not waste a moment to get to the point.

"How are things going with Overton on Cypress?"

"He sent a hand-picked associate—Michael Cassidy. Overton wants Michael to run the file. He says he's ready. I'm a bit worried that Michael doesn't know squat about securities law. I'm in a bit of a quandary."

"Let's not kid ourselves, Odell. In the end we both know who is really running this file."

"The Turk and I have a lot of history. If I'm doing my job, the Cypress board will be following my instructions, but I need Sherman backing me up on all the key technical issues and marshalling our troops for this war."

"True, but you also need Michael Cassidy. Bill Overton insists on it."

"Overton told me it's my call."

"Bill sometimes expects us to read between the lines."

■ ■ ■

At three-forty Jackson skipped down the two flights of internal staircases. He wanted to be waiting for Odell in the Tahoe Boardroom when, in five minutes, Odell would announce to the small working group that Jackson was running the Cypress deal. For the last hour, he had been thinking about the code name for the deal. It would be his call as leader.

The name would be a lot more strategic than Bounty, a bad-luck name if there ever was one. There was a mutiny on the *Bounty*. Maybe that was why nothing had gone according to plan on the file. That's where he had suffered his greatest embarrassment in Odell's eyes, though without that terrible experience Jackson would not have come up with the information that had allowed the General to close the deal. After today's meeting with Torrance, all he had to do was run this deal successfully, and his future would be paved in glory. He would give this deal a name with a better pedigree. An invincible name. Perhaps a Greek god. Apollo. No. Probably overused as a deal name—besides, the gods all had weaknesses. He needed something that would appeal to Odell.

Project Sunmaster. A literal translation of Sun Tsu, Odell's hero. Only Odell would understand the allusion. Their private in-joke. Proof that the lieutenant had absorbed the lessons of the General.

As he made his way around the corner and stepped into the doorway, he almost bumped into Michael Cassidy, who was arriving from the other direction.

Michael chuckled as the two men made their way into the room. "You know, Jackson," he said, pointing at the artwork on the wall, "this boardroom makes me feel right at home. Those grizzly bears are skiing down the mountain at Tahoe. I recognize the scenery. My daughter Elizabeth and I make the trip every February during school break. She's seventeen, an avid skier."

Jackson heard the words but he wasn't listening. Odell was about to give him the nod to run the Cypress file. What was Cassidy doing here so early? No matter. They each grabbed a cup of coffee and sat down. A few litigation partners joined them a couple of minutes later. In all there were soon eight of them waiting. Jackson supposed the announcement in front of this key group of lawyers would make the appointment even sweeter. No one dared to arrive late for an Odell Moore meeting. Jackson intended to run the deal with a tight grip, just as he had learned from the General, and there would be little room for levity once the meeting began. It was not like the General to keep anyone waiting. He began tapping his foot.

Odell dashed into the room a couple of minutes late, sounding breathless, and took his place at the head of the table. "My apologies, people. I hate being late, but Torrance and I just got off the line with Overton, who's been back and forth with the Cypress Special Committee for the past thirty-six hours. They want an active defence to the Turk's takeover attempt. They've left it in my hands to pick the team."

Odell paused and scanned the table. Nodded at Jackson. Moment of truth time. The speech was all prepared once the General made the announcement. Time to smile and begin making eye contact with the partners in the room. A few were smiling back at him. Everyone knew what was coming next.

"Those of you who've been around the office this week may have noticed a new face. Michael Cassidy, to my right, arrived from our L.A. office earlier in the week."

The General dispensing with the polite intro first, Jackson thought. Cassidy waved to the room, to a bit of polite applause. Now for the moment of truth.

"If you have not yet met him you will in a moment. Michael will be first chair on the Cypress deal. Jackson Sherman will be supporting and handling any issues that come up with the SEC along the way."

Jackson could feel the constriction below his stomach. Then a stab of pain as the sharp edges of the words plunged into his gut and twisted. Back and forth, eviscerating him. The General was staring down at his notepad, oblivious to the damage he'd just inflicted. Or maybe he couldn't bear to look Jackson in the eyes. Betrayal. He continued talking, gesturing to Cassidy and then to him, but Jackson could no longer hear the words. Odell sat down. Jackson tried to regain a little focus. He had no idea what was coming next.

Cassidy was now standing at the other end of the table. Talking. Something to do with poison-pill defences. Cassidy didn't even know the first damned thing about a poison pill. He was a music lawyer. On and on he went.

How could this have happened? Torrance had all but telegraphed that he would be running this deal. His test for equity partnership. This so-called advisory role was a bone being thrown, but he was no dog. And now he had to report to Cassidy? How goddamned insulting! That pretender had no hostile takeover experience and didn't have the qualifications to be much more than a lapdog for Overton.

What kind of power did Moore have in this firm that he could override Torrance? Where was Odell's true allegiance? Why would he be putting Cassidy up for the lead when Jackson was obviously much more qualified? None of this made sense.

And then it hit him. Like a foul tip off a Derek Jeter bat, smack on the catcher's mask. Overton must be running Cassidy against him for equity partnership. Overton's boy against Torrance's choice. Why else would Cassidy be here? They were being showcased against one another. Winner take all. Equity partnership to the guy who performs best on this file. That must be what Torrance meant this morning. Except the guy running the file had a huge advantage. And now Moore had given the lead to his buddy instead. Moore was either taking instructions from Overton or he'd disobeyed a request from Torrance. Either way this was a disaster.

He began to imagine the different ways he might torture Cassidy; maybe slip him a poison pill and watch him writhe. He had to eliminate him as a threat to his future. He snapped out of the daydream and began tapping his foot. The immediate task: formulate a plan to fight back.

"Friends," Michael concluded, "we'll have a team of about thirty lawyers on this defence. We meet with the broader group, which includes the securities lawyers, our litigation team, the tax geniuses, and the employment lawyers in a few minutes. The eight of us are the advance team going to L.A. Once we've established a strategy, most of the team will move back to New York. I will remain in L.A. Until then we need to be completely coordinated."

Michael continued speaking. Jackson couldn't believe it. Michael had arrived at this meeting prepared and debriefed, probably by Overton and Moore. Jackson was arriving here cold. He had never felt more disrespected in his life.

Odell took charge once again. "Thank you, Michael. My role is to prepare and then lead the negotiating team from the Cypress board of directors. I understand the nature of the beast we're dealing with. Beating the Turk is our sole priority. These preparations will be all-consuming."

Moore then turned toward Cassidy and continued, "Michael will run the team and make sure we are prepared on every issue before they arise. He, Jackson, and I will set up a base camp in Los Angeles in advance of the first battle. Consider this your final weekend of freedom. We'll get to work in earnest on Monday morning. The Turk's first few moves will keep us in L.A. for an extended period of time. Once we've established the defence tactics, we'll talk about coming back to New York and working from here. First things first. The Cypress board needs to trust us. Prepare your personal lives accordingly. Michael, Jackson, will you step outside for a moment, please."

The three walked out into the hallway.

"I'm counting on the two of you to back me up and run the team beginning Monday," Odell said.

Michael responded immediately. "I appreciate the faith you've put in me. Just to let you know, I'm pumped. Let's drive the ball across the goal line. I can't wait."

Jackson clenched his teeth, keeping his mouth sealed.

"All right," Odell replied warmly to his old pal. "Just don't let me down. Watch one another's backs and we'll be fine. Cass, will you run the next meeting with the broader team? I'm late for an emergency call." Odell hurried off.

Michael smiled at Jackson. "Catch you in L.A. Your flight is tomorrow afternoon. I'm flying out tonight with Dee and Odell. Let's get back in the room and wrap up. This is war."

"I'll join you in a moment."

As Michael closed the boardroom door behind him, Jackson, now alone in the hallway, snapped the pencil he was holding and threw it away in disgust. "Cass my ass," he whispered under his breath. This was war all right.

CHAPTER 6

8:50 p.m., Friday, August 14, 2015

Emily was waiting at the table in the romantic corner of the restaurant. This is where Jackson had proposed to her. Got down on both knees, as if one wasn't enough. The ring wasn't much, but it was what he could afford. She was waiting patiently to replace it once he became a partner. Something like what Dee had.

She knew what she had signed up for: the long hours alone, the phone calls from the office or clients interrupting them at all hours, the weekends when he disappeared to the office without notice, the nights when she crawled into bed by herself. These were sacrifices for their future. She loved the Upper East Side and she was ready for Jackson's babies.

She liked to walk by the private schools in the neighbourhood. One day Jackson would be one of those high-earning partners at TGO and money would no longer be an issue. Hopefully soon. She wanted to be one of those Upper East Side mothers, with a successful husband in a world-renowned law firm, two kids, play dates at expensive apartments, sharing lunch salads with the wives of the elite investment bankers and professionals, the ones who gossiped about their nannies and the latest new restaurant that she just *had* to try. For now she accepted the crumbs that Jackson could offer. He was a brilliant lawyer. His boss at the last firm had told him as much. He also had a relentless drive to succeed. Her role was to nurture. Shortly they'd have a family, she knew it wouldn't be much longer and she really hoped children would mature him and soften the edges.

He had greatness in him, and as long as he could stay out of his own way, she knew eventually it would be recognized. Then they'd be set for life.

She hadn't waited long before the maître d' ushered Jackson to the table. He was rubbernecking every table. Probably taking stock of prospective clients in the room.

"Aren't you a vision," he said. The right words but he lacked conviction. "It's been quite a day, love," he said, as the waiter dropped the napkin in his lap. "I need your help."

Without asking, Jackson ordered himself a double Gray Goose on the rocks with olives and a Cosmopolitan for Emily. After almost five years of marriage he was quite comfortable with her preferences. Or maybe she had become a little too predictable. It would never have occurred to him that she might want something else. She smiled at his self-assurance. She babbled about the day's activities until the drinks arrived. It was time to leave him some space to talk.

"Emily, when I called you this morning, I'd just left Torrance's office."

"The chairman?"

"Just the two of us. He *never* meets with an associate."

Emily sipped the Cosmo. Anything to keep her mouth shut. Let him continue pouring out the good news. She edged forward on the chair.

"He more or less told me I was on the partnership track at the firm. And not just income partnership that they toss out to associates like a bone to be chewed on for a few years. He is seriously considering me for equity partnership."

"Jackson," she whispered, reaching across the table to caress his hand. She wanted to shout his name to the entire world. "Everything we sacrificed for." The tears were welling in the corner of her eye.

"Forget the bigger office. My income would probably triple if the firm has another good year next year."

"I'm so proud of you. I knew that eventually they would recognize the dynamic, brilliant man I love so dearly." Her fingers interlaced with his for a brief moment. He pulled his hand away.

Jackson took a sip of his drink then continued: "That was this morning. He told me I was about to be tested. It could only mean the lead on the next major file, one that had recently arrived at the office. We don't see too many takeover defence files, and this one would be the *perfect* opportunity to make my career." This was supposed to be a good news story, yet the word "perfect" sounded almost sarcastic. Emily withdrew her arms from the table and interlaced her fingers in her lap.

"What's a takeover defence?"

The left side of his mouth frowned. "It doesn't matter, Em." His tone was dismissive. "All you need to know is that it's important and it's work I've been trained to handle. Odell Moore is responsible for the file, and I did a really good job for him on the Bounty deal. I saved the deal for him. He told me he'd spread the word and it must have made its way to Torrance."

Odell singing his praises to the chairman—good news, she thought. Yet Jackson's sentences were racing. A bad sign. Focus him on the positive.

"Wonderful. I just had lunch with Dee today. I'm so glad you're bonding with Odell."

"I was certain I was a shoo-in for this file until this afternoon. I don't know if I mentioned to you that one of our associates from Los Angeles, a guy named Cassidy, arrived in the office the other day."

"Oh, I've met Michael," Emily interrupted. "What a character! He talks as if he was a beach bum with all that California ocean slang. He and Dee and I had coffee together the other day." The words were out of her mouth as it dawned on her that Cassidy's name had been spit out of Jackson's mouth. She felt a small rise of panic in her belly. She had missed the cue. Jackson's face was turning red. If it got to purple the evening was over.

"You know him and you never mentioned it?"

"I … I … had no idea it mattered," she stuttered.

"He's my problem. At our strategy meeting this afternoon, Odell chose Michael to run the file and gave me a secondary role to play." Jackson was almost shouting now. "I'm screwed." Every head in the restaurant seemed to be looking at her. Her fingers were clasped so tightly that they were throbbing. None of this made sense and all she wanted to do was bolt. Would he even notice? He wasn't with her anymore, he was living in his head. Damn. Not the first time either. She took a deep breath. You are not the enemy, the little voice of reason in her head was whispering. You're the only one who can steady the boat and save your dreams. Take on Jackson's bow. Let him ride your wave to shore. Never broadside him with criticism.

"Easy, Jackson." She pushed the words out in a slow rhythm.

"I don't like it one bit," he continued, "I've been squashed. Torrance, the head of the entire firm, more than intimated that this file was mine and somehow Odell trumps him? I tell you, Emily, I won't accept this."

She could feel herself calming. She needed to sound reasonable. Re-take control. That's what Jackson needed. "Why would Odell do that?" she asked in a kindly tone.

"I'm not sure. Cassidy certainly doesn't have the experience to run this file. Bill Overton in Los Angeles must be endorsing him to become an equity partner."

The entire corner of the restaurant could probably still hear all this. The waiter was standing a few steps behind Jackson, ear tilted toward the table. Emily threw a sharp glance over Jackson's shoulder. The waiter took off.

"Jackson, slow down," Emily said quietly. "What if the firm is considering both you and Michael? What's wrong with that? Can't they make both of you equity partners?" Her voice had lowered to a whisper.

Jackson took another gulp of the vodka. She hoped he had eaten lunch today. The waiter arrived with a second, which he exchanged without being noticed, and quickly disappeared.

"At TGO there's a rule. Only one per year." At least the tone of his voice had calmed. This was a private conversation again. But his tone was no less melodramatic. "So it's him or me for all the marbles. No runner-up. If he succeeds on this file, I'm toast."

She reached for the Cosmo and took a long sip. The cranberries balanced the sweetness of the triple sec and she barely noticed the vodka.

That's why she loved them. She needed to balance Jackson. "Didn't you just tell me how much Torrance likes you? He's the chairman of the whole firm."

"That's the point. The associates and partners already know that Torrance has his eye on me. If I don't make it, they'll just assume I failed. I'll be a laughing stock."

It was like 2013 all over again, she thought. That was when one of the partners of the old firm had asked him to handle some kind of securities registration all over the United States. Jackson's research found a potential technical problem in Massachusetts. He advised the partner, who disagreed with Jackson's legal interpretation and overruled him. Two days before closing, the lawyers on the other side pointed out the same problem. Jackson had been right all along. The last-minute correction cost the client $100,000.

A month later at a meeting of the securities lawyers, the partner talked about how it was the duty of the associates to provide the partners with correct advice and not embarrass them in front of clients. He didn't name Jackson but he was obviously blaming him—hanging him out to dry—and it was the partner's fault! Probably no one even knew who he was talking about. But Jackson knew. He came home that night to rant, furious at the partner's lack of character in embarrassing him in public like that. She'd tried to reason with him. To talk him down. The next day she worried about what he might do. He came home that night filled with excitement and energy. He had told off the coward. He made sure everyone in the room knew this guy could not be trusted.

That was the end of the line for Jackson at the firm. Maybe it was all for the best. TGO had been already been approaching him through a head hunter so the story never got out. Emily could not let that happen again. Her words were a starting point, but ultimately her actions were the only way to save him from himself, if that was even possible.

"The fact that Torrance has met with you at all suggests he has a very strong opinion of you," she said evenly.

Jackson shook his head. "I've watched the partners in this firm. They try to keep the associates in the fold as long as they can by making promises, but we're just fodder for their profit-making machine. In the end, it's *their* club and they play by *their* rules. I need to fight back. If that means taking Michael Cassidy down, then that's what we're going to do … and if Moore comes down with him…"

"Jackson, I think you may be taking this a little too hard and too fast. Why would you want to hurt Odell? Isn't he a source of important work for you? Think about it … you asked me to take care of Dee in order to keep an eye on them and to improve your relationship with Odell. He could be an important ally."

"Good point." Jackson picked up the glass, then put it back down slowly. He reached for the water glass instead.

Emily decided to stay quiet and let Jackson deflate on his own.

"You're right. I'm playing this all wrong. Odell is not the enemy. It's Cassidy. I need to come up with a plan to get between Michael and Odell. If I can disrupt their relationship, then I can unsettle Michael. It won't take much."

She nodded to the waiter, who was serving the table beside them. Maybe if she could get Jackson eating, he would calm down.

"Jackson, slow down and think. Your star has been rising. Odell and Torrance as much as told you so. I think you're reading too much into this. Maybe you should just have an honest discussion with Odell about what's bothering you."

Jackson was drumming his fingers on the table. Never a good sign. "Create a distraction for Cassidy and throw Moore a little off balance. But how?" Jackson's eyes half closed. His foot started tapping on the floor. No stopping the cogs turning in his head.

Two waiters in snowy-white coats that matched the tablecloths arrived to set a dish before each of them simultaneously and with a grand flourish. The younger waiter with the thick moustache proudly lifted the domes and announced with a pronounced French accent, "Here we have a yellowfin tuna carpaccio, accompanied by an Iberico ham chutney and sea beans, marinated in lemon and extra virgin olive oil. Please enjoy."

As the wait staff stepped away, Jackson slowly lifted his eyes, which had been transfixed on the plate.

"Did they ever bring the menus? Have I been so distracted that I don't remember ordering?"

"Sweetheart, when I made the reservation I told them we wanted the chef's tasting menu this evening. At some point you're going to have to relax and enjoy this wonderful food."

Jackson sighed. "Emily, you always know how to handle me. Why don't we leave the scheming for dessert?"

She was relieved to switch the subject to something a little more neutral. "You know, Jackson, I've really become fond of Dee."

"That's my girl."

"It's been easy. I think she's sweet and very friendly. I watched her with Michael the other day. He was busy teasing her, wrapping his arm around her shoulder on more than one occasion. They both love Odell and spent most of the day talking about him."

"The Dee I remember from high school is no Snow White. At least based on the locker-room rumours about how fast she moved from first base to third. Unless she's settled down, Odell has no idea what Dee is capable of. He has his hands full with her."

The barely cooked scallop in a warm butter sauce arrived next, and they interrupted the conversation to enjoy the scents wafting off the plates. Emily closed her eyes and took a bite of the scallop. It tasted like heaven.

"Watching you eat that scallop is better than sex." Jackson was smiling now.

His blue eyes softened. She felt a familiar tingle—it went right back to her first night with him. "Save that appetite for later, my dear. We'll enjoy the final course in the bedroom. I assure you that what I have in store for you will exceed even the most advanced capacities of this chef."

"Then I need to cool off for now. Tell me more about Dee."

"Well, here's a bit of news I picked up. Just before he gave her the engagement ring, Odell gave Dee a little trinket. Dee calls it the fertility amulet."

"Really? He doesn't seem the type to believe in superstitions."

"You're missing the point, Jackson." He was always missing the point. Why couldn't he, just one time, do something as romantic as buying her a piece of jewellery for no reason. Even cheap jewellery would mean he was thinking about her the way Odell thought about Dee. "It's just a little silver jug on a chain. She wears it around her neck. I think she's hoping it will do its magic in the fertility department, if you get my drift."

"Do you mean what I'm going to do to you later tonight?"

"Why sir, those are not appropriate restaurant manners."

"Did you want restaurant manners tonight?"

"Maybe not." She smiled then reached for her smartphone. "Sorry, Jackson, it's a text from Dee." Emily read the note quickly and tapped off a quick response. "Dee says she has a bad feeling she forgot to turn off one of the appliances. They're just about to take off."

"I know. They're headed for L.A. So why don't they just send the concierge in?"

"Long story but she doesn't like the idea of the concierge going into the apartment. She sent me the codes. I'll just run up for two seconds on the way home."

Jackson grinned at her and said, "I suppose it's time to unveil tonight's surprise. We're flying to Beverly Hills tomorrow. We have a suite reserved at a luxury hotel."

She could feel herself jumping out of the chair. "Beverly Hills and you're just telling me this now! There's barely enough time to pack. Jackson, how thrilling," she exclaimed. "This is a wonderful sign for your future."

"I wouldn't mind the experience of living like a partner of this firm," he added with a bitter-cocoa-powder tone that worried her. She needed to reground him. Again and again and again.

"So you haven't yet become one of those jaded Upper East Side women who only care about how much money their husbands earn and how quick they can move up the society ladder?" he teased.

"Oh, Jackson, you should know better than that. I'm still a Kentucky girl at heart."

"Why don't we kill two birds with one stone?"

"Two birds?"

"Yes, we'll visit Dee's apartment and you'll get me the amulet," he said.

Her smile disappeared as her stomach sank. "You want me to steal the amulet?"

"I wouldn't call it stealing. Just borrow it. I don't need it for long and don't ask me to explain. Hopefully it's in the apartment. If not, just figure out a way to get it from Dee."

"Jackson, I'm really not comfortable with this. Dee's my friend. She trusts me. Anyway, I'm sure she took it with her—it's not often off her neck."

"Never mind then. It was just an impulsive idea."

And stupid too, she thought. What was he thinking? She needed to keep a close eye on him for the next few days. Keep him focused on the prize. Stroke him and guide him. Show him she trusted him. "You know I can never say no to you."

"That's what I'm counting on for later tonight."

■ ■ ■

Early the next morning, Jackson was at Odell's building. Opening Emily's phone and transcribing the key codes from Dee's e-mail after Emily fell asleep last night was not a sin, he thought. He had a story ready for the concierge, but fortunately no one was at the desk. Maybe he was out on rounds.

As the elevator rose to the penthouse, he noted that his heart was beating a little faster and his palms were sweating. He had convinced himself that he could handle a break and enter calmly and without much emotion, but he was beginning to believe otherwise. He had a flash of his arraignment hearing, where he would plead guilty as charged of snooping. He smiled at the thought.

Once upstairs, he used the code to enter the penthouse suite. Someone had thought about privacy when they designed the entrance. The door opened into an alcove and the light poured into the suite from the left. He tiptoed in. The sound of a toilet flushing. Shoot. He retreated toward the door and froze. At least he could not be seen from the main room from here. He'd forgotten to check with Emily as to whether they had a cleaning lady. Holding his breath, he waited to hear the footsteps or whistling, or some other sound of the housekeeper. Nothing but silence for a long time. Must have been from the suite next door. He stepped cautiously into the living room, then felt his shoulders and neck relax. Jackson admired the glow on the hardwood floors, reflecting the sunshine flowing in through the eastern exposure. He was attracted to some of the African sculptures sitting on various end tables set between the dark grey leather sofa and love seat backing onto the floor-to-ceiling windows. There were three wood carvings of a father and two young sons that might have been done on a Caribbean island, as well as a twelve-inch-high bronze statuette of a female form standing on a pedestal just to his left, at the juncture where the room opened up. The woman's protective gaze was fixed on the father and sons across the room. Jackson reached for the statuette. The woman's lips were slightly turned down, her eyes narrow, as if she sensed a looming danger. It was smooth to the touch, weighing about three pounds. It felt cold and comfortable in his grip as he eased it back to the pedestal he had taken it from.

"So this is how the other side lives," he muttered. "I could get used to this."

Two Impressionist canvasses adorned the walls. He didn't recognize the artists' signatures—not that he followed the art scene.

Jackson made his way into the bedroom and carefully opened and closed the drawers in Dee's night table and walk-in closet. He located her jewellery box but the amulet was not there. She must have taken it with her. He would have to change his hastily conceived plan.

CHAPTER 7

11 a.m., Sunday morning, August 16, 2015
Los Angeles

It was an hour before midday in Los Angeles, and the morning smog had lifted, unusual for this time of year. The boardroom of the TGO offices, set high in one of the Century City towers, offered Odell a crystal-clear view of the Hollywood Hills in the far distance. The invisible mansions in those hills were filled with billionaires, and right beside them, hidden in the ravines, were the coyotes and the homeless. The cute predators and the society of unwanted, all lurking in the underbrush. They lingered just beneath the surface but emerged every so often to remind the rich and successful that they could not be ignored, that they might be threats to the security of their families. Just, Odell thought, like the secrets he did not want to confront. But now was not the time—not with the most important deal of the year within reach.

This was Odell's first visit to L.A. in years. It was also his first brush with the entertainment industry, which was exclusively the business of TGO's L.A. office, where Wild Bill Overton was the master. Michael had obviously been doing well there. Torrance had told Odell that Cassidy was being groomed, but Torrance was cryptic at the best of times. What exactly was Michael being groomed for? Perhaps he was Wild Bill's hand-picked successor as leader of the entertainment group. All in good time. At seventy-two there was still a little tread on Overton's tires, and everyone in the office still treated the founder of the office like a god. Odell couldn't help but notice that even on a Sunday morning, a group of young local lawyers were hanging on his every word.

Odell turned back from the window to the boardroom where the group had cloistered themselves. The space had been converted into a war room, a place where strategy could be worked out to plan for the oncoming attack of Sterling Yildirim's team. Seated next to Odell was the chief legal officer of Cypress Entertainment, Oliver Neville. Oliver had been with the company for fifteen years, having been acquired along with the other assets of a film distribution company that Cypress had purchased. The gregarious, no-nonsense South African had survived the merger and slowly worked his way up the corporate ladder. Those were the early days of growth for Cypress and represented the first of many film and television additions.

The meeting with Oliver and the Cypress board's special committee had ended five minutes ago. Overton had taken a few members of the committee, including a former state governor, out to lunch. Odell was satisfied he had accomplished the first objective for this morning—getting Oliver comfortable with Michael and Jackson. It was not necessary to keep the two of them busy on a Sunday, and he felt a little guilty that Dee was on her own on her second day out here.

He turned to Michael and Jackson, who were seated to his left. "I'm headed back now with Oliver to the Cypress office. We're going to be holed up with the board committees for the balance of the day and probably night. Why don't the two of you take some time off."

"You don't need us?" Michael asked.

"Nothing's really going to happen until the Turk makes the next move. Jackson, this might be the only time you get to spend with your wife. Michael, you're the local boy. Why don't you show Dee the town?"

"Feeling guilty?" Michael asked with a smile. "Happy wife, happy life."

"She wanted to come on the trip, but I don't want her to feel deserted."

"As you command," Michael said, showing his usual enthusiasm for anything Odell asked.

"You sure, General? There's a reason you asked us to be out here with you today," Jackson said.

"Noble gesture, but really not necessary. This may be the last you see of Emily for quite a while." Jackson reminded Odell of his younger self. He wasn't sure what he would do if asked to take a day off when the boss was working. Jackson was probably over-compensating for the disappointment of not running the file. Good that he had responded to the adversity by putting his head down and offering to work harder, but as soon as the pressure on this deal subsided, Odell would explain the firm politics and give Jackson the news he had to be wishing for. He was going to get the lead on the Houston file. High competence and trustworthiness. The key elements when combined with work ethic were going to make Jackson's career just as they had served Odell.

■ ■ ■

The Cypress offices were tomblike on a Sunday afternoon. Oliver waved hello to the sole assistant as he and Odell headed down a long hallway. The hall had no end in sight—sometimes battles with the Turk went the same way, Odell reflected. He felt as though he knew Sterling Yildirim from the inside out.

"I've been following the Turk for my entire career," Odell said.

"I remember him as well," Oliver said. "Down in J'berg in the late eighties the papers called him a corporate raider. You know his name isn't really Sterling?"

"Never thought about it."

"His name has about fifteen letters. Mostly consonants. When he made his first killing it was in the silver futures market."

"I get it."

"Then in '88 he bought up one of South Africa's biggest publicly traded manufacturers. Borrowed a fortune in a leveraged buyout and sold off the pieces. He used other people's money and made a fortune but four thousand employees were put out of work. When you say the name Yildirim to any of my South African friends, they spit on the ground all these years later."

Odell wasn't at all unhappy when the likes of Yildirim's colleague Michael Milken ended up in jail. He thought that might change the Turk's approach. Except all Yildirim did was to rebrand himself. He returned in the new the millennium as a "shareholder activist," whose supposed role was to create value in a company whose management was soft or lacking in vision. Odell had to laugh at the way the media kowtowed to him. Had he really changed? Was he really an activist? Not to Odell. Yildirim was and would always be the pirate—in it for no one but himself and his investors.

"What do you think Yildirim's next move is going to be?" Oliver asked, his South African inflection softened slightly by his twenty years in America.

"The Turk's an enigma. Some CEOs of the companies he invests in swear by him. Others swear *at* him."

They turned into the kitchen. "Let me pour you some coffee," Oliver said, reaching for a Cypress mug. "So we don't know if Yildirim's a good guy or a bad guy?"

"It really depends which script he adopts. In very short order it will rain press releases and he'll be ranting at you on Fox and CNBC."

"Should I be asking our PR people to prepare a counterattack to that bad press?"

Odell added some cream to his coffee and took a sip, while Oliver filled the kettle to make tea for himself. Odell said, "If Yildirim wants to threaten war, he'll begin by publicly outlining the weaknesses of management, the way they're squandering investor money and he wants to curb all the corporate waste. He'll start fabricating rumours about your CEO and his profligate spending habits on the corporate jet, the lavish dinners, the Hollywood parties."

"Hard to counter."

"Exactly. Yildirim knows that. If we say our CEO is honest, it sounds very defensive. Yildirim's goal is to make the market price of the stock drop so that he can take control for the cheapest possible price."

"How cheap is cheap?" Oliver took a teabag from the cupboard and dropped it in his mug. "I can't stand this fake American stuff—talk about cheap—but I can't be without tea. At least I can make it properly." He poured boiling water over the teabag, gave it a quick stir, then added a little milk from a carton in the fridge.

"Pity." Odell smiled at his own very British response. It was a pitiful way to make tea, but Odell was not about to correct the client. Any Brit would use a proper teapot, warmed in advance and sitting in a cozy. Then give it a few minutes to steep. But this was America where everything had to be done instantly and Oliver was South African. They probably rejected all things British.

Oliver shot him a quizzical look. "I don't get it."

"The line is from an old Canadian television commercial for a particular brand of tea," Odell explained. "You call it fake, yet you drink the stuff."

"I spent my first two years as a lawyer working for Hugh Hefner in the Playboy mansion. I learned very quickly to appreciate what was fake."

Odell studied Oliver more carefully. He was fighting middle-age spread, but there was a sparkle in his smile and his sturdy face was well proportioned. He had probably been quite attractive as a young man. "You'll have to give me details some night when we have the time. Sounds like every teenage boy's fantasy," Odell said, then paused before continuing. "Back to the matter at hand. If the Turk can get control by buying as little as twenty-five per cent of the stock at depressed values, he will do just that. He will then get his board seats and replace upper management."

"But he doesn't always use that strategy?" Oliver asked.

"No, in other cases his complaints will be lower key. He won't actively undermine management, but he'll let it be known that there are two or three things he'd do differently. This is usually a telegraph that he'll accept two board seats but will otherwise not actively impose his will as long as a couple of his suggestions are acceptable to existing management."

Oliver blew softly on his mug of tea as Odell was completing his thesis. "I can't believe that we just have to sit back and wait for him to attack. It's not my style and the board will hate it."

"I have a different plan for this defence, Oliver. Something that Yildirim will not be expecting. I've been in touch with our office in Abu Dhabi to get some intelligence on Yildirim's holdings in the region. You may remember three years ago he went into partnership with one of the sheik's sons on an oil refinery plant just outside Riyadh. It was a multi-billion-dollar investment that would keep all the profits in the country rather than shipping crude oil."

"I remember it vaguely. What does an investment in Saudi have to do with us?" Oliver frowned.

"One of the Saudi princes was having lunch with my partner last week and mentioned that the sheik is very upset with Yildirim. He insisted on replacing management with his own people who have no sense of the way things are done locally. They're very worried about security, and it's being whispered that many of the new employees are foreign nationals, hired to save on wages. They're not doing appropriate security clearance."

Oliver leaned against the kitchen counter. "You've lost me, Odell." Oliver took a sip of his tea. He had not bothered to remove the bag. Odell supposed the South African liked it well steeped.

"I've got a team of Middle East publicity experts ready. Let's have them make a big deal about the labour issues there. If we can distract Yildirim right now, he may conclude he has enough on his hands to worry about."

"You want to muddy the waters?" Oliver said, swirling the remaining strong tea.

"We need a distraction to buy us time. Doesn't Cypress have a block-buster movie coming out in a few months?"

"We can never know for sure which of our pictures is going to work for us. It's called *The Survivor*. A movie about a dystopian universe. It's all the rage these days. We're about to spend fifty million on the advertising campaign. It's all superheroes, monsters, and special effects."

"I'm not one to judge," said Odell.

"Nobody is," Oliver admitted. "Even our head of theatrical production was not certain when we green-lighted it."

"What are its chances?"

"We lucked out. The girl playing the lead superhero just got nominated for an Oscar on her last picture. She's only eighteen and her social media presence is enormous. Twenty-eight million followers. The test results are through the roof. We figure it will do at least $70 million at the box. What we don't know is if we're sitting on a $600 million movie."

"And if it does big numbers, won't your stock price move?"

"Anywhere from two to five dollars a share. We have a prequel and a sequel planned. The franchise could be worth billions. That's Hollywood."

"So do the math. If we can buy some time and the stock price moves up, it will make the cost of buying more of your shares too expensive. The Turk is a bottom feeder. If he can't get Cypress at a bargain, he'll just sell the stock he's already bought for a nice profit and walk away from Cypress."

Oliver thought for a moment. "I'll need you to explain this plan to my board and to the CEO as soon as possible. Can you be with me to explain to the special committee and ultimately the board about their duties and obligations to our shareholders?"

"Of course, Oliver. I understand completely. I came to L.A. prepared for some very long days while all this plays out."

"I hope your family won't miss you too much," Oliver said.

"It may be a small consolation for my wife, but she came on the trip. I invited Jackson's wife as well. All on the firm's dime. My best guess is that they're out shopping on Rodeo Drive as we speak."

■ ■ ■

Emily strolled through the extravagant lobby of the Beverly Wilshire Hotel. Incredible. The kind of place waiting just around the corner in her future. The marble floors were freshly polished and the display cases showed off the newest in designer clothing, Panerai watches, Fendi purses, high heels, and fur wraps. Who could have guessed that through the Depression this had been an apartment hotel next to a speedway. In the forties the owners had imported marble from Italy and used it to turn the main building into a showpiece. Later they built a modern second building behind the cobblestone driveway. Now it was at the heart of a high-end shopping Mecca. At least that's what the waiter had told her at breakfast this morning.

Dee was waiting for her at the front door and they eagerly stepped out under the white and royal purple awnings adorning the front of the building. The brilliant sunlight had them reaching into their purses to retrieve their sunglasses. To the left, hotel guests were enjoying late morning coffees at the restaurant tables fronting on Wilshire Boulevard. Tourists were already lining up to take photos at the famous intersection where Rodeo Drive meets Via Rodeo, an exclusive area of high-end stores, art galleries, and restaurants, which were just beginning to open. Emily had to step around a pair of young couples, apparently newlyweds, who were embracing and smiling at their selfie sticks.

"I feel like I'm back in Rome," Dee said.

"It's Jackson's mission to get me there too! Maybe next summer if I don't get lucky."

"Nature just has to work its own magic. But Rome is not a bad second prize."

They walked along the winding European-style lanes, with two-storey buildings on both sides that featured stores offering alternatives for shoppers with hundreds to hundreds of thousands of dollars to burn on designer clothing and jewellery.

After about twenty minutes, Emily stopped in front of one of the designer boutiques. "Dee, we must try on some diamond necklaces. One day Jackson will be a rich and famous lawyer, and when that day arrives, I want to have picked out the necklace I'll want him to surprise me with." Emily giggled.

Inside the store, they sat down with a saleswoman and they each picked out a few pieces to try. Dee was particularly taken with a stunning thirty-carat mixed white and black diamond necklace.

"Darling, this necklace speaks to you," the saleswoman said. "My husband bought me something similar last year. It's my favourite piece."

Emily glanced over at Dee with disbelieving eyes.

"I'm the owner of the store," the saleswoman said. "We're in Beverly Hills, Paris, and Venice. My husband is the designer. Perhaps you've heard of him. Ermando?"

The two women nodded. Ermando's work sat on the necks of half a dozen women at the Oscars.

The saleswoman deftly removed the old chain and amulet from around Dee's neck and placed it in front of Emily on the counter. Dee was intently studying the diamonds that reflected sparkles of light off the mirror. Emily's right hand slithered along the countertop until it covered the chain. She left it there. Dee turned to her and Emily felt her veins freeze.

"So do I buy it?" Dee whispered.

"Are you crazy? That thing must cost a fortune," Emily said just a little bit too loudly. The saleswoman turned her head away, pretending not to notice.

"I'm just having some fun, Em." Dee closed her eyes. "I'm imagining Odell giving me this on a special anniversary. Once I've had the four kids he's promised me."

The moment was at hand. Emily took a deep breath and slid the chain off the table and into her purse. She felt a trace of guilt, but Jackson had told her this was just temporary so she forgave herself the indiscretion—she was just borrowing it for a day or two. Dee probably wouldn't even miss it. At least she hadn't resorted to actually stealing it, as Jackson had insisted. If he needs me to go that far to help his career there must be a method to this madness, she thought.

They had spent another hour or so popping in and out of stores when Dee reached up to her neck. Emily had been waiting with dread for this moment.

"The necklace. Where is it?" Dee said.

"Sorry, Dee, what did you say?" Emily could feel the bile rising. She choked it back. How could she now admit it was in her purse? She still had five seconds to come up with the appropriate lie and return it to Dee. *You were so taken by the diamonds I didn't want you to leave it in the store. The family heirloom is safe and sound in my purse.* The words were all ready to come out. Instead she said nothing.

"The necklace with the amulet. I put it on this morning. At least I think I did." Dee's voice was shrill. "Was I wearing it earlier?"

"Not that I can recall." Emily had cast her lot with Jackson and his future. She was now beyond the point of no return, either on the road with him to partnership or to perdition.

They retraced their steps, going back through every store they'd visited. No one who had served them remembered a chain and jug; the owner of the jewellery store had left for the day. Emily played the role of loyal handmaid. She even got down on hands and knees in the jewellery store.

"I'll check my hotel room. Maybe I forgot to put it on this morning," Dee finally said in the hotel lobby with more than a note of resignation. "I don't know how or when I can explain this to Odell if it's lost."

Emily headed immediately to her room intending to lock the amulet and her shame in the safe, convincing herself that the harm to Dee was minor and the help to Jackson was enormous. She stepped into the bedroom and jumped in shock. A man was reclining on the bed, propped on one elbow, dressed in a beige suit, staring at her. She did a double take.

"*Jehosephat*, it's you, Jackson. Don't you go scaring me like that!"

"I thought I'd check in on my favourite spy. How did the morning go with Dee?"

"I have something for you that you desperately want."

"And what might that be?"

"Your Mata Hari has been hard at work this morning."

Emily lifted the amulet, dangling the chain as she approached Jackson, placing it on the bedside night table. If Jackson could do whatever he was planning and get it back to her quickly, it might not be more than a day or two of discomfort for Dee. Not the end of the world.

"I knew I could count on you," he said.

"Thankfully providence intervened. The necklace came off while Dee was trying on some jewellery. She's terribly upset and I'd like to find a way to get it back to her as soon as possible. Please just do what you have to do."

He took out his phone and snapped a few photos of the chain and amulet in various positions.

"You are truly my angel," he said.

"Are you done with it? Can you give it back to me now?"

"Almost. There's one more thing I need." He put his arms around her waist and pulled her onto the bed.

"Jackson, it's lunch time," she protested mildly.

"Suddenly I'm very hungry," he said, kissing her passionately.

Half an hour later, Jackson got out of bed and opened up his laptop. Emily could barely make out what was on the screen. For about ten minutes he seemed to be engaged in some kind of Google search and then he spent a few minutes on Facebook.

"Is that about work?" she asked.

"Just doing some research on local digital video experts. I guess it's work related." He turned his head to take a look back at her.

"Don't you want to get back into bed with me?" She patted the bed. Emily felt ready for another go.

"Remember, I came here to work, darling," he said, returning his eyes to the screen. A moment later he tapped out something on his smartphone while she was still luxuriating under the sheets. His phone pinged two minutes later.

When he'd put the phone down, he turned to Emily. "There's a hotel about a five-minute cab ride down the road from here. Here's the name and address. A woman selling roses is going to show up at the hotel bar at around nine-forty-five this evening. She'll approach you offering a rose. You need to be there and hand the necklace to her discreetly. I'll take care of the rest."

"Jackson, you promised me this would be temporary." There was not going to be a round two this afternoon.

"Believe me, Emily, the amulet will find its way back to Dee. But now I have to go. Odell sent us away, but I'm returning to prove myself indispensable to him and to the company. There's no rest for a man on a mission."

"I have every faith in your ability, Jackson." She heard the words, but the queasiness in her stomach was telling a different story.

■ ■ ■

Dee returned to her room and began rifling through drawers. Nothing. She needed to sit down and think. Where had she left it? The flashing red light on the phone distracted her. It was a voice mail from Michael with plans to pick her up and head for the beach at two. She glanced at her watch. Five minutes from now. Shoot. No time to get ready. She could feel her chest squeezing like a vise. She had lost her most precious possession; the morning was ruined and now she was about to keep Michael waiting downstairs. She called housekeeping and curtly asked them to report back.

She took a deep breath. It was not a sin to keep men waiting. Perhaps the maid had found the necklace. Once she knew, she would deal with Odell and the amulet later. He probably would not even notice its absence with all his work on this deal. She would just be honest and tell the truth. It had fallen off somewhere. The clasp had been loose. He should have checked that before giving it to her.

She slipped out of her skirt, blouse, and underclothing and dropped them into a small carry bag. Then she pulled on a two-piece bathing suit and a cover-up. After freshening up her lipstick in the mirror, she headed for the valet parking area, between the two towers of the hotel. She pulled her phone out of her purse and texted Emily: "Heading out with Michael. Catch you in the bar this evening. D."

Michael pulled up in a fiery red Mustang convertible. Vintage sixties. The top was down and Michael hopped out of the front seat to greet her; he was a couple of inches taller than Odell, his shoulders were broader and he had to be at least twenty-five pounds heavier. He sported a yellow Hawaiian shirt, denim cutoffs that showed off his muscular thighs, and well-worn sandals. He approached like an old friend, kissing her on each cheek. A strand of blond beach bum curls tickled her face.

"I'm impressed, Michael. Few American men know how to greet a woman with such European grace."

"This is just one of the many things I learned in Montreal."

The valet was already holding the door open, smiling graciously and accepting the bills that Michael slipped into his hand. Michael slid into the bucket seat across from Dee.

"This is the second love of my life. I'll tell you about the first later. In the meantime let's shake it, baby. We're headed to my end of the world. I was debating between Malibu and Venice but decided that Venice beach has far more kitsch, particularly on a Sunday. Prepare to relax and enjoy the surf and sand. Let's roll."

He revved the engine while the car was still in neutral on the cobblestone driveway of the hotel complex. The reverberations were magnified by the surrounding buildings and Michael laughed. He had broken all the decorum rules of the hotel and the city, leaving the hotel staff smirking.

There was little traffic on the San Diego Freeway, but the breeze made conversation difficult, so Dee watched him focusing on the drive. She wondered why someone with that much sex appeal never referred to a woman being in his life. Perhaps there was no room. Eventually they rolled up to a public lot just off the beach in Venice, and he stepped out of the car to open her door.

"Leave all your valuables in the trunk. We're just going to stroll down the beach to get your feet wet."

The sand stretched on forever in both directions. The Ferris wheel on the Santa Monica pier, a few miles north, stood out over the water; a series of bleached apartment buildings on the eastern skyline absorbed the afternoon sun.

Dee took off her sandals, and they headed south along the beach, letting the softly breaking waves lap up over their ankles. The tide was heading out. A perfect place to get to know Michael better and become friends, if only they could get talking. Michael was staring out at the ocean. He didn't seem in any particular rush. She wondered if that was just his personality. Avoid confronting the big issues in his life. Like why he was still single. Or why he and Odell let their friendship slip for so many years. The coffee date they'd shared in New York last week had been a typical first meeting of strangers with a common bond. Social and safe. They both had carefully avoided the elephant in the room. Dee decided to break the ice.

"Michael, I get the sense that Odell feels bad about how you two drifted apart."

"I never took it personally, Dee. That's the way it is with college buddies who go their separate ways. I think I'm as much to blame as he is. In the past, a lot of people didn't take me very seriously."

"Odell among them?"

"It was college. We were young and irresponsible. I developed this Orange County persona to cover up the insecurity of being a math major. As I got older and a little more comfortable with myself, I was able to learn to let my serious side shine through. It took a miracle in my life to do it."

"Odell told me you'd been married."

Michael stopped walking.

"Sorry—is that a sensitive subject?" Dee asked.

"It's a long story. I prefer to start at the end and work backward. The love of my life is my daughter, Elizabeth. She's just finishing high school. It's been just the two of us for many years. Liz was my gift from God."

"What happened to your wife, if you don't mind my asking?"

Michael picked up a smooth stone and skipped it way out to sea. "It all started well enough. Bianca was a law school classmate at Stanford. It was my first serious relationship."

"So you two got married young?"

"I really thought she was the one. Until then I'd just chased skirts. I was the happy-go-lucky guy. She was far more serious. When something upset her, she would get wound tight as a knot holding a ship in port. I glossed over it while we were dating. I just figured it would be a great idea to be married to someone who took life seriously."

"I think that's part of my attraction to Odell."

"Except it was the age-old story. Young married couple, two careers. No time to talk and then suddenly Bianca was pregnant. It was an oops."

"But a pretty good oops."

"The best oops of my life. Except during the pregnancy something in Bianca changed. She went from serious to paranoid. I was working crazy hours to get my technology business off the ground. She was convinced I was out cheating on her. The more I denied, the more convinced she was that I was a lying, cheating scum."

"What about once the baby was born?"

"I worried even more."

Gulls swept along the coast, shrieking while hunting late afternoon sustenance. Dee turned to watch. Maybe they had babies to feed. Nature required them to obey the needs of the young.

"I'll never forget the way she screamed at me. Over and over again. Even while she held Liz in her arms. I swore there was no woman. My business was the consuming distraction and it was bleeding me. The investors were becoming upset, so I worked harder." He dropped his head and his voice with it. She had to strain to listen.

"One day I arrived home from work, Liz was upstairs screaming in her crib, Bianca's bag was packed, a taxi was waiting outside the door. She said she was leaving. I pleaded with her. Begged her to stay. Offered to go for counselling. Anything to get her to reconsider.

"For years I had nightmares about what she did next. She didn't yell. Her face was a blank. A person I no longer recognized. She was very quiet. 'If I don't leave you now, and I mean right now, there will be no Bianca tomorrow and I can't promise you there will be a Liz. Goodbye, Michael. One day you'll thank me for this.' She got in the cab, slammed the door, and took off down the hill. Ten seconds later the cab was out of view. That's how quickly she dropped out of my life." Michael stopped moving and turned to face Dee. "Poof." His voice quivered.

Dee moved closer to him and lifted his shades. Michael's eyes were red. She stepped even closer and hugged him. When it occurred to her what she was doing, she stepped back quickly.

"She walked out leaving me with the baby," he finally said. "Not a word after that." Michael bent over to dig a handful of wet sand out of the ocean froth. The sand slid between his fingers until all that was left was a small half shell.

"Did she…?"

"This shell was once home to a living being. It provided protection. Was the mollusc eaten by one of those gulls? Did it survive? We'll never know. All we have is the shell as a record that something once existed. Did it matter whether Bianca killed herself? Not to me."

Dee was wide-eyed. "Surely Bianca can't have disappeared forever."

"She gave up custody and has seen Elizabeth occasionally over the past fifteen years. Liz became the centre of my life. I still wake up every morning thankful for the greatest achievement of my life. We go out to the ocean to surf from our beach house every morning at sunrise and I feel more connected to her than to any person on earth."

"How did you end up at TGO?"

"I was young and suddenly needed something full time that paid a steady salary. Bill Overton was the only guy in town willing to take a risk on a first-year lawyer, five years older than the rest of the field. I don't know what he saw in me, but he liked the fact that I had failed in business. Told me it built character."

"And no particular love interests?"

"Oh, don't get me wrong, Dee, there have been no shortage of women floating through my life, but I never really wanted to get hurt again, so no one stays for very long. I guess I just never met the right one. Someone as pretty and level-headed as you."

"Now you're making me blush, Michael."

Dee and Michael strolled down the beach, his shoulders completely relaxed, reflecting the sun.

"I'm making it my mission to find someone for you," Dee teased.

"I've heard from Odell that you're one determined broad." They both laughed.

They arrived at a deserted stretch of beach. Michael reached into his pocket and pulled out a rolled cigarette, twisted closed at one end.

"Is that what I think it is?" Dee asked, but she already knew the answer. "It's been a long time since my days in university."

"Don't get the wrong idea, Dee. I save these joints for special occasions. And please don't feel any need to partake."

"Aren't there laws against this?" Dee asked.

"While possession of marijuana in California is still technically illegal, the maximum penalty for an ounce or less is still only the equivalent of a parking ticket citation. No one ever gets troubled on the beach."

"But you're a lawyer in a big firm. Why take any risk?"

"We're not the only ones. We can sit in the surf, which is heading out, observe the world spinning as the sun appears to set, and mellow out into the moment. When was the last time you tried that?"

"Not since the last time I put on my Crimson Tide T-shirt." She laughed. "Odell can definitely use you to loosen him up a little."

■ ■ ■

This had to be one of the better afternoons Arthur Ellison had experienced in the past six months. He sighed with satisfaction, slipping the telephoto lens back into its case and sliding it onto the back seat of his yellow beaten-up Volkswagen Jetta. He slipped behind the wheel and readied himself to pull out of the Venice Beach parking lot to return to the office.

Today was a welcome change from the divorce case that had just wrapped up a couple of days ago. Sitting in the bushes, night after night, hoping to catch the woman in a compromising position with her lover, had wreaked havoc on his back. He got the pictures the husband needed but not without a series of cuts and bruises to go with the back strain. And he just could not shake the extra thirty pounds filling up his midsection. His doctor kept warning him that he was a walking time bomb. Diabetes, hypertension, heart disease. They were all lurking in wait, the way Arthur lurked while focusing his lenses. Acting on the doctor's advice would have to wait. He had a few years of child support payments left to make until his kids were done with school, then maybe he could pack it up and move to Hawaii. Lose some weight. Get the life he deserved.

He'd been thinking it was finally time to get out of this line of work. The competition for L.A. private investigators over the Internet was killing him. There were so many kids out there looking to make a buck on their smartphone cameras. None of them were carrying the overhead of an array of telephoto lenses and a proper investigator's office. None of them took their work as seriously as Arthur. All they were doing was driving down the going rates.

When the text came in this morning that he was to follow the gorgeous blonde from the Beverly Wilshire to wherever she went this afternoon, he had no idea it would lead to a day at Venice Beach. Fortunately, he had a sun hat to cover his bald head and a pair of sandals. He also had a couple of grand that had been e-transferred to his Gmail account.

In half an hour he would go through the digital images, pick out the best ones of the girl and her "uncle," send them as instructed and earn the second half of his fee. They didn't come easier than this. He didn't care that he had no idea who his client was. That was none of his business.

CHAPTER 8

3:00 p.m., Sunday, August 16, 2015

Jackson emerged from the taxi on Colorado Boulevard at the corner of Twenty-Sixth, determined to walk the last couple of blocks. The warm breeze felt good, but he donned his suit jacket that had sat carefully folded on his lap. He straightened the lapels. It was time to do a final run-through on strategy—prepare the plan to get past building security and up to the meeting at the Cypress offices on the corner of Twenty-Fourth. He passed signs in front of the buildings for Lionsgate and Viacom and felt a rush of excitement. Here he was, a kid from Nowheresville, Alabama, about to make a dent in one of the biggest entertainment industry dramas of the year. This would surely make Momma proud. He imagined standing shoulder to shoulder with the General at the press conference once they'd destroyed the Turk.

There was no receptionist in the cramped fifth-floor reception so he stood waiting for a couple of minutes until he could catch someone's attention on the other side of the glass door. He hoped the meeting was taking place up here. He waved to the young woman who finally passed by and opened the door.

"I'm Jackson Sherman from TGO. Can you let Odell Moore know that I've arrived? He should be in the boardroom with Oliver."

"Sure, Jackson. I'm Oliver's assistant, Cynthia. Please take a seat. I'll text Oliver."

Jackson took a seat in a waiting area at reception. The boardroom was just on the other side of a glass security door. There had to be eight people sitting around the table. If he played his cards right, he'd have a huge leg up on Cassidy. Jackson was confident that he could sell Odell on the opportunity.

Cynthia returned shortly. "Excuse me, Jackson, Oliver just sent me a note. They'll be taking a break shortly."

Jackson waited impatiently for about fifteen minutes until the boardroom doors finally opened. He was on his third review of the e-mails in his smartphone when an elderly, diminutive member of the board limped past reception. He had to be in his late seventies, and time had not been kind to him or to his back.

He smiled at Jackson beneficently. "I can't hold it in the way I used to. Time for a little boy's break."

Odell followed a couple of minutes later, holding a piece of paper. Probably something important that had to be dealt with. "Oliver told me you've been sitting out here for a while. What are you doing here?" His tone was brusque.

Jackson stood up and moved closer to Odell. He decided to use a very quiet undertone.

"I figured you'd have your hands full here and would need a second set of eyes and an independent brain to bounce ideas off. I didn't come to L.A. to vacation with my wife. I came to learn, to be helpful to you. For what it's worth, I'm not taking no for an answer. I'll spend the day sitting out here at reception if I have to until you have something for me to do."

Odell shrugged. Time for Jackson to press the case. He'd done his homework on the key board members. Morley Menkoff, the guy who had to pee, was a lawyer by training and ran his own law firm. He had spent the first twenty-five years of his career working on real estate deals for the Berg family in Oregon. They drove the toughest deals in the business with the leverage of their family fortune. Morley was known as a hard-driving negotiator.

"Is Menkoff giving you a rough time, General?"

Odell hesitated before finally responding. "I have to be on my toes at all times with this group. In other situations the board has allowed me to run the show. I provided the strategic advice and we went with it. Not here. They want to dig in and milk every bit of intelligence out of me concerning Yildirim and his tactics on previous deals. And nothing gets past Morley. Everyone on the board seeks his advice. They hang on his every word. Don't let his age fool you. The man is one tough bird."

It was time to show off a little. "Isn't that Governor Noviss of Alaska? I hear he's as charming as the night is long up there in January."

"Yes, Jackson. That man loves to hear his voice and he's quite accustomed to running things. If we end up in a negotiation with Yildirim, Brian is going to be asked to lead the negotiation team, so we need to strengthen our relationship with him."

He used the word "we." Best to assume he was in. "All right, General, what can I do first?"

"We've just been talking about the latest press release that came out during our session. Here," he said, handing over the piece of paper. About time. Jackson began reading: "Mr. Yildirim was quoted as saying 'Visionary CEO's and lax boards. A dangerous combination. Disciplined spending is the only rein keeping profligate spenders from pursing the path to extinction. My goal is to turn the strategy of Cypress away from squandering resources and gambling money on fruitless acquisitions. As a shareholder, I need to have confidence that this board is accountable about improving the bottom-line performance of this company.'"

"Sounds like Yildirim has landed the first blow in this fight," Jackson said, just as Oliver joined them.

"And you two fellows are going to explain to us how to counterpunch? Time to reconvene the meeting." Oliver walked back into the room.

Odell turned to Jackson. "There's a lot of ground to cover, and we'll need to come up with a plan for tomorrow. I've already texted Michael and Dee, letting them know not to expect me."

"When I left Emily, she told me that Michael and Dee were heading out for the afternoon as you instructed." Jackson decided impulsively to push his luck. "If you don't mind my asking, General, how close are you with Michael?"

"We fell out of touch for many years. We're really just beginning to catch up. Any reason in particular why you're asking?"

"Well, before we left New York Emily mentioned that he and Dee seemed very comfortable together. 'Two peas in a pod,' she said."

"Dee's like that. She warms up to people she likes very quickly."

"You're very trusting. I wouldn't be comfortable with anyone spending that much time with Emily."

Odell smoothed his moustache.

"Never mind. I'm overstepping," Jackson backpedalled. A good farmer sows as many seeds as he can, but not too many. Then he waters them religiously, weeds the field, and waits patiently. Something always takes root beneath the surface. Then it grows. It was too early to take this conversation any further. Now that planting season had ended, there was work to do.

CHAPTER 9

Gretl hunched over her computer monitor, twisting her L.A. Kings Stanley Cup champion visor backward so she could better focus on the task at hand. The advances in software allowed her to manipulate the images on the screen before her. She was a Valley Girl by day and an overnight Instagram star with a considerable following of her altered images of reality. Her "Grand Canyon Mashup," which showed four U.S. Olympic freestyle skiers in various stages of descent, superimposing moguls along the fall line of the canyon, had over four million hits. The surreal scenes were designed to parody reality and bring attention to the subject matter. The most controversial of her works was her interpretation of Oxana Mayers, the gold-medal figure skater, emerging from the Gulf of Mexico in the middle of a triple Lutz, dripping in oil that sprayed in a myriad of directions and coating hundreds of birds in the black tarry liquid. That photo was the final nail in the coffin for one of the major multinational oil companies that had been adamant their cleanup effort of a major oil spill was under control.

However, being a master photographer and a surrealist artist was not providing much financial supplement to her part-time waitressing job, and neither job was helping her pay down her student loans. When she'd received the message through her Facebook page late this afternoon asking if she worked with other photographers' images, she jumped at the opportunity. Fifteen hundred dollars for a night's work was a great offer, though she was a little suspicious that one of her exes might be pulling her leg. When the $1,000 advance hit her PayPal account, she waited anxiously for the photos to follow. A photo of a necklace and charm was part of the first package she received. She'd just finished downloading the second set of photos of a woman and her uncle. Her task involved manipulating the data so that the necklace and charm would appear in various photos around the necks of the niece and the uncle. That is what the client wanted and that is what the client would get and more. She never knew when a rave review would drive referral business. She would set up a sequence where the woman appeared to be removing the necklace and giving it to the uncle.

While the assignment required an artistic eye and an experienced hand, the software allowed for such a high degree of manipulation of the images that this job was relatively easy compared to her own artistic works.

"I am truly a binary master," she sang to herself as she fastened the chain around the woman's neck in one beach scene. For fun she took the photo of them holding hands and superimposed the necklace on the uncle's neck. "They'll positively love that one," she said, still focused on the computer screen. "But I hope no one believes that I manufactured the weed! That might get me in trouble. On the other hand, anyone who codes could figure out what's real and what isn't. I wish I had an uncle who was that cool!" Gretl finished around three in the morning and sent off the images to JBOY82@gmail.com as instructed. The next morning the remaining funds were deposited to her account. She definitely needed more clients like this one.

CHAPTER 10

9:00 p.m., Sunday, August 16, 2015

Odell had been sitting at a bar table in the Peninsula Hotel for about ten minutes when he heard the ping. It was a text from the president of California Bank cancelling their appointment. Some board crisis required him to be on a conference call that was running way over schedule and he had to send last-minute regrets.

Odell had been nursing a Johnny Walker Blue at a table just off to the side of the bar against the back mirror. He swirled the caramel liquid. It smelled classy and expensive and went down smoothly, masking the damage it was capable of inflicting on families. That's why he could barely touch it. He could easily have turned out like his sister, Sheneitha. She may not ever have taken a beating like he did, but she was an emotional cripple long before the cancer took her. His mother had slowly gone crazy but she hung in there just long enough to get him to university. For that he would always respect her. Why was he the lucky one? Maybe the better question was when was his luck finally going to run out? He had tempted fate by falling in love with a woman who wanted children. Dee was eventually going to figure him out and then what?

It was just after their discussion about children that he began having trouble concentrating. And now the lapses had returned and along with them moments of anger he could barely control. And then there was the violence. Nothing as serious as what happened in Montreal, but if he couldn't control himself, was he destined to become his father? He'd rather be dead. Anyone who was a threat to children had no place in the world.

He needed to talk. A brunette balayage, in a very low-cut dress with a very high hem, had been giving him the eye from her seat at the bar for fifteen minutes. He loved stiletto heels and hers didn't disappoint.

The woman walked over and sat down in the adjacent chair, making a show of rearranging her hem. Pulling it up a little higher. Her dark skin glowed in the low light above.

"I hope you don't mind company. Care to talk? Perhaps buy a girl a drink? You must love chocolate," she said. She leaned forward in the seat and in a low whisper asked whether he had a room upstairs. With some difficulty he pulled his eyes away from her ample bosom. There was nothing underneath the dress. Heat rose from his neck upward to his cheeks. He was not interested, but some undefined instinct was keeping him at the table. Keeping his eyes focused where they should not.

Maybe she sensed he needed a little coaxing. "Trust me sugar, I'm worth every cent."

"Trust me," he repeated quietly. There was only one woman he could trust. Liberty. No. That wasn't the line. It was "Liberty, she's all you can trust." A song lyric, perhaps? He raised his eyes to an appropriate height. Her lips were thickened with a deep red sheen. A shade his mother once wore. He could not remember when. A trickle of anger began to fill him and within seconds it had turned into a flood, until it burst from his lips.

"I can't trust you at all, can I, Marisol?" The words, uttered quietly, sounded like the hiss of a snake.

The hooker's eyes barely registered surprise. She just smiled. "Call me anything you like, sugar. You shouldn't trust me alone with you. Isn't that why you want me, or are you just the type that likes the tease? Too bad. You're damn fine. Perhaps you want to leave a little token for my trouble?"

"I'm leaving now," Odell said, rising and reaching for his wallet. He left a pair of hundred-dollar bills on the table and headed for the door. The anger had yet to subside. He could barely trust himself anymore and he had no idea if it was time to trust Dee. But he needed to get back to Dee all the same. It was time to talk.

■ ■ ■

By the time Odell arrived at the hotel, Dee was asleep under the covers, even though it was only ten-thirty. She was normally a night owl, but then he remembered it was already one-thirty in Manhattan. A two-piece bathing suit and thin cover-up had been tossed on the floor at the foot of the bed. Why a bathing suit? There was sand on the carpet. He tiptoed around them, undressed, carefully hanging his clothes in the closet, and crawled into bed next to her. She purred. It was not that late and suddenly he couldn't wait to talk to her. It was time to unload. He laid his hand on her shoulder and let it slide down her arm, gently kneading her. That usually worked. They hadn't had sex in over a week but he pushed the thought out of his mind. He hoped she wouldn't misinterpret the gesture. He needed to talk more than he needed to deal with his other frustrations. Still he could feel himself beginning to respond. Could she feel it too?

"You're home. Talk to me, Odell." Her eyelids opened halfway, but her eyes were red and unfocused as if waking from a deep sleep.

"I need to talk to you about my sister and my mother."

"Your father too. I want to know all about your family," she said in a hoarse whisper. She was struggling to bring herself back to full consciousness. He waited a moment until he thought she was really awake.

"All in due time. Let's start with my sister. I told you she died a couple of years ago. What I didn't tell you about was the guilt I still feel about how she lived. How little I saw of her after I left Nova Scotia. My job was to protect Sheneitha. And Dad never touched her. Dee, are you with me?" Her eyes were closed.

"Every word. I'm just resting my eyes. They're burning."

"I was the one my father would go after. Often I would egg him on just so he would leave Mum alone. Get her a night off." He'd come to terms with the violence in his home years ago. It was the 1970s. Everyone knew what was going on inside the Moore row house. The walls on either side were paper thin. No one lifted a hand to help—not at school, none of the neighbours, and the police were powerless because Mum refused to admit to it. Even Mum's family sat quietly, though the three of them regularly moved into her parents' house until Dad sobered up and convinced her to come home.

After the first few beatings, Odell made two decisions. At seven years old he was already making life decisions. Both made him proud—then and now. The first was that he would never let that asshole lay a hand on his kid sister. However, there was nothing he could do for his mother. After the first attack, he'd tried to intervene and ended up gasping on the floor. Dad broke his rib with a knee and then slammed the phone into Mum's cheek when she tried to dial 911. Mum dragged Odell to the emergency room next morning after Sheneitha left for school. "Bicycle accident," she told them. She'd tripped trying to pick him up. The doctors and nurses didn't probe. This was the first of many trips.

The second decision was that he would never let the bastard see him cry again. He was not going to get that satisfaction. No tears and never an apology for Odell's behaviour. It didn't matter how long the beating lasted. Two minutes, two hours. Odell learned to go to a place in his head. The closet. It was the way he neutralized the threat. He'd plan out the next battle strategy, watching the tin soldiers move under his direction. The soul of the little boy being beaten with Dad's belt was not in the bedroom.

Odell continued, "Thank God he travelled so much for work. Weeks at a time. The moment he got into the car on one of his road trips, I could feel the energy returning to our house. He had sucked the life out. It all ended when I was twelve. Mum finally found the strength to leave him. By then she was broken physically and emotionally. Sheneitha probably was damaged from the psychological abuse."

"I love you," Dee said in a muffled tone, falling back to sleep immediately.

What had she heard and what had she slept through? He gently prodded her once more, this time with a little more force.

"Not now," she muttered. "Too tired. Let's wait until the morning." She began to snore.

He got up and collapsed in a chair in the sitting area. What was happening? He had no idea what she was thinking or feeling anymore. She hadn't been talking to him at all. And now she was not listening either. The most difficult admission of his life and she was snoring. Maybe Jackson was right. She was withdrawing. He spent so much time travelling or at the office, they had had really very little time together. In the past week, she'd probably spent more time with Michael than with him. Maybe Jackson was right about another thing. How well did he really know Michael after all these years? Odell studied the bikini lying on the floor. He could feel the embers of his anger radiating heat. This was craziness—he was tired too, and it was late, when it was easy to feel crazy. He pushed the thoughts out of his mind, crawled back into bed. She was not listening because she was exhausted. Exhausted and neglected. He pulled her in close. She didn't resist.

Who was it that Dee was curling into right now? Odell already knew the answer to that question. A dishonest man. Not the kind who told lies or cheated others—he was even worse: the kind of man who hid his secrets so deeply that he couldn't even find them himself and who made sure the woman who was supposed to be his best friend in the world was kept in the dark. He really thought tonight was going to be the night when he told her everything there was to tell. When he was finally honest about the children she seemed to so desperately want.

She would have been awake had he come home at a decent hour. He shouldn't have tried to squeeze in that extra business meeting. The realization hit him. He had no sense of priorities. Always business first. The truth would have to emerge or it was going to destroy his marriage and who knew what else? Maybe Odell's soul.

He just needed to get through this deal. But what was that bathing suit all about? He closed his eyes and within minutes he drifted into a light sleep, watching suspiciously as Dee and Michael ambled down the beach, hand in hand.

He awoke in a cold sweat in the dark. Dee was in a deep sleep, still on her side with her back to him, softly breathing, oblivious to his discomfort. Her long blond hair lay dishevelled, without a care. Odell envied her peacefulness. He couldn't relax for fear of returning to the image of the beach. Damn Jackson for putting these ideas in his head. But he couldn't blame Jackson for the way he was feeling. Odell was the one who was keeping the secrets; Odell was the one who put work first; Odell was the one who'd made the introduction and insisted Dee and Michael spend time together. He fought the urge to hold her tightly and just deal with his goddamned feelings. Instead he lay in the darkness, staring at the ceiling, observing nothing but the blankness that inhabits the middle of the night, depriving the restless of the distractions that daytime offers.

CHAPTER 11

5:15 a.m., Monday, August 17, 2015

Dee was sitting up propped against a number of pillows, finishing a novel on her electronic reader. She had no idea what time Odell had pulled in last night, as she had slept more deeply than she had for ages. It had been a long time since those parties at the University of Alabama. The deeply relaxing effect of a little weed and the halo effect of the morning after. Odell lay inert with his back to her.

He was trying to tell her something last night. It might have been important. Why did he have to come in so late? Why did he _always_ have to come in so late? When were they ever going to have sex again? She rolled into him and reached to caress his shoulder with her lips, then began to nibble on it, tasting sweet and salty. The familiar flavours of Odell. God, he felt so strong. She squeezed her legs together and her eyes shut as the pace of her breathing increased. The desire was overwhelming. It was time to wake him. To take him, right here on the beach—no—in the bed. What was that all about? She froze.

She had not really begun to consider whether or when she should admit to the nature of the escapade with Michael. It had all begun innocently enough. She needed to delve into Michael to make it easier for Odell to rebuild that friendship. Maybe she had overstepped. Gotten a little too personal with Michael.

Odell would understand once she explained how she was helping get their friendship back on track. What he might not understand was why she had to smoke a couple of joints with him in public. Odell could be straitlaced to the extreme. Perhaps it would be best to let some time pass before revealing all the details. On the other hand, how could she expect to build trust in their relationship if she wasn't yet prepared to open herself to potential criticism? She knew him well enough to know he would consider it to be irresponsible behaviour for an adult. She continued arguing with herself until the ping of his phone roused Odell.

Dee watched as Odell, still wiping the sleep from his eyes, instinctively reached for the phone. Always reaching for the phone like it was glued to his hand. After reading the text, he shook his head.

"What's going on?" she asked.

"Hold on, just let me finish this." He skimmed through the text, mumbling every other word out loud.

Just let me this. Just let me that, she mocked under her breath. Why had he brought her along? She walked over to the coffee machine and slipped in a pod of espresso, then climbed back in bed beside him.

"Well, isn't that interesting," he finally said. "One of the largest Middle East oil refiners has been shut down indefinitely by the Saudis. And guess who owns a majority stake in the company? Sterling Yildirim's funds. Allegations of incompetent security. Risks over potential terrorism by ISIS. The sheik had his security forces take over the plant. He claims that after local media reports surfaced, he could no longer trust the owners to fulfil their obligations to the state."

"Who is Yildirim and what does Saudi Arabia have to do with us?" The Saudis and their barren desert, she thought. Just like she was feeling. Right beside him yet completely alone. She could not help herself. So now she was unfulfilled, self-centred, and in need of a massive orgasm. That made her feel guilty. Guilty and selfish. If she could just talk to him for a few minutes she could forgo the sex. Or have the sex and forgo the conversation. Just something to connect to him.

"Sorry." He smiled. "All this is confidential."

"Keeping secrets, are we?" she teased.

He winced.

"Just kidding, Odell. I know all these files are top secret."

"I have a feeling I'll be able to tell you more this afternoon. We have a lot to talk about, but right now I have to get in gear."

"Odell, I just need five minutes. I wanted to tell you all about my day yesterday.

"We'll have plenty of time later."

"Sure, later." She felt a surge of anger. He already had turned his back. What else was new with Odell. She couldn't help herself and raised her voice. "I stayed up as late as I could last night. Finally, I just gave in and crashed. I never heard you come in."

"It's okay," he said.

She really should not have had that second joint on the beach. She hadn't been buzzed like that in forever. More guilt.

"Dee, I'd love to hear all about your shopping and your afternoon with Michael but right now there's likely to be a flurry of activity while we decide if my assessment is correct. I need to prepare for a morning meeting with the client."

"Odell, will you just kiss me?"

He came around the bed to kiss her on the forehead then turned and headed for the shower. Watching his broad shoulders and his tight rear, she had half a mind to follow him in there. The very sight of him now bursting with energy excited her to the core. And it had been a while. He was out of town, or too tired, and on the odd night he wanted it she was too angry. It had been over a week since she'd had the fight with Daddy, and Odell had not even broached the subject. What was wrong with him? He had not even volunteered to speak to Momma since the wedding. Nor had he mentioned his own mother since their visit in June. Was there a callous bastard in there? Maybe it's what made him such a good lawyer.

She closed her eyes and imagined him in the shower. She could hear the water. She could feel the desire building as she imagined what a morning of rushed lovemaking would be worth. She *needed* to feel him inside her. She rose, dropped her robe, and headed toward the bathroom to surprise him. As she reached the doorway, she caught herself. She knew that

Odell, in military mode, was already making his battle plan for the day, laser-focused on defeating the enemy, whomever that might be. She would only be a distraction. He might let her have her way but he wouldn't really be there. What she had in mind was not to be wasted on a half-focused lover. Dee took a few deep breaths. They could resolve this tonight. She'd order dinner up to the room; romantic candle light on the balcony. She shivered with anticipation.

■ ■ ■

A few doors down the hall, Emily's eyes were still closed as she felt for Jackson in the bed, enjoying these moments between the satiny sheets. Her hair was in disarray, the result of their passionate lovemaking just a few hours earlier. She had rarely experienced Jackson so charged up in the middle of the night. She connected with Jackson on a physical and emotional basis unlike any other in her life. As the crescendo built she lost all control, throwing her head back across the pillows, her eyes no longer focused, no longer connected to this world. Screams were coming from somewhere in the room. It sounded like her voice but she no longer felt a connection to the bedroom, to Jackson, or even to herself. He was still deep inside, standing on the floor, facing the bed, one hand supporting her buttocks, the other raised in the air triumphantly, like a cowboy who had just wrestled a steer to the ground. Eventually Jackson collapsed on her saying only, "I couldn't be better."

And then she remembered: handing the amulet off to the flower girl in the bar, and just before that the hooker in the red dress who'd taken the cash off the table then waited two minutes to follow Odell out the door. The bliss vanished. Could she ever share with Dee what she saw at the bar? Or what she was doing there in the first place? She now needed to avoid Dee for two reasons. She also realized that if she brought up the subject now Jackson might be upset that she'd waited. She should have reported to him immediately when she returned to the room last night. In any event she wasn't the type that stole necklaces and spied on her friend's husband. Or maybe now she was.

She had come so close to redemption. After Jackson had left the room yesterday afternoon, she'd resolved to give the necklace back to Dee. Make some excuse about how it had ended up in her purse. What Jackson was asking her to do was wrong. Maybe even criminal. She couldn't go on deceiving her best friend. Really her only friend. She'd dropped the necklace in her pocket and was headed down the hall to Dee's room to return it. No harm, no foul. There was no answer at the door. She was about to send Dee a message about finding the necklace when a text came in from Dee saying she'd left to go out with Michael. Emily decided to wait—to think about it. The window of opportunity slammed shut on her sticky fingers. She would take Jackson on shortly, before another day got started, but he was crossing a line that neither of them could retreat from.

As Jackson left the bedroom, throwing on a robe, Emily curled up in a ball on the bed and hugged her knees to her chest, trying to push down the morning dread. She decided, once and for all, she had not seen a thing at the bar. She felt sick about handing over the necklace: she vowed to no longer participate in this crazy plan. She stood up and walked into the suite's seating area, ready to confront Jackson. He was at the desk, gazing intently at the computer screen, talking softly to himself.

He put his arm around her waist and pulled her onto his lap. Kissed her. His tongue felt like sandpaper and she pulled away slowly. "Precious Emily, I need just one more favour once we get back to New York."

CHAPTER 12

8:00 a.m., Monday August 17, 2015

Michael Cassidy pulled his red sports car into the lot at Century Park East. His usual regimen involved a short morning surf with Liz as the first rays of sunshine filtered in from the east, followed by a drive south along the Pacific Coast Highway before the rush-hour traffic hit. What was the point of owning a car that could hit 130 m.p.h. without breaking a sweat, if he had to let it idle in the choking L.A. traffic and morning smog? Instead he manipulated the curves on the highway at a speed somewhat above the speed limit, feeling the machine grip the road. For the first hour of every morning he was the king, and this day had been no different, at least until he arrived at his office. Lying in plain view on the desk was a single rose wrapped in tissue. Propped alongside was a white envelope with his name written in what appeared to be a woman's hand.

Which one of his recent dates had sent it? Possibly the graduate student with the tight figure he'd picked up just before he began the Cypress deal. He decided to keep himself in suspense and headed downstairs to the coffee shop. While he was waiting in line, he received a text from Odell asking him to meet in the boardroom ASAP. He wondered what Dee had said to Odell about yesterday. It was all in good fun, Michael assured himself. Hopefully Odell had not taken it the wrong way.

When he got to the boardroom, he hesitated at the doorway, turned the doorknob, then waited. Better to start with the apology. Lapse in judgment and all that. Odell would probably see right through the lie. It wasn't any kind of lapse. Weed was a hell of a lot safer than alcohol. Besides, they hadn't done anything wrong at the beach, so why apologize? His thoughts were interrupted by a big snort and a Texas drawl.

"Michael, you comin' in here or you gonna stand out in the hallway all day? We've got work to do, boy." Wild Bill was standing with an unlit cigar hanging out of his mouth and his arm around Odell. Jackson stood opposite them, holding a mug of coffee. The meeting was clearly about business. But why so relaxed?

"Well, boys," Bill Overton opened, "this one has had a Hollywood ending, at least for now. Odell, play the latest news report for these fellas on your thingamabob. I don't get all this new technology."

Michael joined the group and Odell hit the play button on his smartphone.

"This is an exclusive CNN breaking news story. Sources are reporting that American investment guru Sterling Yildirim may be facing a huge economic setback as a result of an oil plant takeover by the Saudi government. The Islamic State has been making threats of attacking this plant for months. Our local office is reporting all kinds of security concerns based on an anonymous piece that surfaced on-line yesterday morning. The Saudi government has announced that they will immediately launch an investigation into the Yildirim organization's role in what they call gross mismanagement. The owner of the plant, a fund controlled by Yildirim, stands to lose well into the billions. Unofficial sources tell CNN that the security at the plant was lax and this might lead to a state expropriation."

"A real tragedy, gentlemen," Bill cut in. He had a huge smile on his face. "The Turk is facing a public relations nightmare. How did you manage it, General?"

"I just gave the P.R. machine a little nudge. The rest was luck."

"You mean you didn't have someone planted in the royal palace whisperin' in the sheik's ear?"

"I wouldn't put it past him," Jackson said.

Michael put his arm around Jackson's shoulder, shaking him hard. "We did it, buddy. The General has worked his magic."

Jackson stepped to the left to pull away from Michael's embrace before speaking. "The General never explains how the magic trick is performed." They all laughed. Everyone except Odell.

"Let's not get too far ahead of ourselves." He spoke in a serious tone. "I may have set the works in motion but that doesn't mean the Turk will follow the script."

He paused while an assistant walked in and handed him a note that he took a moment to read. "Gentlemen, ten minutes ago our adversary issued a press release advising that he no longer had any interest in Cypress, at least for the foreseeable future." Finally Odell smiled.

"Heehaw," Bill shouted. "I'm about to draft me a really large bill, a humungous bill and get it right out to Cypress. Ol' Bernie Jenkins is probably so elated that he'll pay it yesterday. Ya can't give a CEO the chance to get distracted when it comes to collecting payment." He smiled and stood up. "Thank you, fellas, for your commitment. You are free to get back to your lives. But first, would you like to have lunch with me? I'm in the mood for a Texas steer and a big bold Cabernet. And tomorrow I'm gonna book to play a celebratory round of golf at Riviera Country Club. Any of you interested?"

"That's a kind offer, Bill, but I have a number of matters to attend to in order to catch up on my other files before I head back to Manhattan," Odell replied. "But I'd be honoured to join you for lunch, right after I make departure arrangements."

"I also need to head back east, sir," Jackson chimed in, "but lunch today would be an honour."

Michael also chimed in. "Bill, if you don't mind that my golf game's a little rusty, I'll be there tomorrow too."

"Don't worry, son. I find the opening tee shot over the valley below a little intimidating. The starter follows the fine tradition of the club since before the days of Ben Hogan of calling out the name of each guest who steps up to the first tee. The vista for that shot is breathtaking and you'll have the feeling there's a national television audience watching you. Once you get that first tee shot under your belt, you'll be fine."

"As long as I won't embarrass you. I'm not much more than a hacker. I can hang ten but I can't nail a putt."

"I rarely keep score anymore," Bill replied. "I save my competitive spirit for the legal negotiations."

■ ■ ■

Jackson followed Odell back down to the visitors' office where Odell had set up. He had to step quickly to keep pace. The General was likely in a rush to squeeze in some time on the preparation for the Houston deal. The unexpected news about Cypress had opened the door to an immediate opportunity and Jackson was not going to waste a moment. The time to strike was now before Odell got distracted. "General, do you have a few minutes to talk?" he asked, as they stepped off the elevator. "I won't take much of your time."

"Sure, come on in." Odell offered Jackson the guest chair in the sparsely furnished office. A computer and phone were on the desk, as well as the instruction manual for visitors explaining how to log on to the systems. Under the office window was a long work table. Sitting in the corner was a small bottle of water and a couple of oat bran bars in a small wicker basket. The set-up was efficient, particularly for an out-of-town lawyer who needed a place to work. Odell's tan leather briefcase perched on his side of the desk, and after taking his seat opposite Jackson, he opened it and removed a manilla folder.

Jackson launched in immediately. He didn't want Odell thinking about anything other than what he was about to say. Jackson had dodged the bullet on Cypress. The Turk's withdrawal meant Cassidy no longer had the leg up on partnership, but no doubt the Houston deal was next and there was no way he could allow the door to be open for competition. While they were standing around in Overton's office, Jackson had sketched out the first steps of a plan. There was no time to waste.

"I had a chat this morning with Emily and she mentioned that she spoke with Dee after her date with Michael yesterday. Sounds like the two had a very nice afternoon together."

"Great to hear. I haven't had much time to catch up with Dee." Odell absently flipped the file open and glanced down. Force of habit.

"Work has kept you pretty much tied up since the wedding, hasn't it?"

Odell looked up and smiled. "Yes, it's been a little crazier than I expected, particularly with Cypress popping up as a crisis so unexpectedly. But Dee had a fairly good understanding about the life she was signing up for. After all, she lived in a house where her father spent half of every year away from his family in a Washington apartment." Odell looked back down at the paper in front of him. Probably thinking about how to manipulate the investment bankers. Shortly he would probably call his assistant to set up the meetings.

Jackson cleared his throat. It was time to launch the offensive. "I may be the junior lawyer in the room, but Emily and I have been married now for about five years and she's had to survive the life of a young associate trying to impress and move up the law firm pyramid. I've learned a few survival skills over the years." Odell closed the file.

Jackson leaned forward in the chair, resting both elbows on the desk. Moment of truth time. He took a breath, now certain he had Odell's complete attention. "Would you be upset if I offered a little unsolicited advice?"

"I guess in this conversation you have seniority, so go ahead." Odell was grinning. Jackson's shoulders relaxed.

"Okay, the first thing you need to understand is that women are not rational beings, at least not in the way that we men understand. For example, you and I have a conversation and each one of us says what's on his mind. We leave the room with a fairly clear understanding. If you tell me that you have a problem, then I naturally offer advice as to how to solve it."

"Where are we heading with this, Jackson?"

"If I begin the same conversation with Emily, the moment I open my mouth to offer the advice, she shuts down. Conversation over. It always ends the same way. She gets this look on her face, like I'm the enemy. Then when I ask her if everything is okay, she responds curtly, 'I'm fine, no worries.' I've learned very much the hard way that 'I'm fine' is code for 'You've really let me down.'"

"None of this makes any sense to me." There was a hint of irritation in Odell's tone and he looked back down at the file. His fingers reached for the corner. If that file flipped back open, this conversation was dead on arrival.

"Let me put this in terms you use every day. You're one of the best negotiators in the world. You listen carefully to clients and offer advice. I've never seen anybody better at this firm or at my last."

Odell sat back in the chair. Thank God, Jackson thought. "But wives are not clients. When your wife talks to you it's because she wants to talk, not because she wants your advice. You need to actively listen to her."

"Jackson, with all due respect I don't need a lesson in active listening." The sprout of irritation was growing into a weed.

"Please don't misunderstand, General. It means something different in the context of marriage. Active listening means interjecting every once in a while, with a 'really' or 'I had no idea.'" Jackson was using his best falsetto. "Truly active listening taps into her emotions. 'That must have made you feel so bad' or 'Did you find that hurtful?' or 'You must feel so excited.'" He laughed. "Ever use those with a client?"

Odell shook his head. "Not words I would ever use in the boardroom. I'd get laughed out of the business."

"My point exactly."

"I really appreciate the advice and I'm sure that will all come in handy one day, but right now we're still post-honeymoon. With all this Cypress craziness most of our conversations have been short, at least lately. In any event Dee's not a big talker. That must make her different than most women."

"That's probably the worst news you could give me."

Odell's back stiffened. "How's that?"

"Odell, how many relationships did you have before Dee that lasted more than a month?" Jackson was on the offensive, stepping into territory where he knew he did not belong. He needed to keep pushing, but he might end up in deep doo-doo.

Odell stared at him with cold black eyes. Jackson felt the shiver but decided to shut up and hang in. After an endless moment, Odell sighed. "Just one a couple of years ago. Lasted six weeks. When she moved out of the apartment she left me a snarky Post-it note saying it would probably be a week before I realized she was gone." He half grinned at the admission. "She was right," he added.

"So let me give you a little advice." It was time to press on. "If your wife isn't having a monologue with you for at least twenty minutes a day, you have a serious problem. You just don't know about it yet. Husbands are always the last to know. When women become noncommunicative it's because they're internalizing all their problems and that's when you're at your most vulnerable."

"Is there a point here, Jackson?" The tone was irritated, but this was the kind of irritation Jackson was looking for.

Jackson stood up and began pacing, hesitating, as if searching for the right way to break terrible news. That's how it had to sound to Odell. "Emily had a chat with me this morning. She happened to be in the hotel lobby at seven last night when Michael dropped Dee off at the hotel. They'd been out together alone for about five hours."

"So what? I'm not worried about Michael. He's one of my oldest friends."

"Yes, although Emily tells me you know him mostly as a football teammate. She says he was quite the ladies' man."

"That was a lifetime ago, Jackson."

"In my experience people don't really change over time—they just get older." Jackson watched as Odell's eyes narrowed. Was that the first hint of concern? It was time to press the advantage.

"Emily told me that Dee was behaving a little out of balance," Jackson continued. "'Giggling like a teenager' were the words Emily used. Dee was talking about a magical day at Venice Beach."

"What else did she say?" Odell now appeared to be actively listening. Jackson thought he caught a flash of anger, something he'd seen only twice before. Jackson remembered the moment in Odell's office, just before New Year, when his eyes were flashing lightning bolts. And then again in the spring over a disparaging comment Jackson had made about his own mother. He was no longer frightened. He began to wonder whether Dee would be when Odell returned to the hotel.

"Emily had trouble understanding her. She said it was all very odd. Not like Dee at all." Did it matter whether any of this was true?

"Emily and I have been on solid footing for most of our marriage but we did go through a rough patch or two, particularly in the first year. She claimed I was ignoring her. Marriage was a big adjustment. She needed way more attention than I expected. She needed me there to listen to her." Jackson hesitated, laying the snare down for Odell to take one tiny step forward.

"Your point, Jackson? Your point?" Odell asked impassively.

"If Dee's not sharing with you, then maybe she's sharing with someone else." Odell's eyes and nostrils flared momentarily, but just enough. Caught, Jackson thought.

"And that's the final mystery about women," Jackson spoke with certainty, as if he was calling out from inside Odell's head. "When they're truly upset, they begin to act out. And when they stop talking to you altogether, that's the moment you need to confront the situation or risk your relationship."

"Enough," Odell barely grunted through clenched teeth.

Just enough. "Maybe I've overstepped…"

"No." Odell's tone was just a little too harsh. It was time to go. Jackson turned his back and slowly made his way out of the office. "If there's anything else I can help you with, General, please don't hesitate." The door shut behind him. He had waaaay over-stepped.

And that was a good thing.

■ ■ ■

Odell felt entirely out of balance. The story of his life lately. It couldn't possibly be the case that Dee was carrying on with Michael. None of this made sense. He collapsed into the black faux-leather chair behind the desk to gather his wits. After a couple of moments, he texted his assistant in New York and asked her to get them both home tonight. It was time to get far away from Los Angeles and create some separation from Michael. Odell needed to spend time with Dee. He needed to talk to her. But he had this damned lunch with Bill at twelve-thirty. That didn't leave a lot of time. There was no point waiting to get back to the confines of his New York apartment before he confronted her. If not now, then on the plane home tonight. Jackson may be right: she could be very upset that Odell had virtually abandoned her emotionally since the honeymoon. It wasn't just work. He had his own secrets to confront as well.

He collected his papers, and within five minutes he was packed up and in a taxi for the short journey back to the hotel. The palms by the side of the road were waving in a steady breeze. He reminded himself that although L.A. had become the centre of the entertainment universe, beneath its surface it was still simply reclaimed desert. Was this some kind of analogy applicable to his life? The veneer of palm trees and studio lots with false facades of 1920 New York tenements and 1965 streets of Metropolis were no more than bare coverage for the vast emptiness that lay beneath. Once he had stripped away his work exterior, was his soul similarly barren? Had his wife already figured this out in so short a time? He feared he no longer knew if he was anything beyond a conquering lawyer. Plenty of great lawyers had mentored him along the way. No one had ever shown him how to be a good husband or father.

He entered the suite, the apology formed on his lips, the confession behind it pushing its way out from deep inside. He rushed in, not able to hold back for another moment. He was greeted by a dishevelled bed, bikini on the carpet, untouched since last night, breakfast tray on the table, runny egg yolks, picked-at sausages, half-eaten toast, crumbs everywhere. No Dee. He looked back at the damned bathing suit. Maybe she needed to do some confessing as well.

He called out for her again, a loud impatient roar. No answer. Just some gurgling coming from the other side of the bathroom door, slightly ajar. It banged shut, followed by loud coughing and retching.

"Dee, is that you?"

"Don't come in!" she yelled. "I'm no vision to behold, Odell. Please give me a few minutes."

The coughing continued. He needed to get in there. The poor thing was suffering and all alone. How long had he neglected her in this state? "Is there anything I can do to help, Dee?"

"No, sweetie, I'm fine. It might have been the turkey sausages I ate this morning. They didn't sit well. I just need to drink a little water and lie down for a bit."

She finally trudged into the bedroom, wearing the silk bathrobe with the Wilshire logo, her shoulders rounded and her hair unbrushed and limp. Even in that state, she took his breath away.

"Dee, we really need to talk. And we're going home this afternoon. Our flight leaves at five-thirty." He didn't mean for the words to come out so abruptly.

She sat down on the bed and bowed her head. "Maybe we could go tomorrow instead?" She said it quietly, without any conviction.

"New York will be so much better. But only if you're okay. Are you feeling well enough to fly?" Before she could answer, his smartphone pinged. He opened the e-mail. "Good news, Dee. We've been upgraded to business class. Jocelyne had to pull a few strings with the airline." He felt very relieved. He didn't want her to have to fly economy. "It will make the flight so much easier to manage. And we'll be sleeping in our own bed tonight."

Her shoulders sagged for a few moments. She managed a weak smile. "If you really need to go back tonight, then let's do it. Let me just collect my strength for a few minutes."

"We don't need to do anything right away. I have a lunch with Bill Overton. Then I'll pick you up afterwards."

"I'll be ready."

"Yes, my love, but we need to talk." He crossed the suite to check the front door to make sure it was bolted and to double-check that the Do Not Disturb light was turned on. "There are so many things I need to discuss with you." He made his way back to the bedroom, bursting with feelings he did not understand, riddled with concern and uncertainty.

"I've been neglecting you, Dee, and I know it just isn't right. There's so much we have to talk about that I've been bottling up. I tried to tell you last night."

He walked through the open French doors and into the bedroom. She was fast asleep on the bed, propped on the pillows and clearly spent.

He paced the room for half an hour, hoping she might wake up. Finally he penned a note: "I'll be back at three. We'll talk tonight."

■ ■ ■

Jackson had one final call to make before heading back to the hotel. There had to be an opportunity here, but he still hadn't figured it out. Was he going to align with the senator or was he going to protect Odell from the threat that his father-in-law still posed? Perhaps there was still a way to play both ends against the middle.

"Jackson. What's taken you so long to get back to me?" The senator's tone was harsh. He needed to be deflated, just a touch.

"I asked you to give me a week."

"It's passed. What can you tell me about my daughter?"

"Senator, I wanted to let you know that Dee will be back in New York tomorrow. Odell will be heading out to Houston as early as tomorrow evening."

"Then I'm coming to Manhattan. I expect your cooperation, Jackson. I want your promise on the honour of the Sherman family."

"You've had it all along, sir. Goodbye." Jackson cradled the phone and stared up at the ceiling. All the players in the drama were now aligned with Jackson's aim. He had destabilized the marriage, sowed the seeds of mistrust, and was about to set the senator to work pulling at the roots. One way or the other, events would drive the General closer to Jackson and Jackson closer to partnership. As a bonus, if the marriage cratered, he'd have the senator onside for life.

He settled into the desk chair, lifted his legs onto the desk, and closed his eyes. If he'd had a cigar, he would surely be lighting it this instant, blowing rings of satisfaction over his head. Life was perfect.

PART II

CHAPTER 13

Jackson emerged from the subway at Park Avenue South and Twenty-Third Street. It was still early morning but the humidity was already oppressive. Nonetheless it felt good to be back in Manhattan after two days in Los Angeles. The sun was battling for supremacy with the cloud cover. Fortunately the wind was gusting, the turbulence a sign that a storm might be coming—exactly what Jackson was hoping for today. A little lightning bolt that would burn the bridge between the General and Michael Cassidy.

It was only a block to Mary Lou's, Jackson's destination of choice for client breakfasts. The decor was simple but they had a few specials that you simply couldn't get anywhere else in the city. He represented a number of developing technology companies in Soho that he would be visiting later in the morning, but for now it was time to execute the next stage of his plan. He walked in the door and was greeted by the hostess.

"I have a reservation for two under the name Sherman."

"Yes, sir," the perky young woman replied. She couldn't have been more than a year out of college. Hair dyed platinum blond with black streaks in an effort to garner attention. He wondered whether she had been a history or fine arts major. The burden of student loans to finance worthless degrees weighed heavily on so many young service staff in the city. It boggled his mind how short-sighted these young people were. In L.A. every one of them was still waiting for the big break to ignite an acting career. At this end of the country, a paltry few that he had met wanted to be dancers or actors on Broadway; most were simply overburdened with student debt with no idea how to get ahead in life.

"Sherman for two?" The hostess interrupted his thoughts. "Your guest has arrived. Let me escort you to your table."

His guest was sitting, elbows on the table, eyes fixed on his smartphone, no doubt searching for the tourist websites in Manhattan: either directions to the Statue of Liberty or the 9/11 Memorial. Jackson put a hand on his shoulder as he walked by.

"Why, Rodney Ferguson, you Confederate son of a bitch. You finally made it. Welcome to the home of the Yankees."

Rodney stood up and extended his hand. They gave each other a good-old-boy handshake, followed by a bear hug. "Jackie boy, it's good to see you again. I have to say this is a long way from Mobile for me. Arrived late last night." They slid into the red leather booth opposite one another. A waiter delivered a couple of plastic menus and coffee mugs filled almost to the brim. Rodney shared some gossip from Mobile while Jackson planned his opening.

"What brings you to town?" Jackson asked. Rodney had called his cell in L.A. yesterday and mentioned he was on his way. It was an opportunity that had fallen out of the sky. Jackson could not have planned this any better.

"We just sold off one of our trust fund businesses to a hedge fund. I'll bet you've never seen this before." Rodney reached into his breast pocket and pulled out a white business envelope that had not been sealed. He carefully slid the rectangular paper out and turned it with his fingers at each top corner to face Jackson.

"A cashier's cheque for ten million dollars?"

"Daddy never does anything small. He spotted what he thought was an error in his favour in the purchase agreement over the weekend. His lawyers told him to forget it. They're not widows on the other side. Ten million was a rounding error anyway."

"So he sent you to give it back to the hedge fund?" Jackson could not mask his incredulity. He worked on half a dozen deals for the firm's hedge fund clients. Cutthroats all of them. They never slept and never let their lawyers sleep when a deal was on. And they did not make mistakes when it came to dollars. "Let me tell you, Rodney, those guys run the numbers on their deals a hundred times. As far as they were concerned there couldn't have been a mistake."

"I tried to talk him out of it," Rodney whined. "Daddy looks at me yesterday afternoon and says, 'Have you learned nothing about Southern honour, son? We make a mistake, we own up to it. The honour of the Ferguson name comes before ten million dollars. It comes before everything. Go deliver this and make me proud.' After breakfast I'm returning the money."

Jackson picked up the coffee mug and took a sip, to mask his disgust. What he could have done with the ten million that Rodney's family clearly did not need. He took a moment to gather his thoughts and get on to his agenda. "That was quite an effort you and your brother Stanley put in at the America's Cup preliminaries last May."

"Daddy spent eight million on the boat and he won't let anyone know how much the whole adventure cost. Stanley leads the team. Mostly I just cheerlead. Daddy's positioning us to challenge in 2021."

Just like Jackson was about to position Rodney. "Now that you're in Manhattan, can we talk about Dee?"

Rodney reached for a tiny cream container from the white bowl on the table, carefully peeled back the cover, and deliberately poured the cream into the mug, as if he had spent his adult life training for this activity. The coffee looked as clouded as the expression on Rodney's face. Everything with Rodney was work. If you were going to go through life as a polite half-wit, you might as well have a multi-billion-dollar trust fund to fall back on.

"Dee is a lost cause, Jackson. And now she's married. Daddy told me to forget about her once and for all."

"I told you last November at the senator's do, you've got to be aggressive to get her."

"You know that's not my style."

That was Rodney. Always putting up roadblocks before he could get started. "Rodney, trust me it's not too late. You've got your work cut out for you, sure, but nothing worthwhile in life comes without a little hard work and great strategy."

"Strategy? You mean like the gift you suggested I get Dee for the high school prom?"

What was he talking about? Jackson wondered. It took a moment until the memory jogged. "Oh yes. The jewellery. That went over quite well, I remember. She loved the gift. Earrings as I recall."

"She loved them? Come on, Jackson. She never said thank you to me. Never said a word about it. I never even saw her wear them."

"I assure you, she told me she loved them. I was certain I'd passed that on to you."

"Expensive earrings. Five hundred dollars. Remember? I gave the money to you. You told me you'd found the prefect trinket. Trinket you called it. 'She'll love it,' you told me. 'I'll get it for you and send it to her with a note from you,' you told me. All part of the plan to get her to the prom."

That was Rodney. Never quite figuring out the game. Jackson had needed the money. His allowance would not cover the cost and he needed to pay for the tickets to the Stones concert. A pair of gold seats, best in the arena, and a few dollars to spare for condoms. Fortunately, Rodney was so easily distracted.

"Did you go to the prom with her or not?"

"Yes," Rodney admitted grudgingly.

"And whose idea was it to ask her?"

"Yours."

"And who made sure she agreed?"

"You did."

Actually it was Jackson's father leaning into the senator for a personal favour, but that was ancient history. "So maybe my advice is worth taking?"

Rodney nodded.

"Not my fault if you couldn't get her into bed. I can't do everything for you, Rodney."

Rodney's shoulders began to slouch as if the wind had already come out of his sails. "Daddy's been pressing to get Dee out of my head and find a bride. He was sure the sailing would help. It didn't. I just can't move on. Why are you so certain that I have any chance?"

Jackson leaned in with both elbows on the brown linoleum table. "She rushed into marriage with Moore. It's only been a few weeks but I can already tell there are stresses in the relationship."

"How could you possibly know that?"

The server approached, took their order, then quickly moved on to the next booth.

"Let's get to the business at hand—Dee," Jackson said. "According to my momma, everyone who counts in Mobile is saying she should have chosen you. 'Rodney Ferguson is Edward Brabant's choice for his daughter,' she says. Right family, right social connections, the perfect merger." Never hurt to stretch the truth a little—okay, maybe a lot this time. It *would* make a great economic merger and the senator would eventually figure out how to adjust to Rodney's peculiarities. He was an acquired taste but an honest man.

The two orders of chicken waffles arrived in white plastic plates shaped like boats. Jackson was starving and they both launched into their meals. Rodney reached for the syrup. "Real maple from Vermont. Can't get that in Mobile." He smothered the order in sweetness.

"That's why I'm prepared to listen. For my sweet." Rodney laughed at his own idiotic joke. "I'm in your capable hands, Jackson, but I really don't even know where to start."

"Rodney, let me handle the politics. By the time you meet with Dee she'll be putty in your hands and more than ready to leave Odell Moore and return to the South on your arm. Nothing would make her daddy happier."

"This sounds like a fantasy, Jackson." Rodney was looking skeptical. Perhaps Jackson had underestimated how difficult a task this might be. The boat was still in the water. Going nowhere. There was a breeze to be captured here. There was always a breeze, even on a calm day. A breeze that created the advantage if you could just turn your sail enough to catch it. The difference between victor and runner-up. Jackson was no runner-up. Jackson vowed to continue probing until he found the breeze to propel Rodney forward.

"You have to understand that the senator is the root source of tension in Dee's life. They eloped and it shocked him. No formal engagement period, no fancy wedding, and Odell has no pedigree at all in the local community, if you know what I mean." Jackson leaned forward with a conspiratorial grin. "There's no changing the fact that Odell is black." Someone else might have been revolted by the politically incorrect comment. Rodney didn't blink, though he did put down his fork and knife. He might be preparing to stand up and leave. Or not. The wind had shifted, but was it blowing leeward?

"And how would you possibly know all this?" Bingo. The question Rodney had to ask. The sideways push that would inevitably drive them forward together.

"Right from the horse, my friend. Dee is best friends with Emily."

"Jackson, that doesn't sound like a lot to go on."

"To the contrary my friend. To me, it's opportunity come a-knocking."

"How so, Jackson?"

Rodney ran his index finger along the rim of the coffee cup. "I've known you too long, Jackson. What's in this for you?"

"Why do I need motivation? You're my friend. You've always been there for me. It's my turn." That was a whole lot better answer than the truth, Jackson thought. I deeply want to become a partner at my law firm, and part of my plan involves causing Odell Moore to rely on me as a trusted advisor to guide him through the problems in his love life. I can only provide that assistance if there *are* problems, so I'm prodding a little. With Cassidy back in L.A. it's time to bring in another distraction. If the marriage collapses, excellent. The odds that Dee would ever want Rodney—probably not much more than zero. Rodney was a prop. "I'm here for you, my friend."

"The way I'll be here for Dee? Sounds like you're trying to play God here."

"Ye of little faith."

The waitress came by to top up the coffees, breaking the spell that Jackson had been casting. "What exactly are you up to?" Rodney asked.

"Rodney, my boy, I've taken steps to make Odell believe she's having an affair with his old best friend. Never mind how. If I continue to play this one right, they should be at war shortly."

"What can I do at this point?"

"Stay by your phone. You'll hear from me. You booked the suite I told you about?"

"Followed each and every detail."

"First you'll pay her a short visit. After that you'll convince her to visit your suite. Perhaps a dinner while Moore is away. He's headed to Texas tonight. Anything can happen over dinner."

After paying the bill, Jackson pushed his chair away from the table.

"Rodney, my apologies but I have to run to my next appointment. I've got a celebratory lunch to attend after that, but don't worry, my friend. It's time for your star to shine."

Jackson headed to the door, smiling smugly. Plan B was coming together more smoothly than he had expected. Michael Cassidy was a few hours from ruin, and Odell Moore was coming to understand that Jackson was the only person he could trust. He could imagine the offer of partnership from Torrance that would soon be within his grasp. New York was a grand city indeed, and Jackson Sherman planned to become one of its brightest lights shining among the Broadway marquees.

CHAPTER 14

Noon, Tuesday, August 18, 2015
Washington D.C.

Edward Brabant's Senate committee meeting had ended a few minutes early, which was unusual. He had a great deal of respect for Marc Dorion, the committee chair. The man knew how to run a meeting. Brabant quickly congratulated his old friend. They had sat on opposite sides of more issues than he could remember over the course of their distinguished careers in the Senate. The Democrat from New Hampshire was well respected on both sides of the political spectrum.

The two men shook hands warmly. "Well done, Marc. Very efficient use of our time today."

"Thanks, Edward. Tell me, how are Eleanor and that beautiful daughter of yours? She must be sought after by a multitude of Southern boys."

"They're just fine." Brabant felt challenged to explain Dee. He still hadn't come to terms with the fact that she had eloped with the first man to turn her head. What kind of man comes into your house and takes advantage of your daughter like that? Not to mention how embarrassing it was for Eleanor in the community. The man hadn't even had the guts to face up to it. How disrespectful. Instead he'd sent Dee in to mop up the mess. And no word from the coward since the wedding.

Thank goodness he didn't have to deal with it on the Hill. What could he possibly tell people? That his daughter had run off with an older black man. No wedding. No opportunity to at least put on the show of family solidarity and acceptance. Not that he did accept this. A ten-year age difference? What was she thinking? She wasn't thinking. She also wasn't thinking about the grandchildren. How could he explain to the world that his grandbabies would be black? Of course he couldn't use the word *black*. It was no longer politically correct. African American grandbabies—that was his future.

"Edward, I asked whether you and Eleanor were planning any vacation this winter."

"Oh sorry, Marc, I was daydreaming. I miss my daughter, and I was just reflecting how we parents watch them grow up and blossom and then they leave us and set out on their own lives. We have so little control."

"I'd say no control if I were being honest. None at all. We make a career out of arguing, cajoling, and convincing for a living, then we go home. Powerless in our homes." Marc smiled.

"Passengers on a train."

"The best we can do is enjoy the scenery passing us by. Our wives play the role of conductor, particularly insofar as our daughters are concerned."

"Speaking of trains, Marc, I don't mean to be rude but I have to take my leave immediately. I've an out-of-town meeting I have to get to. As always, it's been a pleasure working with you."

It was true that Edward had to leave town, but no meeting had yet been set up. Jackson Sherman had said he should come to New York immediately, and he was going to do it, before there was time to think and talk himself out of it. Eleanor had warned him to stay away from Dee until he felt he could deal with the situation without flying off the handle and so far he had taken her advice, much as it pained him. But Jackson had finally called back last night to say the group was returning to New York from L.A. and it was likely that Moore would almost immediately head off to Texas.

If he could just sit down and talk some sense into the girl. Get her out of that apartment while Moore was away. Just stay calm and make her see things objectively. Spend a few days there if necessary. He knew enough people who could help with the logistics and Sherman promised he would assist in any way he could. The 1:00 p.m. Amtrak to Penn Station would get him into Manhattan at around 4:30. He would send Dee a text from the train.

Odell had been at TGO for almost two years, but you wouldn't know it looking around his office. He had not bothered hanging any artwork on the walls. There were no knick-knacks on the standard laminate desk and matching bookshelves. He believed in keeping his office simple and unadorned. He didn't spend much time there anyway. His job was to be out meeting prospective clients all over the world. TGO had offices in sixteen cities, from London to Abu Dhabi, including the five in the United States, and they all wanted Odell to help pitch the next prospective deal. If he was sitting in his office, he was likely wasting his time.

On the desk was a single photo of him and Dee, taken in Vegas. His arm was wrapped around her. The contrast of his dark skin and broad shoulders with her long blond hair, blue eyes, and slight frame gave him a little chill. In the picture she was a real Southern belle in need of his protection. But how things actually were when they stepped out of the photograph could be deceiving. She was every bit a match for his power. Perhaps that was the attraction drawing them together. He was not used to any of it, but he loved feeling off balance with her. He wondered if he would ever adjust.

He could hear his team whooping it up down the hall in the boardroom, celebrating their victory over the Turk. He'd put in a brief appearance but the red eye home had exhausted him. He also knew this one had been more luck than skill. He'd run a long shot in Riyadh and things had worked out better than he could have imagined. But the Turk would be back at some point. The Turk never disappeared, he would just take on a new form—maybe on a new file if not on Cypress. They were all giving Odell far more credit than his due. Still, a win was a win, he thought. At least he was succeeding somewhere.

He needed to clear his e-mails and then get home to Dee. She had obviously ignored his phone calls this morning and hung up on him while she was at the doctor's office. He felt bad about abandoning her in bed but Torrance had lined up a breakfast meeting with the financiers on the Houston deal once he heard that Odell was returning from L.A. There was no point heading to Houston tonight without the financing in place. Right now he needed to tell Dee he loved her. He needed to show her he loved her. He had to confess his secrets. He had no idea if she would accept him, but he knew when he had to do it. Now.

There was something else bothering him. The necklace. He hadn't seen it on her for the past two days. She'd promised she would wear it always—it was their silly little in-joke just before he gave her the engagement ring, so why was it so important to him? Maybe it was a reminder of the family amulet from Africa that his mother wore, passed along for generations from Elijah the slave, his patriarch. How would Elijah have felt about his marrying a white woman from the South, he wondered. He'd never really considered that before. Elijah had sacrificed his life for his family's freedom. His son, a Union soldier, had escaped on the Underground Railway to Canada. Surely they would be proud of Odell's success in America. But would the marriage bother Elijah? Maybe he would be happy that he and Dee had broken the race barrier.

One thing he did know was how Dee's father, Senator Brabant, felt about the marriage. Deeply opposed might be an understatement. Odell figured once they were engaged he would head out to Mobile and meet Dee's parents. Discuss wedding plans. When he returned home after work the day he proposed, he discovered she had booked the entire itinerary for a Vegas getaway. "A couple of days to celebrate our engagement before you get tied up in another deal," she'd said. Except she had more than getaway on her mind. The day after they arrived, she'd made a bet with him at the black jack table. The first to draw a 21 was entitled to one wish fulfilled by the other. Five minutes later she rushed him to an Elvis Chapel. He didn't even have time to wonder what she would have done if he had won the bet. After the ceremony, he figured it out. He'd bought the tickets to Paris on his cellphone. Her favourite place in the world. It was all so outrageously passionate and impulsive.

Had she married him out of the same passion? He had never given it a moment's thought until a few days ago. She knew there were going to be consequences afterward. She knew her father had ideas about who he wanted her to marry, knew that she was defying him, but she did it anyway. Was their marriage an act of love or rebellion on her part? Odell was no longer certain.

The senator probably considered Odell to be gutless. The last time Odell had spoken to him in April, they were discussing business. Maybe Odell should have raised the subject of Dee at the time. Admitted his feelings. That would have been courageous. That would have been honest. It also might have cost him a deal and his job. It was not that Odell was afraid to deal with the senator. He had dealt with a lot worse in his life. It was just that between all the deals at TGO, there had been no time to attend to Dee's family turmoil.

Besides, Dee said she would handle it herself, and he was more than happy to leave it to her. Whatever she'd tried had not worked, and he had done nothing to fix the situation. Maybe that's why she wasn't wearing the amulet. A form of protest. A way of getting Odell's attention. Why could she not accept that this was his life? She said all the right things about understanding the pressures of Odell's work, but now she was acting as if she needed more attention. He reflexively reached for the office phone and hit the speed dial. He just needed to talk this out with someone, especially someone who knew him well. Michael Cassidy's assistant passed the call along.

"General, I haven't heard from you in all of twenty-four hours. Do you miss me that much?"

Odell heard crackling across the line. "Where the hell are you, Cass?"

"Winding my way along Sunset Boulevard. The cell coverage around these hills is really lousy. I'm heading to Riviera to play a round of golf with Overton. The Old Man thought we deserved the day off after blowing off the Turk. Remember? He asked if you wanted to stay an extra day and play with us."

"Right. I won't keep you long. This isn't about business."

"I didn't think you had it in you."

"This is a marriage question."

"And you're asking me? Are you nuts? I've been divorced forever. But go ahead, I'm here for you."

"I just need an ear. It's about Dee." Odell hesitated before continuing. Maybe this wasn't such a good idea. He was facing the glass wall of the skyscraper across the street. Bright sunlight reflected into his eyes, temporarily blinding him. He kept staring until it hurt.

"You spent the afternoon with her last Sunday while I was with the Cypress board of directors. Did she seem okay to you?"

"More than fine."

"We're going through a rough patch. Not talking very much. I have a bad feeling."

There was no response at the other end for a couple of seconds.

"I gave her a trinket for our engagement," Odell said. "A little silver jug on a chain. She told me she'd always wear it. And she stopped wearing it a few days ago. She's upset with me. And now I'm upset with her. I just don't know what to do."

Still no response at the other end of the line. Odell finally looked away from the sun reflection. He had to close his eyes. Were they still connected?

"Cass, did I lose you?"

"Listen… There is nothing so … that … work … together. Just … to her. I don't think… Just … attention … her."

"You're breaking up." The line cut out. Odell stared at the phone as if it was to blame. "Thanks for the wise advice." The spots in front of his eyes blurred his vision. What else was he blind to?

Odell sat at his desk and closed his eyes. An image of Dee half naked, holding hands with someone else, appeared. He opened his eyes with a start. This was what happened when a man didn't pay enough attention to his wife, when he kept secrets from her. Exactly what Jackson had told him a couple of days ago in L.A.

Odell stood up. He was going home this minute. He needed to talk to her, to unload his secrets, to tell her how much he loved her, how much he needed her. That was honest. He had an overpowering desire to hold her and to comfort her through whatever illness she was suffering. First clean up the e-mails then get out to clean up his life.

■ ■ ■

Michael Cassidy parked his car at the far corner of the Riviera guest lot. The clubhouse was a two-minute walk and he was fifteen minutes early for the tee time, though he had suddenly lost the urge to play. He steadied his left hand on the steering wheel of the red Mustang and tilted his body across the stick shift, straining to reach for the glove compartment. His right hand fumbled around, feeling for the envelope that he had stashed there this morning. Hanging hard to his right, he felt as off balance as the moment after dawn this morning, when an unexpected wave had built under his surf board too close to shore.

Pulling himself upright, he spilled the contents he'd grabbed onto the bucket seat beside him. A hand-signed note and a gold chain. He opened the note and read it once more.

Darling
Let's do this again soon.
All my love
(s) Dee
p.s. Here's a little token of my affection

Nine little words. *Darling* could mean nothing. A simple term of endearment. And they'd had a good time together so why not do it again? *All my love* could be read any number of ways. At least yesterday, when the *token* was just a token. He lifted the chain above his head and over the convertible roof. The sun reflected beams off the tiny red stones embedded in the silver jug. Odell's jug. The unexpected wave with its threat of a surf pound that could fling him to the beach, head first.

He slipped the note and chain back where it belonged for now and carefully locked the glove compartment. Then he wiped the sweat off his brow. What was Dee thinking?

CHAPTER 15

2:30 p.m. Tuesday, August 18, 2015
Manhattan

Odell wiped at the perspiration that had gathered on his forehead. Maybe he was coming down with what Dee had. He settled in behind his computer screen and began scrolling down his inbox for any e-mails that might have arrived in the past few hours. Just five minutes and he would be off. He then quickly checked through the e-mails in his spam folder, which blocked unknown senders but sometimes caught important messages.

Most of the e-mails were obvious trash: new vitamin supplements, how to enlarge his penis, and the odd charity request for funds. One e-mail heading did catch his eye:

"General Moore: the following photos require your immediate attention."

His interest was piqued, and he knew that the second layer of security would evaluate each of the downloads before releasing them, so he hit the "permit" icon and within a few minutes the e-mail would be transferred to his inbox.

There was a knock on the door, and Jackson let himself into the office. He had certainly grown to feel comfortable around Odell. One minute with Jackson and then he'd be off. He began jamming some papers into his briefcase while they chatted. Jackson would surely get the message.

At that moment the computer pinged.

"Give me a moment, Jackson. An e-mail just came in. Might be the Houston deal."

General Moore,

While your troops have been fighting the good fight, your wife Dee has been keeping secrets. If a picture is worth a thousand words then take a few minutes to examine the novel below.

This e-mail was obviously sent by someone who knew his business nickname, though anyone who followed the press would also know it. However, no one outside a select group knew about Dee. Without giving any further thought to the firm's policies, he began downloading the photos. One by one the pictures appeared on his screen.

The first showed the backs of two people walking down a beach together. It wasn't possible to make out who they were but it was clearly a young blond woman and a taller man with massive shoulders and curly beach-blond hair. The photo had obviously been taken with a long-distance telephoto lens but there was no way to tell anything about the couple. The second was taken as if it was a close-up. There was no question about the subjects now sitting on the beach. Michael was passing what appeared to be a cigarette to Dee. A series of three or four shots followed with each of them taking a puff.

Odell had no idea she was a smoker. The fifth was a close-up of Dee taking a haul on what was obviously a joint. He could feel the colour draining out of his face and the anger rising. This was the escapade to the beach? Maybe Jackson was right. Odell had been far too trusting. And Michael? Smoking a joint in public while in the middle of a deal? What if Odell had needed him? What kind of shape would he have been in to assist? Then there was the reputation of the firm. Who the hell was this photographer? What if he'd been hired by Yildirim's people to follow them all? Did Odell have to alert the firm of the risk? He was not about to bring his wife into this. He fought to regain control. He had to stop speculating and get some perspective.

He continued downloading the photos, now frightened about what would follow. Nothing could have prepared him for the next series of shots. This was a skilled photographer with serious long-range lenses. The next few shots focused on Dee in full frontal wearing her bikini top, a cover-up wrapped around her hips. Then she hugged Michael close. She hugged him. What the fuck?

A Victoria's Secret's model would be wearing more than what Dee had on. The late afternoon sun was sinking on the horizon. She was wearing the amulet—the jug caught a glint of sunlight and became the focal point of the picture. In the next shot she was holding the chain in her left hand, the jug hanging down below her waist. The following shot showed the amulet sitting on Michael's neck. Odell uttered a low growl. How could she do this? His special engagement gift to her ... and here she was stoned out of her mind giving it to him to wear?

He might have been able to understand her taking it off near the beach ... even handing it to him for safekeeping. But to ask Michael to wear it? Dee could have slapped Odell across the face and it would have stung less.

The rational side of his brain continued to search for an explanation. His training as a lawyer required him to examine a problem objectively, from all perspectives before jumping to any conclusions. The arc of his career had followed this approach, amassing all the evidence before taking a decision ... never behaving rashly ... always taking emotion out of the equation before responding.

Weigh the evidence. Was it a gift? The amulet. Fertility. They were stoned on a deserted edge of the beach. She was wearing practically nothing.

He finally understood how his clients felt when under siege. They responded to their knee-jerk emotional response. They wanted to counterattack, to destroy the enemy regardless of the personal cost. He had learned to let them emote, didn't try to challenge the emotions, let them simmer down, and then approached them with cold logic. But here he was in their shoes. His entire life was being threatened by the man he thought to be a close friend, a man he trusted. He was gasping as the photographs cycled before his eyes, he was having difficulty regulating his breathing. He grabbed the arms of his chair. "Think rationally ... control yourself ... breathe. There has to be another explanation."

"Everything okay, General? Maybe you're coming down with whatever Dee has. Emily told me she wasn't well. And your colour is way off."

He had completely forgotten Jackson standing by the doorway. How much time had passed? He had no idea.

"No, Jackson. I'm fine."

"Can I help?"

Odell could feel the entire story pushing its way out. He had to share it with someone he could trust. He opened his mouth but no words came out. He took another deep breath, placed both palms on his desk, and pushed himself upright, feeling his composure return. There was another way to deal with this.

"Let me ask you a question. A friend of mine is experiencing some marital problems. He's worried that there may be another man involved with his wife. What does he do?"

"That's simple," Jackson answered. "Does he have any evidence of the infidelity? In that case it wouldn't be much more complicated than to lay the trap by asking an innocuous question that will either confirm or deny the hard evidence."

"Thanks. Let me think about that one. You know, Jackson, I think I've underestimated you." He needed Jackson to get out. Immediately. Jackson got the hint and turned to leave.

After the door shut, Odell dialled Michael's cellphone number. Jackson's approach sounded logical but neither of them were courtroom lawyers accustomed to trapping witnesses into admissions of guilt. It didn't matter. Taking action was empowering, even if it led nowhere.

Michael was almost whispering as he answered Odell's call. "General, I'm really not in a position to give any more marital advice today. I'm on the second hole. Not allowed to speak on the course. Club rule and Wild Bill is staring me down here."

"Has Dee given you a necklace?"

"Sorry, you're breaking up, Odell. I can't hear you."

Odell slowed the pace and raised his voice. "Did … Dee … give you … a necklace?" There was a long pause at the other end of the line.

"Yes, but I need to—"

"Okay, Michael, that's all I needed to know."

"Yes, Odell, but you need to understand the whole situation—"

Odell hung up and slumped back into his chair. He didn't need to hear any more. He understood the whole situation. Perfectly. His left hand rolled the mouse. One by one the pictures scrolled across his computer screen. Damning evidence. Damned Cassidy. She smoked with him on the beach, held his hand, hugged him. She'd given him the fertility amulet. What else could that possibly mean? Only one thing, he thought. Cuckolded by my best friend. How could she betray me?

He paced his office, clenching his jaw, the caged tiger dreaming of the kill. Odell ran his tongue over his lips, recognizing a familiar taste. Vengeance mingled with fresh blood. "Screwed by my best friend, who's screwing my wife." It didn't matter how many ways he analyzed the photos; the conclusion did not change. He rushed out of the office toward the elevator, backtracked to ask his assistant to cancel all his scheduled calls for the afternoon, and raced out the door. The sidewalks on Sixth were filled with people but he took no notice. Blind rage drove him and his instincts directed him.

■ ■ ■

After leaving Odell's office, Jackson made a short fist pump then began softly whistling "Dixie." The pieces of the puzzle, one by one, were shifting into place. Returning to his office, he closed the door, sat down behind his desk, and hit the pre-programmed long-distance number on his office phone.

"Hello, Rodney. Have you arrived at your hotel yet?"

"Yes, the cab just dropped me off."

"Excellent. Call Dee on her cellphone and ask if you can pay her a visit. Remember the key is to get her to meet with you. Focus on the prize."

CHAPTER 16

2 p.m., Tuesday, August 18, 2015

Dee willed herself into the coffee shop on Lexington and Eighty-Third, passing an assortment of young women with their laptops flashing on the wooden counter running along the front window. It took a moment before she spotted Emily sitting in their regular booth, nursing a double espresso with a twist of lemon in a neat white demitasse. Dee ordered a chai tea at the counter and took a seat. An almond croissant sat in the centre of the table on a dessert plate with two forks. It had been cut in half, the paste oozing out onto the plate. Any other day and it would have been a perfect touch.

"Sorry I'm late," she said. "I'm moving at half my normal speed today, and the gynecologist ran a little late. Thanks for getting me in to her on such short notice."

"Is everything okay?"

"I'm upside down. She ran some blood tests and said they would call if it was anything serious."

"Come on, Dee. What else did she tell you?" Emily picked up the cup and took a sip of the coffee, which didn't really hide the knowing smirk.

Dee wanted to smile but couldn't find the energy. "You know what she told me. It took her sixty seconds to run the pregnancy test. I only wish I felt like celebrating. I've been throwing my guts up for two days now." Between the fatigue and the queasy stomach, nothing felt right. The shopping spree with Emily on Rodeo Drive the day before yesterday could have been a hundred years ago.

"Congratulations!" Emily shrieked. "News like that should have you feeling on top of the world. Have you told Odell?"

"Not yet." She watched Emily tentatively, then looked down and stirred the tea. Why *wasn't* that her first reaction, she wondered, until a plausible explanation occurred to her. "I didn't want to tell him over the phone," she said.

"Of course," Emily said, but her eyes told Dee something else. Dee felt her cheeks flushing with embarrassment.

Emily reached for half the croissant and licked at the almond paste. Then she took a nibble. It sent a wave of nausea coursing through Dee's stomach. She covered her mouth and dropped her head. Tried to gather her composure, then raised her head, barely holding back the bile. She needed to swallow, but it had to wait. "Swear you won't tell a soul. Not even Jackson. Not until Odell knows."

Emily nodded.

"I need some time." Dee was not ready to share the news with Odell. She'd crawled into bed last night at three in the morning sick as a dog. Him and his stupid idea to fly home when he saw she wasn't well. Why had she allowed Odell to talk her into flying when she was in such obvious distress? They could have stayed at the hotel for one more night. What was the big rush to get back to Manhattan? Probably another deal. Another secret deal. She could feel the bile rising and sipped the tea to push it back down along with her anger.

Even though they had not been married long, she knew not to argue with Odell. She could tell by his resolute eyes: she already knew them all too well. He had made a decision, and he was not going to be moved. Just like her father. So she'd given in and had the worst night of her life. The plane pitched and rolled in a storm and she wanted to die. She hadn't spoken a word to him all night. She was afraid of what she might say.

This morning, with her back to Odell, she'd reached for him across the bed, stretching her arm out behind her. He might be stubborn and resolute when he'd made a decision, but this morning Dee had appreciated his determination. It reminded her of Daddy. She found it strangely comforting. It was time to forgive Odell. He'd been right about one thing. She was thrilled to be back in her bed in Manhattan. It was beginning to feel like home for her and for the new life she might be carrying. She felt a rush of love overpowering her.

Normally when she reached out, he would turn inwards and spoon her. Some mornings it would lead to passionate love. She purred and extended her arm farther as her fingers sought him out, but all she felt were crumpled sheets. Where was he? Then she turned. Odell was gone. It was only seven-thirty.

"Odell knew you weren't well. Why did he rush off to work this morning?" Emily asked.

"He left me a text. Something about another deal. It's always another deal."

"Yeah; it's been like that for five years," Emily sighed, playing with her half of the croissant. "But here's the bright side. You're married to a big-shot partner in a big-shot firm."

"That's not what attracted me to him." Now her anger was directed at Emily. Dee stared at the untouched half-croissant. She felt like picking it up and throwing it. Where was this all coming from? she wondered.

"Easy, Dee. I just mean Odell is like the number-one deal guy in America. At least that's what Jackson's always saying."

"The number-one deal guy hasn't been around much in the last month, he's been so busy flying all over the country for work. Dallas, Houston, and I can't even remember where else. Then when he finally gets home, he's off in his own world. I'm frustrated, if you know what I mean."

"I get it. You're newlyweds. You want to know everything about him. You want to be spending every spare minute in bed with him."

"And I'm not. Until a couple of days ago it was the only thing on my mind. That's why I insisted on going to L.A. He promised me we'd have time together."

"Instead you spent it with Michael."

Dee blushed. "It wasn't like that."

"Sorry, Dee. I didn't mean anything by it."

"How did you and Jackson adjust when you first got married?"

"By the time we got married, we'd been together a few years. It's a process. You both have to put in the time and effort."

Dee sighed. "You have Jackson all figured out, while I still barely know Odell." A tear formed in the corner of her eye.

"It took me awhile. It all started with his mother issues. When boys act out, you can bet it's because either Momma or Daddy laid a number on 'em growing up." Emily picked up the lemon twist and popped it in her mouth.

Dee grimaced. It didn't take much to turn her stomach. "Isn't that bitter?"

"It's like marriage. Sometimes you just have to suck it up. I didn't tell you about the day I stood up to Jackson's mother? She never lets him forget that he doesn't measure up to her sister's son. Cousin Earl always outperformed him in his momma's eyes. Even now Jackson's just an associate while Earl runs his own law firm. Every time his mother mentions Earl, he cringes. Last trip out to Mobile I stepped into it, told her that Jackson was already a star in my eyes."

Dee had barely spent any time with Marisol, her mother-in-law. Just that one brief visit. And his father was dead to him.

"Jackson took me apart for it later in the car. Didn't want me interfering. Thought he could defend himself. I was making him look weak." Emily tightened her shoulders and her voice got loud. "My ass. Why do you think he works in New York? Can't be far enough away from that poison." Emily flushed. "Whoo, it feels good to get that off my chest."

Dee noticed the woman at the next table staring at them. Why couldn't she mind her business? What else had she overheard? She threw her a glare. It wasn't working so she picked up the croissant, ready to fire it. She could feel the warm almond paste seeping onto her wrist, trickling down her arm. What was she doing? She dropped the squished croissant on the plate and fumbled with her napkin.

Emily's shoulders slumped back a little as the colour in her cheeks began to drain. "We're a team, but his momma is off limits."

Dee continued to rub at the paste, which had stained her blouse cuff.

Emily's eyebrows raised slightly. "Do you think Odell might be keeping something from you?"

Dee felt a short piercing pain in her chest. Right through the middle of her heart. She didn't want to admit it but that was exactly what she was coming to believe. "It seems as if he wants to talk about something but he just can't find the time or opportunity." She involuntarily reached down and patted her firm belly. "I'm giving him some space, though the timing of this … this…" She could not say the word. "Well, it really couldn't be worse."

"Don't say that, Dee. Don't even think that. You know you don't mean it." Emily patted Dee's hand.

Dee paused, remembering her first kiss with Odell, outside her father's house, with Odell's limo waiting. Earth-shaking. Her life was never going to be the same. "I knew by that second evening that he had a depth to him behind the façade he presents to the world. But every time I try to reach behind the curtain, he shuts down. He's holding back. I can feel it but I can't explain it."

"Just cry it out," Emily said, pulling a tissue from her purse and handing it to Dee.

Dee dabbed at her cheeks.

"You love him and that's all that matters. That and the rock on your finger. Let me see your hand. That thing must be at least four carats." The stone radiated hopeful light.

Dee finally smiled. "He pulled it out while we were in bed. I still had so many questions." Like the scars on his back, she thought. How did he get them? Another thing—like his father—he wouldn't talk about. She kept her thoughts to herself. "But I had no doubts, I don't even understand why. I barely knew him. And I knew there were going to be acceptance issues. I went home to Mobile and tried to have it out with my father a few weeks ago. He left in a huff. Momma told me to give him time."

"Maybe that was part of the attraction. Forbidden fruit?"

"That's not it, Em. Odell's the one. I know he's carrying a lot inside him. He just won't let me in. I'm such a failure," Dee said, sighing and feeling tears start.

Dee knew there was nothing Emily could do or say to make her feel better. Her tears were now falling in torrents but she no longer cared who might be watching. She was the author of her own misfortune. Between Daddy's reaction to the marriage and Odell's distance from her, this marriage—only several weeks old—was turning into a fiasco.

"I think you need to sit back and take a breath," Emily said in a comforting tone. Then a small smile crept across her lips. "Do you realize you have almond paste all over your wrist and you just wiped it on your chin? Why don't you take a moment and go freshen up?"

"I also need to pee." Dee laughed, though she had no idea why.

■ ■ ■

Emily needed to take stock. Dee was falling apart and Emily couldn't let on that she was not far behind. Jackson's plan was working out, but not without a cost. Dee was the one suffering—likely from morning sickness— so at least she had an excuse for the nausea. Emily was battling guilt. That snivelling rich jerk from Mobile would be calling at any time. Jackson had insisted that she encourage Dee to meet with Rodney. He swore it would be the last thing he asked, but Emily still was not comfortable—this was not what friends do. She reminded herself that once Jackson made partner, Michael Cassidy would drop into the background. Dee and Odell would eventually make up and all four would live happily ever after. She and Dee would forever be best friends and if Emily was lucky, they could share pregnancy stories.

Dee returned to the table and sat back down. The colour had returned to her cheeks and all traces of the almond paste had been removed. As if it had never been there. Like the necklace. Dee's phone vibrated. Emily steeled herself. Jackson was going to want a full report later. Dee pushed the phone across the table with her fingertips as if it carried some disease. "You take it." Emily let it ring, but it persisted. Damned Rodney. "Pick it up," Dee ordered. "I can't handle the news either way." Shoot. Of course. The number was local.

Emily nodded a few times then said thank you and disconnected, wondering how she would be feeling right now if the call was for her. Probably beyond ecstatic. She pretended it was. "It was Dr. Brown's receptionist. The medical tests all came back negative. You have started a normal pregnancy and the severe morning sickness is a great indication." She raised her voice two octaves. "Isn't that the best news ever?"

Dee didn't light up at all, and Emily knew she would have to carry the excitement for both of them, rocking back and forth, clucking just a little too loudly. It didn't seem to be working, though the woman one table over was staring again.

Dee's phone vibrated again. "This one's from Alabama," Dee said. "Sorry, Emily, it might be Momma—I should at least say hello." Dee answered the call and listened for a minute. "Well, Rodney, thank you so much for the good wishes. You've always been a kind and thoughtful man."

There was a pause while Dee listened.

"Rodney, this is so out of the blue. I'm not quite certain of my afternoon schedule and I'm out right now. I'm at Eighty-Second near Second, if you know where that is."

Emily leaned over and whispered. "An old friend?" Dee nodded.

"If you have the energy, meet with him, it may do you good to hear some stories about home."

Dee nodded, then spoke into the phone. "Certainly, Rodney. Let's make it at 3:30 at my apartment." She hung up and began crying again. "Rodney Ferguson is the last person in the world I want to see now."

"He'll be a distraction, and then you can send him on his way," Emily suggested. This was the last favour she was doing for Jackson. Dee wasn't the only one who needed to vomit.

Emily gathered up their purses and handed Dee's back to her. Dee reached for it and the strap slid through her fingers and dropped to the floor. Her eyes glazed over. Emily put a supporting arm around Dee's waist and slowly walked her outside onto Lexington. The foot traffic was light.

"Just take a few deep breaths. Enjoy the moment. God must be smiling on you."

Although it was a short distance back to the apartment, in the stifling heat it felt as if it was taking forever. The storm the weather channel predicted had not arrived yet, but it was on its way. Emily kept up a constant and excited chatter. She needed to behave normally. Like an excited best friend. Ignore the fact that Dee just needed to get horizontal and fast.

They finally made their way into Dee's building. Giancarlo, the concierge, rushed up to greet them and stepped up to prop Dee from the other side.

"Can I help get you into your apartment, Mrs. Moore?" The smell of his minty mouthwash was overpowering. Dee's face turned green.

Dee shot Emily a look that was shouting for help and urging her to keep moving. "We're fine, Giancarlo," Emily said. The two women stepped onto the elevator and after the doors had safely closed Dee began to cry all the way up to the penthouse and inside the apartment.

"Thanks for all your help, Em. I don't know what I'd do without you." Dee reached out for a hug. Emily could feel her own tears boiling up behind her eyes. She quickly turned to leave, then stopped. She suddenly remembered what she had forgotten to tell Dee.

"Dr. Brown said to call her office tomorrow to set up your next few appointments. Congratulations, Dee."

3:00 p.m.

Exhausted, Dee lay down in the bedroom. What would she do without Emily's understanding? And why was Emily the one to care? Where was Odell? How could he run off once again this morning, leaving her in this state of … this state of… She couldn't finish the thought. She could feel the anger rising again. How was she going to tell Odell the news? And when?

Dee fell into a light sleep, dreaming about her father and a child running in circles in their backyard in Mobile. There was laughter and Daddy was chasing from behind, pretending that he couldn't keep up. Dee saw the child trip, hitting her head on a rock. Blood was flowing everywhere and Daddy bent over to help. He turned the child's head upward, trying to revive her. Dee screamed. It was as if she was staring into a mirror. She woke with a start, thankful it was just a dream. It didn't take a dream reader to figure that one out. Too many unresolved issues with Daddy. She fell back into a restless sleep. A persistent buzz finally woke her. She shook off the fog, realizing the disturbance was coming from the intercom. She got up quickly, though she felt disoriented until she heard a familiar voice. She cringed when she heard Giancarlo speaking.

"Mrs. Moore, there is a man down here by the name of Ferguson saying he has an appointment with you."

It was just after three-thirty and she remembered the call. Rodney. Darn. "Please send him up." She was really in no shape for a visit and determined to make excuses. Within a minute there was a knock at the door.

Rodney walked in, with a wide grin. She felt terribly embarrassed by her appearance. His grin was beginning to turn into a grimace. He followed her into the living room and took a seat on the couch.

"Dee, I can't tell you how much I've missed you. Are you all right?"

"Rodney, I really appreciate your coming by, but I'm feeling a little under the weather right now. Do you mind if we do a rain check? I'm sure I can make some time later this week if you don't mind. Why don't you text me in the morning when you know your schedule, so we can make arrangements."

"Certainly, Dee, I'm so sorry to impose. I had no idea."

"No, Rodney, I'm the one who's sorry. Please excuse my rudeness. I think I've got a touch of a stomach virus. I really should have called you but I fell asleep."

"No problem at all. You get better, ya hear. I'll be in touch tomorrow." He turned and headed out the front door.

Dee closed the door and crawled back into bed.

■ ■ ■

Rodney wandered into the elevator. He could hear Jackson's voice piercing the fog in his head. That's it, you just accepted a lame excuse like that? And later this week? What does that mean? You're telling me she didn't sound good? Something was bothering her, probably her marriage and you didn't capitalize?

But what was he to do? It certainly wouldn't help to be rude, would it? What would Jackson do in this situation? Certainly not slink off with his tail between his legs. Rodney would never be able to explain this failure, piled on top of all the others.

Time for the new Rodney to take charge. He resolved to give her a couple of hours. Maybe three? But he couldn't walk in on her and Odell. Jackson would tell him that was idiocy. He'd give her a few hours and then return. *Seize the moment, Rodney. You only live once.*

CHAPTER 17

Dee was again startled awake by the buzzing intercom. She reached for her phone on the night table and called downstairs.

"Another guest, Mrs. Moore. Mr. Brabant? Can I let him in?"

"I'm sorry, Giancarlo. What did you say?" Dee jumped out of bed in a panic.

"He says his name is Edward."

She choked down the wave that was threatening to send her rushing to the bathroom. "Please send him up." Her heart was racing as she did a quick run around the unit, eliminating signs of poor housekeeping. He'd be sure to notice—not that he would say anything. More proof of her weak character.

She glanced at her watch. On most nights Odell couldn't be expected before 7:30. Why hadn't Daddy given her any notice? He must be here on business. Maybe he was coming to open the door to amends. She felt a darkness surrounding her and walked over to the back of the living room to open the curtains. The late afternoon daylight poured in, and it began to calm her. She willed her heart to slow down. Took a few deep breaths.

When the buzzer sounded, she opened the door and stared at her father. Speechless.

"May I come in?" he asked a little stiffly. "I sent you a text almost three hours ago. When you didn't respond, I worried. I hope you don't feel you have to ignore me."

She realized she had been holding her breath. A rush of feeling gushed out with her exhale. She stepped forward suddenly and threw her arms around his shoulders. "Oh, Daddy, I'm so glad you've come around. And the timing couldn't be better. Sorry about the phone. I just got up from a nap and I must have turned the sound off. It's the jet lag. We just got back from L.A. late last night." She began to cry. "Excuse me." She reached for a tissue from her pocket and dabbed at her eyes, then smiled broadly. "Come on in."

Edward closed the door behind him and followed Dee through the hallway and into the living room to the left. "You would not believe what happened to me on the way over here. Those darned teenagers selling candy bars at Grand Central. Must have lifted my wallet while I was reaching into my pocket for change. Thankfully I keep a billfold in my pocket. Otherwise it might have been very embarrassing with the taxi driver."

"Well, Daddy, I'm glad you're able to keep your sense of humour."

"The cards can all be replaced. Not like my family."

"Daddy, that's the nicest thing you could say to me right now. Please sit. Make yourself at home. Why don't you take a seat in the living room and just relax. I need a few minutes to make myself pretty. Then I'll fix you a snack."

Dee headed for the bedroom.

■ ■ ■

After she closed the bedroom door, Edward realized he had arrived empty-handed. Eleanor would kill him if she found out he hadn't brought a housewarming gift for his daughter. There were all kinds of stores on Lexington so he should be able to find something quickly.

"Dee, you take your time," Edward called out. "I'm just going to stroll the neighbourhood while you get ready. I'll be back shortly."

■ ■ ■

Ten minutes later Dee heard the front door open. She panicked. Only Giancarlo had the code to get in—so it must be him, no way it would be

Odell at this hour. And if Giancarlo came all the way back here? He saw she hadn't been well when she entered the building, yet he still gave her that wolfish look with his disgusting breath. She needed to stop him. She reached for her phone to call Odell. It wasn't there. She must have left it on the living room table when she greeted Daddy. She'd have to pretend he was home. That would scare off an intruder.

"Who's there? Odell, can you get the visitor at the door." She held her breath and hoped the front door would close.

Odell stormed into the bedroom. "Get the door? You know I wasn't home. What's going on? I've been calling. Why haven't you answered?"

She could barely speak she felt so flustered. It couldn't be Odell. Yet here he was, angry as a wasp. "I'm sorry, darling. I just don't feel myself today." She walked past him to the living room to get her phone on the coffee table. She scrolled down the list of callers. Odell, Odell, Odell, Odell, Odell, Daddy, crap. She could feel the colour draining from her face. And the worst was yet to come. Daddy.

Odell had followed her into the living room, stopping at her side. "Dee, do you have the amulet?"

He had noticed and he had beaten her to the punch. But the amulet wasn't important anymore, thank goodness. Not with what she had to tell him. Then he'd be an ally to help her deal with Daddy. "I have something better than the amulet. That's what I wanted to—"

"Don't deflect. Just answer the question," he ordered.

It took every bit of self-control to hold back the sudden burst of anger. No one talked to her like that. She managed an even tone, but it was sapping every ounce of energy. "I've been meaning to tell you, Odell, but I didn't know how to break the news. I must have misplaced it while we were in Los Angeles. I searched high and low in the room and I even left a message with the concierge that if they find it they should notify me immediately, but I've heard nothing so far. I feel terrible about it. I know how important it is to you."

"And you didn't give it to anyone?" Now it was beginning to feel like an inquisition.

"Odell, why would I do that?"

"Tell me, Dee, what were you doing on the beach with Michael the other day?"

This was all so confusing. All she wanted was to share the good news and he was behaving like a … like a… "Why are you behaving like a jerk?" She threw it at him hard. Did he know about the joint? Probably. He was asking questions like a lawyer laying a trap. Who could have told him beside Michael but if so why question her like this? Nothing to be defensive about but she knew it would have been a whole lot easier if she had told Odell. "Michael and I had a very pleasant afternoon together. You asked him to spend the day with me. Did you forget?"

"I don't think I can be more plain about what I'm asking, Dee. What did you do together on the beach? Did you walk? Did you sit? Did you eat? The question is fairly simple. I just expect a simple answer."

"You *expect*?" she asked. She felt herself tensing. She did not like his tone of voice and she felt a well of anger rising inside her. This one bigger and bolder. "You can *expect* all you want but until you begin to treat me with a little respect, you can *expect* me to turn around and leave this room." She found herself raising her voice to him for the first time in their marriage.

"Is it so difficult to answer my question?" His voice sounded a little calmer this time. Smug bastard. Did he have an ounce of emotion in him? Did he ever show emotion? If it was there, she'd find it.

"You abandoned me this morning when you knew I was sick as a dog. Work. It had to be work. It's always work. Every time there's a choice to make, it's work before Dee. And then you come barging in here thinking you can talk to me like one of your lawyer flunkies? No, forget that, General," she sneered. "I'm sure you treat all your lawyers who glorify you with a lot more respect than I'm getting today. I told you, it was a day at the beach, no more, no less. Simple question, simple answer." She was not going to give an inch. He still had a lot of apologizing to do and the list was getting longer.

"So you didn't smoke a joint with him?"

"Is that what this is about? A freaking joint? You're giving me a rough time over a little marijuana. Since when did you become Mr. High and Mighty to judge me? I'll have you know I toked on plenty of joints in my days at 'Bama and I can tell you I am no worse the wear for the experience. There's nothing wrong with being a little out of control from time to time."

"You mean like you are right now?" The declaration of war.

"Oh, here comes Mr. Perfect, who's never committed an infraction in his life. There's nothing wrong with smoking a joint in L.A."

"Dee, it's against the law," he said. His voice was getting a little louder.

"Don't go getting all sanctimonious on me. And don't you yell at me." She could feel her temperature rising, the pitch of her voice rising in tandem.

"I am not yelling." Now he was yelling.

"Okay then," she shouted, raising her hands to shoulder level. "Cuff me and take me in. Arrest me." There was a long silent pause between them. She knew immediately she had taken it too far. How to retreat? This was foreign territory for her. Probably for him as well.

She began to sob. "I'm sorry, Odell, I don't know what's gotten into me." The rollercoaster had dipped and her stomach was reeling.

"Listen, Dee, I'm only talking about honesty here. Why is it that Michael told me today that you gave him the amulet?"

"It's … it's … simply not possible, Odell. It never happened."

"Dee, I've seen photos of the two of you on the beach. You gave it to him."

She felt the band in her stomach tightening. "You were spying on us?" Her voice hardened once again. "You call that trust in a relationship? You took pictures of us? I don't know you at all, do I? The books all say don't get married until you've had your first fight. I should have said no to you when you swept me off my feet." Dee turned her back. "There's a very ugly character beneath that wonderful controlled veneer you present to the world."

"Don't try to change the subject. This isn't about me."

He put his hands on her shoulders and turned her to face him. His hold on her was uncomfortable. Almost as harsh as his words. "I didn't spy on you and I didn't take any photos, but someone sure as hell did and they sent them to me. The photos tell the story. You gave him the jug, you smoked with him, you did God knows what else with him when you were stoned together on the beach wearing a very revealing bikini." Odell paused. "Did he take advantage of you?"

Dee couldn't help herself. She began laughing. "'Did he *take advantage* of you?'" she repeated in a mocking voice. "Are we living an episode of a nineteenth-century British melodrama? In North America we ask, 'Did he *screw* you?'"

She felt his grip on her shoulders tightening. "Get off. You're hurting me!" she yelled, twisting until his grip released. She could feel a searing pain just below her shoulder blade. "I've never been so insulted in my life and I will never forget what you just did to me. Never. I don't know where you got your information but someone is lying and it isn't me. Yes, I had the joint, mea culpa, nail me to the cross, and let me die there so you can absolve yourself of all your sins, you son of a bitch. Get out."

He was not moving. Not an inch. Maybe she was finally getting through. She just needed to hurt him a little more so he could share the intensity of her pain. She crossed the room to get away from him. She detested him. "And before you go, I just wanted to share the good news. I'm pregnant. Congratulations."

"Is it his?" Odell was barely whispering now.

"It's been three days since the beach. We only just met a week ago. You and I never use protection. Of course it's his, you moron."

The rage overtook her. She picked up the nearest item, a glass vase, and launched it. She didn't intend to hit him, but she needed something to break along with her heart. The vase missed Odell by a few feet and crashed into the wall, breaking into a thousand shards behind him.

Her defiance broke along with the glass lying on the hardwood floor. She sagged, mouth agape, overflowing with remorse. He just stood there holding his forehead with one hand, rubbing his eyes with the other. Odell's cry was brief, anguished. It was more like the howl of a wounded animal. Was it guilt or recognition that he was behaving like a fool?

Dee ran to the hall bathroom. She needed to be alone. Even when she was with him she was alone. Anguished, she slammed the door, sat down on the toilet seat, and dropped her head into her hands.

She heard a door close. She waited a minute until she was certain he was no longer there. She could not face him. Not now. Maybe later. If she ever felt normal again. Maybe when he was ready to apologize. The buzzer sounded and she nearly jumped out of her skin, suddenly realizing that her father had returned. Maybe he'd been right about Odell all along.

She trudged to the front door and opened it. "Come in, Daddy" was all she said.

The senator walked through the doorway. She hung her head. The broken glass, the flowers, the puddles on the floor. What must he be thinking? She gave the door a nudge with what little remaining energy she possessed, before turning and heading for the couch in the living room where she sat down. It was all too much.

"What the blazes is going on? My dear, you've been crying and this looks like a war zone. I was gone for less than an hour." She was certain he was figuring it out.

"You didn't run into him in the hallway? He just left a moment ago." It was virtually impossible for them not to meet. It made no sense. Could Odell have seen Daddy coming and ducked into a corner? At this point she wouldn't put anything past Odell. How could he leave the apartment in the middle of their first fight? Coward.

Edward's face was beet red. "He must have been going down one elevator while I was coming up in the other. Did he raise a hand to you?" The pitch in Edward's voice lowered an octave and turned icy quiet. "Because if he did I will wreak my vengeance on him personally." He spoke each word slowly, as if he was already plotting his revenge. Then he rushed across the room like a protective bear. "No one lays a hand on my daughter," he growled.

"Daddy, you're overreacting." She stepped back from his reach and looked her father straight in the eye. She couldn't give him any ammunition here. "We had a fight. It was loud, it was nasty but we will reconcile.

Eventually. I'm not without fault here and he didn't touch me." There was no way she was conceding to Daddy that Odell had manhandled her. That would be all he would need. Besides she knew Odell didn't mean to hurt her. She wanted to rub her shoulder and decided against it.

"Not possible, angel. You are perfect."

She smiled weakly. "Please come and sit down, Daddy. I'm afraid I can't be the best host this evening."

"Dee, at least let me clean this up for you."

"Daddy, you're my guest. Just leave it. I'm the one who made the mess and I'll get to it later."

He reached into his jacket pocket and pulled out a small gift-wrapped box. "Here, Dee, this is for you."

She unwrapped it slowly. It was a tiny sculpture of a couple of white turtle doves. Was this a peace offering? Maybe the two of them could make some real progress today.

"It's beautiful, Daddy," she said, placing it on the mantel just under the Pissarro. "Thank you."

"Listen, Dee, your mother thinks I behaved badly when you first told us you were married. I may be a thick-headed man but perhaps I did over-react at the time."

"I know you care about me, Daddy."

"You know me. I've never been a man to beat about the bush. I say what's on my mind. When you first told me, I believed this was a mistake. He's almost ten years your senior."

How often was Daddy going to raise such an old-fashioned argument about the age difference? And when was he going to admit to himself the real reasons for his objections? She would never get through to him until she forced him to confront the prejudice. For the moment she allowed him to vent. "How much can you have in common? There are so many reasons why this can never work. It's not too late to pull yourself out of this."

"I thought you came to apologize for overreacting."

"I'm no longer certain my first reaction was wrong. The evidence is all over the floor."

"You don't understand, Daddy, I love him. I want to build a life with him."

"Build a life? You call this mess a foundation to build a marriage? I only see anger and reprisals and pain coming your way. Shattered glass lying on the floor. That's going to be your life, Dee."

"Daddy, you're misunderstanding."

"You barely know this man who has bewitched you, taken advantage of you, then left you stranded here in this prison of an apartment in a city where you're alone, where you have no friends, no family. Just torn-up flowers and puddles of pain. Am I really the one who's misunderstandin'? Please come home with me, Dee. I'm beggin' you."

"It's too late, Daddy." This was overwhelming. She needed to lie down, but not yet. There was only one way to get through to him. Muster her final resolve and finally tell the goddamned truth about who she was, other than the frail daughter in need of his protection.

"My dear, it's never too late. I know plenty of people in the judiciary who can help. Let me take care of everything."

She felt her anger rising again. She would not be treated like a child. "Daddy, I don't know how to make myself more clear. Stay out of my business." The words were launched like a rocket.

She saw the shock register on his face. "Dee, I've never seen you in this state. Calm down. We're havin' a discussion about how I can help."

Storm clouds had moved in and the sky was dark and threatening. There was a flash on the eastern horizon followed by a crash of thunder. The lights in the building flickered a few times and went out completely. Through the window, she saw the lights in the adjoining buildings were out as well.

She was distracted for a moment then regained her focus. The veneer of Southern softness had been scraped away.

"Another discussion? Is that what we're having, Daddy, or is this a lecture? Another one of your lectures that I've choked down sweetly for over twenty years? The lectures the dutiful father gives to the daughter he's doting over. That may be what you think but let me tell you what I feel. Smothered."

"Horse crap. I always provided the best for you."

"Oh yes, Daddy. Always providing for your Dee. Always molding her into the person you want her to be? I finished high school desperate to get out of your house, determined to get some space in my life. You insisted on two years of state college, before you'd let me leave town for university. It was no more than a glorified finishing school for women. Cows waiting in line to mate. You were probably betting I'd be engaged and never leave Mobile." Dee fought to control the trembling in her voice. "It was disgusting but I swallowed it down for you. Two years of my life— a complete waste of my time. Maybe you finally understood I needed to get away from home. I needed a university degree and a life of my own. Why did it take you so long to figure that out? Do you know how hard it's been on me to be your daughter, with your family history?" The tears were beginning to well up.

"I don't know what you're talkin' about, Dee." She could tell he knew exactly what she meant.

"Oh, don't think I haven't studied the family background. I know about the Klansmen past. I've just choked it down for all these years."

The lights came back on, causing Dee to flinch involuntarily. Now she could see, and not just feel, the anger etched into his eyes. But the battle lines had been drawn.

"And your support for Governor Wallace? Tell me, Daddy; it's rumoured you wore the hood as well. At least that's what all the other kids told me in elementary school. They were getting it from their parents, after all: your so-called friends. Did you know that, Daddy? I got to lie in bed at night and imagine the horrible things that you might have done to black teenagers. Have you found forgiveness from your God for those acts? From your Christian God? From your Jesus who turns the other cheek?" The tears were now streaming down her cheeks as she began to wail.

"Daughter, I have no idea who you are or who you've become, but this outburst worries me, more than any other evidence, that somethin' is very wrong with this marriage. I made the trip here on instinct, feelin' I needed to share advice based on my years of experience, but now I'm certain I took the right steps visitin' this evening because you are in need of assistance, whether or not you're prepared to admit it. You're not behavin' normally. You're comin' with me." Edward stood up as if preparing to take action on his words.

Dee could feel the hysteria rising from her very depths. Once more she was screaming. "Daddy, I am staying right here. This is my life. With my husband. I will live it as I choose."

"Dee, you're outside your own mind."

"Out of my mind?" she yelled.

"Not what I said. You're not thinkin' straight and there is definitely somethin' the matter."

Edward was approaching her, yet she sensed a new presence in the room. It must be her imagination. She crossed her arms under her breasts. Took a deep breath. Faced him down. Lowered her voice. Lowered the boom.

"I am not moving one inch, Daddy. I'm pregnant."

She was certain now that she heard a movement coming from the front door and just out of view. Odell arriving to apologize. Perfect timing. She might as well leave the room and let the two of them go at it. At this moment she just wanted to be alone. Let them both go to hell.

Her father took no notice: there was no slowing Edward Brabant when he launched into his own tirades and Dee could feel one coming on. He stood as if addressing an audience, readying himself to make an impassioned presentation to swing the mood of the Senate. He began speaking quietly and as he spoke she could feel the passion rising from within him.

"Dee, your sanity is slippin' and now you are goin' to complicate all our lives with a black child. I will not abide by this."

His voice had risen to a roar as he crossed the room grabbing for her arm. As she pulled away from his grip, she began to feel faint. She collapsed, hitting her head on the corner of the glass coffee table. The crash was thunderous. Blood spattered everywhere as she lost consciousness.

"Oh my God," Edward whispered as he knelt over her. Just then a blow struck him on the back of his head and he collapsed on top of her.

■ ■ ■

The attacker stepped back. This was not what he had come to do. He had come to apologize. Instead he began doing what the voice in his head told him he had to do once again. What had to be done to people who betrayed him. This man was always going to be a threat to Odell, as long as he lived. He heard movement coming from behind the bedroom door. Another threat? If so, he'd have to deal with it quickly. Nothing was going according to plan. He lifted the cellphone from the floor and dialled 911 then headed to the bedroom to deal with that threat.

PART III

CHAPTER 18

Detective Stavros Micolonides felt the approach of the witching hour as his partner pulled the car to the curb. Still eleven minutes to go. It would be long after midnight before they got back in the car. He and Rachel Brodinsky stepped out of her black Impala, nondescript except for the car seat filled with stuffed animals in the back. Another crime scene—another late night. They didn't get too many on the Upper East Side, though Mac, the name he had been rechristened with at the Academy, had come to understand after thirteen years working homicides, eight with Rachel, that only one thing mattered. Dead was dead. That was how they made a living.

They were directed upstairs by one of the officers controlling entry into the building. The press had not yet arrived. It wouldn't be long. Mac stopped at the doorway of the penthouse to scan the room. He noticed the small pool of water about six feet to the left of the entrance, watermarks on the wall, and fragments of glass and long-stemmed flowers strewn on the floor nearby. Each spot had been tagged and labelled, and the photographers were taking shots from various angles.

Mac stepped carefully around the evidence, then stopped. His trained reflex was to study the scene before the body. Nice apartment. Floor-to-ceiling windows letting in the New York moonlight, expensive artwork on the walls, an assortment of sculptures. Jennifer, his wife, would know if it was any good. She had studied art in school. One gigantic piece had a blue iceberg floating around in a northern landscape. Very surreal.

Not much furniture, though. Just a fancy couch, love seat, and a shattered coffee table. No dining room furniture.

The victim was lying on his stomach, his head resting left side up on a rust-and-chocolate-brown-striped area rug. He had to be at least in his mid-sixties, portly, Caucasian, and dressed in a tailored suit. The blood around his scalp had ruined the collar of his white dress shirt, but it wasn't nearly the amount Mac would have expected from a head wound. A second and far more substantial puddle of blood had pooled on the corner of the rug and dripped onto the hardwood floor.

A small sculpture lay askew a few feet away, and fragments of glass were all over the carpet, presumably the remnants of the shattered glass coffee table.

Rachel bent over the body on the floor, sniffing him up and down.

"Well, if it ain't Mac and Cheese," a shrill voice echoed from across the room.

Mac was willing to bet that Rachel was now glaring at the medical examiner, Mariella Cabrerra. He could never figure out why the nickname bothered Rachel so much. She came by it honestly—she had solved the Barino case last year by sniffing out a poison in the parmigiana that the victims had eaten for dinner. The story had made its way around the precinct like wild fire.

"What do you have for us, Mariella?" Mac asked.

Had Mariella been sleeping when she got the call? She'd made no attempt to tie up her frazzled hair, which stuck out in all directions in various shades of grey. Her voice sounded like chalk scraping a blackboard.

"The victim shows obvious signs of blunt-force trauma to the back of the head. Too soon to say if that killed him. Bleeding's a little light for this type of homicide. I'd have expected more like the pool on the floor over there," she said, nodding toward the edge of the carpet.

"That's not his?" Rachel asked.

"No. There were two bodies. The second victim was a woman. Still alive. The pool came from her head wound. The officer in the kitchen has the details." Mariella's hands were carefully feeling the man's neck, separating it from the damp collar. The blood had begun to crust.

"If you get a little closer, you can see there are some abrasions around the neck. Note the bulging left eye and deep red circle around it. I expect we will find the same in his other eye. Also not consistent with the head trauma. There's more to this than meets the eye. Certainly not a slip and fall. Likely a homicide. I can't say much about time of death but if I had to guess, I'd say it's been about four hours. I'll need to get him back to the lab before I can give you anything concrete."

Mac made his way to the kitchen. The stainless steel top-of-the-line appliances shone, probably brand new, and a couple of empty pots sat on the stovetop. The beat cop had his back to him, standing over a granite countertop, scribbling in his notepad.

Mac tapped him on the shoulder. "First of all, who's the vic?"

Startled, the officer turned around. Olive skin and barely any facial hair, probably straight out of the academy. He fumbled to close the notepad. The wrong thing to do since he'd obviously need to refer to his notes. Rookies.

"Sorry, detective. I'm officer Devanathan. Please call me Dave. I was the first responder to the 911. The victim had no ID."

"Call me Mac. This your first homicide, Dave?"

The officer nodded.

"If you have a soul, they never get any easier, but the first one is always the toughest."

Rachel had just joined them in the kitchen. "The vic is very familiar but I can't place him."

"How does he smell?"

"Shut it, Mac."

"All right then," Mac said, turning to the officer. Maybe it wasn't the best time for sarcasm. "Take it from the beginning."

"We think it might have been a robbery gone bad. The apartment belongs to Odell Moore. He works for TGO, one of the big-time law firms in midtown. According to the concierge, Moore shares the apartment with his wife. She moved in recently but hasn't been around much, at least that's what the concierge tells us. Mrs. Moore arrived home at about two-thirty p.m., and there were at least three visitors that he knows of over the course of the afternoon, including Moore himself. He's definitely not the body on the floor. Moore is a tall, athletic African-American. The concierge didn't see him leave the building. However, it's a small building and the concierge does rounds four times a day, so there are periods where the front desk is unattended."

"Any witnesses?"

The officer went on to explain that he had interviewed the neighbour, a music professor at NYU. She'd been practising her cello and was disturbed by yelling from about five-thirty p.m. onward. At one point she heard a crash and the door slamming, and then later on, around seven p.m., there was another huge crash. A few minutes later she heard some footsteps in the hallway. She was too frightened to come out of her apartment and couldn't be certain about the timeline. In between the crashes, there was a power failure in the building. Finally she worked up the courage to go out into the hall and found the door ajar.

"Can she identify the assailant?" Mac asked.

"She's of no use to us," the officer said. "An anonymous 911 call alerted the paramedics, and when they arrived, the neighbour was lying just inside the entrance of the crime scene—she'd passed out. At first sight, they assumed she was one of the victims. She came to just as they arrived, although she was pretty woozy. The last thing she remembers were the bodies on the floor and all the blood. Nothing else."

"What did the paramedics find?" Rachel asked.

"There were two bodies on the floor. The old portly guy was lying on the legs of a young blond woman. She was still alive. The concierge identified her as Mrs. Moore. We had time to get some photos before the paramedics took her away. We left the male on the carpet. His body position was adjusted when they lifted the woman out from under him." The officer showed him an image of the bodies in their original locations. The male victim's head was askew, as if deliberately pushed into a very uncomfortable position.

"Tough way to die," Mac said.

"What does the neighbour know about the Moores?" Rachel asked.

The officer flipped his notepad open again. "She said they'd never been introduced. She'd only seen Moore at a distance. The wife is a relatively new addition, and they said hello to one another in the hallway, but that's about it."

"Which way is the bedroom?" Mac asked.

"Just behind us," Dave answered. "Through the French doors. Nothing relevant as far as I can tell."

Mac would be the judge of that. One of the doors was ajar, the other bolted in place to the ceiling. Not much decoration on the walls and the bed covering was rumpled, as if someone had been sleeping on it and hadn't bothered to straighten it out. One of the Moores might have taken an afternoon nap. Probably the missus. Nothing notable on the night tables. High-end furniture. Four-poster canopy bed. Jennifer would probably say it was very romantic.

He walked over to the closets—two walk-ins facing each other. He opened one of the doors and was surprised at its depth. A series of starched white shirts, French cuffed, were hanging on one side, evenly spaced. Opposite them hung an assortment of dress suits, a dozen in all. Six navy and six black were also spaced about an inch apart. Mac reached in to feel the material. Silky smooth. They weren't selling these in the downtown warehouses where Mac paid cash. The labels were Italian. The back wall was narrow and filled with an array of colourful ties. Something for every occasion from funeral to business meeting to wedding. The man dressed to impress.

The pairs of polished black and navy shoes were also carefully aligned on shelves, just off the floor. Nothing stood out except for the three tin soldiers sitting on the floor in the corner, just beside a shoe box. They were the only thing out of order in the entire cupboard. Mac kneeled and picked them up in his gloved hands. A Union general standing over two

Confederate privates, lying prone. He put them down and lifted the lid on the box, which had been left slightly ajar. It was a collection of Civil War soldiers of various ranks and an 1860 silver dollar. Probably collectors' items. Maybe Moore was a buff. There was nothing worthy of note in the woman's closet, but this was just the beginning. Who could tell what might be relevant when they had a better understanding of the case?

Mac headed back to the body in the living room. He got down on his knees. The bulging eye was a distraction. Mac closed his eyes for a moment. He couldn't shake the feeling of familiarity with the profile. Finally he opened his eyes and stood up.

"I saw this guy on *Face the Nation* last Sunday."

"You still watch cable?"

Mac ignored Rachel's comment. "Some big shot on the Senate Appropriations Committee in Washington."

"I guess they'll have to find a replacement for him."

"He's a hardliner on sanctions for the Russians and the Chinese. What a shit show this is going to turn into."

"You can Google him back at the precinct. Our first assassination!"

Dead was dead. It didn't matter to Mac how it was labelled.

CHAPTER 19

10:30 a.m., Wednesday, August 19, 2015

Odell stood over the anguished profile and a bulging eye. The distressed gurglings from the throat were almost soundless. Odell's body tensed. His fingers clenched, the muscles in his arms taut. Slowly the dream image diminished and the spasm relaxed. It was chilly and damp, so he kept his eyes closed as he curled into a ball and pulled the blanket up to his neck. The dream continued. He heard the plea for mercy. "No," Odell shouted. His head jerked off the pillow and his eyes blinked open. The blinding pain behind his eyes caused him to shut them quickly. Slowly he opened them again. Dull light poured in from all directions. He raised his arm to shield the light. This was a completely alien environment. Morning? There were no windows in sight. He guessed early dawn, but where the hell was he?

He pulled himself into a sitting position, elbows on thighs, head resting between his palms, and rubbed his temples. That helped ease the pain. Why was the floor concrete? He heard a voice from a distance.

"Moore's finally up. Maybe this morning he'll be a little more communicative."

Was the voice a continuation of a dream? No, the voice and the pain in his head were real. His training kicked in and he remembered his college football coach saying, "It's only pain. Get up." He stood, attempting to focus on the two silhouettes on the other side of the iron bars. How had he managed to get into a cell? Had he been knocked out and abducted?

"W-what's going on? How did I get here?" The fog wasn't lifting.

He tried to focus on his jailers. One was short and thick, dressed in a polyester, off-the-rack suit, probably from a deep-discount warehouse. His tie was half done up, collar open, a day-old growth of beard, and he could probably use a shower. Odell felt that way himself. The taller figure had a prominent sloped nose, close-cropped blond hair, and was wearing a form-fitting brown suit, sipping a cup of coffee and staring at him. He felt like a zoo animal on display.

The shorter one began. "We apologize for leaving you in the jail cell overnight, but we didn't have any options."

"Have I been arrested?"

"No. We brought you in late last night. You don't remember?"

"This isn't funny at all. I have no idea who you are. Do you know who I am?"

"Yes. You're Odell Moore. The lawyer. We introduced ourselves last night. I'm Detective Stavros Micolonides, though feel free to call me Mac, and this is my partner, Rachel Brodinsky. We met outside your building."

"So what the hell are we doing here? Why didn't you let me go back to my apartment?" Could he believe anything they were telling him? He'd never seen these two in his life, much less last night. "Show me your badges."

Each detective obliged. "We tried talking to you last night," the one called Rachel said. "You became belligerent. Very aggressive. Unfortunately you left us little choice. Besides your apartment is a crime scene."

"A crime scene? This is outrageous. I demand you release me. My wife must be beside herself with worry." He patted his pockets. "Where's my cellphone?"

"We've taken it for now and we'll return it to you shortly," Rachel said. "You have to understand, Mr. Moore, while you're not under arrest, you're currently a person of interest in a murder investigation. We need to have a long talk. Why don't you gather yourself together while we step away for a moment. We'll be back shortly."

It began to dawn on Odell that his last recollection was walking the streets of midtown Manhattan yesterday afternoon, at least assuming that today was Wednesday. Everything after that was unreachable. The amulet … something about the amulet. And an e-mail. His mind was a complete blank. He hadn't had this kind of total blackout in almost twenty years, since that night in Montreal when he was out bar-hopping with Michael Cassidy. That entire night had been a blank, too, and he'd barely had anything to drink. Just the same terrible headache the next morning.

■ ■ ■

"Moore's showing signs of some kind of trauma," Rachel said to Mac after they left the room.

"But nothing like the victims," Mac said.

"Nothing explains his behaviour last night. He was walking around aimlessly like a street person, and he didn't respond to a single question. And you have to remember, Mac, he's a big powerful lawyer in a big powerful firm."

"He may also be a big powerful actor."

"He carries himself like a Hollywood actor, doesn't he?" Rachel said. "Perfect leading-man material. Fallen lawyer turned villain."

"We have to play this by the book and continue to show the man some respect, at least until we have some corroborating evidence pointing at him. Or else someone's going to come down hard on our heads."

They re-entered the holding cell. Rachel took the lead.

"Mr. Moore, I think it's time for us to have a discussion. My partner and I have a lot of questions for you."

"Not until you tell me what's going on. And I want to speak with my wife."

"Follow us, sir," she said. "We'll take a room, get you a cup of coffee, and try and figure this whole thing out together."

■ ■ ■

Odell followed the two detectives up an oak-stained wooden staircase that creaked as if it was built a hundred years ago and into a cramped room that contained nothing but a rectangular beat-up table and three wooden chairs. He sat down. The chair was uncomfortable. It wasn't built to hold a man with long legs, and he had to extend them out under the table. Rachel placed a cup in front of him. Black coffee. He preferred it with cream, but left it for the moment. This moment was about recovering equilibrium. He needed to figure out how long they were going to hold him. And when to call a lawyer. The last thing he needed to do right now was say something that would be used against him later, but he knew if he invoked his right to an attorney now, they would perceive it as guilt and he might not get out of here. He needed to get to Dee. She was the priority right now. At least his capacity to reason was returning. But how long should he continue to go at this alone? He might be one of the best corporate lawyers in America, but in here he was completely out of his depth.

"Am I under arrest? If so, please explain the charges." Odell knew he needed to project an outward calm—his secret for success in dealing with difficult situations.

"No, sir, you're not under arrest," Mac said. "We're just holding you for questioning as a person of interest."

"You mean I'm a suspect?"

"I didn't say that."

"Well, if I'm not a suspect, I assume I am free to leave."

"I didn't say that either."

"Then you're holding me. You're telling me I'm not free to leave?" Odell sat upright and tucked his legs under the chair. He could feel the muscles in his thighs tighten, the same way they used to when he ran the quarterback sneak in college. Pent-up explosive energy.

"No, sir, not just yet," Mac said.

Person of interest. Regarding something that happened last night. But what? This was all still a puzzle. He was normally very good at solving them. Not today. He could feel the pain behind his eyes blurring his judgment. His patience was being strained, and the detectives continued to speak to him in riddles.

"I have no idea what you want from me." He couldn't hide the sharp edge in his voice.

"Mr. Moore, we appreciate that you're upset," Mac said. "Why don't we start with your explanation about what happened before we picked you up last night."

He took a sip of the coffee and almost sputtered. Someone had added sweetener. He expected black to be black.

"Will you listen to me. I've been trying to explain—I have no idea why I'm here. I woke up in the cell this morning but I have absolutely no recollection of having been picked up last night. I'm still searching for my last memory. Everything's a blank." He watched Mac drumming his fingers on the table. Was he buying any of this? Odell took another swig of the coffee.

Rachel cut in. "Mr. Moore, you have to understand we have a murder scene to deal with, and that murder scene happens to be your apartment. You can appreciate we have to try to figure out what happened. What do you remember?"

"Murder scene?" His stomach fell through the floor. "My wife. Is she—?" He couldn't bring himself to say the word.

Neither detective spoke. Odell wondered which one had been designated to give him the bad news.

"No, sir, she's not dead," Rachel said in a softer tone of voice. "She was taken to the hospital last night. We don't have word on her condition."

"Then I'm leaving. I have to get to the hospital immediately." Odell was halfway to the door before Mac interceded to block the pathway.

"You don't understand, sir," Mac said. "Your father-in-law is dead. Senator Brabant was found lying on your living room carpet. There's no question in our minds that this is a homicide. So you're not leaving until we understand your involvement."

"My father-in-law? In my apartment?" Odell felt his resolve draining.

"Dead," Mac said, staring into Odell's eyes.

Odell held the stare briefly then tried Rachel. He'd negotiated enough deals to know whether he was making headway. They weren't buying it. Maybe he hadn't shown enough shock. Or maybe they were expecting contrition. Or guilt. He had no idea what they wanted from him, but whatever it was, they were not finding it.

Odell had half a mind to push his way past Mac, but caught the foolish impulse.

Mac crossed his arms. "Sit down, sir," he said firmly.

The mirror to the right was giving nothing away. There might be a number of people watching him through the one-way glass. He backed up and took his seat. It was getting closer to the moment when he would have to invoke his right to an attorney, but if he did so, wasn't there a risk in this chess game that they would arrest him? He had no memory of how he got here. His father-in-law was dead and his wife seriously injured. It was only a matter of time before they pieced out the relationship between Odell and his father-in-law. Then he'd never get to the hospital to tend to Dee. It was time to regain control of the situation. That was his specialty, even when he had no leverage.

He summoned all of what calm he had left and slowed his speech to a very measured tone. "I'm not suffering from complete amnesia here. I'm a partner at TGO in midtown Manhattan. Have you heard of them?"

They nodded.

"I practise corporate law, and unless I've been sleeping for more than twenty-four hours, it's Wednesday, August 19, 2015. You tell me my father-in-law is dead and my wife is in the hospital and I am telling you I have no information about any of this. I only know I could never harm my wife."

He heard the words "I could never harm my wife" coming out of his mouth before he thought about them. His mind went back to what Michael told him about the violent episode in Montreal so many years ago when he had blacked out. And to the homeless man on the street just a few months ago. And the recent memory lapses. Could he really be so certain?

"How would you describe your relationship with your wife, Mr. Moore?" Rachel asked.

"Never mind that. She's in the hospital, all alone. What kind of person do you think I am that you won't let me go to her side?"

"She's not alone," Rachel said. "Your mother-in-law is with her."

How could Eleanor have gotten here so quickly from Mobile? he wondered.

"She was the emergency contact on your wife's phone," Rachel said as if reading his mind. He had better be a little more careful with his thoughts. "The hospital called her immediately last night," Rachel said, with a trace of accusation in her tone.

He knew what they were both thinking. Why wasn't he the emergency contact? Even Odell didn't have a good answer. Dee had not bothered to get a New York number since she'd moved. Maybe she hadn't updated the emergency contact either. Odell didn't even have one in his phone. Too many years being alone.

"Let's get back to your relationship with your wife," Rachel said. She was rubbing her nose. Disconcerting.

"We're newlyweds. We've never even had a fight."

"That's not the information we have, sir," Mac said.

Odell felt confused. What was he talking about? He might have been irritated with her and she with him, but what was the detective getting at? "I beg your pardon?"

"Sir, you were in your apartment last night. You saw your wife. You argued with your wife. We think you fought with her."

"Nonsense."

"Mr. Moore, we've already spoken to your neighbour. Your wife was heard screaming and at one point there was a violent crash. The concierge saw you enter the building late yesterday afternoon, and your neighbour told us she heard a man's voice she believes was yours."

Rachel took a photo from an envelope she was carrying and tossed it on the table.

In the photo, he saw the wreckage of his apartment and his father-in-law lying on his stomach in a pool of blood on his carpet. If this is what he'd done to the senator, what did that mean about Dee?

Odell's mouth hung open. He could feel his eyes losing focus.

"Right now, sir," Rachel offered, "we don't know who killed the senator or who hurt your wife. We're guessing the trauma she sustained is related to the fatal injuries suffered by your father-in-law. We're waiting for reports from the hospital and the preliminary report from the medical examiner. We have a lot of questions. Our timeline has you placed in the apartment around or possibly just before the time of death. You've got to *think*, sir."

Rachel leaned forward. "No disrespect intended here, Mr. Moore. We know you must be terribly upset, but you have to understand our position. Your father-in-law, a well-known American political figure, has turned up dead in your apartment, your wife is in hospital and can't tell us what happened, and we found you wandering on the street after the event."

"Help us, Mr. Moore," Mac said. "The police commissioner and the mayor are pressuring us to provide some answers. We're hoping that once you've recovered a little, your memory of last night will start to return so we can get to work on finding the person or persons responsible."

If Dee died there was nothing left to recover, no point going on, Odell thought. What could he say, what could he do, to get out of this jail, out of this nightmare? They had to believe they were already talking to the person responsible for all this. Rachel was speaking but he was no longer processing any information.

"Why don't we give Mr. Moore a few minutes to collect his thoughts. Maybe once the caffeine kicks in, he'll begin to remember things," she said.

The two detectives left the room, while Odell battled his impulse to slam the table.

CHAPTER 20

Mac returned to his desk and reached for a handful of pistachios out of his New York Giants mug, tossing a couple into his mouth. Helped him think. He looked twice to see that Rachel was out of sight, then spit the shucked shells in a perfect arc into the garbage can beside the desk. She had gone to check if there was an update from the medical examiner. They decided to let Odell Moore stew for thirty minutes. Give him time to think. The amnesia card never played well because it was never true. At best it was partly true. Just give the suspect enough time and rope to trip over the deceit and volunteer a statement recalling a detail during the "blackout." If they kept the pressure going long enough, Moore would slip up again. He and Rachel had both twigged to one line in that first interview. "I only know I could never harm my wife" were his exact words. As Rachel had pointed out, "He didn't say 'I could never hurt anyone.'" People usually said what they meant, whether or not they realized it.

Mac decided it was time to make himself appear a little more understanding. He stepped back into the room, sat down opposite Moore, and crossed his hands on the table. "Just so you don't worry too much about your wife, one of our officers called from the hospital and advised us that she's in stable condition."

"Then I need to get there now. I can come back for questioning later. My wife needs me." Moore began to rise.

"Please sit down, sir. Remember, we're not charging you with anything, though you're free to ask for counsel to represent you, but you do need to tell us what you know before we'll consider releasing you."

Moore settled back into the chair. "This whole situation is unfathomable. I don't remember anything."

"Let's run through this from the time you left your office yesterday afternoon," Mac said.

"It was about three-thirty or four, maybe four-thirty."

"Is that the time you normally leave the office?"

"No, I left early."

"Any particular reason?"

"All I can tell you, detective, is that I was upset. I can't recall what it was about. The afternoon is blacked out."

Moore began to stroke his moustache. Likely a nervous habit.

"How often do you black out?"

"When I was in university—that's not entirely true. I've had a few minor lapses lately, where I go into a trance but no serious blackouts."

Mac opened his notepad and took out his pen. "Is there anyone who will corroborate this? Did you ever seek any medical treatment for the condition?"

"No. The other times were when I was a teenager. One of my work colleagues in California can corroborate a blackout I experienced when we were college students together in Montreal many years ago. And Jackson Sherman, an associate of mine here in New York, witnessed a brief trance I experienced a few months ago."

"I'll need your associate's contact information in case we need to speak to him to corroborate."

"Of course. His name is Michael Cassidy. He was my college roommate, and he now works for TGO in L.A. He can tell you what happened during the blackout. I only remember waking up in our apartment the next morning."

Mac took detailed notes. "And you don't remember any of the details?"

"Not a thing."

"And there's no one who can vouch for where you were last night. No friends; no family?"

Odell's nostrils flared. A sign his composure was wearing thin. "I keep telling you, I don't remember. As for family, I'm estranged from my father, my mother is in a long-term care facility in Canada, and my sister died a few years ago. My wife is my only family in New York. I have nothing to offer you." Moore threw both arms open. "Speak to Drew Torrance in my office if you want a character reference."

Clearly the subject of his family was a touchy one. Kids from troubled families grew up to be troubled adults—who ended up in prison cells.

■ ■ ■

Rachel was staring at a note on her desk when Mac returned. She did not want to watch his reaction when she broke the news.

"We're having company in a few minutes. Our favourite guests. FBI."

Mac tossed the file down on the desk. "What the hell do they want?"

"I told you, Mac. It's an assassination. Washington has gone nuts. They're insisting on a joint investigation." As much as she knew that Mac did not like the idea of working with the feds, someone was going to have to put in the hours going through the list of potential political enemies, checking the senator's appointment records for the past few months, his personal and Senate e-mails for evidence of a stalker. He probably had no shortage of opponents and maybe even political enemies, but narrowing down the list was going to be a painstaking task. Let them do it.

"Moore will be lawyering up any minute," Mac said, "so we're not likely to get any more out of him today. He's claiming amnesia. But we have him placed by a witness in the apartment some time before the death."

"Not completely accurate, partner," Rachel said. "His voice was *heard* in the apartment by a neighbour who later fainted in the Moores' doorway. The same neighbour admitted she had only seen Odell Moore from a distance. He wasn't actually *seen* in the apartment, just in the lobby by the concierge."

Rachel began to rub her nose, a nervous tic that drove her mother crazy and for which she had been teased mercilessly as a child. She found her greatest inspiration arose from moments of deep reflection, and at those times, her left hand involuntarily moved to the bridge of her nose, tracing the thin ridge back and forth. She knew it was difficult to watch without a grimace. That and the sniffing, which was not a habit at all.

About six years ago she had taken her golden retriever to the vet. At the beginning of the appointment, the doctor sniffed the dog's coat. "I have a very sensitive nose," he had said, "and if I can get a baseline when they're healthy I can usually detect the odours of illness later on." Rachel had a very powerful sense of smell and decided to do it on her first homicide investigation, knowing it was going to open her up to being teased. But ever since she had started solving more crimes than anyone in the precinct, her colleagues learned to tolerate and even encourage her. Criticism of Rachel was taboo, even if the occasional wisecrack was not.

"I just got the preliminary ME report. Senator Brabant suffered blunt force trauma to the side of the head." She continued to fill him in on the details from the report. The angle of the blow suggested it had been administered from the rear, likely by someone who was left-side dominant. Some kind of metal object was used: possibly something from the apartment. The CSI team was checking the site for objects with traces of the victim's blood, and the ME was running some additional tests. There was blood spatter on the floor, and it would take some time to analyze which belonged to the senator and which to his daughter.

"Mariella doesn't believe that the hit to the head was the cause of death. The victim's larynx was crushed and she discovered traces of redness on the victim's neck about an inch and a half thick, consistent with asphyxiation."

Mac slowed down the pace as they neared the door. "Sounds like strangulation," he said.

"Yes. Very strange. You'd think the danger would have subsided when the perp clobbered the senator, probably knocking him out. To then choke him to death suggests either that the killer intended all along to kill him or simply got lost in a moment of uncontrollable rage."

"If it was a professional hit, the killer wouldn't have been this clumsy. The strangulation instrument may have been a belt. Hardly the hit man's instrument of choice."

"Right now all we have is Moore, but it's still early," Rachel said. "We'll keep pursuing the Moore angle, but there's still way too much that we don't know yet."

"Meaning we don't have enough to hold Moore much longer without charging him." Mac crossed his arms as Rachel reached for the door handle.

"Exactly. We're going to have to kick him loose for now. At least let's take one last shot before he walks out the door. Once we know more, we'll bring him back in."

"He has no idea of the media shit storm he'll be walking into the moment he leaves here. We don't have to worry about him disappearing; his privacy is gone."

Just as Rachel was about to turn the handle, an officer called out. "Moore's counsel has arrived. She's asked for some privacy."

CHAPTER 21

12:45 p.m., Wednesday, August 19, 2015

Odell was alone with a woman out of a fashion magazine. She was short, and her form-fitting black dress was simple but elegant, yet it was the kind of dress that might turn heads: she dressed to attract attention. She wore no makeup except a touch of eyeliner and deep red lipstick. It was clear that from the moment she entered a room she was in control, that she was a woman to be taken very seriously.

"Mr. Moore, my name is Carrie Tinker. I'm a criminal attorney."

Not just a criminal attorney, Odell thought. A saviour. "*The* Carrie Tinker?" Odell asked. He didn't know much about criminal lawyers, but everyone in Manhattan knew of Carrie Tinker. She was one of the few lawyers in the city who got more press than he did.

"I'm small but I'm tough," she continued. "Your law firm keeps me on retainer when there are criminal issues to be sorted out on behalf of their clients. I got the call this morning and I'm here to represent you."

"I know how good you are." For the first time since he woke up, the overwhelming headache was beginning to lift. Maybe the nightmare with it. She had to get him out to see Dee.

She smiled. "There's a lot for us to work out. Let's start with why you're here."

"Can we start instead with getting me out of here? My wife needs me."

"Indulge me for an hour or so and tell me everything you told the police this morning, as well as whatever you can tell me about last night."

"Can't we do that after we leave? I never want to see the inside of a police station again." He could feel his shoulders tensing.

"Let me tell you why I don't think that's such a good idea. Your life has changed dramatically in the past eighteen hours. Besides, you have nowhere to go. Your apartment is a crime scene. It's been sealed and it may be a week before you can return."

"I have no intention of going home." His tone was dismissive. Not what he intended. "Sorry, I didn't mean to sound rude." He needed her help. His voice softened. "I'm heading straight to the hospital. You heard about my wife."

"That's part of the problem. The whole world knows about your wife. By tomorrow they'll know what she likes to eat for breakfast. You also have no idea what's waiting for you outside the doors of this station."

"That's not the point—"

"It's exactly the point," Carrie said gruffly. "The media has been camped out here and at your apartment since two in the morning when the picture of your father-in-law was posted on-line. There had to be a leak in security—maybe one of the paramedics trying to make a buck. The tweetosphere is going crazy. Over fifteen million views on Facebook alone. Every major outlet in the country is waiting for a sound bite for tonight's news. The bloggers are out there as well, waiting to broadcast a compromising picture or video of you leaving the station."

"I'll deal with it. I just need to get out of here." Calm insistence generally worked.

"Do you even know where she is?" Her tone of voice matched his.

"No." Odell began to feel the pressure in his head building again. The walls of logic that surrounded him were crumbling. Carrie didn't need to ask the next question. He had no idea where to begin the search for Dee. By now the whole world knew where she was. Everyone but him. This was an embarrassment.

"A United States senator was killed last night. That potentially turns the murder into an assassination. Your life has changed in unimaginable ways. You may be used to being famous in the community of big law and big business, but this morning there's no one in America who doesn't know who you are. You will be hounded until you give them what they want."

"What is it they want?"

"Right now it's your head. And if you don't leave here with a strategy, they will remove it without an ounce of contrition."

She reached into her briefcase and pulled them out one by one: the *New York Times*, the *Wall Street Journal.*

He scanned the headlines. They were all about the same. "Murder in the condo of celebrity attorney." "Odell Moore being held by the NYPD for questioning." How could this be? His right elbow had been resting on the table. He lifted his forearm, dropped his head into his hand, and began kneading his temples with his thumb and middle finger.

"You're an overnight sensation and will suffer the penalty that all American celebrities have to live with. Your privacy is gone. Your life as you knew it is gone—not forever, but for the foreseeable future and at the minimum until I get you cleared."

"So what am I supposed to do?"

"Let me figure out how to get you to your wife. The first thing you're going to do is take advantage of the relative privacy of this small room and tell me the entire story, down to every last detail you can remember. I'm not here to judge you, merely to protect you."

"Are they going to release me today?" Even he was beginning to wonder whether they should.

"Based on my experience and the media scrum waiting outside the station, you'll be out sometime late this afternoon. Just in time for the evening prime-time news cycle. They won't have enough to charge you but they'll be ready to feed you to the hounds. If they can get a few grungy photos or videos of you in the media, you're all but guilty. So let's focus. Start by telling me what you've told the police and then take me through the story from the beginning."

"Pretty much nothing."

"You've been here over twelve hours and you haven't talked? You're as smart as your reputation would lead me to believe."

"You don't understand. I can't remember anything that happened since yesterday afternoon."

"Nothing? Okay, let's start with background. What's your relationship with the senator?"

"We met last November at a fundraiser in his home in Mobile, Alabama. I was working on a deal for a TGO client. I went down to Mobile to lobby the senator to approve federal financing for the deal."

"His role on the Appropriations Committee?"

"Exactly. I was down there with my associate Jackson Sherman, who's from Mobile originally. He gave me the lay of the land. Everything had been carefully planned."

"So you met with the senator."

"Jackson had screwed it up. We were supposed to be meeting at his downtown office in Mobile, but at the last minute the meeting was moved to the estate. We had ten minutes alone with the senator before the cocktail party began. Nowhere near enough time, but we had no choice."

"So the meeting was the beginning of a relationship."

"Yes, and in the process I met his daughter. I followed her out of the party and into the gazebo at the rear of their estate. We talked for half an hour and it was all over for me. Dee had an uncanny ability of unsettling me. She still has it. I didn't understand it at the time but I was falling in love—something I was certain was never going to happen."

"That was not in the plan?"

Odell laughed. He was surprised he had it in him. "After that, nothing went according to plan, including my entire life." Odell went on to explain how Dee had convinced her father to invite him for dinner at the senator's house the next evening with the Canadian ambassador. Because Odell had been born in Halifax, the senator thought they would make interesting dinner companions. Odell jumped at the invitation and the chance to cement his relationship with the senator. What he had not bargained for was the surreptitious romance with Dee that blossomed under the senator's nose, the frenzied lovemaking, the ache when Dee was not around, her insistence at running off to Vegas, the Elvis Chapel, the laughter, the I do's, breaking the Champagne glasses as a sign of good luck, running to the airport to get to Paris, not bothering to book the honeymoon suite at the Ritz, bumping the Arab businessman who kept it on reserve for his harem for an extra $20,000 tip to the concierge.

"Do you regret rushing to marry Dee?"

Odell reflected for a few moments. "For the first time in my life I didn't have a plan. It started to go sideways when the honeymoon ended."

Odell bowed his head. He should be feeling some sense of relief for confessing to all he knew: except he still knew nothing—nothing about what happened between leaving his office and waking up in the cell, nothing about himself and what kind of violence he might be capable of. Instead his pulse was racing and his head felt light. He needed to get out of here and be with Dee but he no longer had control over his life. At this point Carrie Tinker was in charge.

"I have enough to go on for now," Carrie said, "but I need more information if I'm going to properly represent you. I hate surprises. We'll need to meet at my office. How is ten tomorrow morning?"

He could barely move, much less make a decision, and was grateful for the concern reflected in her dark eyes. His head was nodding but when was he finally going to the hospital? "That means I can go care for my wife tonight?"

"Give me time to figure out where she is and whether you'd be met by police at the door. If that were caught by the press, it would make your situation impossible."

"Then when?"

"I can promise you that as soon as you leave my office tomorrow, I'll have all the information you need. Then you can go live there if you need to."

Carrie stepped out momentarily, then returned, this time holding an overstuffed brown handbag. She waited until Odell's gaze fell on the bag. "Aren't you going to ask?"

"You mean what's in the bag?"

"It's a surprise."

"I thought you hated surprises?"

"Only when I'm on the receiving end." She dropped the bag on the table. "They're going to have to release you any minute. They've already told me they don't want you leaving the city without advising them. I suggest you take that request very seriously."

"Where the hell would I go? There is only one place I belong. At the hospital. My wife needs me."

"Tomorrow. For now I'm told that Dee's mother is with her. Your presence would only add to her pain now."

"What do you mean?"

"She's going through a very difficult time. Her husband is dead. She may have had to identify the body. Meanwhile she has to focus on her daughter. What do you think she's thinking?"

"I don't care." His fists balled up. "I'm the husband."

"Stop being so bullheaded."

His hands relaxed. "Like the Minotaur," he said, "sitting in the centre of a maze, with no idea how to navigate my way out."

"Don't forget, you haven't been ruled out as the perpetrator of the attack on her husband and daughter. You can't just go marching in there and expect a normal reaction. For all we know, her attorneys may be in the process of obtaining a restraining order against you. If you show up, you may push her over the edge and force her to take dramatic action to keep you away. That will allow the media, like Theseus, to slay you."

"Carrie, this is so confusing." He closed his eyes, trying to draw on some inner strength, looking for the resolve he had taken for granted would always be there in times of crisis. For the first time in his life it had abandoned him. Maybe he could funnel some from Carrie.

She put her hand on his arm. "Odell, for the next day, just listen to what I tell you. I've arranged for lodgings under an assumed name where you're more likely to find some privacy."

"What about work?"

"The media are already camped out at TGO, and I'm fairly certain that Drew Torrance will tell you to take some time off to deal with your family."

"He doesn't want me around, does he?" he said and then sighed.

"Both you and they are about to be examined under a microscope."

He didn't cringe at the thought. He just accepted it. This was becoming the new normal.

"We'll work with experts starting tomorrow. Once I understand all aspects of our story, we'll plan our own media campaign to begin restoring your credibility. Don't read the newspapers or watch television. Stick to the sports channels. For the next little while, there's a risk you'll be portrayed as a villain or even a monster. Every reporter in the country will be digging into your past."

"There isn't much to find."

Nothing in the public record, anyway, he thought. His recent memory lapses could be cobbled together to make anyone wonder about his self-control. The lapses had begun just after Easter during the Bounty deal. He'd finished a debrief meeting when Jackson said he had a gift from his mother for Odell. An 1860 silver dollar. Jackson apologized, saying it was probably worthless but that it had great sentimental value to his mother. He called it her good luck charm. He made a joke about his mother's sending an apple for the teacher—in her view, Odell was the teacher as well as the boss. He sounded embarrassed about the whole thing. Odell laid in to him. You don't disrespect your mother regardless of what she's done.

After Jackson left that day, Odell had felt lightheaded. He knew he had not been very polite to Jackson. It had hardly been a gracious acceptance of the gift. He'd needed some air and went for a walk up Sixth Avenue toward Central Park to clear his head. Next thing he knew he was sitting on the sidewalk. A cop was threatening to give him a citation for accosting a homeless man. The man had approached too closely and according to the blue jacket, Odell was prepared to fight him. Did he need to mention this incident to Carrie? Maybe tomorrow.

But now she was saying, "Let's hope you're right, but you better start thinking about anything that someone might uncover so that I can stay ahead of it. We need to let this cycle pass and slowly supplant the message in the media with our softer, kinder, and gentler version of an Odell Moore who could not possibly have committed the acts you may be accused of. And understand it's irrelevant whether you're charged. Unless someone else stands trial for this, you'll be convicted daily in the court of public opinion, on the call-in shows, the blogs, and most of the rag journals."

"Why would I care about that?"

"Often those unsubstantiated sources find their way back to the mainstream. Journalism isn't what it used to be. There's far too much pressure to build audience, and opinion often replaces truth, if truth even exists anymore."

Odell stood up to stretch. "Ironic, isn't it?"

"How do you mean?"

"This is what I do for a living in the corporate context. I study the opposition, come up with a strategic plan, hire communication experts, control the messaging, and then run point on every possible contingency. Suddenly there's a complete stranger running my life in the exact same fashion."

"Speaking of fashion, it's time to open the bag. A gift for you, so to speak." She was not smiling. "I'm going out to confirm you can leave. When I return I'm going to want your clothes, so get changed."

After she left the room, he turned his back to the window, stripped, and turned the bag over. His childhood poured onto the table. Quickly he put on the clothing, an outfit for Odell Moore that bespoke his current status. Suspected criminal. Not yet charged, but that was bound to happen. The man staring back at him in the reflective glass was old and worn out. His face was unshaven, his eyes bloodshot, and his cheeks gaunt. He was wearing a baggy grey sweatshirt with a hoodie pulled down over his forehead and a tattered trench coat that smelled faintly of piss. His blue jeans were threadbare and stained, the ill-fitting running shoes tied loosely. It was an outfit a street person might be wearing.

That was pretty much how Odell felt right now. Homeless, without direction, no family, without hope or memory. He had brought this upon himself. That was what the image in the mirror was whispering to him now.

He folded his dress shirt, tie, and suit and carefully placed them in the bag. A moment later Carrie opened the door and took the bag from him.

"Give me five minutes, then join me in the hallway," she said.

■ ■ ■

Odell stepped out of the room and walked over to stand beside Carrie and her male assistant, who was about Odell's height, shape, and colouring. Odell's wardrobe fit him well. They walked down the corridor together and paused just inside the front door of the station.

Carrie headed out the door and toward the limousine accompanied by a black man in an expensively tailored suit who was partially covering his face from the prying camera lenses. The swarm of reporters descended on them, screaming out their questions. "My client has no comment" was all Carrie was prepared to admit. She had prepared for the moment with additional security opening a path to the passenger door of the black limo that she reserved for her white-collar clients. Eventually the press would figure out that they had been duped—handsome, athletic black man—one as good as another. At least the body double had slept and shaved. An innocent man in front of the cameras.

Odell hesitated then slowly shuffled down the other side of the staircase, turned in the opposite direction, and hopped in the cab. No one ever pays attention to a black bum going in or coming out of a police station. He might have escaped detection for the moment, but he wouldn't be able to avoid the media forever. For now he appreciated the solitude, sat back, and asked the driver to take him downtown, to the address Carrie had given him. He checked into the hotel off Wall Street; the room was reserved under the name Curtis and prepaid cash for three nights. His clothes stunk and he headed back out the door to find replacements.

Half a block down he froze. Directly in front of him, a parked car with a fake wood back panel: Dad's station wagon, all beaten up and rusted.

Mum nicknamed it the Woodie. He couldn't catch his breath and bent over, balancing his hands on his knees, closing his eyes tightly. A young boy in pyjamas was standing beside Mum on the front stoop watching the Woodie disappear down the hill. Freezing rain was falling on the misshapen roofs of the long row of attached houses across the street. Huffs and puffs of maritime wind were shaking the rotting siding and loose shingles were flying. "Free from Isaiah for the week," Mum whispered. Odell wasn't sure whether he was supposed to hear her. She smiled. He'd forgotten Mum's smile. She kissed him hard on the forehead and squeezed him tightly. "You're growing big as your father," she whispered. He pulled away hard. The searing pain in his back, like a swarm of wasps, tore at him. Dad's farewell gift.

Except when he got home late that afternoon, Dad was parked at the kitchen table. His lucky coin in one hand, a stubby in the other. The ashtray was filled with butts and a couple of empties lay on the cracked floor, the suds blending in with the bubbling linoleum.

"Where's Mum?" Odell asked.

"Sleeping." Mum didn't sleep in the afternoons. She cleaned houses then she came home and made dinner. "Wake her up and there be hell to pay."

He opened his eyes. Funny the tricks memory played. He couldn't remember anything after that, except playing Civil War games on the hardwood in his closet with his tin soldiers. They never stood straight on the cheap carpet in his bedroom. The Union general always won. Except this time Odell pushed his thumb against the neck of the Confederate general until it snapped. It was the only time he remembered losing his temper. At least it was a memory.

He grabbed a few items at the first clothing store he could find, then picked up a bag of essentials at Duane Reade: a tiny bottle of coconut-scented shampoo, white soap that was an inch thick, toothpaste, a toothbrush, desperately needed deodorant, a hair brush, some clips and hair extensions, complete with instructions, and headed back to the hotel. The nondescript room was no more than a queen-sized bed with a night table, a flat-screen television mounted on the wall, and a bathroom desperately in need of a renovation.

Odell hopped in the shower, ignoring the mildew stench of the greying shower curtain bunched in the tub. Four days ago he was confidently preparing a team for a cross-continent battle, on top of his world. The world he dominated. But there was a second world to deal with. How could he have been so blind as to take his new wife for granted, oblivious to a festering rift with his father-in-law? As usual, the world of his personal life had taken a back seat and it had now collapsed all around him.

He squeezed the shampoo out of the tiny bottle and worked it hard into his scalp. The smell reminded him of growing up. His Third World. The world dominated by his father. He rubbed until it hurt. Until he could feel the childhood pain once again. It didn't help him remember what he had fought so hard to forget.

Could he have done any of this? Could he have thrown Dee to the ground with a force sufficient to shatter the coffee table and then just walked out the door? And what kind of man assaults his father-in-law in front of his wife? Odell knew he was capable of doing such things. Dee was not the first woman in his life to visit the emergency room. Was he just like his father? If Michael was to be believed, there was little doubt. Michael—his oldest friend—the man he could no longer trust. It was over twenty years ago but if the story Michael had told then was true, the violence had been incubating in Odell as it had in his father, just waiting to detonate his life.

Whether he had done this to her or not, he was certainly responsible. There was no escape from the past and no washing away the guilt or the uncertainty about everything in his life.

CHAPTER 22

5:30 p.m., Wednesday, August 19, 2015

Carrie Tinker was one of the toughest criminal defence lawyers in the city. She was in her late forties but could pass for ten years younger. While she was still a student her law school professors had tagged her as someone to follow. At the time she had a punk hairdo, a photographic memory, and a deep sense of justice for the oppressed. Today the oppressed included some of the most high-profile defendants in the city, television personalities, a pro football player, and now one of the most famous lawyers in the country. Not bad for a kid from Poughkeepsie.

This case would be particularly challenging. At this point she had no reason to doubt that Odell really did have a memory problem. Fortunately he had the means to afford the defence he would need if he were to be charged, a good possibility at the moment. The psychiatric expertise concerning amnesia would be expensive to procure and prepare and she had a lot to learn about the subject. But she was getting way ahead of herself. The best defence revolved around finding other potential suspects. That was where her attention needed to be focused. Hopefully the police would not fall into the trap of taking the easy bait, which at the moment was Odell. But if they did, someone like the senator must have enemies, and her job was to ferret them out and put them on display at trial.

Carrie got out of the limo and walked purposefully to her office building. A horde of reporters was waiting. She had ignored the reporters outside the police station, but here she had home field advantage. These were the moments that had built her career. She walked through the mass and climbed the six steps to the doorstep of the building, giving her a height advantage. The cameras pointing up at her would make her six inches taller.

"Ladies and gentlemen, it would be premature to speak on behalf of a client who has not been charged with any offence. I have only recently been retained on this matter and have yet to ascertain the facts. What I can tell you is that my client, Mr. Moore, mourns the passing of his father-in-law, Senator Brabant, and is deeply concerned about the well-being of his wife. Any attempt to pursue him at a moment in time when he is in shock over such tragic circumstances would not only be premature but unconscionable on your part.

"I will have a statement for you once we know more of the facts. The police are conducting an investigation and it is not normally my custom to interfere with their work. Let them bring the guilty party to justice. My client intends to provide any assistance he can but his first priority has to be his family. I have no further comment, thank you." With that she turned into the building, ignoring the many questions being shouted at her. She quickly made her way up to her offices.

When she stepped out of the elevator and into third-floor reception area, she was greeted by her assistant, Marg Da Silva, who had been working for Carrie for her entire fifteen-year career. Together they headed to Carrie's office. Marg knew the routine on days like this.

"I heard you coming, boss."

"Hard to miss, wasn't it?"

"They're still yammering outside. We're all used to it by now."

"Marg, there's someone I need you to get for me right away."

"Mr. Torrance?"

"Please."

"Arlene has him on hold waiting for you," Marg said with a thinly veiled smirk.

"Can you get in touch with Jones and have her check whether any restraining orders have been filed against Odell Moore in the last twenty-four hours. I also need to know where Dee Moore is. Hospital and room number and anything else you can find out about hospital security."

Once inside her office, Carrie put on her wireless headset before connecting. She preferred to pace the office while she was on the phone. The energy that ran through her needed a regular outlet.

"Drew, I'm sorry, this must be a trying day for you and the firm."

"Carrie, the television trucks and reporters have been camped outside our building all day, hoping to get a quote from anyone from the office clerks on up. I had our crisis management team in the door and hard at work since early this morning. They were my second call. You were my first."

Carrie cut in. "And the world has already inferred that as the only person of interest right now, the NYPD must be considering him a leading suspect. Social media is already crucifying him."

"I've placed our entire staff under a gag order. Plenty of law firms have been caught up in scandal surrounding a rogue partner over the years—"

"A rogue, Drew?" Carrie interrupted. "Isn't it a little premature for that?"

"Let's not play games, Carrie." There was an immediate hard edge to his voice. "I'm pretty certain Odell has not done anything wrong, but I'm not going to publicly stand behind him until the police clear him."

"Sorry, Drew, you know me. Once I get involved in a case, I defend my clients to the end of the earth."

"And my job is to defend the integrity of the firm. Can you let Odell know I've placed him on temporary leave of absence?"

"I've already told him to expect it."

"At this point he has more pressing matters to deal with in his life, and none of us will benefit from his being here with the cloud of this case hanging over his head. He should be with his family."

Carrie could read between the lines. At this point Odell was a liability to the firm. It didn't matter how much he billed—if he was the lead suspect in the murder of a sitting senator, Torrance needed to distance the firm from the rogue. She also knew this was going to be their last communication until Odell was cleared. There was too much risk to the privilege of her communications with Odell. They could not be compromised by any third-party conversations. She had terminated her relationship with TGO this morning before heading to the jailhouse.

"Did the referral to Marty Brigham work out?"

"Thanks for recommending him. I'm sitting with him now."

"Best we end the discussion right here then."

She disconnected, feeling a tinge of pity for Moore. She'd been on the other side of this drill with corporate CEOs and the contingency plan to disown and disavow the employee being shamed in the press. Cut out the cancer. Save the patient. Life goes on.

■ ■ ■

Drew Torrance had his hands full. It was not enough that he had to manage partners on four continents on a daily basis. Now he had a murder investigation involving one of his own and over one hundred partners around the world who wanted to know what was going on. From the moment the news broke on social media, the e-mails started flying across the TGO network. He had been working since four this morning dealing with his public relations firm, a crisis management expert, and the firm's new criminal counsel, Marty Brigham.

They had been holed up in Drew's office for the past two hours with a parade of internal staff passing in and out: Simon Lester, who was the firm's general counsel; the head of the technology group; each of the department heads; the head of personnel; and the head of the associates group. The message was tailored to each group, but the consistent theme was the same. Only one person spoke for the firm—Drew Torrance. He would not abide leaks of any nature. Arlene had been monitoring the flow of traffic in and out of the office until he finally stepped outside five minutes ago and told her, "No one else. I need to think." They were finally alone, Drew behind the imposing desk and Marty sitting across from him, his laptop open, furiously typing notes for his to-do list. It was the first five minutes of silence Drew had had since the first call came in at 3:00 a.m., from London of all places. One of the assistants had forwarded a post on LinkedIn to the local managing partner, who called Drew in a panic. Odell Moore was an overnight sensation. The butt of thousands of Twitter comments, most of them ugly. A ticking time bomb that had just exploded all over Drew's office.

Drew watched Marty at work. Marty could stand to lose thirty-five pounds but his suits were tailored to minimize his girth. The bald head gave him gravitas. Carrie had given him credibility.

"I'll get in touch with the precinct handling the investigation and volunteer that the firm intends to be compliant in any police investigation into the death of the senator," Marty said.

"Will the police and FBI investigations be coordinated?"

"Hopefully. If I tell them that we're proactively doing all their legwork, I'll earn points on two fronts. First, it will allow you to tell the media that we are voluntarily cooperating with the police investigation."

"And that will keep me ahead of the media curve," Drew said. He stood up and walked over to his trophy case, picking up the Michael Jordan autographed basketball, absently spinning it on his right index finger.

"It will also allow me to assert lawyer-client confidentiality in respect of the thousands of e-mails relating to client matters. Finally, it will signal to the police that the firm has nothing to hide here."

"Why would we have anything to hide?"

"What's particularly tricky in this case is that Senator Brabant is not simply Mr. Moore's father-in-law. They had business dealings. The media has already been reporting that they were involved in a transaction six months ago, and the police investigation may lead to a review of the business relationship between them."

"The Bounty deal can't possibly have anything to do with this," Drew said, a little too quickly and too harshly. He knew immediately how it must sound to Marty.

"Let me sound a little jaded here. Last year the senator threw his support behind a deal involving your firm. Presumably there were millions in legal fees. A few months after the deal closes, your big-name partner, who ran the deal, marries the senator's daughter. Perhaps his support of the business transaction was an engagement gift for the happy couple."

Drew's face began to turn red. "That's not at all the way it happened, Marty." Torrance placed the ball back onto the display case with a little more force than necessary.

"I don't have to tell you that it doesn't matter what actually happened."

"I understand," Drew said, sighing. "All that matters for now is how it all looks. And the way it looks right now puts this law firm front and centre in the investigation."

"Once it begins, that investigation might go on for months, and during that period TGO will not be able to escape the media circus."

"How can you help me deal with that?"

"You've hired PR experts for that. I can only handle the legal end so let's not get ahead of ourselves. Let the police investigation unfold. Maybe the senator's death has nothing to do with Moore. On the other hand, you need to prepare your partners for the possibility that somehow this relates to your Bounty file."

Marty reached into his file folder and took out a small stack of papers. "I told your head of technology to review Moore's e-mails for the past few days for anything that might stand out as unusual." It would take days, maybe weeks, to assess everything related to Moore in the TGO computer system. If there was anything pertinent to what had happened yesterday, Marty figured it would likely be very recent. He slid the papers across the desk to Drew. "Can you make any sense of these?"

Marty handed a series of over a dozen digital images to Drew, who flipped through them carefully. Drew showed no visible reaction at all to the images, including the one that showed a man and woman smoking what appeared to be a joint.

After examining each photo, Drew separated out four images that had been printed off the computer downloads, and laid them out on his desk, trying to reconstruct the sequence of events and the meaning behind them. This was worse than he could imagine. "The male subject in the photo is Michael Cassidy, one of our L.A. associates. He just spent a few days in our New York office and ran the Cypress deal back in L.A. You probably read about it."

Marty nodded almost imperceptibly, though Drew read it as a bluff. The criminal bar was probably not following an entertainment industry takeover battle.

"The woman is Dee Moore. What a mess. Can you tell me anything about the sender?"

"It's well cloaked. I'll get my technician working on the trace. Actually, that may be a bone we can throw to the police investigation. They'll be able to trace the source much more easily than anyone I can hire. If I can earn their trust, they might even share the information with me."

"What's my biggest immediate risk here? My partners are going to want to know."

"A subpoena for all your records. FBI trucks parked outside, officers going up and down the elevator banks, hauling out computers, and live media coverage of it all."

"You must not let that happen, Marty. That's a priority for me." Drew's cheeks flushed. He had single-handedly engineered the merger of three average firms many years ago and willed TGO to become one of America's legal powerhouses. More than anyone, he understood that despite all this success, it would only take one scandal to rip the heart out of this partnership. That was exactly what had happened at Arthur Andersen. He was not going to watch his life work come undone. There was no place in this moment of crisis for lax leadership or errors in execution. No delays, no excuses, and no failures.

"I'll do what I can. This voluntary disclosure of the e-mails might be a start in the right direction. Let me organize with Simon Lester." Marty was sounding calm and confident and Drew appreciated it. He needed a team around him that was focused and dispassionate. Odell might be a key partner at TGO but no one partner was bigger than the name brand. Its protection was Drew's primary concern. Marty needed to understand that.

"Marty, make a deal with the FBI and the NYPD. No subpoenas, no trucks, no seizures. This is priority number one. I don't care how much it costs or what we have to do to make this happen. Do you read me?"

There was a knock at the door and Drew's assistant, Arlene, stepped inside.

"Sorry to interrupt, gentlemen, but the police are on the line. They would like to come down tomorrow and interview Jackson Sherman and make arrangements to get in touch with Michael Cassidy and anyone else in the firm who worked recently with Mr. Moore."

"Jackson Sherman is here but Cassidy is in L.A.," Drew said. "We can set up a video conference. Does that make sense?"

Marty nodded in agreement. "Complete cooperation, Drew. I'll work with Arlene and your people to set it up promptly."

Drew stood up dismissively. "If we're finished, I have a crisis to manage. Go work your magic."

CHAPTER 23

7:50 p.m., Wednesday, August 19, 2015

Odell wrapped the frayed white hotel towel around his waist and walked over to the single window. The scars on his back still burned. At least the shower worked. He stood in the grey twilight, dulled by the creased blinds. The paint on the windowsill was cracked. He unlocked the bolt and lifted the window. It rose only about four inches. Probably protection for depressed jumpers.

The jumpers couldn't hit Wall Street from this room, which faced out onto an alley. He stared blankly at the dull red brick wall just a few feet away. There was an entire world beyond that wall and he had to assume it was there. Just as he had to assume that his wife was recovering in some hospital room, he didn't even know where, wondering why she had been abandoned. Some husband. Desperately, he tried Dee's cell a couple of times. The call was directed immediately to voice mail. He didn't have Eleanor Brabant's phone number. Other than their brief encounter at the senator's dinner party, he had not ever spoken to her.

He reached for the television remote control and turned on the news channel, ignoring Carrie's advice. Not that it mattered, since he wasn't paying attention. He just wanted some noise in the room.

The shame clung to him like plastic wrap as he realized that since the wedding, he had not taken the slightest interest in mending fences with Edward or Eleanor. You reap what you sow, and his field was now fallow. He had some lessons to learn about family but at the moment his failure to invest in getting to know anyone in Dee's family was a huge liability.

Eleanor had no way of knowing whether I might be capable of killing her husband and injuring her precious daughter, he thought. She probably hates me; what kind of son-in-law elopes and makes no effort to reach out to his in-laws, particularly when he knows they're upset. Worse still, if she asks me point blank for an explanation, what am I supposed to say? I don't remember?

He began pacing the length of the room. He needed to remember something. Start with the last memories. The Cypress celebration. He hadn't felt well. Needed to get out. He went back to his office. Sitting at his desk … Dee and Cass… Something about Dee and Cass.

Connect with the feelings, Odell … jealousy … and… He could feel the anger building. The fragments of memory cutting at him. He needed to fight the pain behind his eyes… It's only pain… The e-mail … photos… Did he call Cass? Yes. Twice… The second time about the amulet… Of course… Cass was wearing it in the photo… Why would Dee give to him? … Betrayal by Dee? None of it made sense … except that Cass was wearing the amulet.

Odell lay down on the bed and closed his eyes. The photos flashed across the screen in his head. He had rushed out of the office, needing to confront Dee. Right away. What had he done to her? How could he hurt her?… the belt … the bulging eyes … and his father … the source of it all … the beatings in his room … the belt … the pain … the escape to a different part of his mind … the closet… Then the peace offering.

Odell blacked out. He slept fitfully. After five minutes or maybe an hour, he was awakened by a discussion between the newscasters.

"Still no results on the autopsy of Senator Edward Brabant. The FBI has agreed to a joint investigation with NYPD. They're hoping that forensics will provide sufficient leads on the assassination. Speculation is rampant as the police are compiling a list of the senator's known adversaries both in the U.S. and abroad. However, an unnamed source has told CNN in an exclusive that the police are theorizing that the killer was left-handed."

"Thanks, Margaret. The White House and the governor of Alabama have already confirmed that there will be a lying-in-state in D.C followed by a formal state funeral in Mobile, but only after the senator's daughter stabilizes further. She is currently in hospital in New York and her condition is described as critical but stable."

Odell felt his stomach heave and he rushed back to the bathroom, vomiting into the rusty toilet. The odds that he had done this had just climbed dramatically. He needed to talk this out with Carrie. How could he have done such a thing?

But he had done it once. He had decimated those three thugs in Montreal. He had the training to kill with his bare hands. But that was twenty years ago and they deserved it. At least that's what Michael told him, but could he trust anything Michael ever said to him? The lying, cheating scum. Could Dee, or her father, for that matter, have provoked him to such violence? Only questions and no answers. He reached for the remote in disgust, turned off the noise, then launched the device against the wall. It shattered, the pieces falling on the carpet.

It was early still, but he didn't feel like another walk. Too much risk of being identified. It was going to be a long night and he worried that the horrifying dreams were lying in wait. He backed up a couple of steps, dropped on the bed, and propped a couple of pillows behind his head. He might not have any of the pieces, but he'd learned to conduct the Civil War manoeuvres in his head on transcontinental flights.

Odell closed his eyes and a battlefield slowly emerged. On this night his troops were outnumbered, in disarray after the last retreat. If they lost again tonight, the entire line would break. The outcome of the war was resting on General Moore's shoulders. He began calculating his strategy. Part of him wanted to call for a retreat, to fall back and reorganize. Instead he launched an offensive. The battle went on for hours. His troops were finally beginning to advance in a battle of attrition when he began to drift into restless sleep.

CHAPTER 24

9:30 a.m., Thursday, August 20, 2015

Mac Micolonides arrived at the TGO offices five minutes early for the appointment. The lobby area was as big as the entire floor of the precinct. The receptionist behind the long granite desk stood up as soon as he stepped off the elevator. She had obviously developed a sixth sense for greeting customers. Or Torrance had warned her to keep an eye out for the cops. A moment later a woman came to receive Mac and ushered him toward the boardroom complex.

"I'm Arlene Tousignant, Mr. Torrance's assistant. He asked that you be given anything you ask for. We have a boardroom all set up for you." Mac noticed a hint of a French accent.

They passed a series of unoccupied boardrooms of various sizes and shapes until they arrived at the end of the hallway.

"This is the video-conference room," Arlene explained. "Mr. Cassidy is waiting in the boardroom in L.A., and our counsel, Mr. Lester, will be joining you on this side at Mr. Torrance's instruction. The hookup will be ready to go in about two minutes if you would like to sit down and make yourself comfortable. There is coffee, and an assortment of herbal teas and cookies just behind you. Can I serve you anything?"

Exactly what they were missing at the precinct, Mac reflected. Mac thanked her and politely declined. A moment later a man entered the boardroom carrying a laptop. He was wearing a ginger sports jacket that matched his bushy moustache, a white shirt, and a checkered tie. His red hair had substantially thinned on top and was beginning to grey. Mac guessed mid-fifties, give or take a few years. At some point, he knew, hair began disappearing from where it was needed and began growing where it was not welcome. Little red tufts were sprouting out of his ears.

"Good afternoon, detective. I'm Simon Lester, general counsel for TGO." He had a British accent. "Mr. Torrance has instructed me to sit in on the interviews and provide any assistance you may require." Lester sat down across from Mac, opened the laptop, and began to peck away at the keyboard.

"Just taking notes if you have no objections," Lester said.

The video technician at the end of the room was playing with two remote controls, and moments later, Michael Cassidy appeared on the screen. The reception was remarkably crisp, and the camera focused exclusively on Michael. Cassidy said hello and Mac noted the slightest delay between the audio and the video. Less than a quarter of a second but enough to be distracting since he needed to focus not only on the content but on the demeanour.

They dispensed quickly with the pleasantries and Mac got down to business.

"How long have you known Odell Moore?"

"We were roommates at McGill University in the mid-nineties, and we played together on the varsity football team for a couple of years."

"You'd say you know him well?"

"I knew him as well as you can know a roommate. I studied math and he was an arts student so we never attended the same classes. Besides football practices and gym workouts, we also spent a lot of Friday and Saturday nights together meeting young women, if you know what I mean." Cassidy smiled. No tension in his face and no tells. At least not yet. "Our paths separated for twenty years until Odell joined TGO a couple of years ago."

The out-of-sync audio was bugging Mac more than he had expected it would. Time to find out what else was out of sync. "Anything unusual about him that struck you while you were students?"

"Nothing in particular. He was pretty straitlaced."

"When we interviewed Mr. Moore yesterday, he mentioned something about having a blackout in your presence."

Creases formed on Cassidy's forehead and he was not rushing to answer. The first hesitation. Mac made a note.

"To put it in context, we always had one another's backs. You never know when someone's had too much to drink in a bar or a parking lot, or you're picking up a woman whose boyfriend is returning from the washroom. Things can go wrong quickly. We were big and tough but there was occasionally a drunk wanting to take us on. I found Montrealers fairly open-minded so there was very little racial tension. Aside from the odd bloody nose that one of us delivered, nothing to speak of—except for one Friday night." Cassidy paused and turned his head. Mac couldn't make out whether there was a window at the other end. Or perhaps he was just staring off into space.

Mac needed to bring him back. "But that Friday night was different?"

Cassidy refocused on the camera. "Yes. Very different. It was our last night out together before I was scheduled to return to Malibu after final exams. We hit a bar on Crescent Street, the centre of downtown. It might have been one in the morning. We were chatting up a couple of thirty-somethings at the back of the bar. Today you'd call them cougars. A fellow came up to us at the table and began with a racial slur aimed at Odell. He had maybe fifty pounds on me, close to seventy-five on Odell. Odell is pretty solid at six feet two; this guy was an ox. He had a black ponytail and a long scraggly beard. He put his hand on the woman's shoulder and asked her to dance. Her eyes were begging for help and Odell was right beside her. He asked the thug to remove his hand. Very quietly. He didn't ask a second time. Suddenly Odell is up on his feet and the guy is howling in pain."

"What did Odell do to him?"

"It all happened at lightning speed. Odell must have dislocated the guy's finger. Then he got him in some kind of wrist lock and frogmarched him out the back door into the alley with me following. I had no idea that

Odell's karate expertise was so … precise. That's when I noticed the cut on the back of the leather jacket."

Michael closed his eyes, as if reliving it for the first time in years.

"White angel wings wrapped around a bleeding red skull. The guy is part of some motorcycle gang and it hasn't occurred to me that gang members don't travel anywhere on their own. Who stops to think in that kind of situation? I'm just covering Odell's back and I follow behind as quickly as I can… If I had just taken a half moment to check my own back… Two other leathers are following behind me. One of them shoves me into the wall. As I'm falling, I notice the other holding a knife. I scream out to Odell just before my head hits the concrete wall."

Michael opened his eyes.

"I was down for about a minute. When I picked myself up, the three gangbangers were lying in a heap in the alley. Odell was standing over them with his belt in his hands. I don't know if he planned to hogtie the leader, all I knew is we had to get out of there."

"Was Moore hurt?" Mac asked.

"I thought he might have been. He was rubbing his eyes and walking in circles. I checked him over and couldn't find a scratch anywhere. Anyway I grabbed him and we took a taxi back to our apartment. Odell fell asleep as soon as he hit the bed. I was a little worried he might have a concussion so I woke him every half hour until morning."

"What happened then?"

"He woke up with a killer headache and absolutely no recollection of what had happened that night. He asked about the women. Did we sleep with them? I tried to tell him what happened, but he just acted confused."

"Did you take him to the hospital the next day to get checked out?"

"He refused to go. Said he was fine. Wouldn't even go to the university clinic. We've never spoken about it since. Until today I really gave it no thought at all. I would have chalked it up to a big drunk except Odell barely drank."

"And that was the only time it happened?"

"I've never met a man more in control of himself. Yes, that was the only time."

"Thanks, Mr. Cassidy. Those are my questions for now. If you don't mind, as we proceed through our investigation, we may be back in touch with further questions."

The technician disconnected the feed, and Mac had a few minutes to reflect before his interview with Jackson Sherman. If this had happened once, was it possible there were other incidents subsequent to that? Guys who dissociate and become violent, in Mac's experience, did so periodically. The serial killers usually had some kind of trigger that set them off. What would trigger a big-time lawyer? Mac reminded himself that the rich and famous were not exempt; they could just afford better counsel.

■ ■ ■

Jackson made his way down to the video-conference room on the forty-fourth floor. Odd place to have a meeting unless they were going to be taped. If it had been his decision, he would have made sure the cops were nowhere near the boardroom complex where clients milled around. It could not be good for business to have the police in your offices.

He walked in and a short stocky man rose to greet him. He was dressed the way Jackson imagined a detective would, in ill-fitting clothes. Cheap clothes meant modest income. The guy was smart enough to make detective, so why choose this profession? Simon was sitting at the table busily typing away. No doubt Torrance's eyes and ears to what was about to transpire.

After shaking hands, he took the seat at the boardroom table kitty-corner from the detective. He had read in a business article about negotiations that sitting across the table from someone was more confrontational. Jackson wanted to project honesty and a spirit of collaboration. A man who had nothing to hide. There was still plenty of space between them at the long table.

Was the video equipment recording? He could not really tell. From his position, the camera, if it were on, would not have a good view of his facial expressions.

"Mr. Sherman, my last name is lengthy and Greek, so feel free to call me Mac. Thank you for taking the time to meet with me. I am one of the detectives working on the Brabant homicide and I'm trying to gather some background as part of our investigation. Your boss tells me you've done a lot of work with Odell Moore."

"Yes. I led the Bounty file last year."

"Bounty?"

"Sorry—force of habit. We're not allowed to refer to the companies involved in a major transaction in order to protect confidentiality. There are all kinds of Securities Commission rules, so we just give every file a code name to be safe. It's public now, but when you've been working on a deal for a year, it just becomes second nature."

"So you've worked with Mr. Moore for a year."

"Longer really. I've been at the firm around the same amount of time as Mr. Moore. Maybe just a little less. I joined the firm in the hopes of working with him. He's legendary in the business."

"So I understand. How would you describe his demeanour lately?"

"Nothing out of the ordinary. When we're working on a deal, he's extremely focused. Never gets flustered. He's very methodical."

"Does he ever lose his temper?"

Was Mac beating around the bush to ask Jackson whether he thought the General was capable of killing someone? It was not good news for him if Odell was arrested for this. Any hopes of partnership would probably fly right out the window if that happened. The firm would probably send Moore spinning out the door faster than an Alabama twister, whether he did it or not. Emily was right about one thing at their dinner. It was only a week ago but it felt like another lifetime. Without the General's sponsorship, Jackson would have to get back in the line with the other associates. It would take years to rebuild his political capital with enough partners to get the votes to become an equity partner. Then again, if Odell were cleared, Jackson would be back in the running, where his only obstacle was Michael Cassidy. He could not control the outcome of the investigation, but perhaps he could point it in the right direction.

What should he say about the episode just before Christmas on the Bounty file? They had not been working together for long when the deal hit a snag over the purchase price. Jackson assumed the General would handle it. That is until the General called him down to his office and told him to get down to Mobile and fix it. He could tell by the look in Odell's eyes that he better not return to New York without a solution. He couldn't explain it but at that moment Jackson felt a fear he had never before experienced. It was as if the General had all of this pent-up but well-controlled anger ... but what would happen if he ever let it loose?

"Sorry, Mr. Sherman. You haven't answered. Does Mr. Moore ever lose his temper?" Fortunately the detective had not lost his with the hesitation to answer.

"Sorry for the delay. I was giving that one careful thought. Not that I can recall. The man never loses his cool," Jackson said. "Mr. Moore is always in control."

Jackson saw that the detective was taking notes. He leaned back a little in his chair. He figured that would project an air of detachment.

"Anything unusual in his behaviour lately?"

"Meaning?"

"Sorry if I'm being a little vague here. Did you notice any episodes where he seemed disoriented or spaced out?"

This was probably something that Jackson should disclose. Unrelated to any murder motive. Besides, if he had noticed it, others probably had as well. "There have been a couple of instances when he's zoned out."

"That you experienced personally?"

"I had come by his office with a gift for the boss my mother had sent from Mobile. She insisted. Her personal good luck charm. A silver dollar minted in 1860, though not the Confederate version. That one would probably be worth a lot. Besides I don't think Mr. Moore would have appreciated it, given his background and all."

"His background?"

"Yeah. He's more than just black. His ancestor was a slave whose son fought for the Union."

"I get it. Sorry I interrupted."

"This coin must have been worth, well, a dollar, but she was convinced it would influence Moore to make me a partner. Not that he has any final say, but there is no arguing with my mother on things like that. So I just gave it to him and made a joke about my mother's superstitions." Jackson caught himself before going on, remembering how the General had really let him have it. He'd chastised Jackson *never* to make light of his mother, with an intensity that almost knocked Jackson off his chair. He'd flashed scary eyes. Now it was twice that Jackson had seen it. No mistaking Odell's intensity this time. Unvarnished anger. Once again, he kept that thought to himself. "Then he kind of drifted away for a minute. Don't know where he went, but then he was back. Perfectly normal."

"Doesn't sound all that serious," Mac said.

"There was another incident, just after we closed Bounty. He was taking me for lunch."

Mac began scribbling in his little flip pad.

"We were walking along Sixth Avenue and I was telling him a story. The light turned red, at least five seconds before we arrived at the intersection of Forty-First. He stepped right out into traffic. A cab driver almost killed him."

"Where were you?"

"Standing with everyone else on the corner. I screamed out to him. He didn't flinch or hesitate. Just kept walking. It turned out it was just a bruised knee and some bleeding. He was lying on the pavement for a good minute or two before he finally understood what had happened to him. Completely disoriented, but I figured he was just not paying attention."

The clicking on Simon's keyboard had taken over the room. Jackson and Mac both turned in his direction. Simon smiled. "Don't mind me," he said.

"You were out with him in Los Angeles recently?" Mac asked.

"Yes. Last week."

"Did you notice anything unusual?"

"He was in top form in the boardroom. You understand I can't disclose any details of what went on. Privilege and all that."

"So no signs of blackouts or space outs?"

"Come to think of it, last Sunday we were sitting in a meeting with clients and he zoned out a couple of times. If it was anyone else, I wouldn't have noticed."

"Meaning?"

"You know, sometimes the partner running the meeting gets caught not paying attention or tries to sneak a peek at his smartphone and gets caught."

"So why point that out?"

"After a year working with the General, I never saw it happen. Not even once. And here it was twice in the same meeting." Mac jotted down a couple of notes. Jackson couldn't figure out what that had to do with anything.

"Any signs of tension between Mr. Moore and his wife?"

"We were on different flights home. My wife went shopping with Dee in L.A. but didn't mention anything in particular." What about the trip to the beach? Should he bring that up on his own? Slippery slide, that one. Mind you, if he could cast Michael as a potential suspect in the case, that would be the perfect ending.

Who knows, maybe Cassidy *did* have something going on the side with Dee. She fell head over heels for Odell. Maybe she was that type. The flirty blond bombshell. The type Jackson always avoided. The type who might have had an affair with her husband's buddy. Wouldn't that be ironic. Maybe Cassidy took a separate flight from L.A. to New York that no one had yet discovered. Maybe he went to visit her at the apartment. Jackson didn't know any of the details surrounding the murder of the senator, but it was possible to imagine that Cassidy was there, part of a love triangle. Maybe the senator walked in on them. If it had been Odell walking in, it would have been Cassidy lying on the floor.

It probably wouldn't take the cops more than half an hour to check the flight manifests from LAX to see if Cassidy was a passenger. If he was devious enough, though, he would have flown somewhere else and rented a car. Or maybe he rented the car in L.A. and flew from somewhere else. The possibilities were endless if Cassidy didn't want to get caught cheating with Dee. The cops would probably check all that out as well. If that were the case, the reasonable possibility that Cassidy was somehow involved might be enough to get him booted out of the firm. Or at least delayed entry to partnership. Anyone with that kind of cloud hanging over their head was never going to make partner at TGO.

The notoriety might ruin Cassidy's life and with it his prospects for partnership. These conjectures flashed through Jackson's mind at warp speed, and he just as quickly decided to plunge ahead. He leaned forward and put both elbows on the table. Lowered his voice just slightly, like a conspirator who needed to share a secret. "My wife told me that Dee spent the afternoon on the beach with Michael Cassidy, a good friend of Mr. Moore and an associate in our L.A. office. All that was happening while Mr. Moore and I were working on the deal. It's not the first time they were alone together. I don't mean anything particular by that. Just saying."

Mac was taking copious notes now. Jackson had to repress a smirk. Simon might be watching him, though he too was busy clacking away at his keyboard.

"You mentioned that your wife went shopping with Dee Moore? Tell me about their relationship."

"They've become friends since Dee moved to New York. Dee didn't really know anyone here when she arrived and Emily had time on her hands. I suggested they get acquainted. Emily went through a similar adjustment five years ago."

"Adjustment?"

"Emily's from Kentucky. This can be a cold city. Anyway, they became friends."

"My partner, Rachel Brodinsky, will want to speak to your wife, today if possible. Can you please let her know? We need to learn as much about Mrs. Moore as possible."

Jackson nodded.

"Now if you don't mind, I'd like to ask you a few questions about the senator and your relationship with him."

"Our families have known one another since I was a child growing up in Mobile."

"Any other connections?"

"You probably know that Mr. Moore met with the senator on the Bounty file. I can't say more than that other than that is how they first met."

"So Mr. Moore needed the senator's assistance for a client matter."

"You can draw your own conclusions or ask Mr. Torrance, but I'm forbidden from discussing any client matters."

"Any idea how Mr. Moore and his wife met?"

"It was the same night as a fundraiser for the senator in Mobile. That's the reason I began working with Mr. Moore. I grew up in Mobile and knew the social landscape. I provided the background for Mr. Moore on his first meeting with the senator. Who knew he was going to fall in love?"

"You're saying it happened the same night."

"I can't say anything for sure. All I know is that a few months after we closed the Bounty deal, they were married. They eloped you know. Anyone who is anyone in Mobile is still talking about it." Shit, another case of loose lips. Once the detective got through with all the follow-up questions it would be obvious to a child that there was no shortage of animosity between the senator and the General. If that wasn't motive...?

Half an hour later the interview wrapped up. Jackson felt as if he had delivered Moore up on a skewer ready for the roast. He left the room kicking himself.

CHAPTER 25

10:00 a.m., Thursday, August 20, 2015

Odell walked briskly along Wall Street. Yellow cabs streamed past him and darted around cars trying to make right or left turns. Everyone in a rush to get somewhere. The morning smelled familiar—like money. For the first time since he'd started work in Manhattan a few years ago, he wondered why it had always been so important. Right now, he felt as if his life might not be worth more than a plug nickel after what he'd learned last night. These thoughts accompanied him to his destination, a six-storey red flatiron in lower Manhattan, not far from the courthouse. He walked up three flights to the offices of Tinker and Company. The receptionist sitting behind the black minimalist reception desk flashed a friendly smile. He supposed everyone who walked in professed to be innocent.

"You must be Mr. Moore. Ms. Tinker is expecting you. She's just finishing up a meeting in the boardroom and will be with you momentarily."

Odell took a seat, ignoring the photo on the front page of the *New York Times*: his father-in-law, lying askew beside the shattered coffee table. Instead he focused on the glass walls of the main boardroom that permitted the light to pour in from the windows overlooking the Wall Street neighbourhood. The sheer curtains behind the receptionist were drawn, shielding the identities of the half dozen silhouettes seated around the table. The men rose to leave, circulating quickly around the room before heading toward the door like sharks on the hunt. Probably the Valentine insider trading case she was defending. He recognized Steve Valentine from a distance and lowered his eyes to avoid having to exchange looks. He was aware, nevertheless, that they all tried not to notice him on the way out the door.

Carrie was the last to leave and walked purposefully back toward her office, signalling to the receptionist that she would be back in a moment, giving Odell a quick wave on the way. She returned a couple of moments later, her lips now a glossy red. Did she believe the fresh coat of lipstick gave her super powers? he wondered. Regardless, he would take all the help he could get. He lifted himself out of the chair and followed Carrie into a small room adjacent to her office. The files were arranged on the table waiting to greet him.

"Well, Odell, we have quite a day in front of us. Would you like some coffee?"

"Water would be fine, thanks."

Carrie walked over to the credenza and poured a tall glass of ice water and handed it to him, before resuming her seat opposite him.

"I've been in touch with TGO, and they're poring over everything in your computer and phone system. Do I need to worry that they're going to find anything incriminating?"

"Nothing," he replied.

"This isn't a cross-examination, Odell. Maybe you can be a little more expansive?"

He reached for the glass and took a long sip. He held the ice water in his mouth until he could feel his brain freezing.

"The news reported that the killer was left-handed," he said.

"So."

"I'm left-handed."

"So is ten per cent of the population. That's thirty-two million Americans alone. Even if we limit ourselves to the twenty-one to sixty-four demographic, that's still nineteen million suspects, give or take. Let's get one thing straight here, Odell. I am not here to try you. I'm not a judge. I'm not a jury. I'm your lawyer. My job is to defend you, and until it's proven beyond a reasonable doubt that you did this, you are not guilty. I don't have to explain why. You know the rules from first-year law school. Leave the case to me. And no second-guessing. Do you read me?"

"It's just that I can't remember a thing about the evening, though the afternoon is beginning to come into focus. I've been getting the memories back in flashes."

"Then you still owe yourself the benefit of the doubt, don't you? There is one incoming e-mail that I wanted to go through with you. Perhaps you can give me some context."

She pushed a red file folder containing the photographs across the table. As he flipped open the cover, Odell grimaced at the sight of the images that had disturbed him so much. He had seen them only two days ago though he now felt as if an entire lifetime had interceded.

"How did you get these?"

"I've told TGO I can no longer share any information with them, but when they called about these photos we agreed to an exception since it impacts both you and the firm."

"I don't know what to make of this, Carrie. I was really upset when I first saw this on Tuesday."

"Who are these people?"

"The man is my oldest friend, Michael Cassidy. He works out of our Los Angeles office. The woman is my wife, Dee. She accompanied me on a business trip to L.A. last week. I was tied up in a potential takeover transaction; Michael was on the file as well but I had given him the day off and suggested he show Dee the sights. They must have gone to the beach."

"You sound surprised. Dee didn't tell you about this? It happened last Sunday."

"Long story. I was completely tied up with a deal and then she became ill and we just never got a chance to talk."

"You sure that's the only reason she didn't tell you?"

"No, I don't know anything anymore."

"Sorry to push you, but I need to know." Her eyes narrowed and he couldn't help feeling that he was being evaluated. Did she believe he was naïve or lying? Which was worse?

"I can't explain what they're doing smoking a joint in public together. In the best possible light it shows incredibly poor judgment on Michael's part. If he has any hopes of becoming a partner at TGO he should know better than to avoid this type of illegal behaviour. We can't afford public scandal even on something as mundane as marijuana possession. As for my wife, what can I say?"

"Any idea why she was hugging him?"

"Are you asking if they were having an affair?" The feelings returned in an overwhelming rush. "How the hell should I know?" His palm exploded onto the table. Carrie jumped but would not break eye contact. Odell finally dropped his head. "Sorry," he mumbled.

Five seconds later her assistant opened the door. "Everything okay in here, boss?"

"No worries, Marg. Mr. Moore is just a little upset." Marg left the room but did not shut the door all the way.

"There's a whole series of photos relating to a necklace. Why do you think that was so important to the photographer?"

"That second set of photos left me speechless. The necklace and jug on Michael's neck is a gift that I gave to Dee the night I asked her to marry me. It has great sentimental value to us." Odell stopped dead and looked up at Carrie. Her head dropped perceptibly and her lips pursed as if she'd just heard a whopping lie from a client. She did not have to say a word. What could he add? He was not the one telling the lie—unless it was to himself.

"I can't for the life of me understand why she would give it to him. I called Michael before I left the office Tuesday to confirm that he had it."

"And did he?"

"Yes, but the call was cut short."

"So who do you think would send this?"

"I have no idea and I've been racking my brain. The e-mail came to me anonymously; I don't know who took the photos or why. My first assumption was that it might be someone from Sterling Yildirim's organization."

"The Turk? How does he fit into all this?"

"I was working on a deal at TGO. Yildirim was on the other side. They've been known to stoop to any level to upset the opposition when they're trying to take control of a corporation."

"Could they be blackmail photos?"

"Yildirim has withdrawn, so it doesn't really make sense that it would be them. Maybe they orchestrated this before they changed their minds. I really don't know what to make of any of this. All I can tell you is that I decided Tuesday afternoon to confront Dee with all of this. I was really upset."

"And did you?"

"I don't remember." His head hung low.

"You told me a few moments ago you've been getting flashes of memory. How did they come to you?"

"I closed my eyes."

"Then try it again. Close them."

Odell shut his eyes.

"Take a few breaths and stop thinking. Just float."

Odell could feel the beginning of a separation between the moment and space. A part of him was leaving his body and crossing the room. It felt familiar.

After thirty seconds he heard Carrie's voice. Softer than normal. "Okay, talk to me about the last thing you remember."

"Walking up Sixth. Obsessed with the photos. I had this bad feeling even before we left L.A. that something had happened between Michael and Dee." His eyes were still closed, his fists clenched.

"Relax, Odell. Feel yourself breathing. Relax your arms, your shoulders. Long controlled breaths. Feel the lightness. Engage your senses."

"I'm getting a jumble of images. Smoke hanging in the air. Smells like gunpowder. Union soldiers running amok. Get into formation. Liberty, she's all you can trust. I hear the snap of the lashes. My father's belt. I'm seeing the face again. The agony. The man choking." His eyes exploded open. "I strangled the senator. That's the vision. A faceless victim choking. Do you know how he died?"

"No, not yet."

He searched for traces of duplicity in her eyes. He could find none. "Not very good, is it?"

"Keep working on the memories. It's a little too early for you to be convicting yourself. Right now the firm is working with the police on tracing the source of the e-mail containing the photos to you." She had her own experts reviewing the digital images to confirm their authenticity but it would take a couple of days.

"When can I move back home?" he asked.

"It might be another week or so. Possibly longer. The CSI unit is scouring your apartment for fingerprints and DNA evidence. The processing takes a number of days, and results are often inconclusive, particularly insofar as ruling you out as a suspect are concerned. I expect your fingerprints and DNA are all over the apartment. They should be looking for third-party markings that may tie into video-camera evidence in the building. You need to let me know who else has a grievance with you or who has had access to your apartment in the past few months. My job is to cast doubt and help point the finger at someone else."

"I wish I could remember what happened." He deserved to be guilty.

"I'm also exploring the theory that Dee was the intended target," Carrie said.

His head shot up. He could feel the adrenalin rush. Every nerve in his body was now tingling.

"What do you mean?"

"We know your father-in-law was murdered, but we can't rule out the possibility that Dee might have been the intended victim. Remember there are two victims here. Maybe the senator was just in the wrong place last night."

"Andreas Moore."

"Pardon me?"

Odell's throat suddenly felt parched. He took a long sip of water. "After the divorce, my father remarried. He had a second family. Two children.

Just like us. A boy and a girl. The boy is twenty-five. I had no idea they existed until last year. The son called me out of the blue one day at the office. Said he was calling from Detroit. He'd just been arrested on drug possession charges. He'd read some press about me. Saw I was this big successful lawyer. Could I recommend a good lawyer in Detroit?"

"And he wanted more than a lawyer?"

"I didn't want anything to do with my father. I spent years overcoming what he did to me as a child. I wanted no connection with him. Forgive me if I felt no kindred relationship with anyone who happened to call himself my father's son. I gave him a name and I wired him $10,000."

"That sounds a little inconsistent to me."

"The money meant nothing to me. Neither did he, but there was no point referring him to a decent lawyer without money for a retainer."

"So why are you concerned about him?"

"He called me in March to thank me. He beat the charges. Could I maybe get him started down a new path. I told him politely that I felt I had done all I could ever do for him. He called four more times. I stopped returning the messages."

"And you think...?"

"Maybe he came to find me. Or to hurt me. Or to hurt..." Odell slammed his fist. "I'll kill him if he even so much as touched Dee."

"Stop torturing yourself. I'll put my investigator on it."

"Carrie, right now I don't care about me or any half-brother. My wife is my priority."

"You mean after your life."

"I mean before my life. Nothing else matters."

"As far as I know there are no restraining orders outstanding so I suppose your wife's family hasn't taken any legal action."

"Against me?"

She did not respond immediately.

He resigned himself to the reality, sitting in the office of one of the most famous criminal lawyers in the country. "Against me."

"You told me there was great antagonism by your father-in-law as a result of your marriage. He ends up dead in your apartment. What do you think your mother-in-law must be thinking?"

"I have so much to make up to her. I don't even know where to begin."

Carrie's eyes narrowed. Her voice hardened. "You're one of the most skilled advocates in New York. Rely on your instincts."

That might be true of Odell the corporate attorney. He wondered whether Odell the murder suspect had any instincts at all, beyond short-term survival.

"That should be your first priority," she continued. "The firm wants you to take some vacation time until this blows over, so it would be helpful for you to be at your wife's side, if only for the PR value. I'm sorry, I don't mean to sound callous, but my job here is to protect you."

"I still don't know where Dee is," he said sheepishly.

"Sorry, Odell, I should have told you. She's at New York Presbyterian. It's at 168th and Broadway. I'll get the room number from my assistant and text it to you. I've been told the family engaged private security to screen anyone trying to enter the room. It's as much for your mother-in-law's privacy as anything else. There is potentially a murderer on the loose, and until the police have more information it makes sense to have someone stationed outside the door. Your big challenge will be making your way through the media scrum still camped outside the hospital. Fortunately, they're not permitted inside."

"I'm not sure which is worse. Facing the media or Eleanor Brabant. Regardless, I need to get up there immediately."

"For now there's nothing for you to do here or at your office. It should be a few days before I have any concrete information. I'll also have my investigator conduct our own review to figure out who else might have been in your apartment. In the meantime, good luck. God speed to your wife and family."

Three hours later, Odell stepped out of the subway across from the hospital. He was dressed in hospital greens, a pair of sneakers, and a small tuque that covered the dreadlocks poking out from underneath.

He jammed his hands into his pockets, slouched and shuffled across the street. As he got closer to the entrance, he saw the media lounging outside the door. There could be only one person they were staking out.

The next shift was about to start, and a slew of hospital administrative staff came pouring in to replace the group that would be leaving in fifteen minutes. Odell found a group of four orderlies who were joking together and tagged along at the rear, keeping his head down and falling into their rhythm as they moved past the reporters and cameras. He made his way through the corridors, following the signs to the south elevators and then up to the neurology ward.

CHAPTER 26

5:00 p.m., Thursday, August 20, 2015

Rachel arrived at the apartment on Eighty-Third Street, half a block east of Second Avenue. She reminded herself that an Upper East Side homicide was a murder like any other, though the witnesses might identify themselves as upper class or upwardly mobile. Rachel had spent most of her adolescence through to her twenties working on her own identity. Was she gay first and Jewish second or vice versa? Those were the years when everyone tried to put her into a box and there was no comfortable fit.

After she met Janet, everything changed. Janet's love inspired Rachel to accept who she was. To develop her potential as a cop and then as a detective. Janet gave her the greatest gift in her life—a daughter. Now Rachel was a wife and a mother and a cop. A guilt-ridden mother and a guilt-ridden wife and a damned good cop. And all that mattered was that she had come to accept it. She was never going to assuage the guilt and she was learning to live with it. But the only way she could live with it was to become one of the most diligent detectives in the precinct. Her job today was the same as it was every day. Discover the facts, rely on her intuition, sort out the lies and misconceptions that witnesses inevitably carry around, and uncover the truth. "Uncover" was an interesting choice of words when it came to truth. It suggested it was lying beneath the surface. It was time to peel back the layers of Emily Sherman.

Emily nodded a greeting as Rachel entered the apartment but avoided making direct eye contact. She escorted Rachel immediately to the kitchen and offered tea. The room was functional and tight, typical for a working couple with no kids. Rachel had already begun the profile. Witnesses often took you to the place they felt the most comfortable.

They sat at bar stools at the counter. Not a lot of room to manoeuvre. She bet Jackson Sherman rarely spent a moment in here other than to grab a morning coffee and maybe a beer at the end of the day. He probably knew his way to the fridge and back. The dilapidated appliances had probably been there beyond their useful lives. The grime on the burners had built up. It made Rachel feel comfortable. Almost at home. Her mother had been a great cook but the oven had shown the evidence of decades of use.

"Do you do a lot of cooking?" Rachel asked. As good an icebreaker as anything.

"Jackson isn't home very much, particularly at dinnertime. Still, I'd rather prepare something fresh than eat one of those frozen dinners."

Rachel moved into explaining the purpose of her visit. "I'm trying to gather as much information as I can about Dee Moore. I gather the two of you are friends?"

"Can you tell me how Dee is doing? I'm worried sick and the hospital tells me they're not accepting visitors. Something about security around the senator's death."

Rachel hesitated, trying to frame the answer. Emily's face turned pale.

"I don't have a lot of details. All I can tell you is that she is being carefully monitored and we are all waiting for her to regain consciousness."

"What about the baby?" Emily's face had tensed. She appeared to be genuinely concerned.

Rachel swallowed quickly, hiding her surprise at the revelation. If Mac had taught her one thing in the years they'd worked together, it was the importance of a poker face. Moore had never mentioned that his wife was pregnant. Had his wife withheld it from him? Odd. "She told you?"

"Of course she told me," Emily bristled. "We're best friends. How could she not share that?"

"I didn't mean to offend you."

"I know it's your job to ask questions." Emily grabbed a tissue and dabbed at her eyes. Then she took a long gulp of her tea from the porcelain mug.

"You spent a lot of time together?

"I'd say so."

"Have you been to the Moore apartment recently?"

"Just a few days ago. Dee asked me to check some appliances for her after they left for California last week. She texted me the access codes so that I could get in. Is that important?"

"Our CSI team is dusting for prints and checking DNA. There will be a number of unmatched identifications. I just want to rule you out. Would you object to my taking your fingerprints and doing a DNA swab?"

"None at all. I hope you catch the monster that did this."

"And you were not at the apartment Tuesday?"

"I walked Dee back to the building at around three in the afternoon or so. She had just found out about the pregnancy. She needed to lie down. I escorted her upstairs but I didn't go in with her."

"Who else knew about the pregnancy?"

"We were all just back from L.A. and she had just got the news while we were in the coffee shop."

Rachel caught herself thinking about Janet's pregnancy. She had felt like the husband, going through it all vicariously. But she needed to focus on Emily Sherman. It was time to take her through her story step by step. Maybe there was some jealousy between the two friends when only one was pregnant. "Tell me about L.A."

Emily recounted the events until the moment they had both received the news from the doctor's office.

Rachel watched Emily's eyes carefully. They were shimmering. Love or something else? "So you knew about this before Odell Moore did?"

"Yes, and to answer your next question I have no idea if she told him. I just know she was planning to."

"How was her state of mind. Excited?"

"Dee was completely upside down. Her hormones were all over the place. One minute crying, the next laughing. Not herself. At all."

Rachel nodded, suggesting she understood.

"Do you have any kids?" Emily asked.

"Yes, a daughter. My wife carried her."

"Then you wouldn't have experienced it first hand, but you've probably observed."

There were moments during the pregnancy when Janet behaved like she was from another planet. She claimed to love every moment of the pregnancy, but she conveniently forgot the screaming sessions, the odd tantrum, and her feeling that Rachel was letting her down. All that was forgotten at the miraculous moment of birth.

It might make life more challenging as a detective, but the ability people had to reshape their memories to screen out bad behaviour or stories not consistent with what they thought of themselves was essential to maintaining sanity. Particularly in a marriage. She knew that every marriage had its challenges and some made people crazy. In Rachel's experience, crazy enough to kill.

"How was Mrs. Moore's relationship with her husband?"

Slight hesitation. "It was wonderful during their courtship. After all, she's pregnant."

Emily said the word pregnant as if she was describing a state of being just short of euphoria. Perhaps she was projecting. Rachel made a mental note and filed it where she kept the rest of her insights.

"With all the sex they were having once they started dating, she had to know it was a possibility. In case you're wondering, we never discussed whether she used birth control. I'm just guessing. After all, how else do you get pregnant?

Indeed, how else? Rachel thought, with a dose of sarcasm.

"I never asked, but I just assumed that was part of the big rush to get married in Vegas. Whether Dee admitted it to herself or not, I'll bet that somewhere inside she just knew. They say women know right away. After the honeymoon Dee seemed more tense."

"Were they fighting?"

"No, no, no. Nothing like that. At least as far as I know. I don't want you to get the wrong idea here. Dee and I are not lifetime pals. We just met a few months ago when she relocated to New York."

The response sounded a little defensive. It was time to probe a little more. "But there was something you noticed?"

"Dee had some issues to get off her chest. Dee thought Odell did too. They couldn't find the time with all the work pressures." Emily frowned.

"So as far as you know there were no big issues, though?"

"Dee had just found out she was pregnant. Literally that afternoon. It was so exciting. I think she found it overwhelming. The morning sickness was really taking her down."

"Would you say depressed?"

Emily took a sip of tea. Held it for a moment in her mouth before swallowing. Took her time to answer. "Um, I would say she was trying to figure out how to cope."

An interesting revelation. "Cope with what? Are you aware of anyone who might have posed a threat to Mrs. Moore?"

"She didn't trust one of the concierges." The words jumped out of Emily's mouth and her pace picked up. "I don't remember his name. Something Italian. He's very attractive. Tall, slicked-back hair. The type who thinks he's God's gift to women. She thought he was creepy. That's why she had me instead of him check her apartment. She was worried he would go through her things."

"Was she seriously worried?"

"She thought he had an alcohol problem. I saw him. The look he gave her last week scared me." Emily shivered slightly.

Rachel made a note to get information from the concierge. It was time for a more thorough interview with him.

"What about the relationship between Dee and her father?"

"Her father was a subject that Dee steered away from while they were dating because of the deal Odell was working on. Dee was surprised at the level of her father's outrage that they had eloped. I know she really wanted to patch it up."

"What was the problem specifically?"

"It wasn't just that he was caught off-guard. The senator was opposed to the marriage. She went down to Mobile after the honeymoon to talk to him but she told me it didn't work. Her father was really upset with her and even more upset with Odell."

"And what about your husband and Mr. Moore?"

Emily dropped her eyes. "What about them?" It was more of a whisper.

Rachel's antennae went up. The first note of defensiveness. There was something Emily Sherman was holding back. "How was their relationship?"

Emily's back straightened and she took a sip of tea. Then another. A stall tactic.

"Jackson was Odell Moore's go-to man. He played an important role in all of Odell's recent transactions. They spent a lot of time together."

Emily sounded tense, her response careful to the point of sounding forced. There was something more to be discovered. There always was, Rachel thought. All in good time.

CHAPTER 27

Odell exited the elevator just outside the nurses' station in the neurological wing and ran into his first challenge. There was no way to enter the patient area without a security clearance for visitors. He pulled off the tuque and stuffed it into his bag. He smoothed his moustache and approached a nurse who appeared to be responsible for guest clearance and asked if she could page Mrs. Brabant. The nurse gave him a funny look. That's when he remembered he'd forgotten to change his clothes. She must be wondering why an orderly did not have ID. There was nowhere to sit so he leaned against the wall, shuffling his weight from one leg to the other. Waiting.

He was expecting a broken woman in mourning for a lost spouse. A woman whose distress and lonely vigil had worn her away to nothing. A woman many years older than when they'd had dinner last November. Someone in need of assistance and company to take care of Dee.

Fifteen minutes later she stepped out. Her blond hair was tied up tightly in a bun. Her eyes were made up, radiating strength from some kind of reservoir. She was wearing a floral pattern dress, carrying a small black purse. The lines on her face were deeper than the last time he'd seen her, but her shoulders were pulled back. Taller than he remembered. All puffed up like the mother bear protecting her cub from a predator. How did she manage it?

"They let you out on bail?" she said curtly. There were going to be no pleasantries.

He was planning to start with an apology. He was planning to express his sympathies. The woman had just lost her husband and was worrying about losing her daughter. His tongue tied around his feeling of guilt. She'd probably been spending every moment with *his* wife. He'd spent every moment shuttling between a jail cell, a run-down hotel room, and a lawyer's office. Some newlywed husband. He lowered his gaze. "I wasn't arrested." He couldn't meet her eyes.

"Sorry. I heard the nurses gossiping about what they're hearing and reading in the news." She didn't sound at all sorry.

Odell summoned his strength and looked Eleanor straight in the eyes. Earnestly. It never failed him. "I've come to be with my wife."

"That's not happening. What in the world is going on? What are you doing in scrubs? You look like an orderly here. And what have you done with your hair?"

Shoot. His change of clothes was in the knapsack slung on his shoulder. He'd forgotten to remove the hair extensions. Odell Moore the strategist, the perfectionist, the man who knew how to play others, was dead. Remorse had swallowed the old Odell. He had no idea who was left inside.

He met her eyes again, trying to match her ferocity. "Dee needs me. I'm her husband. And you know very well that I can insist on entering. I just have to tell them who I am. I called you out here as a courtesy."

"And I'm her mother," she said, calling his bluff. "As far as I'm concerned, until you're cleared, I'm taking no risks with her safety. Charged, not charged, it's all the same to me. You're a risk to my daughter's safety. You want to come in today? I can't stop you. But you're not going to be with her alone for one minute, and I'll be advising my lawyers to present a motion for a temporary restraining order. Is that what you really want? A public fight with me? You know and I know that it doesn't matter one iota who wins the fight, you would lose."

He saw immediately that he was no match for her strength. He shifted the knapsack to his right shoulder. "At least tell me how she's doing."

"They operated on her before I got here to relieve the pressure building in her brain. The doctor called it an acute subdural hematoma."

"Did they translate that into English for you?"

"One of the residents explained it was a bruise to the front cortex of the brain as a result of the fall. She split her head open on the coffee table. It left a gash on her forehead and caused some internal bleeding between the brain and the meninges, which is the sac protecting the brain. There was a lot of blood, but the actual gash is only a couple of inches long."

"The police told me she's in a coma."

"She's been unconscious since they brought her into emergency but she shows responsiveness. They say she's not in a coma."

"When do they expect her to wake up?"

"She'll wake up when she darn well pleases. There's no science here. It's all art." Eleanor hesitated. She sounded frustrated.

"They have no idea, do they?"

"He said—these were his words—it's 'not uncommon for some kind of brain function damage to present in this type of case.' Doctors and their magic language. Double negatives. *Not uncommon.* Does that make it common? That's why I didn't pursue law as a career. You lawyers—and politicians. The lot of you can't be trusted."

Odell already knew that about himself.

"The staff here in obstetrics and neurology have all been checking in on Dee and monitoring the baby. They say she's about two months along."

"Dee's pregnant?"

"She didn't tell you?"

He stared at her blankly. Dee might have told him that afternoon when the police told him he'd been in the apartment. He had no recollection. Maybe it was not uncommon for someone who suffered blackouts. Or maybe the revelation had triggered the blackout, which incited the violence. Odell could feel a slight dizziness coming on. Something inside him was becoming convinced that Dee must have told him.

He had to stop speculating. His normal rational response system had hit the wall. His stomach was in free fall. He could feel the joy, frustration, and something undefined welling up from deep within him. He wanted to cry. He just shuddered.

Eleanor waited for a moment, maintaining a blank stare, and then continued. "So far they see no evidence of risk to the pregnancy. Of course they'll be monitoring her continuously, and I'll feel a lot better when she regains consciousness." She reached into the purse and handed him a tissue.

Odell stood still, trying to recompose himself. No tears.

"She didn't tell you, did she?" There was an edge of contempt in her tone. Eleanor's eyes narrowed.

"She might have." He stood there for a moment feeling the intensity of her focus, trying to figure out how he would explain this.

"This is not the kind of thing that a wife might or might not tell her husband." Her tone was withering.

The knapsack slid off his shoulder. He let it fall to the ground and it hit with a familiar thud. Like his life.

"It's nothing like that. My brain is a complete blank. I have no recollection of anything after about two-thirty in the afternoon on Tuesday."

"How could that be?"

"I don't understand it myself but the whole afternoon and night are a blank. I woke up in a police station cell Wednesday morning. They told me I was walking on the street near the apartment Tuesday night and acting oddly—I was incoherent."

"So you have no memory of what might have happened?"

"The police told me I'd been to the apartment late in the afternoon. She might have told me then."

"The whole story defies belief."

Odell nodded his head. If he were Eleanor, he'd be saying the same thing. "Even I don't understand it."

"And you can't even tell me you didn't do it?" Eleanor's tone had changed ever so slightly. As if she wanted to believe he was not capable of doing something so awful. "You can appreciate why I'm being cautious."

"I feel so helpless and I don't blame you one bit."

"Blame me?" Eleanor's eyes flared. Odell was losing the battle for credibility once again. At this rate she would never let him through the door.

"Not what I meant—I mean I don't blame you for finding this hard to believe. Please let me help out in some way." He was hearing himself beg. He watched for any sign of give from Eleanor. He could see none.

He continued nonetheless. "You'll be here for an extended period. Where are you staying?"

"I've been at Dee's bedside since I arrived."

"I'll have my assistant book you a hotel room nearby so you can take some breaks. There must be matters to attend to concerning Edward."

"That is kind of you," she said, though her cold tone of voice showed no sign of gratefulness. But her eyes once more betrayed a little give. Odell realized he had taken this as far as he could for the moment.

"You should get back to her—I don't want to keep you from her—but I'll be sitting in the waiting area. I have no intention of leaving the hospital. I don't care how long it takes until you finally agree to let me in." She looked as if she was thinking something like "When hell freezes over." He said firmly, "I'm not leaving."

"As you wish. I'll come out with updates when they're available." With that she turned and walked back into the secured patient area.

He could not have expected any better. He found himself alone in the waiting room along with half a dozen chairs, stained a light wood grain, with nondescript lime cushions. A small-screen television hanging from the wall was playing the New York breaking news with subtitles and no sound. A couple of small end tables held the dog-eared magazines, and a few toys were splayed across on the floor.

He found a bathroom and changed into the clothes in the knapsack— a T-shirt and black jeans. He also removed the hair extensions. He had no plans to leave the hospital, so no more need for a disguise. Then he returned to the waiting area and arranged a couple of chairs facing one another and propped his legs up. He had never felt so alone. In all those years as a bachelor, he was often alone but never felt lonely, never felt he was missing anything. He had kept his secrets to himself. Never felt a need to share them. Now he was alone once again and all he felt was a void. An aching void. His secrets had come back to overwhelm him.

He closed his eyes for a moment and settled into his feeling of being cut off from the most important people in his life. He thought back to the summer Dad moved out. It had been two months since Mum finally got the court order denying Dad custody and access. Odell and Sheneitha went to visit Gramps on the farm, their summer vacation. Gramps still called him Odie, even though it felt a little childish. It sounded a lot better than when his father used the nickname. They were picking blueberries together, in a field overrun with wild bushes, about half a mile from Gramps's house. Odie's favourite place in the world.

"A boy can't divorce his father," Gramps said. He didn't sound like Gramps. He sounded more like what Odell imagined the Confederate general toy soldier would sound like if he were a real person. Barking orders. Mean. "Your Dad loves you." This time a lie spoken as if it were the truth. Gramps had never lied to Odell before.

"He has a funny way of showing it."

"Ya gotta judge a man by what's in his heart, not by what the booze does ta him. We're simple people, growed up on the farm and what. And we all made mistakes. Mistakes ya gotta forgive."

Odell nodded his head. "Gramps, you may love him but I don't think he loves us."

"'Course he does. All dads love their kids. Some just can't show it. I'll make sure your dad straightens out. Just let him visit here once in a while. I'll be around so's you don't have to worry."

"I may change my mind later, Gramps, but for now Sheneitha and I need to keep our distance." An odd choice of words for a twelve-year-old. Maybe not so odd for an aspiring lawyer. He'd thought that's why Gramps shook his head when he heard the words. Got down on a knee so he could look Odie straight in the eye. Except something in Gramps's expression felt different. Odie came rushing over. He wasn't certain which one of them needed the hug. Gramps pushed him away with a violent shove that almost knocked him off his feet. He clenched his fists tightly. His face became an unrecognizable block of ice. This person was no longer Gramps, as if he'd been taken over by a space alien or evil ghost from the movies. The look frightened Odie more than his asshole father ever had.

Gramps released his fists and looked down as if studying his hands and what they were capable of doing. He did not raise his head. Just began speaking matter-of-factly. "In that case, Odell, you're dead to me. You're no longer my flesh and blood." No belt ever scarred him as much as those searing words. Gramps stood up, shoulders slumped, turned his back and trudged away, leaving Odie alone in a sea of blueberries. Gramps kept walking until he shrunk away to nothing. That was Odie's final visit to the farm. Odell had never heard from him again. Why?

It still gnawed at him, sometimes unbearably. Odell started and his eyes flew open at a sudden realization, one he had kept from himself for over thirty years. Maybe it said more about who Gramps really was and about his relationship with Dad when he was a boy. Regardless, nothing could excuse what Dad had done to Odell. And nothing could excuse Odell. Even if he hadn't done this to Dee, his jealousy over Michael was at the root of his not being around to protect his wife from what had happened. Odell had failed her. Perhaps that was just as evil as being the perpetrator of all the violence.

Maybe everything would have turned out differently if he had put Dee first. Instead, his father-in-law was dead, his wife lay unconscious and pregnant, and Odell was living in a waiting room. His only friend might have cuckolded him. No family, no friends, no wife, no close work associates, no trust. He didn't even trust himself. He needed Dee to wake up. The constants in his life right now were half a dozen lime chairs.

CHAPTER 28

8:00 a.m., Friday, August 21, 2015

Mac sat behind his desk in the precinct. The furniture bore the scars and divots of abuse from generations of detectives. He didn't keep family pictures or any other evidence of a personal life on his desk, though he kept a stash of baby pictures of the twins in his desk drawer to remind him of the days before he and his wife, Jennifer, needed to worry about the kids' future. Not that they didn't worry as young parents, but when the twins were kids, the problems were so insignificant, at least compared to them as teenagers. He might not have said that last weekend, but with teenagers sometimes the world changes overnight. This morning, work was an escape from the mess he'd left behind.

Rachel and her partner, Janet, didn't have any problems with their daughter, Kailey, at least according to the evidence in a picture frame on her desk. Some photographer had captured the two women giggling in Central Park last year, holding hands with Kailey, swinging her in the air. Kailey's head was thrown back, her curly auburn hair flying in the wind, her mouth exploding with unbridled laughter. Everything about relationships these days was considered normal. Did it really make a difference if a child had an absentee father as long as she had two mothers? It really wasn't fair to call a biological father an absentee, though. All he contributed to Kailey's life was a test tube full of sperm. He probably didn't even know she existed, that the potential of life that he deposited at the bank might one day be realized in this joyful being. Was Kailey even aware that she had no father in her life? Was Kailey more or less likely to have problems growing up deprived of a father figure? This was a subject area he never felt comfortable raising with Rachel.

Yesterday Mac had been pretty sure it mattered. Yesterday he'd been on a different page. A chapter of life where Mac understood fatherhood and children. This morning Terry announced that he was not going to college. All those applications they had completed together never got mailed. His brother, Evan, was part of the conspiracy. Jen tore a strip off the twins, but it was not going to change the immediate future.

Jen had ranted at Mac on the cellphone on the way to the precinct. It was all too much for Mac to deal with in the middle of this investigation. He sat and he listened and he said nothing as her voice filled every inch of the void in the car, like a balloon that continued to expand, until there was no room left for Mac and his silence, which only fuelled Jen's anger all the more. "When are you finally going to be a father?" It was the last thing she shouted before the line went dead. He knew she didn't mean it, but that didn't mean it was not true. There was no upside in defending himself. And no one on the other end of the line to listen. He knew from experience that this was not the moment to try and call her back. On the weekend they would all sit down; hopefully there would be enough of a break on this goddamned investigation.

The media pressure on the case was growing. The senator's public profile had led to a *New York Daily News* article this morning listing the various organizations that might have a bone to pick with the senator over the past year for public stances he had taken against their interests. Most recently he had been at the forefront of the protest against the growth of Russian-led organized crime across America and Chinese cybercrime designed to destabilize American business. Anonymous sources said to be close to the senator had mentioned that he was working on a bill to have the government impose harsh sanctions on the Chinese in the event that any cyber disruption of American business or government interests could be linked to sources in the Chinese government. The newspapers were openly speculating as to whether the death of the senator might be a warning to other U.S. legislators that none of them were secure if they pursued this type of aggressive legislative approach to these problems.

The cooperative investigation between the NYPD and the FBI fuelled public fears that this was being investigated as a political assassination. Various witnesses placed the senator in a morning meeting in Washington, and his secretary had told police that his calendar had no notations for the afternoon on the day he died. There was nothing to suggest to her that he wasn't in Washington. Normally he was quite meticulous in keeping her advised of his comings and goings. She speculated he must have gone to visit his daughter. Not exactly rocket science. The on-line conspiracy theorists, who were being monitored by Homeland, however, were speculating that he might have been lured to New York.

Mac knew it was all horseshit. He and Rachel had been briefed by agent Albert Copertino last night. The FBI had run a complete review of the senator's e-mail, calendar, and travel schedule over the past month. There were no calls from blocked numbers, no unusual e-mails, no individual meetings in the calendar with Chinese or Russians, of an official or even of a social nature. Other than strong official statements issued by the Chinese ambassador two weeks ago, vowing that any anti-Chinese legislation would be met with swift diplomatic and political reprisal, there was no chatter of any nature directed at the senator. His assistant confirmed that she had no idea that he was planning to be in New York. His last meeting was chaired by Senator Marc Dorion. When questioned, Dorion told Copertino that Brabant had mentioned something about a meeting in New York that he was rushing to get to.

The senator's credit card showed a one-way train ticket from D.C. to Manhattan, booked the day of the murder. The evidence pointed to a trip that was impulsive—not forced. There were no charges after the time of death. Whoever took the wallet didn't bother checking the pocket with the billfold. Odd, if theft was the motive. Who leaves the cash behind unless they're in a big hurry to get out? There was no way to figure out whether it was the assailant who took the wallet—at least based on what they knew to date.

Senator Brabant had ended up at his daughter's apartment. Maybe he'd gone to settle the score with his son-in-law. Or maybe Rachel was right last night when she told him it was possible that he had come to reconcile with his daughter. Rachel would eventually interview the widow.

The building security cameras recorded the senator's two visits to the apartment. They also showed a number of others, no more than a handful, other than tenants, going in and out of the building on the afternoon of the murder. The concierge kept a log of visitors to the building only before 7:00 a.m. and after 7:00 p.m. Workmen were allowed in only if they had work orders and written permission to enter the building. The concierge recalled one visitor to the apartment with a heavy Southern accent, though he could not remember the name. Because of the power failure and the paramedics' visit on the night of the murder, the concierge admitted he had kept no records of who was coming in or out that evening. His shift normally ended at eight.

Rachel had reminded Mac last night that while they could not rule out Moore, it was still not entirely certain that the senator was the intended victim. Her sixth sense told her there was more to this story than met the eye, and they still had to keep an open mind about the possibility that the killer might have been after Dee Moore. Of course, the prime suspect when the wife is found lying in a pool of blood after evidence of a passionate fight is the husband. Unless the investigation led them in another direction, Odell Moore was still the prime suspect. For whatever reason, that was bugging Rachel.

She was convinced this was a crime of passion, likely an unplanned death. Mac reread the coroner's report for the fourth time. Had he missed a critical detail that might point him in a new direction? The preliminary report confirmed the blunt force trauma to the side of the head had cracked the senator's skull but suggested further testing was still required concerning the cause of death. The bloodstained statuette lying on the floor had been applied by the perpetrator from behind. It was likely, therefore, that the senator was overcome by a surprise attack, especially as there were no signs of a struggle. Although he was in his late sixties, he was a vigorous man with a large build. Anyone confronting him would likely have had to engage in a fight before knocking him out. The angle of the blow also suggested that the assailant was left-handed and at least six feet tall and therefore probably male.

They had checked the statuette for fingerprints and DNA. Moore had a cleaning lady in once a week but her prints were not on the statuette. Not surprising, since she wore rubber gloves when she cleaned. There was one set of prints that did not match Moore's but the prints did not match anyone in the system and the DNA was inconclusive. Mac made a mental note to have a chat with the lab technician.

He was rechecking the list of potential suspects when his phone rang. It was Rachel. He answered without enthusiasm.

"Do me a favour, Mac. Open the top drawer of my desk."

"Why?"

"To everything, there is a season," she said.

"You going pop music on me?" he asked. "Please don't continue." Mac winced. He'd heard Rachel sing.

"It's Ecclesiastes, you philistine. Just open the drawer."

"You keep a Bible in there?"

"Partners have been murdered for being less irritating." Rachel laughed. "Will you just open the drawer. I'm not trying to get philosophical here." Mac stepped over to her desk and pulled open the drawer. A Tupperware with four cupcakes. "Are these Ginnie's?"

"Yes. From the Seventh Avenue store. I got your favourite. Pistachio and chocolate butter cream. Take one. It will help you think. Might also improve your mood."

No question. Ginnie made the best cupcakes on the island. Mac nibbled the frosting.

"You're a saint," Mac said and licked his lips. "The amnesia story might check out, partner. Cassidy confirmed the story about Moore blacking out twenty years ago, but he added a new twist. Moore became very violent. Seriously injured three motorcycle gang members in a back alley. Uncontrolled rage protecting the honour of a woman."

"Not the same as blindsiding your father-in-law in your apartment."

"Unless your father-in-law has a beef with your wife."

"It seems he did," Rachel said. "Emily Sherman told me the senator was deeply opposed to the marriage."

"Then maybe we have Moore's motive. The senator could not resist meddling and Moore could not resist taking action." Mac could no longer resist taking a bite of the cupcake. It was devil's food speckled with nuts and he bit deeply enough to hit the green butter cream centre. "I dunno," he mumbled through the explosion of flavour. "Maybe it's not such a stretch to connect the two. What else did Mrs. Sherman tell you ?"

"She had access to the apartment, and she was the first person to find out that Dee Moore was pregnant. She's been married five years so maybe she was jealous. But it's really a stretch to get from there to murdering your best friend over her getting there first."

"Unless there's more for us to discover." Like the fact that he had to dig deep into the cupcake to get to the filling. He didn't hesitate to take another bite.

"She also said there was a problem between Dee Moore and the concierge. Possible stalking issues. I'll go speak to him next. I also get the sense that there's more than meets the eye to the relationship between Mrs. Sherman's husband and Odell Moore. She was hiding something from me."

"Your talent is reading people."

"I feel like she's holding onto information she didn't want to share with me."

"Funny you should say that," Mac said. "Jackson Sherman sends off a vibe that's bothering me." He squeezed the rest of the cupcake into his mouth. His partner knew him well. For a brief moment he no longer cared about anything but the party on his tongue.

■ ■ ■

Ninety minutes later, Rachel returned. Mac was busy organizing files on his desk.

"Busy boy. Too busy to clean up your desk?" An empty cupcake holder lay beside the files—rainbow coloured on the outside, speckles of devil food crumbs clinging to the inside rim, matching the remnant crumbs scattered across the desk.

"I owe you a big one," Mac said, sweeping the mess with his right hand into his left palm. He dropped the paper in the trash can beside the desk while he threw back the remaining crumbs into his mouth. Rachel's eyes widened. "My mother taught me it was a sin to waste," he said, without a trace of defensiveness. "She lived through the food shortages in Greece during the war, before she emigrated. Drilled it into us."

"Same with my grandmother. I used to chalk it up to her being a Jewish survivor." Rachel dropped into her desk chair facing Mac.

"What happened with the concierge?"

"Other than being a drunk, he has a solid alibi for the time of the murder. He needed help getting the building generator in order and a few maintenance people were down with him in the basement from just after the time of the blackout until at least ten minutes after seven o'clock. The 911 call had already come through by then."

"So we're back to Moore. He's the one claiming amnesia, which I still don't believe for one moment. What Jackson Sherman described amounted to not much more than the odd zone-out. Hell, when I'm stressed that kind of thing happens to me. Moore's still the logical starting point. Big enough, strong enough, and based on what Cassidy told me, violent enough."

"On the other hand, Cassidy's story about the violence is twenty years old. We just don't have anything yet beyond the circumstantial. Not enough to build a case."

"It's only a matter of time before the conspiracy theorists start running amok if we can't make an arrest. Thank goodness Al Qaeda and ISIS aren't claiming responsibility, because if that happens hysteria will reign. Imagine a new way of hitting back at America. Killing their elected officials."

"Sorry, Mac. We can't bow to that kind of pressure, and right now Moore is just not looking good to me as the perp. Let's wait on the fingerprints."

"I almost forgot, we're going to have some company," he said. "TGO's counsel and his computer specialist want to meet with us. They've come up with some evidence but aren't quite sure what to make of it. I've asked our computer forensic team to join us."

■ ■ ■

An hour later, two well-tailored suits arrived along with a smartly dressed young woman and a second woman in a powder blue blouse and jeans.

"Detectives, I'm Marty Brigham representing TGO. I would like to introduce TGO's general counsel, Simon Lester; my associate, Leslie Stevens; and Ellie Cooper, my technology expert."

They gathered together around the interrogation table, and Marty opened the discussion.

"TGO have been working through Mr. Moore's correspondence for anything unusual, and in the process we discovered one e-mail with a number of photo attachments." An e-mail exchange? Between whom? Mac wondered. Their working theory was that if it was Moore it was unplanned. Were it not for the strangulation they might only be looking at murder two or manslaughter. An e-mail tied to Moore might turn this into a planned murder gone wrong. A murder with an accomplice. A conspiracy.

A voice shook him from his reverie. "Perhaps you'd like to share all this with us," Rachel said. Mac smiled inwardly. He bet she had guessed that he was off on a mental rant.

Marty slid a folder across the table and paused to allow the detectives to go through the e-mail and file of photos. After about a minute Marty resumed. "Mrs. Moore accompanied Mr. Moore on a business trip to California last week. She took a trip to the beach while Moore was working. Someone tailed her and took photographs, documenting her whereabouts and activities. We don't know who took the photos or why they were taken." He paused again. Mac thought it might be for effect.

Mac had already jumped far ahead of them. If Moore had hired the photographer, he wouldn't be receiving the covering e-mail that sounded more like a tease. And the package would not be sent to the office server. When the jealous husband hired the private detective, the photos were generally hand-delivered in a brown envelope and in person. Judging from the photos, though, Moore had good reason to be worried.

He and Rachel would have to sit down and parse the cover e-mail carefully, line by line. That could wait until later. He'd also have to go back and interview Michael Cassidy again in light of these revelations. Cassidy could have admitted all this in their interview, but he obviously thought no one knew. There had to be a reason why Moore's counsel wasn't here, unless the firm thought he might be behind all this. Or if they were not sure.

Lester jumped in, "We don't have to tell you, Detective Micolonides, the male subject of the photos is another lawyer at TGO, Michael Cassidy."

Mac nodded over at Rachel. She must be coming around to his view on Moore.

Marty continued, "Ms. Cooper has verified that the photos have been doctored."

Rachel snapped forward in her chair. "Doctored?" she said.

"As you will discover," Ellie Cooper said, speaking directly to the police technical expert, "the code on the photos had been digitally altered. I've recreated the original photo which shows no necklace. The necklace is a separate picture that was superimposed on the original."

This meeting had taken a sudden right turn. Mac needed to get behind the wheel. "So if I understand it correctly, one or more doctored photos were sent by someone to Odell Moore at his office e-mail address. Let's say that I'm prepared to agree for the moment that someone was trying to mislead Moore about a necklace and his wife. How is this of any relevance to our investigation?"

There was a knock at the door. On the other side of the frosted glass stood someone short. He had a pretty good guess who it was. The door opened.

"Sorry I'm late, though I was not officially invited," Carrie Tinker said. Mac noticed her lips were flaming red. It was really difficult to focus on anything else. The woman knew how to make an entrance. But how did she know the precise moment to arrive? Brigham had probably orchestrated this.

"Carrie, we were just getting to the necklace," Marty said. "Perhaps you can help shed some light."

"My client, Mr. Moore, tells me the necklace was an engagement present that he gave to his wife. That she *appears* to have given it to his old friend."

"Why do we care?" Mac asked.

"That's what we've yet to figure out," Carrie responded. "We were hoping for some assistance from your end. If someone was stalking Mrs. Moore, it's possible that the target of the murder was not the senator, rather it was his daughter. If that theory is correct, it's entirely plausible that the perpetrator had come to attack Mrs. Moore and may have been surprised to find the senator in the apartment. In that case he or she may have panicked, attempting to kill her and killing the senator in order to clean up any witness trail."

"That's all very interesting." Rachel stood up and began to pace. Then she stopped directly in front of Carrie. "We've also been operating on the assumption that Dee Moore might have been the intended victim. But if that's true, isn't your client the most likely killer? He received the e-mail and photos. He didn't know they'd been doctored. Maybe he reacted in a rage. Raced home. You better than anyone know what could have happened next."

Carrie knows how to keep a poker face, Mac thought. Rachel sounded convincing, but Carrie was experienced enough not to react. Rachel continued, "Our experts will go through Mr. Moore's computer records and follow the e-mail trail back to a source."

Mac stood up ready to spring to action. "I'll get the warrant process going."

"Whoa… Not at all necessary, sir," Simon responded in a stiff British accent, handing Mac a piece of stationery with the TGO logo at the top.

"This letter contains the necessary authorization. If you're prepared to send someone back to our offices with me, I can get you immediate access. Obviously we would prefer to move ahead with this as discreetly as possible for reasons I don't need to explain."

■ ■ ■

After the visitors left, Rachel took her seat at the desk opposite Mac and rubbed her nose slowly. "Isn't that visit a little more than coincidental? Perhaps there's more to my theory than I had imagined. What if someone was trying to interfere in Moore's relationship with his wife?"

"Part of me wants to believe it was Moore spying on his own wife. She's a bombshell in a bikini. Maybe he's another O.J. Rich and famous, beyond the law, driven by impulse with a jealous streak a mile long."

"Add to that a history of sudden violence that he admits to, and all the ingredients are there. I have to admit it's a possibility. We know that the marriage was sudden and unplanned. If she fell for Moore so quickly, maybe she was also falling for his pal. Maybe she's that type."

Rachel picked up the cover e-mail and read it out loud. "*General Moore, while your troops have been fighting the good fight, your wife Dee has been keeping secrets. If a picture is worth a thousand words then take a few minutes to examine the novel below.* Who writes like this?"

"Exactly what I was wondering while we were sitting in the meeting. How do you account for the e-mail? Would Moore send it to himself, at the office, and come up with a cover that looked like it was written by a third party who knew him? When would he have had the time to come up with all that?"

Mac reached into his New York Giants mug to grab a fistful of pistachios. He was still chewing when Rachel began to speak.

"The sender of this e-mail writes like someone who thinks he's very smart. He's trying to be poetic. A picture worth a thousand words."

"True. He didn't have to write anything." Mac spat a few shells into his wastebasket.

"And he addresses him as General. Suggests it's someone who knows him. Maybe even someone who works with him."

"Maybe someone who used to work at TGO who's carrying a grudge," Mac said.

"A really big grudge. We can run it down," Rachel said, "but just hearing the words coming out of my mouth sounds far-fetched."

"We can check with Torrance if there is anyone with a history." Mac put a couple more nuts in his mouth. "Let's go back to the beginning. Dee's father was opposed to the marriage. He came to New York. What was he trying to—"

"Sorry, Mac," Rachel interrupted. "It's time for a new perspective." Rachel's mind went back to the day she came out of the closet. She had put it off for years, petrified that her parents would disown her. She had been dating a woman for about six months and it was time. Rachel's sister gave her the courage to break the news. They took it much better than she expected—almost shocking for a couple of Eastern European religious Jews. It was her uncle Yossi who went crazy. He thought demons had taken over her soul. "We can still save your *neshama*, your soul," he kept telling her one Sabbath. She learned there was such a thing as Jewish exorcism and Yossi was prepared to put her through it. There was no reasoning with him.

Returning to the present, she said thoughtfully, "There may have been other relatives or close friends deeply opposed to this marriage."

"So you think there could have been a number of people in Mobile who were very upset with the marriage beside her father?" Mac asked.

Rachel slung her purse strap over her shoulder and headed to the door. " I'm going to pay a visit to the senator's widow in the hospital. Maybe she can shed some light on what was going on in Alabama."

Mac responded, "Here's something else that's peculiar and you may want to check out with Mrs. Brabant. There's an Alabama number in Dee's cellphone inbox on the day of the murder. The number isn't listed in her contact information but the call lasted about four minutes so it wasn't a wrong number. I had the number checked this morning; the caller is an R. Ferguson from Mobile, Alabama, though the cell tower information indicates the call was placed in New York."

■ ■ ■

Rodney was feeling a little jumpy. He stood in front of the bathroom mirror in his hotel suite. The circles under his eyes were even more prominent than yesterday. He hadn't slept a wink since he'd arrived in New York. The senator was dead, Dee was in the hospital, and Rodney knew more about it than he had admitted to Jackson. Jackson had insisted that he remain in New York. But Jackson didn't know what Rodney knew. He needed to leave town quietly and quickly, before anyone figured out his role in all of this. He had behaved dishonorably and if Rodney stayed in New York, it was only a matter of time until his daddy found out.

The moment his name became publicly associated in any way with the assassination, it was going to bring scandal on the Ferguson family. The media would twist the whole story until he became the next Squeaky Fromme, the woman who shot at President Ford. They would come up with some nickname for him by which he'd always be remembered. She was Lynette before she went to jail. He needed to calm himself. He reached for a Xanax in his toiletries bag.

They had last spoken yesterday. Jackson had implored him to calm down and take advantage of the opportunity. Now was the time, he said, for Rodney to stay calm. They were going to indict Moore for the murder any minute and then the path would be clear.

Jackson's logic was beginning to make sense. "Once Odell Moore is arrested," Jackson argued, "he'll languish in a jail cell for months." I could step in to help Eleanor Brabant in the hospital, Rodney thought. I could be the first smile to welcome Dee when she regains consciousness. Jackson's words were still ringing in his ears from their call this morning. "I'm telling you, Rodney, none of this was planned, but in my wildest dreams I don't think it could have worked out better. Just stick to the plan. When you're hunting big game, you have to be prepared for the unexpected twists and turns of fate.

Jackson had been compelling. Still Rodney was not cut out for all this intrigue. He choked down the sense of dread and turned on the television to catch the latest on the investigation.

CHAPTER 29

Mid-afternoon, Friday, August 21, 2015

Rachel reached for the banana on the passenger seat of her vehicle. In the middle of an investigation, she rarely ate at fixed hours. Janet packed a paper bag for Rachel every morning, including a couple of fruits and mixed nuts, insisting that she take the snack bag on the road. Some days Rachel would shove them in her locker when she arrived, throwing them out a couple of days later when the fruit began to rot. Most days, though, she was mindful of Janet's advice. She made no admission of failure on the other days. That was marriage: loyalty, fidelity, and the odd white lie if it didn't hurt anyone. Rachel peeled open the fruit and lovingly took a bite, realizing that these small touches, regardless of the annoyance of the nagging, were what helped to grease the joints of their marriage. She still felt an emptiness though. Kailey had been asleep every night for the last four days when she got home. A couple of nights Rachel had crawled into bed with her for fifteen minutes. Kailey was dead to the world, sucking hard on her thumb, a habit she and Janet could not agree on how to handle. Damned investigations.

Pulling away from the hospital, she voice-dialled Mac on the hands-free.

"Mrs. Brabant had been speaking to her daughter regularly even if her husband had not. Dee Moore had no friends in New York, other than Emily Sherman. She had no idea Rodney Ferguson was in New York. The Brabants and the Fergusons are casual friends in Mobile, and Rodney and

Dee were classmates many years ago. It's no secret that Rodney has pursued Dee for years, but his affections haven't been returned."

"Interesting." Mac responded. "Maybe he was unhappy with the elopement and came to New York to have it out with her. He calls, she shuts him down, and he goes ballistic. After that, maybe the senator walks in on them; anything's possible in the heat of the moment."

"That makes him our next stop if he's still in town. Have our boys ping his phone and triangulate his location. I'll pick you up in twenty minutes."

When Rachel swung around the front entrance to the station, Mac was waiting for her outside. He got in and immediately began sharing the latest news. "As it turns out, Ferguson is staying at a local hotel. He's there right now. Interestingly, the address is just a few blocks from the Moores' apartment. I also discovered his cellphone account shows numerous incoming and outgoing calls from someone at TGO."

"Given that he's from Mobile, we can probably guess who that would be."

"Let's go discover what falls out when we give Mr. Ferguson's tree a little shake."

They arrived at the hotel, a boutique on Park Avenue. The desk clerk was tending to the floral arrangement sitting on the polished reception desk, and two other attendants were busying themselves doing nothing. All were dressed in black shirts and slacks. Mac asked the desk clerk to ring up to Mr. Ferguson's room. "Just tell him a couple of NYPD investigators would like a word with him," Mac said, flashing his badge. The desk clerk nodded and Mac returned the badge to his breast pocket.

Rodney was waiting for them at the doorway to the penthouse suite. He was dressed for happy hour: a navy sports jacket over an open-neck starched white shirt, and charcoal slacks. His gold monogrammed cufflinks stuck out beyond the sleeves of the jacket.

"Forgive me," he said, "but would you mind showing me your badges. One cannot be too careful these days with intruders."

The two detectives took out their badges, and Rodney spent a moment or two going through the motions. He then ushered them into the suite's dining area. A crystal chandelier overhung a table with seating for six. Off to their right was a plush zebra leather couch surrounded by matching love seats.

"Nice place, Mr. Ferguson," Rachel said.

Rodney appeared flustered as he responded, "We've done well with our family investments. I must say I never expected my first trip to New York would put me in such proximity with New York's finest. Is there any accuracy to the TV portrayal of crime and punishment in the city? That's about as close as I've ever been before today. Not even a speeding ticket in Mobile." The words tumbled out of his mouth stiffly.

Mac responded immediately, deliberately trying to calm Ferguson. Rachel took it as his signal that Rachel would play the tough cop today if necessary. "We get asked that question a lot, Mr. Ferguson. Suffice it to say most of our job would be a little too boring for the big screen. Those shows combine a year of action into one hour. I think even reality TV producers would get very bored following my partner and me around all day."

"So, how can I be of assistance? Please make yourself comfortable."

"We prefer to stand if you don't mind, sir," Mac replied. "We're investigating Senator Brabant's death, and we're curious about what brought you to New York at this time. We understand you have a connection to the family. Maybe you can shed some light on their background."

"Actually I'm here on family business. The senator's death and the relentless television coverage have been shocking. I mean, I know the man. He's an old family friend." Ferguson played with the cufflink on his right sleeve.

"Why don't you tell us about your relationship with the family?"

"My parents and the Brabants have known each other in Mobile for as long as I can remember. The families probably go back to Civil War days together. I was a classmate of Dee's. I hope she's recovering."

Rachel stepped a little closer to Rodney. "We understand that your relationship was a little closer than just classmates."

"Dee and I dated in high school, and I won't hide the fact that I was always a little more interested in her than she was in me."

"Have you had any contact with her lately?"

"Listen, detectives; you probably have more information about me than you're letting on. I'm assuming you haven't shown up here on a lark. Let me tell you what I can."

Rachel stared impassively at Rodney. Time to play the tough bitch. Why was it that when Mac came out tough, he was just being a cop, but when Rachel did it, she was a dyke? While she was still a beat cop, the odd gang member had used the word after she walked away, when she was still in hearing distance. As for the rest, she could hear it in their eyes.

"Yes, I did call Dee when I arrived in town. I wanted to catch up. I went to visit her at about three or three-thirty on the day of the murder and left shortly afterward. She was feeling ill and asked that I postpone. I left immediately."

Rachel edged into Rodney's personal space. "We're treating everyone who entered that building as potential suspects. Can anyone account for your whereabouts between five and seven that afternoon?"

Her hunch that this might rattle Rodney's composed air began to pay off. A few drops of sweat were forming on Rodney's brow. The fingers on his left hand were now furiously flipping the cufflink, back and forth, back and forth.

He took a while to respond. "I'm afraid that I can't. I was probably out walking at the time."

"Probably?" Rachel said. She stared at him a good five seconds. She finally spoke, her tone brusque. "We also note that you've had considerable communication with someone at TGO's offices. Do you want to tell us about that?"

Rodney just stood there, now sweating a little more. Always a good sign.

Mac continued, "You know, Mr. Ferguson, we can take steps to find out on our own who that is and then return with more questions."

"Well, er, yes, I have had communications, uh, with a friend of mine there." His voice was now shaking perceptibly.

"And who would that be?" Rachel said. It was more a demand than a question.

"Jackson Sherman is an old friend from Mobile. We speak occasionally. He works for TGO."

Rachel advanced once more. "Do you consider 'occasional' to be over twenty separate communications over a one-month period? Mr. Ferguson, do you really want us to believe you're hiding something from us? If so, we can take this questioning down to our station."

"No, ma'am, there will be no need for that." Rodney hesitated. The colour had rushed from his face. They didn't want him fainting, at least not yet.

"Mr. Ferguson, do you need to sit down for a minute?" Mac asked.

Rodney collapsed onto one of the love seats and put his face in his hands.

"Do you need a moment?" Mac asked, sitting down facing him.

"No, I'm fine," Rodney said, pulling himself together. "It was Jackson Sherman's idea for me to come out here. He thought that Dee and Odell were having marital problems. He wanted me to try to break up the marriage. The whole plan was foolish to start with, but I was willing to try if there was any hope that Dee might return my affections. But murder? Never. Not Dee and not her father. I couldn't imagine violence in any proportion. Check with my friends in Mobile. They'll tell you. Rod Ferguson is basically a wimp. Wouldn't hurt a fly … has no backbone… Won't stand up to his daddy or to anyone else for that matter. If not for his daddy's fortune he would be a nothing." Rodney began to cry. "I cannot believe the nightmare. I swear to you I had no part in any of this."

It was time to close the deal. Ferguson was about to spill every last drop. "What was Mr. Sherman's interest in all this?" Rachel asked.

"He thinks I don't know. Jackson's always treated me with disdain. He thinks I'm an idiot. That I could never see through him. He's always underestimated me."

"Yet you've spoken to him on twenty occasions in the past month," Ellen prodded.

"When I was desperately in love with Dee in high school it was Jackson who got me the prom date. I would never have had the courage to ask Dee."

"We're really not interested in going back that far," Mac said. His tone was impatient.

"Let him finish," Rachel said.

"He came up with the plan. He took $500 from me, pretending to get her a gift. I'm not that much of an idiot. I knew it was a fee to enlist Jackson's help. I just pretended. He did get me the date, which was worth ten times $500 to me. I've come to learn that Jackson never does anything unless there's something in it for him."

"So how does that apply to now?" Mac asked.

He called me to meet with Dee in New York. Told me there was hope for me. Why would he do that? Why meddle in her marriage? I keep asking myself that question."

"You think he might have had an involvement in the death at the apartment?" Mac asked.

Rodney raised his head. His eyes were red. He really was crying. He took a moment to control his quivering lip. "For as long as I've known him, Jackson's been a schemer. A cutthroat at getting ahead. He was a cruel child. BB guns, firecrackers, and the like. Mostly childish pranks. But could he kill a person? He was always telling me how the senator was his career secret weapon."

Mac nodded at the inconclusive answer. Rachel knew he was not convinced.

Rodney seemed to gather his control for a moment. "Jackson called me the other night in Mobile. He sounded a little agitated about some fellow named Michael Cassidy. Kept calling him a rival. It's no secret that Jackson is gunning for partnership. I don't know how or whether that fits in anywhere.

"I'm just so sorry I've allowed myself to get this far involved. My parents will never live this down if the family name becomes associated with the murder. Our family will be finished in Mobile, even if I'm cleared later. Please, you must believe me."

What Ferguson had admitted so far, Rachel thought, was not much. Certainly not enough to cause any reasonable person to conclude they were associated with the murder. She was certain he was still hiding something. She and Mac would eventually pull it out of him, but not just yet. "Mr. Ferguson, that will be sufficient for now. I am advising you that you are a person of interest in this investigation, so we would like you to remain in town for the next few days. I'm sure you don't want us visiting you down at the Mobile police station with further questions. But if you must leave town earlier, please notify us of your whereabouts."

"Yes, ma'am."

"We're also asking you to refrain from any further communication with Mr. Sherman, at least for the next two days," Rachel added.

"Absolutely and thank you."

As Rachel and Mac were heading to the door, Rachel turned back with an afterthought. "If you really want to clear yourself as soon as possible, I have one more question."

"Sure. Anything."

"When you went to visit at three-thirty, did you enter the apartment?"

"I sat down on the couch but I didn't stay more than two or three minutes. Dee was ill."

"Would you be prepared to give us a set of your fingerprints and a voluntary DNA sample so we can officially rule you out as a suspect? It involves no more than a cheek swab—I have a kit in the car."

"Whatever I can do."

"All right, I'll be back in a couple of minutes to take the sample. I appreciate your cooperation."

The two detectives turned to leave. Stepping into the elevator, they could barely control their laughter.

"They don't come apart at the seams any faster than that," she said.

"Unless he's an incredibly good actor, I think he's telling us the truth. He tells us Sherman was meddling in the marriage. Do you think he might have been the one to send the e-mail to Moore?"

"Could be," Rachel said.

"If there is any way to link the e-mail photos to one of Sherman's accounts, we're golden."

Rachel thought for a moment. "We still haven't matched the fingerprints on the statuette used to knock the senator senseless. Let's pay a visit to Mr. Sherman and come away with a print. Otherwise we'll need a warrant, and right now I don't want to scare off our new prime suspect. I still don't get how the senator figures into all this."

"If Sherman's fingerprints are on the statuette, I don't really care why he did it. Maybe it was a surprise visit to Mrs. Moore gone terribly wrong."

They headed back to the station to find that the technical wizards had left them a report concerning the unusual e-mail that Moore had received. While it had routed through five different servers, one of the addresses had been connected to a credit card account in the name of Emily Sherman.

"Well, Mac," Rachel sighed with satisfaction, "all signs are pointing to our friend Mr. Sherman and possibly his wife as well. If the fingerprints match, perhaps we have our man. Then we just have to tie it all together."

"We'll pay a visit to Mr. Sherman first thing Monday morning."

CHAPTER 30

Odell had lost track of how many hours he had spent in the waiting room. Because it was without windows, the days and nights had become as indistinguishable as his sense of self. He had not bothered with dinner and his stomach was beginning to grumble. The cafeteria was probably closed, so he figured it was time to finally get some fresh air and a bowl of soup at the sandwich shop next door.

He reached down for his knapsack. Settling it over his shoulder, he turned toward the door and saw an enormous pair of black Nikes. He lifted his gaze. The shoes were filled with tree stumps in blue jeans and a torso covered in a loose-fitting L.A. Rams T-shirt. Odell stood up to face the giant who was holding a large brown paper bag that was stapled shut. Why was he always smiling? The lying, cheating, toking scum. Odell could feel his own heart beating faster, and although he pulled himself up taller, he was still a couple of inches shorter than his opponent.

"No one invited you to this party," Odell spat out.

"You have a strange way of greeting friends."

"Get out, Cass. You have no business being here." Odell's back stiffened, and he felt his thighs tightening. His stomach was beginning to churn. It was the feeling just after an opening kickoff when the adversaries stood opposite him on the first play from scrimmage. It was the moment when victory was still an unknown, and he was excited about first contact. The crashing of bodies, smacking of helmets. Until he had delivered the first body blow, he would not feel normal again. He often kept the ball on the first play just to get in the lick. Except the physical violence on the football field had not been about revenge. He had never understood revenge before this moment, but it was an overpowering feeling. His mouth was dry but he could taste it. The coppery smell of fresh blood.

"I have every reason to be here." Cassidy sounded unreasonably reasonable.

"Get out before I do something you're going to regret." Michael's eyes grew a little wider. He lifted the paper bag in front of him as if it could provide some protection. Despite the size disadvantage, Odell knew he could have Michael in a submission hold in under three seconds. Dead in thirty with a simple choke hold, if he wanted.

"At least we're in a hospital," Michael said.

This was no time for a sense of humour. "Fuck you, Cass. If you've come to be with Dee, you'll have to clear it with her mother. Just get out of my face."

"Forgive me, General, if I tell you that I have no idea what's generating all this hostility. I flew all the way out here to be with you. Figured America's most wanted man might want some company."

Odell was stern in his response. "I may have been a fool but stop treating me like one. I saw the pictures from the beach. I can't begin to imagine how you could have taken advantage of Dee like that. I can't sleep anymore." Every time he closed his eyes, he saw Michael holding Dee. Kissing her. Making love to her. But now and without warning, Odell deflated, collapsing into a lime chair. He had lost the battle without Cassidy having to raise a hand in defence. "I give up, man. If she prefers to be with you, when she wakes up, I'll get out of the way, but for now I can't be in a room with you."

Michael took a seat facing Odell. "You look like crap and your brain is fried. I've got no idea what you're talking about. The only thing Dee and I shared on the beach were a couple of joints and too many stories about you and how much she adores you."

"Bullshit. Why else would she give you the amulet?" Odell could feel his temperature rising, his energy renewing as he thought of the missing amulet. He clenched his fists. They could finally settle this once and for all, though he'd have to haul himself out of the chair.

"I told you on the phone." Michael was speaking calmly.

"You admitted you had it." He could feel the urge to strike Cassidy growing once more. It was just a short leap to grab him by the throat. Cut off his air supply the way Michael had cut off Odell's life.

"Then you hung up on me. You never listened to my end of the story. She never put the necklace on me. Never handed it to me. I never even saw the amulet until it turned up on my desk the next day. I thought she'd written me a love note but it didn't make any sense. I sent the note to your lawyer to have the handwriting analyzed. Carrie thinks someone else was framing me and playing you for the fool."

Odell sat there evaluating. It might be true and it might not. But why would he have flown all the way out here to be with Odell if he still had eyes for Dee? If he'd slept with Dee? If he was the father of the child? Odell was coming to understand what he always knew. That Dee could not be unfaithful, that the timing of the pregnancy meant it had to be his. That he was behaving and thinking like a moron.

"I had some vacation time coming, and Overton saw I was worthless to anyone with everything going on here. He told me to take the weekend and get the hell out. I decided you probably needed some company. So I got on a flight this morning. Last-minute economy. My back will never be the same."

Odell's shoulders sagged. He could feel the tension begin to drain. "What's in the bag?"

"Chinese take-out. You hungry?"

8:45 a.m., Saturday, August 22, 2015

Odell was awakened from his doze by a tap on the shoulder. Eleanor was standing over him. She was wearing sunglasses. Who knew what was hiding underneath? It occurred to Odell that she was probably going through an experience worse than his. She had lost her life companion and had not had a moment to come to terms with that new reality. He had only briefly taken a moment to consider her pain, her grief. He'd still not uttered any words of consolation to her. At least nothing that he could remember. How could he ever come to terms with Eleanor if he could not take the time to feel for her loss? And what did he have in his life right now besides time?

"She wants you," Eleanor said. There was a softness to the tone that he was unaccustomed to hearing. These were words he was not expecting her to say.

Odell shook off the sleep with a jolt.

"She regained consciousness?"

"Just briefly. She's very weak and her recollection was fuzzy, but she asked for you."

"And you're prepared to trust me?"

"She doesn't remember much except another man in the room with her and Edward just before he was murdered. She couldn't identify the man but she is certain it wasn't you. Go be with your wife. I have to take care of all kinds of arrangements for Edward. I'm sorry for what I've put you through." She didn't need to apologize to him. This wasn't about Eleanor. It was about Dee. It was about finally getting to be with Dee.

He felt every muscle in his body going limp all at once to the point where he had trouble keeping his balance. His body shook uncontrollably. She crossed the gap between them and squeezed him close.

"I promise you. I'll do better," he said.

"I know," she said.

8:00 a.m., Sunday, August 23, 2015

Odell stood with his back to the window, watching Dee. She lay flat on her back under white sheets, her eyes closed and her head bandaged. Wires connected her to a nearby monitor and IV pole. The door had been left ajar, and he heard the familiar clicks on the floor as it eased open.

Eleanor tiptoed into the room—ironic given that Odell was anxiously awaiting Dee's re-awakening. The next time she came out of this sleep, he would be sitting by her side waiting to greet her. A husband secure in the knowledge that he had not harmed his wife. That he had not killed her father. Had Dee not woken briefly for Eleanor, he would still be wondering. This was not a gift he would waste.

The sunlight pouring into the room highlighted the black circles under Eleanor's eyes that had grown to the size of tea bags. She had forgotten the sunglasses, or perhaps she felt she no longer had to put on a show of strength for Odell, or for Dee for that matter. Odell understood that sleeplessness all too well. Her shoulders were slouched and whatever residue of energy that had been carrying her was completely dissipated. Had he been so wrapped up in himself that he had not noticed the worry lines that now defined her face?

Eleanor stared intently at him, closing the gap between them, but not in an aggressive manner. He felt uncomfortable with the warmth of the woman's smile. Her eyes softened exactly like Dee's did, every time she told him that she loved him. She once did love him.

"The Lord is watching over her, Edward," she said with a tone of finality.

Odell stood quietly, debating whether to say anything. Then he stepped forward, encircling her in his broad arms. The tears began streaming down her cheeks in torrents; they probably were the first tears she'd shed. She sobbed quietly, shaking softly, releasing her pools of boundless grief. She gradually accustomed herself to this embrace, resting her head on his chest for what felt like an eternity. Eventually she gathered control of herself, took a half step back, and stared into his eyes. That was when he finally understood.

"Thank you, Odell," she said. "For a moment I was sure you were Edward."

"I'm terribly sorry for your loss." The words were out of his mouth before he thought about them. Such standard words of comfort, which he'd used often enough at funerals for clients' families. Except this time was different. He actually felt her emptiness. Terribly. The feelings had been consuming him for days, but those were his own feelings of loneliness. His own disconnectedness from his life, from Dee, and from the world.

For the first time since his wedding day, he felt reconnected but in a completely different way.

He'd heard about this from a client who had a life-saving bone marrow transplant. The doctors had just about killed him with the chemo, brought him to the point where he felt he was no longer alive, to prepare him for the injections. Then the rejuvenation began. Fetuses grow in the womb, cells doubling every few moments, until there are sufficient billions of cells to differentiate it from other life. Adults were not meant for this type of rebirth. The cell growth resulted in pain beyond any agony imaginable. But it was a rebirth that had saved a life.

Odell felt Eleanor's unbearable pain. A pain different from anything he had experienced. A pain born out of intense love and loyalty to one person. He understood that when Dee woke up he would need to share his pain with her, so that he could begin living.

"Do you believe in God, son?" Eleanor asked in a soft voice. An angel voice from a film.

His eyebrows knit together as if he was suddenly in touch with something very painful. He cleared his throat. "For many years in my childhood I had a very difficult time believing there was a God. There was no one looking out for me or my sister. Not on earth. Not anywhere."

"And yet you turned out all right."

"By the time I left high school and headed for university I began to understand that there was some power that had blessed me with unusual talents and allowed me to find a way to survive a dysfunctional family life. If I had any doubt, it all melted away the day I met your daughter—it took me that long to get there."

"She told me the powers of the universe had drawn you together. It was an unstoppable force."

"My friend Michael would have attributed it to two opposite and attracting forces. The laws of nature are governed by Newton's rules, not God."

"Einstein showed us that Newton wasn't always right. And Einstein was convinced there had to be a God," Eleanor said. She smiled.

"Regardless, Eleanor, I deeply believe that from the moment the two of us laid eyes on one another, some greater compelling force drew us together. You might call that your God, and I admit that it was more than simple chance."

She walked over to the bed, sat in a chair, and took Dee's hand. Dee's head tilted involuntarily toward her shoulder.

"She'll be back with us soon, Odell. Come sit with me."

He pulled up a chair on the other side of the bed and sat. Finally he dropped his head and spoke very quietly. "Eleanor, I've been such a fool for the past few weeks. I've said some things to Dee that I can't ever take back. I don't know if she'll ever forgive me."

"That's marriage, dear. Finding ways to forgive. It's a never-ending process but it starts with forgiving yourself."

CHAPTER 31

9:30 a.m., Monday, August 24, 2015

The previous week had been a firestorm of publicity and mayhem at TGO, a result of the persistent attempts by the media to get a comment from anyone in the firm. The reporters were all still camped out downstairs from dawn until dusk. When Jackson had entered the building at seven-thirty this morning, he had passed a security guard stationed at reception. The turmoil couldn't be good for the firm but it might be good for him. On Thursday and Friday, he had noted that the partners' offices were empty, many of them taking Torrance's advice to work from home for a few days until the media moved on to another story. Judging from the media presence outside the lobby early this morning, it was going to be another bad week for TGO. With Odell sidelined and everyone distracted, Jackson had boldly approached Torrance late on Friday and told him he would volunteer to take on the next deal in the door. There had to be something coming. He'd heard rumours there was a deal in Houston.

Torrance's assistant, Arlene, had called to let him know that the detectives wanted to have another word with him and would meet him in a boardroom. Now, just outside the boardroom, he stopped to button up his jacket. The General did that whenever he was about to step into an important meeting. He donned his mask of confidence, remembering that this was how Moore had navigated Bounty. If the detectives were back for a second interview, what could they want from him? Maybe more details about Dee. The innocuous questions the woman detective had for Emily were no bother, as long as Emily had not left anything out when she reported the discussion to him. He drew a deep breath and turned the door handle.

The detectives were admiring the artwork and had their backs to him. He decided to take the jovial approach. Not a care in the world.

"Hello, Mac. Nice to see you again."

"Mr. Sherman, this is my partner, Rachel Brodinsky. We're here to ask you a few questions, if you can spare the time right now. If not, we can arrange a more convenient time for you to meet with us at the police station."

"I have half an hour to spare right now. How can I help you? Has anyone offered you some coffee or tea?"

"Thanks," Rachel answered. "We got our java on the drive to Midtown."

Jackson couldn't help but note the physical contrast between the tall, slim Rachel and her stocky partner. Which one was going to be the bad cop?

Mac began the questioning. "I don't think we'll be here for too long, Mr. Sherman. We just have a few questions about Dee Moore."

"How can I be of assistance? I know you've spoken to my wife. She's the one with the relationship with Dee."

"We're also interested in Mrs. Moore's Mobile connections."

"Dee's connections?" They were starting with a curveball. "So you're not convinced that the senator was the target of an assassination attempt?" he said. No sense hiding his surprise about that point. Who'd be interested in hurting Dee? If she was the intended target, it had to be someone she'd upset or rejected. Someone who might be blinded by sudden rage. Jumping Jesus—that idiot!

Rodney had been there. Jackson as much as sent him—set the whole thing up for him. What if? What if Rodney had walked into the apartment expecting Dee to come running, but she pushed him away? What if it got ugly? Rodney didn't have the courage, but he also didn't have a brain in his head. Maybe he snapped. If Rodney had become a suspect, the smoking gun might point back at Jackson. That would ruin him. Besides Rodney would probably unravel like a kitten playing with a spool of wool. It wouldn't take them five seconds to figure out all the connections.

Jackson had invited both the senator and Rodney to see Dee on the same day. Accessory to murder … conspiracy to commit murder. He had to get control over his own vivid imagination.

Mac reached into a cardboard accordion folder he'd brought with him and carefully pulled out a plastic sleeve holding several pages of material. He handed the package over to Jackson. "We brought some documents and were wondering if you mind explaining them for us?"

Jackson's stomach sank as he withdrew about a dozen pages of material from the plastic covering. Not at all what he was expecting. But not nearly as bad. This was no longer about Rodney.

He flipped through the pages, trying to control his facial expression and his eyes. He knew they would give away the anxiety he was feeling. The photos were obviously taken from Moore's computer. But there was no way they could tie them to Jackson. There had to be at least four dummy accounts between him and the e-mail. Could they have pierced the chain so easily? Even if they did, all it proved was that he sent some photos to Odell concerning Dee and involving Cassidy.

He knew he had only a few moments to decide whether to contrive an elaborate lie or tell some version of the truth. What would the General do now? He flipped the pages slowly, pretending to scrutinize each picture, formulating the response. He had no sense of how much time was passing.

Jackson had to become the General, think like the General. Think like Sun Tsu. Time was not important to the General. It was all about the preparation. Do not focus on the adversary. Focus on the plan of counter-attack. Give up information that they are already likely to know through their own intelligence gathering.

"Yes, I recognize them," he finally said. "They were delivered to me anonymously and I wasn't sure what to make of them. I assumed they related to the day that Michael Cassidy was entertaining Dee in Los Angeles. My wife had spent the morning with her. I also recognize the necklace, at least through the stories Emily has recounted. Dee told Emily a story about the jug being a sentimental engagement gift. I'm a little surprised that she gave it to Michael. I know that Odell and Dee hadn't known each other for long before marrying, and when I got the pictures I hesitated."

"What do you mean by that?" Rachel asked.

"Well, it really wasn't any of my business, but obviously someone was trying to encourage me to reveal this to Odell. Why else would I have received it? It was really none of my business and I almost sent it to trash, but finally I concluded that Odell deserved to decide for himself."

"But you didn't send it to him directly? How come?" Rachel asked.

"I decided to do it anonymously through an e-mail account not directly tied to me. I didn't feel right about confronting Odell with this information directly. After all, he's my boss. I figured if he knew how much I knew he might feel too embarrassed to deal with me. That would be a career killer around here."

Rachel began touching her nose. "So you were worried about appearances?" They weren't buying the story. He could tell by the way she asked the question. All that pretend inquisitiveness.

"It wasn't an act of kindness so much as self-preservation. You never know how someone is going to react. I didn't want him shooting the messenger."

"That sheds an awful lot of light on the matter for us," Mac said. "Could you hazard a guess as to who might have sent it to you?"

Jackson paused to create the appearance of giving it some thought. The cranking of the gears in his head was disturbing the dyke. She was rubbing her nose now. Very unattractive.

"Dee and I know many of the same people in Alabama from our years growing up together. The worst kept secret in our little community in Mobile is that a fellow by the name of Rodney Ferguson was madly in love with her. I still keep in touch with Rodney from time to time, and I know for a fact that he still carries a torch for Dee. He may be mildly obsessed. He was shaken to the core to discover that Odell had scooped her up. Perhaps he's the one who's been secretly following her. I ran into him recently and Dee was the only topic of his conversation. Anyway, for what it's worth."

"Interesting," Rachel said half out loud.

Jackson figured the deflection would buy him a little more time to think. They couldn't ignore the possibility that Rodney might be involved. The more Jackson thought about it, the more he became convinced that old Rodney wouldn't harm a frog. They exploded when you stuffed them with firecrackers. Jackson learned that as a child one Fourth of July. He made a note to get back to Rodney and check whether he had an alibi. Even if Rodney did not, what was Jackson worrying about? Okay, maybe they'd figure out he was the mastermind behind the photos, but they could not possibly have any evidence of him being involved in the murder. On the other hand if they did, he'd need to establish his alibi. Otherwise there would be no way they would believe him, even if they had no evidence. He had an alibi. A very expensive alibi. A last resort. He would take care of that tonight.

"Mr. Sherman, you've been quite helpful. We appreciate your candor," the female cop said. Holding out her hand, she continued, "If you wouldn't mind returning the package, I'd like to make sure we keep control of all the outstanding copies. Would you mind passing it back to me. We appreciate you taking the time. My partner and I have a few other matters to discuss with Mr. Torrance before we leave."

■ ■ ■

After he closed the door behind Jackson, Mac quickly put on a nitrile glove, lifting the plastic-covered package off the table and reinserting it in the cardboard accordion folder.

"Rachel, for chain of custody purposes, please note that at 10:04 a.m. I received this package from Jackson Sherman. We'll take it together to the lab to process for fingerprints. It couldn't have been much easier than that. We have two rats here trying to jump off the ship, each pointing at the other. Who do you make for this?"

"Ferguson strikes me as the type who's afraid of his own shadow, but we both know the type of rage that jealousy can generate."

"We can't be deceived by the show he puts on," Mac said in agreement.

"On the other hand, Sherman strikes me as a very smooth operator. I would say he's one of those types that's too clever by half. I'm convinced he was playing us. Of course, that doesn't mean that either of them actually did it. Taking a page out of your book at this point, I'd say let's allow the evidence to lead us to our conclusions."

Drew Torrance entered the room.

"How is the investigation going, detectives? I hope you're getting closer to tracking down the perpetrator. All of this media speculation is not good for my law firm. Is there anything I can do to help?"

Mac piped in. "Actually, sir, you can assist us with one more matter that we haven't yet run down. Do your people all have electronic access cards when they move among your office floors and when they go in and out of the building?"

"Yes, that's the norm for Manhattan law firms. What with GPS on the cellphones, if we wanted to, we could monitor them 24/7. Of course, that would be a complete invasion of privacy, but our firm policies actually permit us to do that. I guess few of our employees read the fine print of our policies. Sorry, I don't mean to make light of all this. What would you like?"

"Would you mind sending us all the records for the afternoon of the murder."

"You'll have the information no later than first thing in the morning. To save you time, I've had Simon Lester do some sleuthing for me. Odell's assistant, Jocelyne, informed him that Odell left the building at four-thirty that afternoon and was unaccounted for after that. I spoke to Jocelyne myself. When pressed, she admitted that Odell seemed quite agitated. She was worried. As for Jackson, he was out of the building from 3:00 p.m. onward at a client meeting outside the office. He didn't return.

"I assumed you might also be interested in Michael Cassidy's comings and goings. He was definitely in L.A. that day."

As the three of them got up to leave together, Torrance turned to Rachel and said, "In just one week, my firm's image has been wrestled through the mud, and these events are testing the strength of my partnership.

I'm counting on you to find the person who committed this crime and bring him, or her, to justice."

"That's what the city pays us to do, sir," Rachel said.

"If the murderer happens to be a member of this firm, it will be a tragedy, but one that I am prepared to live with. It's the uncertainty that is wreaking havoc on us. I need you to understand you can count on me for cooperation, regardless of the outcome."

"Thank you, sir," Mac responded as they shook hands and the two detectives got on the elevator.

"A week is nothing compared to what he still may be facing if Sherman is involved in this," Rachel said after the doors were safely closed.

"Very classy approach. Unfortunately for him, all we can do at this point is what we're trained to do. And that will take time."

"And he has to live under the microscope of media scrutiny. Tough job."

10:30 a.m., Tuesday, August 25, 2015

The building records arrived the next morning as promised. Mac flipped through them page by page. They confirmed what Torrance had told them about Odell and Jackson.

Mac stepped up to the white board with a timeline and photos of all the players. Rachel took a sip of her chamomile tea, then sat forward in her chair behind the desk, leaning on her elbows.

"Go ahead, professor," she said.

"The videocam in the lobby was functioning until the power went off and never reset. At 3:30 p.m. Ferguson enters the building. There is video image of him leaving at 3:40.

"At 5:15, the senator arrives and leaves shortly afterward. Moore is on video just before six. The neighbour reported some yelling coming from the apartment, presumably Dee, followed by a loud crash at about 6:15. It could have been a little later.

"At 6:25, the senator enters the building once more; again there's some yelling reported by the neighbour. She wasn't sure of the precise time, except it was definitely before the power failure. Again male and female voices.

"At 6:46, the power goes out in the neighbourhood; a few minutes later the security desk is left unattended for ten or fifteen minutes."

Rachel interrupted. "The concierge was attending to the generator. Presumably, in that hiatus, the perp enters the building."

"Right," Mac said. "Unless he was already in the building. The neighbour reports hearing a crash a few minutes later just after the power comes back on. After that, no further noise is heard coming from the apartment, but she did report footsteps in the hallway. She couldn't tell if it was someone coming into or leaving the apartment. We have no idea if it was one or more people. At 6:58 a call is placed on Dee's cellphone to 911."

"We still don't know how the perp got access to the apartment," Rachel said.

"We do know that someone wearing a Yankees cap left the building by the rear door just after seven. We have the video. His face was obscured by gloved hands."

"I thought you said the video system went dead after the power failure."

"Cheap technology wins out," Mac said. "The back-door camera was makeshift and operated separately. It had a two-hour backup battery."

"If our perp is Moore we know how he got in. Rodney Ferguson and Jackson Sherman are another story. And any of them could have waltzed right out the front doors once the video system went down. Wait a minute." Rachel opened her notepad. "Emily Sherman told me that Dee had given her the code to get into the apartment the day they left for L.A. If she had it, do you think she might have given her husband the access code?"

Mac flipped through his notepad and stopped. "The front door access code had an eight-hour battery, so Sherman could have used it to get in. So when could he have arrived?"

"I felt there was something Emily held back in her interview with me." Rachel jumped to her feet and started pacing, rubbing her nose. She was on a roll.

"Sherman's meeting was at Broadway and Twenty-Eighth, which would have left him ample time to hop on the subway to Lexington and Eighty-Second. It's only a five-minute walk from there to the apartment, so there would be plenty of time to spare. There's nothing in Sherman's calendar until the next morning, so likely not working at the time. We can't rule him out."

"We also can't rule out Ferguson, either acting alone or with Sherman."

Rachel continued to pace. Four steps toward the wall. Four steps back. "Moore has no alibi, no memory, and his mother-in-law hadn't spoken to him since he married Dee Moore. There's also no video evidence of him leaving the building."

"So let's leave him on the list, but since when is not speaking to your mother-in-law suspicious behaviour?"

Rachel laughed, finally dropping her hand from her face. "In these circumstances it's a little abnormal, but point taken."

"You'd think a big-shot lawyer could manage his own family."

"They're just as incompetent as the rest of us at managing their personal lives."

Mac immediately thought about his deceptive son and his wife's intense anger. What would he do about that? Only one option. "Maybe Moore went to confront his wife over those photos. Maybe jealousy was a motive."

"Except there's no evidence she and Cassidy did more than hug each other. They were alone on a beach. If they had kissed, or done anything more, wouldn't the stalker have caught them and sent it along? Way more provocative than sharing a joint." Rachel mocked a toke on an imaginary joint.

"Never thought you were the type."

"You kidding? Lesbian with acceptance issues trying to fit in? Not since I joined the force, of course, but I had my share," Rachel said. "I still don't get the alteration of the necklace photos. Deliberate deception? Almost certainly it was Jackson who did it."

"Maybe his wife understood the importance of the necklace to the marriage. She easily could have learned that from Dee Moore."

"Does that make Emily Sherman a knowing accomplice in all this?" There was a tremor of excitement in Rachel's voice.

"Wait a minute. Why would Sherman want to excite Moore enough to run home and murder his wife? We're running in circles again." Boom. Another theory shot dead.

They headed to the morgue to speak to the medical examiner. Mariella Cabrerra had been one of the top M.E.s in the city for over twenty years. She was thorough and had a reputation for being very careful with her procedures, though at times she got lost in the details, all of which fascinated her. It was her scrappy voice that grated on Rachel's nerves. Today she was wearing a hairnet, so the loose grey ends, like her autopsy, were under control.

"Mac and Cheese. Here to discuss the unusual Brabant case, I assume? I place the time of death at approximately seven p.m., give or take twenty minutes, based on the degree of rigor in the body."

"That would correspond to just after the time of the power failure," Mac interjected. "What is it that makes the case unusual?"

"You've heard of a trifecta?" She paused as if waiting for an answer.

"Sorry, I assumed the question was rhetorical. We've been to the track from time to time," Rachel said impatiently.

"If there was such thing as a murder trifecta, this would be it. First, there was a blow to the side of the head with a blunt instrument which fractured the temporal bone with obvious indications of an epidermal hematoma. This type of blow would not normally lead to death, but would be enough to stun the victim. I told you previously that the angle of the blow's descent suggests it was applied from the rear, possibly left-handed and the assailant was at least six feet in height."

Rachel raised her left arm and brought it down toward the back of Mac's head, mimicking the attack.

"Something like that. Second, there were abrasions to the neck consistent with strangulation with a one-and-three-quarter-inch-wide instrument, possibly a belt. There are no contusions anywhere else on the senator's body, which suggest there is no sign of a struggle, and no DNA evidence under the senator's fingernails. He must have been near unconscious when the strangulation commenced. Third, the victim also suffered myocardial infarction. He was suffering a ninety-five per cent blockage in the carotid artery, so in some respects he was a walking time bomb. It wouldn't have taken much to trigger a heart attack in normal circumstances.

"So what is not yet clear is the sequence of events. Did the hit on the head trigger the heart attack which killed the senator before the asphyxiation took place? Did the strangulation trigger the infarction? I haven't quite decided which event was the technical cause of death. And there's a contusion caused by the strangulation. Again suggesting that the force was applied at an angle consistent with someone who is left-side dominant."

Mariella then bent over and pantomimed. "This time I'll handle the re-enactment. Mac, get down on the floor."

"Why always me?" he complained.

Mariella dropped her right knee onto Mac's back, then looked up at Rachel. "Cheese. Watch my right arm levering the neck while my left arm pulls upward on the belt. It's more likely that your perp is someone comfortable with his left arm doing the pulling of the belt."

"Ow. My neck," Mac yelled. "You're killing me."

"Sorry, Mac. I got a little carried away."

Mac stood up and rubbed the side of his neck. "Excuse me, Mariella, but you lost me at hello. How did the senator die?"

"The point is, Mac, I'm not certain yet. The blow to the head might have triggered the heart attack that killed him, or he might have suffered the heart attack while he was being strangled, or he might have been suffering the heart attack that might not have killed him had he not also been strangled."

At this point Rachel was ready to jump out of her skin. Mariella's voice was killing her. She thought she might be able to wrap this up without need for an interpreter. "If I understand it, if the same perp hit the senator, then strangled him, this is all academic."

"Correct. It would only matter if there were two perpetrators, which I suppose you still need to rule out."

■ ■ ■

The old wooden floors creaked reliably as the detectives made their way out and back to their desks.

Rachel opened up her file. "Let's assume we have one killer who did both acts. The senator got bopped, then was strangled and died. Open and shut murder."

"All we're missing is the perp."

Rachel suddenly put her hand up. "I forgot to tell you that I spoke to Michael Cassidy last night. While he admitted to being in possession of the famous necklace, he said he received it in an envelope with a note signed by Dee Moore. She never actually gave it to him personally. And she certainly didn't give it to him at the beach."

"We know the photos were doctored to look as if she did," Mac said. "Who sent it to him with a note signed by Dee? And why?"

"Someone else must have come into possession of that necklace and taken photos of it in order to doctor the photos sent to Odell Moore by Sherman. If I had to guess, Jackson sent the necklace to Cassidy to incriminate him."

"Well done, Watson, but we still can't rule out Rodney Ferguson."

"Do you think playing Holmes is going to help you?" Rachel asked with a grin. "Maybe he took the pictures in a scheme to upset Moore. That would mean he had to be working with Jackson. We know Jackson sent the e-mail to Moore. Maybe they've both been playing us, in which case the M.E.'s assumption that we have two perps might also be a possibility."

Mac reached for a fistful of pistachios. "Remember, it was Emily Sherman who had access to the apartment so she might have photographed the necklace in the apartment."

"So now we have a conspiracy of three? But what's the motive and why kill the senator and almost kill Dee? It doesn't add up."

"Loose ends. Too many loose ends," Mac said. "Not enough evidence. And we're still waiting for the results of the DNA analysis. The CSI people collected a few hairs at the scene."

"Don't get your hopes up on that front. Even if the hairs match someone other than Moore or his wife, we'll never know whether the hair was left on the day of the murder."

Mac shucked a couple of pistachio shells with his teeth. "I have to admit I don't believe Ferguson has the guile to pull this off. Sherman? Maybe. The two of them together? I just don't buy it."

"Remember the Barino case. At first you didn't believe me. Dutiful daughter, Generation X, poisons her parents. Combine jealousy, deep-seated anger, and circumstance and any of us are capable of murder. It takes only a moment to pick up a statuette and use it as a weapon when rage takes over."

Mac walked over to the white board and started jotting a few more notes on the timeline. "Okay. Let's take it from the top. Emily Sherman had access codes to the apartment. All Jackson Sherman has to do is read a text on his wife's phone in order to get them. He was involved in sending along the photos to Moore. He could be the one who doctored the photos. But did he have motive to kill the senator or Dee?"

Rachel's hand stroked her nose. "Rodney Ferguson admitted that Jackson was very upset with Michael Cassidy for standing in his path to partnership, so I could see him trying to ruin Cassidy in Moore's eyes in an attempt to eliminate the competition. That would account for the photo mischief. But why go to the apartment and why kill the senator?" That was the sixty-four-thousand-dollar question. "Say he had access to the building. No one was expecting the senator to be around. As far as anyone knew he was in D.C. Maybe Jackson was headed there to confront Dee with his proof of her alleged escapade with Cassidy."

"Why would he do that?"

"Blackmail. Use the photos to get Dee to influence Moore to support Jackson's partnership. Except he walks in. She's going at it with the senator. Then…"

"Hold on, Rachel; what about this? Sherman or Sherman and Ferguson walk in as the senator and his daughter are scuffling." Mac paused. Perhaps it was because he had nowhere to take this story.

Rachel closed her eyes, trying to relive the scene. Her hand was well positioned. "Remember we're in the midst of a power failure. Maybe Sherman or he and Ferguson enter the apartment and believe she's being attacked. One of them reaches for the statuette and hits the senator on the back of the head not realizing who it is until it's too late. Impulse and opportunity add up to manslaughter."

"Here's the weakness. Both Sherman and Ferguson have known the guy for years." Mac spit a pistachio shell, which missed the waste basket.

"Disgusting," Rachel said. "Almost as disgusting as the strangulation. I can't figure how it fits. That's almost a fetish. The senator is dazed. Dee's already fallen and is out cold. Maybe she saw Sherman, maybe she didn't. But why take off a belt and use it? That's the sign of someone who's enjoying the violence."

"Perhaps there's more to Sherman than meets the eye. I think we should speak to police in Mobile. Maybe they know something. Anything."

A female clerk trotted over to Rachel and handed her a file. Stacey Keenan lived for technology and chasing down the results. It might take a village to raise a child but it took a team to solve a murder. Rachel couldn't understand how Stacey could hole up in a windowless room all day processing, but nothing was more exciting to her than watching the glee in the eyes of the detectives when she announced a match on fingerprint results.

"What do we have, Stacey?"

"The prints on the statuette are a match to the prints of Jackson Sherman you had us test." She was smiling broadly.

"I guess that locks it for me," Mac said. "We have our perp. Let's pick him up."

"Not so fast, I'm not there yet. We still have too many unexplained facts," Rachel replied. "We're missing the instrument used to strangle him. We have no witness who saw what happened. A man was caught on camera leaving the rear exit of the building wearing a black Yankees cap. We need the belt, assuming it was a belt. We need the hat. There are too many loose ends."

Mac's phone rang. He put it to his ear, quickly picked up his pen, and frantically jotted down some notes, like the pen was on fire. At the end of the call, thirty seconds later, he made two excited slashes at the bottom of the page.

"It was the FBI. They thought we might be interested in a couple of calls that the senator made. The first was outgoing to Jackson's extension at TGO a week before the murder. The second was a call placed by Jackson's cell to the senator the day before the murder."

"You think Sherman may have been setting him up?"

"I think we have enough to bring him in and charge him. Let's go convince the A.D.A.," Mac said.

"It shouldn't take much. The mayor's under huge pressure. I don't think she even cares whether we arrest the right person."

"Once Sherman's in custody, we can execute a search warrant at the apartment. Maybe that'll get us what we need."

"I have a better idea, Mac. Let's ask Sherman to come see us before he lawyers up. He has no idea how much we know."

"And I'll speak to Torrance first. I have an idea about how he can be helpful. Let's bring Ferguson in as well. Let them both know they're suspects. They might roll on each other."

2:00 p.m., Tuesday, August 25, 2015

Rachel was standing in front of the white board staring at the photos of the senator and his daughter pasted at the centre of the board. Underneath, the timeline was all laid out. The arrows pointed all over the place. If the timeline was supposed to put everything into perspective, it wasn't working for her. Nothing about the upcoming arrest of Jackson Sherman made sense. There was no way to construct a motive that wasn't crazy-talk. Why did he want either of them dead? He might have been a misguided jerk or, better put, too smart by half, but why strike the senator and why choke him? And he'd spoken to the senator the day before the murder. Had he lured the senator to New York in order to kill him? Not unless there was a part of the story no one yet knew. And if he knew the senator was coming, he would have expected him at the condo. It did not add up.

Her desk phone rang and she walked across the room to pick it up. The DNA lab results were available. Incredibly they took one-quarter of the time of a normal case. Not really a surprise given the victim. The blond hairs were confirmed as Dee Moore's and most of the grey and black hairs on the carpet were complete matches either to the senator or to Odell Moore. There were a number of other hairs, some showing 0.1 per cent or less and a couple showing a 3 per cent resemblance to Moore. Who knows whether a concierge had been in the apartment and when the last time the carpets had been vacuumed? Not much help. She would let Mac know before the day was out.

The inner voice was whispering to her as she rubbed her nose. There was something she was missing and it had to be obvious.

CHAPTER 32

6:10 a.m., Wednesday, August 26, 2015

Jackson stepped off the subway at Fifty-First and Lexington, rather than transferring to the M train on Fifty-Ninth and getting off at Rockefeller Plaza as was his usual habit. He was up earlier than usual, having decided there was not much point lying in bed worrying. He needed to do a little walking—the hot spell had finally broken, making it a pleasure to be out and about. The predawn light left a grey hue on the horizon. He used to go fishing on the bay with his daddy at this time of day. The fish always bit best before sun-up; they could hear the flies better than they could see 'em. You'd think after centuries of experience they might have learned a thing or two. Natural selection and all that. But fish were bound to be fish and it was simply the luck of the draw as to which ones took the bait. Maybe survival was just luck.

His own luck was not holding. Moore still had to be the prime suspect but they had Jackson on the e-mail. If they figured out exactly what he was up to, it might cost him his job. He'd need the General to save him, and the General might be on his way to jail soon. Neither alternative led to a good career result. How was he going to wiggle off this hook?

He arrived at his office at six-thirty and opened his e-mail to find a note from Drew Torrance inviting him to stop by the office at eight. No details. He was as perplexed as the first time he'd been summoned to the Den. Was this going to be another good-news meeting? Not in this environment. The only thing normal about TGO these days was the crown prince of abnormality, which had reigned since the murder in Odell's apartment. It was as if the senator's body had been found on the floor of the staff lunchroom. Tension filled the corridors. What was Torrance, the king of TGO, even doing here? He was supposed to be in China, working on the secret merger with the second-largest Asian firm. Secrets in this law firm were very difficult to keep. Jackson guessed a murder investigation trumped an Asian merger.

Jackson walked in just before eight. "What can I do for you, sir?"

"Jackson, please take a seat." Torrance offered one of the chairs on the other side of his desk. Message received. This was to be an official conversation with the chairman of the firm.

"Listen, Jackson, this police investigation has affected the firm badly. As long as the senator's murder goes unsolved and there is speculation that someone in this firm is involved, it's affecting our reputation in the media, with our clients, and with our suppliers. And it's not just New York that's feeling the brunt of this. Our offices all over the world are fielding difficult calls from clients. I don't want to even hazard a guess as to the number of potential new clients we're losing over this. Now, the whole thing is nonsense to me. I'm convinced that Moore is not involved in this in any way, but I've told the police my lawyers will turn over every rock to assist the investigation. We must be beyond reproach in this matter…" Torrance was in another trance.

Here we go again with the pregnant pauses, Jackson thought. After a long hesitation, he finally spoke. "So where do I fit in, sir?"

"I've promised the NYPD the complete cooperation of every member of this firm with ties to Odell or his wife, and everyone that had a significant role to play in Bounty. That includes you and your wife."

"I'll do everything I can to help."

"The detectives on the case gave me some homework. Because of the sensitivity of the file, I didn't want to delegate the task. Normally Simon would handle this. The time records indicate that you had an afternoon client meeting that ended at five o'clock on the night of the murder. You didn't return to the office?"

Time to slow down and think, Jackson thought. He took out his smartphone to check his calendar. Torrance must already know I didn't return to the office. Is this investigation turning on me? How much did Torrance know that he wasn't letting on? Torrance could make his career but he could also break it in less than sixty seconds. Moore was far more valuable an asset to Torrance, so the sooner someone else went down for this the better.

"Well, sir, if I recall we're talking about the Dovecraft meeting. I left the building at about five-fifteen, roughly fifteen minutes after the meeting ended. I was chatting with the client's accountant for a few minutes in the lobby before heading over to the subway. I had thought about coming back to the office, but with the Cypress deal done I figured this was a rare opportunity to spend a few hours with my wife. I decided to surprise her by getting some groceries and cooking her dinner. With all the shopping, I figure I didn't actually get home until seven-fifteen."

"Did you keep your receipts?"

Jackson hesitated momentarily. Since when does the chairman of the firm deal with such minutiae? Was Torrance doing this with the cops or was he conducting an internal investigation? Which was worse?

"I doubt it. I stopped at the local grocery store and paid cash. The same goes for the bottle of wine that I picked up on the walk to my apartment. I picked up one of Emily's favorite Cabs. Something really special."

"That's all I needed for now. Thanks, Jackson."

Jackson returned to his office, wondering whether he should be worried. What was Torrance's motive? With Odell on indefinite leave, the firm would need him more than ever. Someone had to run the Houston financing. A partner would have to be nominally in charge of the file, but Jackson was certain he could run it. Torrance had probably figured that out as well. Maybe this was Torrance's way of signalling that he should prepare for another NYPD interrogation. If the detectives came back with more questions Jackson had better be smooth. Was the NYPD behind this meeting? Was it a heads-up to prepare him for an interrogation? Torrance could not afford for Odell to be gone and Jackson to be tied up in knots with the detectives, instead of preparing for the biggest file of the year. The firm's clients had to come first. He could never get a clear read on Torrance.

He shut his office door and began to muse aloud as he paced in little circles. "I've admitted to forwarding on the photos to Odell. Bad judgment but not a crime. So why check on my alibi? Unless they've concocted some way to connect dots to the murder."

Fifteen minutes later the phone rang.

"Mr. Sherman, this is Detective Mac. We still have a few questions that we need answered so we can close the book on the firm. I would really appreciate it if you could come down to the station this morning. How is ten-thirty?"

"I can make it for about eleven," Jackson responded tentatively. The dots had come full circle, hanging like a noose around his neck. The chair waiting for him at the police station was about to be kicked out from underneath. Only an idiot would walk into that station house unprepared. He immediately dialled the number of Mark Shumaker, a litigator on the forty-third floor whom he trusted and had worked with on Bounty.

"Mark, a client of mine has been arrested on a felony charge and needs immediate criminal counsel. Who would you recommend?"

"Try Chuck Smith or Elise Orber. Only use Chuck if your client has admitted he did it. He has a great record for plea bargaining the charge down to something that will have your client spend the minimal amount of time in prison. Hiring him, unfortunately, is read by the prosecutors as a sign of guilt. You may be innocent until proven guilty in this country, but in this city, if Chuck's representing you, the only question is what crime you're guilty of committing."

Jackson placed a couple more calls. He still had not arranged the online bank transfer that he had promised Betty Carolli. Now unavoidable. She was constantly complaining about the level of her student loans so this would help both of them. Their late-night meetings had been going on for a few months, most of them work related, but he'd never had sexual relations with her, at least according to the Clinton definition of the words. At some point he'd explain it to Emily. She had to be with him in the corner the police were painting him into. I just need people on standby, he thought. He picked up the picture frame and gave Emily a final kiss. "You I need more than anyone else," he said to the photograph.

■ ■ ■

Mac was chomping on some pistachios, spitting the shells into the wastebasket across the room. Rachel pushed her chair away from the desk and grabbed his Giants mug.

"Mac, you know that habit sickens me. You're behaving like a fourth-grade student."

"Correction, Rachel, I'm behaving like a professional athlete. Gimme back my nuts."

"Don't get smart. Can't you throw the shells out like a civilized human being?"

"Rachel, one wife in my life is more than I can handle at the moment." He had been right in his assessment of Jen's mood. Once she calmed down and had some time to think about Terry's childishness, Jen and Mac were partners once again, helping their son with a solution. He didn't want to go to college and there was no forcing him. They'd spent the weekend talking with Terry. Assessing what he really wanted from life. First Jen had to listen. He wanted to make his own decisions about his life—even if it meant learning them the hard way. Wasn't that the way with kids? They couldn't and wouldn't learn from your hard experience. They needed their own.

Mac suggested to Jen that maybe six months in a factory job would teach him about what life without an advanced education was going to be like. They discussed it again last night and Jen very calmly advised Terry this morning that he was welcome to choose his life path, but as long as he wanted to live under her roof, it meant getting a job and paying rent immediately after graduation. Crisis averted, at least for now.

"Did you come up with a motive for Jackson Sherman last night?" Rachel asked.

"To be honest I'm dealing with other things at home right now. I still like Sherman for this. He's on his way in. You're the one with the intuition. What's your take?"

Mac was ready to spit another shell. This time he caught the impulse and tucked it with his tongue into the upper corner of his mouth. Manners.

"With Sherman's prints on the statuette, even if we have no proof concerning the strangulation, we have him on assault," Rachel said. "Maybe even attempted murder."

"The A.D.A. spoke to the lieutenant early this morning. He's confident he has enough right now to get an indictment from the grand jury on manslaughter, but he really needs to bring first-degree murder charges. The D.A. is up for re-election shortly." The salt in the shell began to irritate his upper gums.

"I guess the strangulation makes it politically impossible to walk away from first-degree murder. Imagine if our jobs depended on getting elected. That would be a pain in the ass."

Funny how pain and pressure made life more problematic, Mac thought. "There has to be corroborating evidence in Sherman's apartment. If we charge him we can get an immediate search warrant and then we'll discover whether we can support all this circumstantial evidence." Mac brought his fist up to his mouth and caught the shells. His mouth felt better and he hoped Rachel had noticed how he was evolving.

"I brought Ferguson in an hour ago," Rachel said. "I have him sautéing in a room with a view. We'll let them see each other when Sherman arrives. By that time Ferguson should be crapping his pants, imagining what Sherman might be telling us."

"What do we need Ferguson for?"

"Ferguson may be an upper-class twit, but I sense he's still holding out on us. We'll also need his testimony as corroboration for Sherman's crazy plan."

■ ■ ■

Jackson arrived on time, taking directions from the desk sergeant, heading up to the second-floor detective unit, which was calmer than he had expected from his experience watching crime shows. There were no suspects in handcuffs, no hookers sitting in the hallways swearing at the passersby, and no obvious drug dealers waiting to be charged after a long New York night. Perhaps the morning riff-raff had been cleared out or maybe he had been directed to a quieter end of the station. The two detectives greeted him and led him into a small interrogation room, completely nondescript but for the mirror, which his vast television experience told him was the one-way window that allowed outside observers to watch the interrogation.

Mac surprised him by pulling down the blind. "You wouldn't believe how many witnesses are convinced that people are standing outside the door watching them while we ask questions. TV has done a lot to make our jobs more difficult," Rachel complained. "For now, we have a few questions for you."

"How can I help you today, detective?" Rachel had taken the seat opposite him. Fat detective Mac stood off to his right, out of view. Emily had warned him. Rachel had pretended to be all nice and understanding to Emily until she'd started zeroing in on Jackson. Not to be trusted.

"There are a few things we're still trying to figure out," Rachel said. "Did you have any communication with the senator before the day of the murder?"

At least they were starting with an easy one. Jackson had been preparing this answer for a few days. "He called me to ask some questions about Odell Moore after he and Dee eloped. After all, I was the one who'd made the introduction to the senator."

"What was his state of mind?"

"What would be yours if you find out your child got married without inviting you to the wedding?"

Rachel opened her mouth slightly and dropped her head, like his answer was cheeky. Bitch. She probably didn't have kids. Control yourself, Jackson. "Sorry, I didn't answer your question. He was very upset."

"And was that the only conversation you had?" she asked.

If she was trying to set a trap, she was not very good at her job. Only an idiot would deny the second call. They must have reviewed the senator's cellphone records. "He was agitated. Wanted me to do something about getting the marriage undone. I didn't have the heart to tell him there was nothing I could do. I told him my best guess was that he needed to speak to his daughter directly."

"And you knew his daughter?" Rachel asked.

He thought he'd answered that yesterday. Was she deliberately trying to throw him off balance? Were they going to try and trip him up? *Control yourself.* He began blandly, just like the General would. "I thought I told you, previously. Dee and I go back to elementary school in Mobile." Jackson began tapping his foot rhythmically, as if he was reciting a poem to a steady beat, keeping his sentences short. "I was a couple of years ahead of her. Our parents were acquaintances. At one point I think my father and the senator were young lawyers in Mobile. I guess you could say Dee and I were friendly acquaintances. Never more than that. As for her father, I last saw him on the evening I introduced him to Mr. Moore. That was last year." *Tap, tap, tap out the answers.*

"And there was nothing unusual that took place in that deal involving the senator?"

"That information would be subject to solicitor-client privilege and I really couldn't speak about it. If you want to ask any further questions related to the deal, I suggest you ask Mr. Torrance in order to get the permission of our client."

"No need, but thank you for pointing it out, Mr. Sherman. We're just trying to ascertain if there might have been any animosity between anyone in your firm and the senator."

"None that I am aware of."

"All right then, let's get to the night of the murder. You told Mr. Torrance what, exactly?"

"I told Mr. Torrance that I left the client meeting around five o'clock."

"You told him five-fifteen."

Don't react to the dyke's pettiness. It answered one question. Torrance was working with them. Not a good sign. "Right, say five-fifteen. Then I headed to the subway. Did some shopping for groceries. Paid cash." Tap, tap, tap. Maintain control. Moderate the pace.

"Do you often stop for groceries on the way home?"

"Never actually. Most nights I'm working until ten or eleven at night. Sometimes later if there's a deal going on. My wife does the cooking, though she doesn't need to make me dinner. We order takeout to the office. One of the students picks it up."

"But on this night you didn't work late?"

"No. We were on a break between deals. I was feeling guilty and I thought I would surprise Emily and make dinner that night."

"Can you tell us what time you did the shopping and when you arrived at your apartment?"

It was time to slow down. Make it appear as if he was thinking back to that evening—working carefully to be accurate. "I wasn't punching a clock, you know. I think I got home around seven; might have been seven-fifteen."

"Mr. Sherman, had you ever been to the Moore apartment before?" The question from fat detective Mac arrived like a dart to the side of his neck. Jackson turned to face Mac, who was standing with his arms crossed.

"My wife's been there."

"So we should take that as a no?" Mac persisted.

His foot was no longer tapping. Moment of truth time. What was the right answer? Nobody knew about the visit before he left for L.A., and what did that have to do with a murder in any event? Was he really going to have to admit to breaking and entering when all he did was a five-minute snoop of the apartment? Both feet were rooted to the ground.

"That is correct."

"Well then, Mr. Sherman, perhaps you could explain to us how your fingerprints were found on the statuette that was used to assault the senator."

The trap snapped shut. He had no idea what Mac was talking about, but it was clear what was about to happen to him. His feet were planted and there was nowhere to run.

"Detectives, will you give me a moment; my cellphone is pinging me." Jackson took out the phone and typed out a short text and then returned his attention to Mac.

"I believe at this point I would like to invoke my right to an attorney before the questioning goes any further."

■ ■ ■

The detectives left the room, and Mac figured the time was ripe to harvest Rodney Ferguson, who had been sitting on his own in the interrogation room for over an hour and a half. Ferguson's face, a pale shade of grey, greeted Mac on the way in the door. Time to capitalize.

"Do you know why we brought you in, sir?"

"No."

"You have not been completely truthful with us, have you?" It couldn't hurt to start with an open-ended bluff. They never told you everything on the first meeting.

Ferguson started crying. "I knew you were going to take this the wrong way... The night Senator Brabant was ... was ... I can't even say the word." He honked his nose.

"Control, Mr. Ferguson." Mac handed him a tissue. He blew his nose and shoved the soaking tissue into the pocket of his sports jacket. Today he was wearing a summer tweed. He began to play with the cufflink on his right wrist.

Rachel slipped into the room, taking her place beside Mac.

"Start with the night of the murder," Mac said.

"I went back to Dee's apartment. Around seven, give or take. Just after the power failure. I decided to confront her. To be a man. To tell her I loved her. The lobby door wasn't locked. Someone left a newspaper on the floor to prevent it from closing. Upstairs the apartment door was ajar. I had to walk in a few feet to see around the corner ... the bodies lying there on the floor... I almost screamed and I'm ashamed for what I did next."

"And what was that?" Rachel asked.

"I didn't check if anyone was alive. I didn't even call 911," he squeaked. "If my daddy ever found out I don't know what he would do. My cowardice was unforgiveable. Doesn't matter if anyone else finds out. I have dishonoured the Sherman name." His nose began to run. He brought his sleeve toward his face but caught himself. Mac did not offer a second tissue. "I panicked and ran all the way down the stairs and out the door. I didn't stop running until I got back to my hotel. I swear it wasn't me. Not that it matters anymore. My life is over just the same."

"I notice you play with your cufflink with your left hand, Mr. Ferguson," Mac said. "We all have our nervous tics. My partner likes to rub her nose. It allows her to figure out who the murderer is."

Ferguson was the deer in the headlights, now staring at Rachel. She was rubbing her nose and smiling. "What hand do you write with, sir?" she asked.

"I want a lawyer." It sounded almost like a wounded howl.

■ ■ ■

They returned to Jackson. Mac figured they might as well be on hand when the lawyer arrived. There was a knock on the door. Before Mac could respond, a tall woman strode into the room. This one meant business. "Detectives, good morning. Your discussions with my client are at an end." Turning on her heels to Jackson, she said: "Mr. Sherman, a pleasure to meet you. I am Elise Orber. Perhaps next time it will be under better circumstances."

Turning to her right, she faced Mac and Rachel with an expression of disdain. "I don't believe that Mr. Sherman has anything further to say today, so if you don't mind we will be leaving."

Mac faced the attorney. There were few moments in the day when he felt he had any advantage over defence counsel, particularly once they dug into a case. Every once in a while, he and Rachel had a slight knowledge advantage over the defence, so he couldn't help but enjoy those moments, however short-lived they may be. While the goal of the exercise was justice, the players were all subject to human frailties. The business of prosecution played out as a war, with battles, and you took your pleasures from the small victories, all in the name of ultimately achieving justice.

"Ms. Orber, I'm afraid I have some bad news for you. Your client is being charged with the murder of Senator Brabant. Shall we read him his Miranda rights?"

"No need to Mirandize him. Mr. Sherman, they are about to process you. No more talking to anyone. Period. Not here and certainly not in jail. We'll connect when they are done and we can have a private discussion at that time. Do you understand?"

"Yes, ma'am."

Rachel cut in, handing Elise Orber a document. "This is a warrant to conduct a search at Mr. Sherman's residence. It's vanilla for this type of case. Our officers are executing the warrant as we speak. I am sure we'll be in touch again."

"Emily," Jackson screamed out.

"Sorry, sir, it's Elise, not Emily," Orber said.

"My wife is Emily. She has no idea. They're probably going to destroy our apartment. Ms. Orber, you have to do something."

"I'm on my way."

Police officers came to escort Jackson for processing. Elise headed for the door. She was already focused on the keyboard of her phone.

"All in a day's work, counsellor," Mac said to her on the way out.

Elise dropped her hand, stopped, turned, and shot back immediately: "You know the routine, detective. This is a twelve-round match. There's no advantage to winning round one on points. See you at the bail hearing."

"We should be finished processing him by tomorrow morning."

"Somehow I suspected you were going to take your time processing him."

"What do you mean, counsellor?" Mac asked innocently.

"Your D.A. will want to have her moment with the media just before the prime-time news cycle this evening, then you, your captain, and the police commissioner can heave a sigh of relief and hope to heaven that you've charged the right person. I'll tell you right now, I've been on this case for all of five minutes, and I already know you're going to have an impossible time proving motive. Just wait until I've dug into the case."

"It's out of our hands now."

"But the wheels of justice have to turn and I have to make a living. In the end you will have succeeded in ruining a promising young attorney's legal career but that's about it. A killer is still on the loose in Manhattan. That's on your heads." The door slammed behind her.

Mac chuckled. "Chalk up one point for the good guys," he said.

"I don't know, Mac. We're missing something critical here."

Rachel began rubbing the bridge of her nose. A good thing it never bothered him. Why was it that he could handle the nose rub and she couldn't take the shells? That kind of argument never worked at home on Jen and he figured he best just swallow it for now. Women.

Two hours later, Rachel took a call from the officers executing the search. They had seized the home computer, and in the closet they'd found a black New York Yankees cap. They also seized every belt in sight. Next step would be processing at the lab for DNA testing. "No way a smart lawyer would be stupid enough to keep the murder weapon."

"Some of them like to keep souvenirs, Rachel. Possession of a black Yankees baseball cap could make him and a million other Yankee fans potential suspects so it's not terribly compelling on its own. The belt would help."

CHAPTER 33

2:00 a.m., Thursday, August 27, 2015

In the middle of the night Odell woke up with a start. A woman was screaming in the hospital room next door—then nothing. He heard footsteps racing toward the room, nurses shouting, followed by a Code Blue announcement over the intercom. Nothing was waking Dee. He jumped out of the lounge chair provided by the nursing staff and checked her monitors, then put his head against her chest to feel her heart beat and the rhythmic rise and fall of her chest.

The pace of her breathing was equal and unrushed. The peace that was missing from his life. He had become accustomed to the high pressure of his lifestyle, which forced him to keep moving, solving everyone else's problems without having to face his own. These past few days had forced him to slow down and examine his choices. It was a difficult task for the child of an alcoholic. Never certain about whom he could love because he barely loved himself. He'd built a convenient wall of intellect around his core. Solutions to business problems were logical; the more he could dissociate from emotion, the more successful he became as a transaction lawyer. Smile a lot and ignore emotion. Rely on intelligence before taking action. Do not ever allow emotion to interfere with sound judgment. Those were the keys to his success. They were also the locks that kept him from developing any kind of mature relationship. Not with Dee and not with himself. The time had arrived for a radical change. If only Dee would come back to him. If she could ever forgive him.

If she couldn't or wouldn't, if he lost her and the baby, then life support would be of no value to him.

He put his arms around her, laid his head on her shoulder, and shook uncontrollably. Almost forty years' worth of tears came pouring out of him onto the bedsheets. He felt a hand caressing his hair. It must be another dream.

"I'm back, love," Dee whispered and then closed her eyes once more.

CHAPTER 34

2:00 p.m., Thursday, August 27, 2015

"Good afternoon, Jackson. You've got a lot of explaining to do."

Elise Orber began every first meeting with a client the same way. No question who was in charge; no time for small talk or empathy. Where was the upside in getting to know them personally? These were all one-shot deals. Take the case, fight it, get a result, get paid, and move on to the next. She'd watched some of her competitors get vested emotionally in their clients and their troubles. Big mistake.

She was about to enter the ring for a fifteen-round heavyweight fight and all that ever mattered was that she had the tools to go the distance: patience to root out fact from fiction, razor-sharp wit, intimidating size, and a wardrobe that spoke to her pride in being a large woman. Prosecutors hated her and juries identified with her. Today she had chosen a black and white checkered dress, cut low in the front to more than hint at a substantial bust. The red scarf around her neck set off her shoulder-length auburn hair. She understood how to take command. The room was small and a guard stood by the door. This made her physical presence loom even larger, important for this second time they were meeting. Round two. Establish control of this relationship.

"How does it feel to be a star, Jackson?"

"Glad you arrived with your sense of humour intact," he replied.

"Let me tell you how I work. You're going to have one chance to tell me this story. You're a lawyer. I don't have to tell you that everything you tell me is confidential, but as of this moment there are over a hundred million

Americans convinced you killed the senator. We have to move quickly to establish your alibi, assuming you have one. I spent some time last evening with your wife."

"What did she tell you?"

"Please don't interrupt, Jackson. I'll ask the questions for now. The police crawled over your apartment for five hours, leaving the place turned upside down. Emily is in shock."

"She's tougher than you know. She'll bounce back."

"I don't think you appreciate the scope of this mess. Your image has appeared in every media outlet around the world, and the vultures have descended on your apartment building. She was caught completely off guard by all of this, and she's now living the nightmare that's only going to get worse each day of your incarceration. I advised her to shut down her social media accounts. The haters are out there attacking both of you— calling you the New York Strangler." She reached into her handbag and pulled out a pad of yellow paper and a Bic pen.

"I've made quite a mess of things," Jackson said. He sounded almost matter of fact. Hardly recalcitrant and definitely not defeated. A most interesting combination. She needed to find out how hard he could be pushed.

"It could get worse. I wouldn't rule out the possibility that they may drag Emily into this as an accomplice, if only to pressure you into mistakes. You're going to need her as an ally to beat this, and I suggest you get to work on that from here as soon as possible."

"I assume I'm not getting out any time soon." Most clients would be in a panic over what the police might do their spouses. No reaction yet from Jackson, which meant he was either a sociopath or innocent. No way to tell which just yet.

"I wouldn't hold my breath on bail. I'll make the usual plea. After all, you have no priors and a spotless record. The judge will laugh at me. Even astronomical bail is likely out of the question. You're accused of killing a sitting politician." She paused to let this sink in and to switch to a more philosophical tone. "Do you believe in God, Jackson?"

"I go to church on occasion."

"Then pray to Jesus for a miracle. Otherwise, you're going to be re-manded back here. For a long time. Make yourself comfortable."

"Jesus has better things to do with his time than to worry about my loneliness in here. I'll just start making friends with the boys in the cells on either side of me," he said with a heavy trace of sarcasm.

Was he kidding? She was not about to take chances. Back to the bitch-slap. "No talking to anyone, do you hear me? No one in here will be your friend."

"I was kidding. You don't have to be so mean. Besides, I don't have enough tattoos to be relevant in here. When can you get Emily to visit?"

"We'll get to that. You have one chance to work with me, Jackson, and it begins this moment. Do you understand? I don't care what you did or how you did it, but you can't lie to me, even by omission."

"I understand," he said in a defeated tone.

She was accustomed to the depression that only deepened as her clients acclimatized to their new accommodations. The entire weight of the judicial system was now geared to compress him to dust, to sweep him up and throw him in the waste bin. At this point guilt or innocence was no longer relevant to the system. Once they were remanded, they were prisoners with few rights. The system treated them as guilty until acquitted. She saw it almost every day in her practice. Judging by the statistics, the odds of the offender being innocent were very low in any event. Almost all of them had done something illegal—even if they had been arrested for something else. But the system was also designed to process them like meat. Move them through, grind them up if they could not afford counsel, or plead them down to lesser offences if they could. Elise knew it was almost never about innocence. Only the level of guilt.

"How was your night at Rikers?"

"Better than my worst nightmares. Since I was a child I had this fantasy of being imprisoned on my fortieth birthday, and here I am a few years early. At least no one attacked me last night, and when I came down to breakfast this morning I was shown some respect. I guess there is a hierarchy for murder in here, and taking down the Man gets you brownie points. Who knew?"

"Keep up the sense of humour; it'll keep you sane."

Her questioning began with Jackson's background with the senator, Dee, and Odell. She also had him trace his career arc. Not because she cared even a little bit about him, but this case might make her career, if she played it right. Based on the little she knew, the prosecution's case was entirely circumstantial. Sure, they had his fingerprints on the assault weapon, but if she could prove he'd been in the apartment prior to the murder she could explain that away. No witnesses had emerged, and if Mrs. Moore woke, hopefully she could deny it was Jackson and that would be that. If she didn't wake up or, worse, if she died, the public relations would be a nightmare (Jackson a double murderer comparable to the serial killers), but even so, without witnesses the prosecution would still have to make a case for motive in order to secure a conviction.

She needed a sense of who Jackson was and how he fit in the world. She needed to find his motive. She also needed to understand how he behaved when he was telling the truth. There was no point starting with the alibi until she had established a baseline. How did he tell a story when the facts did not matter, when it was more likely than not that he had no motive to lie?

After a couple of hours, she felt she was ready. "Let's go back over your alibi and the statements you gave police."

"I told them I was out shopping for groceries and making dinner for Emily during the window of time when the senator was killed."

"Will Emily corroborate that?"

"I assure you I was not at the Moore apartment. I'm prepared to take a lie detector."

He hadn't answered the question. His pattern up until now was to deflect only when he didn't know something. Elise guessed that Jackson had no idea whether Emily would corroborate. That told her everything she needed to know. "I've heard that one before. In any case, a lie detector is of no value to your defence."

"Do you hear me, Elise? I was … not … there." She could hear his foot tapping to the beat. The tone was emphatic. Was he really using righteous indignation?

Why did new clients always insist on piling up the obfuscation in a first interview? she wondered. She needed to make it plain to them that she wasn't an idiot. A slap across the face might work in ordinary circumstances, but the verbal equivalent would have to do.

"Let me make this simple for you, Jackson. Where were you?"

He sat there as if he was evaluating what story might work on her. He was going to be a most challenging client.

"Don't make me pull teeth, Jackson."

He stared at her for a good ten seconds. Long enough to contrive the lie or to force himself to finally tell the truth. Closed his eyes for a moment then opened them wide just before he spoke. "I was in the apartment of one of our first-year corporate lawyers. She works in our anti-trust department." He stopped. Took a deep breath and exhaled. "We've been having an affair for the last year." He looked at her as if waiting to be judged. That was not her job. "I love my wife, but I need some variety in my sex life."

Elise registered no response at all. She had heard worse. "Name and contact info? I need to speak to her."

"Betty Carolli. We work very long hours together and one thing just led to another. The woman is insatiable and prefers married men. She keeps telling me she doesn't want attachment. It started after our last holiday party—"

"Whoa, Jackson. I don't need her life story or yours. I just need her to corroborate your alibi. Does Emily know?" Emily probably had no idea or she would have said something yesterday. She had not been as shocked by the police search as other wives Elise had observed. Probably had had a tougher childhood than most Upper East Side wives. However, there was no accounting for how a woman was going to react to a cheating husband. Some of them would rather their husbands be murderers. They'd spent a few hours together last night and she didn't show the anger of a woman scorned by her unfaithful husband. No question Emily had no idea this was coming.

"From Emily's perspective I was already working insanely long hours so she never perceived any change of behaviour at my end."

"Anyone else observe you two?"

"Unlikely. No one in the office knows. I'm trusting that Betty will swear to my whereabouts on the night of the murder. I just hope she doesn't lose her job over it. The firm has a non-fraternization policy among its employees. It's never enforced. Given the crazy hours we all work, these things are fairly commonplace. The rumour mill suggests a couple of partners were threatened with sexual harassment suits a few years ago. These things just happen."

"How do you explain your fingerprints on the statuette?"

He looked over at the wall. An involuntary deflection. Perhaps this admission was far more painful than his infidelity. He wouldn't look back at Elise as he began to speak. "Dee texted Emily the access code to their apartment when she and Odell were catching a flight to L.A. The next day I used it to go to their apartment." His tone was still steady. Surprising for his first criminal admission. Breaking and entering, in most cases just a misdemeanour for a first-time offender with a slap on the wrist for a penalty. Probably a felony to which he would have to plead guilty if added to a murder charge.

"So Emily gave it to you?" That would make her complicit. It would also give the police all kinds of leverage to threaten her as a conspirator on the B and E and who knows what else.

"She doesn't know I took it. Emily would consider it an invasion of her privacy. I'm not sure if the greater sin was breaking into the Moores' apartment or stealing the contents of one of Emily's e-mails."

"Why would you do such a thing?"

"You mean the trip to the Moores'? I was snooping. I walked around the living room admiring the artwork. I probably picked up the statuette just to play with it. I don't even remember doing it but that's a plausible explanation for my prints."

For a guy sitting in a jail notorious for its violence, he was a little too relaxed. Was it because he was too stupid or too smart? She had already decided she could never put him in front of a jury. They would hate him at best and disbelieve him at worst.

"Why would you be snooping, Jackson?"

"Part of me just wanted to experience how the other half lived. Also, Emily told me about a cheap necklace with a charm on it in the shape of a little jug that Dee owned—it had sentimental value to her. I thought she might have left it in the apartment. I just wanted to take a picture of the necklace."

"What for?"

Jackson sighed for the first time. "It was a scheme to upset Odell Moore and Michael Cassidy, the associate I told you about. We're competing for equity partnership."

He probably meant that in the past tense. He *was* competing for equity partnership. Now he was competing for his life.

"But you didn't get it?" she asked.

"You mean the necklace? It wasn't in the apartment. Ultimately Emily took it from Dee and gave it to me."

"Well, Jackson, that explains everything. I'm now completely convinced you didn't do it."

"It's a little early for such heavy sarcasm, Elise."

"I have to give you credit. If you're as scared shitless as you ought to be, you don't show any outward sign. This story just keeps getting better. Tell me once more. Why did you call the senator the day before the murder?"

That piece of evidence was going to be used against Jackson.

"I told you, he wanted my help to break up the marriage. As if."

"As if, what?"

"As if I would assist him at the risk of ruining my relationship with Odell."

"So you told him to come to New York on the day that someone else murders him. And you might have been the only person in the world to know he was going to be here."

"Tough coincidence."

"Yeah. Coincidence."

She turned away from Jackson. "Ladies and gentlemen of the jury. My client was a brilliant young lawyer on an upward trajectory in the firm. He had an affair with a co-worker, broke into his boss's apartment intending to photograph some jewellery, and played with the sculpture. His wife ultimately stole a necklace from his boss's wife, the boss he hoped would make him a partner. It was all completely harmless. He even reached out to a U.S. senator who tried to enlist his help in destroying his boss's marriage. This is typically what successful lawyers do in big law firms."

She held out a dramatic arm in his direction. "The defendant is an honest and sincere man. He has a beautiful wife. Right here sitting behind me, the picture of despair." She turned and pantomimed pointing her right arm behind her at the imaginary defendant's table. Then she turned back toward the imaginary jury. "I won't put him on the stand, but if I did, he'd tell you he didn't do it. He may break and enter; he and his wife may steal. He may have lured the senator to New York on the day of the murder. But he could never commit murder. Not in order to become a partner in a big-name law firm. After all, who would do such a thing? It's just bad luck that his fingerprints are on the murder weapon. He was in the apartment, but only to snoop. That's how his fingerprints got on the weapon used to assault the senator. Of course he must be telling *me* the truth. He would never lie to *me*. The story is just so compelling."

She turned back to Jackson, having ended the soliloquy. "What kind of a bird brain do you take me for?" She stood up as if she were preparing to leave.

"Wait." There was finally a note of desperation in his voice.

"Jackson, I'm seriously worried about whether we can work together."

"I know the story sounds idiotic but it's true. You need to understand what life is like at TGO. Then maybe this story will begin to make some sense to you."

Jackson spent another hour rehashing his history with the firm and his relationship with Michael and Odell and filling in some blanks from the first round. She listened carefully, taking notes, having him repeat portions of the story a few times. There was not an ounce of contrition for his stupid behaviour. Jackson was the kind that couldn't imagine that what they'd done was wrong. They also manipulated the facts and lied to themselves. So much so that the lies had become the truth in their heads. She had learned through hard experience that if there were variations between the retelling of versions of an event, it was much more likely her witness was telling the truth. Only the liars had a carefully rehearsed script from which they would not deviate. On the other hand, there was nothing normal about Jackson. He had far above average intelligence. The type that thought everyone else were idiots. Those guys were often pathological liars and tough to catch.

"And are the police going to find anything incriminating on your computer?"

"I've erased everything that someone might conclude was incriminating."

"Unless you've professionally wiped your hard drive, you can assume they'll find every deleted e-mail and attachment and a complete history of your Internet roaming, so please don't leave out a pertinent fact that they will uncover. I need to know."

Jackson blanched. Had it finally sunk in just what kind of mess he had created? He pushed both hands through his hair and lifted his head. The colour had returned to his cheeks and his voice was commanding. "I had a plan. A good plan. I commissioned a photographer to follow Dee when she went to the beach with Michael Cassidy. I hoped the photos could be used to cause Odell to believe his wife was having an affair with Michael. It all sounds quite childish now, but at the time it had all the ingredients of success. Emily found the necklace and charm, and I had an expert superimpose images of the necklace around Michael's neck implying that Dee had given it to Michael, then I had the necklace delivered to Michael, purportedly from Dee. All of this was done to make Odell jealous and angry at Michael. It all worked like a charm."

"Like a charm. Look where it got you."

"All of that may be immoral on my part but how does it add up to anything other than bad judgment?"

"There's the understatement of the millennium. Maybe if Dee's father hadn't been hit over the head with the statuette you fondled, the rest of this exceedingly bad judgment on your part may only have demonstrated that you're an idiot." Elise paused for a moment to reflect. "However, I don't know if it amounts to any kind of motive for murder."

"I had absolutely no reason to hurt the senator or Dee Moore. Why would anyone think I did?"

Elise stared at Jackson across the small table. She began to speak at a rapid clip. "There are all kinds of holes in the case against you. Supposedly you showed up at the apartment at the exact time the video system was down. No evidence of you entering or leaving. I interviewed the Moores' neighbour this morning. She didn't recognize your picture. Nor has anyone else in the building that I showed it to. You can spend all this precious jail time remembering the route you took to Carolli's. Once you give me that, my investigator will contact every building in her neighbourhood and any business with street-facing video on the route. That might provide corroboration that your story is true. They say the senator was beaten and strangled. They seized all your belts and I'm assuming they will find nothing. They also took a black Yankees cap that they found in the closet."

"What's the big deal about a Yankees hat?"

"I was hoping you could tell me."

"No idea."

"They're also going to have to show motive. You have none. Moore was your sponsor for partnership. Dee and your wife were best friends. Nothing fits together in their case, except for the fingerprints."

She took a paper and a fountain pen out of her briefcase. "My retainer letter. You need to sign it."

Jackson signed his name quickly without reading the three-page document. He signed with his right hand. That would be helpful evidence based on what she had read in the papers to date. A left-handed client would be a liability.

"Sounds like you have some confidence in my defence," Jackson said.

"Without an alibi witness, my friend, a jury that decides it doesn't like you might find a way to convict. You prepared to risk your marriage over this?"

"Emily will find a way to forgive me. I made a mistake. Speak to Carolli and get her to confirm the alibi."

"Will she still love you when you admit to her that your chances of ever working in New York again are about as good as the Cubs winning a World Series?"

"I prefer the odds of Hillary becoming president. So my life will change. She'll stick by me. I know her."

"When this story gets out, you'll be a laughingstock. So will she for having all this go on under her nose. Not too many wives I know would put up with that." At least the defence was beginning to take shape. She'd laid it all out and she was beginning to feel confident that she could win this case. The next landmark case might come to her instead of Carrie. They might be drinking buddies, but Elise had been living in the shadow of the tiny eclipse for too long. "Think about your options. I can build you a credible defence. It'll cost you your job and possibly your marriage. Lethal injection or fresh start? Your choice."

Elise recognized capitulation when she saw it. Jackson didn't have to reply. He'd get her the alibi witness and deal with his marital problems.

"There's no chance we can avoid a grand jury. All these revelations will probably seal your fate with the firm and you'll continue to be the media poster child for a few days until they find a new whipping boy to destroy. At least you'll be alive, but you're going to be stuck here for a long while. Is there anything that you haven't yet told me?"

Jackson smiled for the first time.

"Don't allow yourself the luxury of smugness, Jackson. Between us, there's little chance I'm putting you on the stand to testify. I think I can create enough reasonable doubt. But nothing creates doubt more than other suspects. The investigative work is going to be expensive. This whole damned defence is going to be expensive, but if you follow my lead, you'll walk out of here one day."

"The decision to testify is my right, Elise, not yours." Jackson's voice sounded remarkably firm. Almost emphatic. The challenge of having a lawyer for a client. "It's not your life on the line."

Elise's face turned red, but her voice was barely above a whisper, the voice she used to drive home anger. "Jackson, there's only one boss here. Take it or leave it. There are lots of lawyers out there who would be happy for the publicity of this case, win or lose. Hire one of them if you want to run the case your way. It's your ass, after all. But if you want to continue *this* relationship, let's get the only ground rules in place that count. I won't ever tell you how to run a business deal and you won't ever tell me how to try this case."

Jackson stared at her as if taking her measure. He didn't seem to be intimidated. Or flustered. A good sign. He'd hold up well in court. Unlikely to wilt under the pressure or the intimidation of the process. "Deal," he finally said, holding out his arm. The handshake was firm, the eyes unreadable.

"Can you please make arrangements for Emily to get here. She knows I couldn't have done this … and she'll eventually forgive the alibi."

Elise signalled to the guard that it was time to leave. Between the press following and the legal fees, this case was a career builder. As long as he didn't testify, she didn't have to worry about what was true and what was only true in his head. The pathological liars were the worst types. They believed their own bullshit.

CHAPTER 35

Friday morning, August 28, 2015

Emily was wearing her only pair of blue jeans and a yellow loose-fitting T-shirt. She'd never felt more ugly in her life. Her hair was a windblown mess from the ride on the ferry. She hadn't slept in two days and the mirror was now an enemy. There were no mirrors at Rikers but Jackson's frightened eyes when she entered the room confirmed just how awful she looked. He made no effort to get up to meet her. Maybe his leg was chained to the wooden table. She had no idea how prisons worked but she now had a very good idea about how spouses were treated.

Elise had warned her about the dress code but nothing could prepare her for the indignity of clearing security. No dresses, no leggings, no tight clothing, no layers, not a hint of sexuality. The list of prohibitions went on and on. She'd caught the earliest ferry to the island and avoided eye contact with the other women. Many of them had children in tow. Some speaking languages she could not understand, some a form of English she'd never heard except on television crime shows.

She had to clear three separate metal detectors. The first woman guard reached inside her bra. The last two opened her jeans from the front. One of the women stuck her thick hands inside her underwear. Emily closed her eyes and held her breath. She was not going to let them see her cry. She held it along with her sense of violation, which was ready to spill all over the concrete floor.

She took a seat opposite Jackson. "What have you done?" She could barely control the anger. "They've ransacked our apartment, treated me like a criminal and they're telling the world you're a murderer. How could you do this to us?" She wanted to cry. She had promised herself whatever happened she would not cry. Jackson needed her.

"I'm sorry, Em." He would not make eye contact. He was looking at a spot on the table, right at the edge where his arms rested. He'd never behaved like this, not even with his mother. She pulled on every ounce of her reserve energy to stem the tears. She sniffled for a moment and caught her breath.

"Just tell me what you did. I can deal with it. I'm stronger than you think."

"I didn't do any of the things I've been accused of."

"Then why you, Jackson?" She reached across the table and touched his forehead.

"No contact," boomed a strong male voice from the corner. Emily jerked and removed her hand.

"You know I couldn't physically hurt anyone, much less strangle the senator and hurt Dee."

"That doesn't answer why you. Be honest with me, Jackson."

Step by step he revealed the story, from the visit to Odell's apartment to the affair with Betty Carolli. "I absolutely did not do this. Elise is telling me I have a solid defence. But I need you beside me. I need you to forgive me. I did some terrible things and I'm sorry."

The floodgates opened, releasing all the emotions Emily had been damming up. She made no effort to stem the tears. After an eternity, she pulled herself together. She ought to feel spent. Instead, she could feel a new energy filling the void where her dignity used to live. An energy fuelled by something she did not recognize. Whatever it was felt liberating.

"You violated my privacy. Broke into Dee's apartment after I told you not to."

"I'm sorry, Em."

"Shut up," she whispered. Then she smiled. The way the fox smiled at the gingerbread man. "All those years I sacrificed for you. I gave up my job for you. I stood by you even when they wanted to kick your sorry ass out of the last firm. I defended you in front of your bitch of a mother. I was always there for you, Jackson. Always. Always. You cost me a friendship with Dee. I have nothing left in the world. Nothing." She pushed her chair back from the table and stood. She understood the new feeling. Pure hate. She turned around and headed for the doorway.

"I know, Emily. I've behaved like a fool," Jackson shouted.

There was nothing left to say to Jackson. Ever.

CHAPTER 36

Monday morning, August 31, 2015

It was a dreary, rainy New York day. The type of day where you just want to crawl back into bed for another hour—unless you've been sleeping for over a week. Dee's spirits were not the least diminished. The wires were all disconnected, and she hoped to be discharged in the next couple of days. All the fuzz had lifted, and the headaches were no longer punishing. She could not bear to hear them say, "We're taking good care of baby Moore." It hadn't helped with the pain one bit. She was down to Tylenol 2s and her patience for the nursing staff was increasing with them. None of the painkillers managed the ache in the corner of her heart where her father used to live. Yesterday morning she'd spent half the day crying with Momma and the other half just talking with Odell, the barriers between them coming down.

Momma had mentioned this morning that the police were planning to show up shortly with some questions. Dr. Cameron had finally lifted the ban. He said her head could stand a little stress, but not too much. He didn't like to take any chances with his concussion patients.

Odell paced beside the bed. "Aren't we a pair?" Dee said. "Neither of us remembers a thing about the most dramatic night of our lives."

"I guess that's what trauma does to you. Your brain locks out the memory to protect you. But you remember some aspects of what happened to you that night."

"No. Nothing."

"But you told your mother that you saw enough of the attacker to know it wasn't me."

"I lied. I have a memory of a noise. I'm certain someone entered the apartment. But I have no memory at all after that."

Odell's face turned pale before her eyes. "But that means it might have been me."

"It wasn't you."

"You can't be certain. Why would you lie to your mother?"

"When I first woke up, I was pretty confused. You weren't beside me and that confused me even more. My head was pounding. She told me about Daddy and I asked for you. She told me she couldn't let that happen. Not unless she was sure. You're not capable of this, Odell. And I need you. So yes, I lied. Not my first sin. Not my last."

"How can you trust me? Even I don't."

"If this is going to work, I mean us, we have to trust one another. You need to open up to me. I can't know only part of you."

Odell sat for a moment. Had she gotten through to him? Yesterday he'd told her about the childhood abuse and his father's alcoholism, but she knew it had to be just a starting point. He was staring off into space, either considering where to begin or avoiding her again. They were on new ground and it was soft and uncertain beneath. She waited until he finally spoke.

"Before law school I bought a '68 Chevy for five hundred dollars and decided to drive out to the Rockies by myself. Greatest summer of my life. During the day I hiked the mountain trails in Montana, moving from campsite to campsite at night. I had a lot of time to think about my life, especially about what my father did to me and my sister. I realized I was no longer a child. I could no longer play the victim. Not if I wanted to be an effective advocate for others. I decided to confront my father."

"How long had it been since you last saw him?"

"Almost ten years. I had three days in the car to plan out everything I was going to say to him once I got to Halifax."

"Were you worried about confronting him?"

"Never occurred to me to be frightened. I would never cry during the beatings. After growing up in his house, I was never afraid of anyone, except myself. Nothing played out the way I planned it, though."

"What do you mean?"

"Once I got there, I froze. I walked into his office, sat down opposite him, and suddenly I was tongue-tied."

"Like your worst nightmare, when you can't scream?"

"Something like that. Time lost all meaning. He had just finished chain-smoking his third cigarette. Neither of us had spoken. That's when it dawned on me that I had the power. His eyes spoke of a fear that relaxed me, got me started talking. I left his office three hours later. I made him listen to everything I experienced, everything I felt. He just sat there and took it."

"You finally took control of your life."

"I finally felt like a man. I never had another blackout until a few months ago. Now they're back and recurrent."

"Something triggered this. I'm no doctor, but I guess that there's still something in your past that you haven't resolved. It's only by sharing that you stand any chance of figuring it out."

"But in the process, I may discover that I killed your father."

"You didn't do it. We both know you're not capable of that. I don't care what kind of trance took over. You would never hurt someone you loved. You risked your own life for Sheneitha."

"Nothing special. A brother stands up for his sister." Odell's phone vibrated.

"It's okay, Odell. Take it."

"A text from my lawyer asking me to call." He excused himself, walked into the hallway, and made the call.

"Odell, I have some urgent information that you must hear. I've been trying to reach you since Thursday afternoon."

"My phone has been off, Carrie. Sorry. I'm tending to Dee. I've been unplugged from the world for a few days. She's finally up."

"Wonderful. Does she remember anything?"

"Not much."

"I'll be brief. I have some news that you may find shocking. First, Jackson Sherman has been charged with the murder of your father-in-law."

"Jackson? That makes no sense. Jackson is a friend. I know him. He couldn't possibly be a murderer."

"Second, the firm has discovered that it was Jackson who sent the e-mail to you with the photos. Jackson was the person who had Dee and Michael followed. The story is even more bizarre. A number of the photos were doctored. The necklace which appeared to be transferred from Dee to Michael was added to the original photos. It was a complete fabrication. I spoke to Michael. The necklace was sent to his office in an envelope purportedly from Dee."

"He's told me about it. He visited the hospital."

"I've sent it out for handwriting analysis but I need something in Dee's handwriting to compare them."

"Jackson was deliberately trying to make me jealous? Why?"

"Only he knows. Jackson is now living his own personal hell, but that's not your problem. The police have confirmed to me that you are no longer being considered as a suspect in the investigation. From this point forward, you can focus all your energies on Dee's recovery. We'll talk more later."

"So the nightmare is over?"

"Let's hope so. By the way, you had mentioned your half-brother in our interview. My investigator found his name in the system. He's in the middle of serving a three-month sentence in Detroit for assaulting his girlfriend."

He stared at the smartphone, somewhat bewildered, then turned it off. Odell felt something in him finally unlock. Cass wasn't conning him. Odell wanted to believe there was nothing between Michael and Dee, but the lawyer in him could not relinquish the trace of skepticism in a corner of his heart. It was beyond time that he trusted the only two friends in his life. He headed back into the room and crawled onto the bed beside Dee.

PART IV

CHAPTER 37

Saturday morning, April 23, 2016
Nova Scotia

The flight touched down at the international airport outside Halifax a few minutes ahead of schedule, leaving Odell plenty of time to pick up the rental car and head out on a short detour along the coast of Nova Scotia. Too many bad memories in the city, best avoided. Besides, Odell never tired of visiting Peggy's Cove and its solitary lighthouse on the rocks. The red dome topped the whitewashed tower, a warning for centuries to sailors arriving from the Old World. The lighthouse was also witness to the crash of Swissair flight 111 just off the coast, which took the lives of over two hundred souls, many of them U.N. diplomats. The lighthouse could stand guard, but it could not protect.

He headed back to the main highway to complete the drive. The road was dry, and the day was remarkably warm for this time of year. The spruce trees crowded route 103 on both sides. Miles of green branches, indistinguishable one from another. Despite his best efforts, his mind began to drift. The last time he'd been in Lunenburg was the bus trip he took from Halifax with Sheneitha to celebrate her eighteenth birthday. No other family invited—no risk of ugliness. He was only eighteen months older but his responsibilities, until that night, were of a different order. He ordered the first round of beers and then the second. There were more afterward, he couldn't remember how many. Freedom Day, she called it. They both puked their guts out in the harbour that night and suffered terrible hangovers on her first full day of adulthood. No matter. It was still a proud achievement. He had gotten her to the finish line unscathed. Until Dad had finally left eight years earlier, it had been a challenge. Since then the two of them only had to deal with Mum's growing depression.

Sheneitha moved out the following week and took a job at a grocery store an hour outside the city. She earned enough to support herself over the years, until the cancer started eating her up four years ago. Odell deposited support payments in her bank account monthly. Two girlfriends managed her care: the best that could be bought in the province. Odell visited sporadically and flew in for her last two days on earth, sharing stories with her friends in the hospice. He buried her on the third day.

After that coming-of-age night in Lunenburg, he'd returned to Halifax, packed his bags, and left for his second year at McGill. The Royal Institute for the Advancement of Learning. A very fancy title for a university that went back over 150 years, back to the days when his ancestor was still a slave. There was a memorial to the founder of the university, James McGill, at the spot where his bones were interred at the centre of the campus. Odell used to spit on it when he walked by. McGill was reputed to have owned some slaves. Ironic that it represented what Odell thought was his new life of freedom from his past.

Now he knew better. He still was not free. He took the Mahone Bay exit heading toward the southern shore. The bay had become a haven for vacationers from the mainland of Canada along with the regulars who enjoyed the small-town Maritime charm. The area was a great place to vacation and an even better place to hide. Here you could be anyone you wanted to be. The car slowly rounded the west side of the bay. The sailboats were all in dry dock, and the water off the downtown shoreline, though still ice cold, was inviting. He parked just off Bluenose Drive and stepped out into the brightness reflecting off the water. He left his windbreaker in the car.

He needed to walk, to feel nineteen again, with the nightmares behind him and the promise of a new future ahead. He passed an assortment of partly finished hulls in makeshift boatyards, the imposing red shakes of the maritime museum, a bright red barn that defied the seasonal erosion caused by the salty air, and an assortment of inns and restaurants for the tourists, crammed close to one another, rising up from the harbour, all serving lobster and crab. The locals were out walking, smiling at one another, hands thrust into pockets. Just another day. Just as he remembered them over a quarter century ago. Nothing ever changed in Nova Scotia. Children grew up to become their parents. That's why he'd had to leave.

He felt a sudden hunger and walked into the Old Fish Factory on the waterfront.

The young blond server smiled broadly. "Good afternoon, sir. Here for lunch?" It sounded like she was singing. "My name's Katie. Are you one of them big-city critics?"

"Pardon me?"

"You're dressed like you come from Montreal or something. Y'know we have some great acting talent out here. Y'wouldn't really expect it up here in Lunenburg, eh?"

"What do you mean?"

"Everyone here knows the Lunenburg Players. Tonight they're putting on a production of *Othello*."

There was only one Lunenburg player he cared about. The private detective had taken less time than Odell had expected to track his quarry. Isaiah had left Halifax a few years ago. Now he lived in a cramped apartment in nearby Chester and could be found most evenings at the local playhouse. Odell decided to wait until the evening to make contact.

"They're a group of seniors who put on a Shakespeare play every year 'bout this time. They're amateurs, though they get the odd retired TV actor. This year they got one of the stars from *Corner Gas* to play Cassio. He's right funny. They're performing it this week at the town auditorium down the road in Chester. Opening night last night was a little rough but I'm sure they'll do better tonight. I can sell you a ticket if you're interested. All the retailers downtown help push tickets. It's not Stratford or anything like that, but it's all about good fun and the proceeds go to charity. Showtime is seven o'clock, that is if you wanna see it. I hope I'm not bein' too pushy."

"I'd like that, thanks. Can you bring me a ticket with a lobster roll and a Diet Coke, please," he said, handing her back the menu without opening it.

"Yes, sir." She turned and headed for the kitchen.

While he waited, Odell thought about home. Dee was glowing in motherhood. Edward was now two months old. And she was already planning the timing for the second. Since the senator's funeral, Eleanor had made regular visits and had moved into the guest room during the ninth month. She planned to stay for another couple of weeks so the timing for the trip was ideal. Odell's extended leave of absence from TGO had ended a month ago but he had decided not to return. The break had given him plenty of time to get to know himself and his bride. He had steadfastly refused the psychiatrist's open invitation to begin therapy. At least not yet. Thankfully the blackouts and trances had subsided on their own.

Maybe he was living happily ever after, especially since the police showed no further interest in him now that Jackson was in custody and awaiting trial. It was still hard to imagine that his protégé was capable of murder. Why would Jackson want to harm his wife's best friend or the senator for that matter? Maybe something else had pushed him over the edge and he just snapped. Or he'd experienced a moment of irrational rage. Odell was quite familiar with that. You never knew who was capable of what.

He hadn't visited his sister's grave since the burial. If not for Dee, he might never have returned. "I've managed my life quite well until recently. I don't need to go through my childhood again with a fine-tooth comb to satisfy someone else's curiosity. Living it once was enough," he told Dee last week for the fourth time. She was behaving like a dog with a bone. Her strength had returned and with it her resolve.

"If you're not going to a doctor, then at least reopen your relationship with your family. Maybe your mother can fill in some blanks. Go see her in Montreal."

"Last time I spoke to her she barely recognized who I was. She has her moments of lucidity but the nurses in the hospital told me she may never come back to who she once was."

"You need to go home, then. You need to visit your sister. We all need to go home at some point," she kept insisting.

He finally relented, particularly since the nightmare about the distended head, the belt, and the gurgling had become recurrent. Sharing it with Dee had not helped. Maybe there was something in Nova Scotia that was a key to resolving the problems of the past. Sheneitha had been so brave, enduring the pain of the final months of the ovarian cancer that inevitably consumed her. He needed to visit her grave. And he needed to deal with his father once again. He didn't understand why, he just knew he had to do it, though he was not yet prepared to share that with Dee. Not yet, but soon.

He began fidgeting with the stainless steel knife on the table. Through the eyes of an eight-year-old, his father was the physically imposing tyrant who ruled his life. At twenty-two Odell had finally sized up Isaiah for what he was: a weak middle-aged man, lacking in self-control. A man who'd pushed away everyone in his life and replaced it with alcohol and anger.

"Coward," he said out loud, banging the knife on the table for emphasis. Good thing the restaurant was half empty. No one turned around.

And now? Who knew what kind of senior citizen Isaiah might be? A retired salesman playing the lead in *Othello*, a role well beyond his age range.

■ ■ ■

At the other end of the restaurant a man sat sipping his coffee, reading his Globe and Mail, oblivious to everything going on around him. A theatre ticket was sitting on the table. After Moore left the restaurant, the man quickly paid the bill and headed back to his grey sedan. He slipped in behind the wheel and followed Moore at a safe distance. It was not yet time to make contact. He was waiting for instructions.

CHAPTER 38

7:00 p.m., Saturday, April 23, 2016
Lunenburg

Odell approached the Chester Playhouse. The locals obviously took great pride in the auditorium. The front was covered in marine-blue cedar shakes outlined with freshly whitewashed lines. It was elegant in its rustic simplicity. The room might have held three hundred people when completely sold out. The front of the theatre was filled but the back three rows were empty, except for the back-row seat Odell was in. The stage was simple. The playhouse group probably functioned on a shoestring budget and did not invest in elaborate sets or costumes.

He settled in to watch Isaiah perform, transformed for the evening into someone else: a man of great courage and strength and greater weakness. The mighty general. It required a whole lot of imagination on the part of the audience, but they were game and enthusiastic in a very Maritimes way. He had to admit it was not a half-bad performance. The concluding speech might have been Othello but it certainly was not his father:

> *I pray you in your letters,*
> *When you shall these unlucky deeds relate,*
> *Speak of me as I am; nothing extenuate,*
> *Nor set down aught in malice. Then you must speak of one that lov'd*
> *not wisely but too well.*

Maybe Isaiah was capable of love now, but that was not the father Odell had grown up with. Then he was a man driven by hate.

After the final curtain call, Odell waited patiently by the backstage door. Would his father even recognize him? It had been at least twenty years. When Isaiah finally strolled through the door, Odell fell into step behind him. When he turned down Pleasant Street, Odell stepped up beside him.

"Good evening, son. I be wondering if you'd ever show up."

"You recognized me?" Odell was genuinely surprised.

"I been following you since McGill. The national championship game on CBC, then nothing for years 'til your name started popping up on Google. Big-shot businessman, *GQ* most eligible bachelor list, America's top lawyer."

"You forgot to mention murder suspect." Odell did not mask the sarcasm. "I didn't come to talk to you. I don't want anything from you. There is just something you need to do tonight." Odell's tone was harsh but Isaiah didn't seem bothered. His head held high, his mouth relaxed, as if he were at peace.

They kept walking.

"Where are we to?" the older man asked.

"It's a surprise. Just a few minutes from here. We don't need to talk."

"But we should talk. I got a lot to say."

"Don't waste your breath."

"No point telling you how sorry I am. I was a shite father. Weak and right drunk most of the time. Not much to show on life's scoreboard ever since I tore up my pitching arm. I was only nineteen but it felt like my life was over. So many errors."

"Is that your excuse? Your baseball career didn't work out so you beat Mum and me to compensate?"

"For what it's worth, the past few years been peaceful. Since I left Halifax, I ditched the anger and the alcohol. Got into a twelve-step program. It's hard work, but what else I got to do in retirement. Gives me hope I might be able to apologize. Gotta tell people I'm sorry. Gotta mean it. My sponsor warned me that I'd face moments where the demon would drive me to the drink. She was right." Isaiah reached into his pocket and pulled out a coin. "My eight-month gold coin from AA. Not a drop since last August."

"Congratulations," Odell said dryly and without a trace of feeling. "I'm not interested."

They continued wordlessly for another few blocks until they had crossed into the cemetery. The mist was now cold and damp. It smelled of pine and renewal.

Odell walked with purpose, and he could hear Isaiah labouring to keep up, breathing a little more heavily. The terrain was uneven, and the day's warmth had melted the remaining snow, leaving a muddy mess. They passed an open gravesite. Just a rectangular hole in the ground, waiting for the next funeral, perhaps tomorrow.

Odell finally stopped in front of a headstone and shone his phone's flashlight on it. "Read it," Odell ordered.

"Sheneitha Moore 1974 to 2013." He staggered slightly. "I never knew. She been dead almost three years and nobody tell me?"

"She insisted," Odell said. "Sheneitha told me and Mum that she would rather have no visitors than you. She made me swear not to let you know, not when she was sick and not when she was dying. She told me I would know when it was time."

The two men stood by the grave for five minutes. Neither spoke.

"Ya mind if we go sit down?" Isaiah finally asked. There was a wooden bench a few yards back. They sat down beside one another. "She be the first woman I ever fell in love with. Back in high school."

"Mum? You had a very odd way of showing it." Odell turned his head and spat.

"You don't get it. I adored her. But she had her eyes on someone else."

"What the hell are you talking about?"

"She only had eyes for my cousin Roy. Quarterback of the football team. A year younger'n me. Remember Grampa's brudder Joseph, what died ten years ago. His kid. I was the best pitcher in the county but Roy had more talent than anyone. Tall and handsome. He could have had anyone. I never had a chance." Isaiah began massaging his elbow.

"What happened to Roy? I don't remember ever meeting him."

"Got a scholarship to Northern Colorado University then played semi-pro in the States for a few years. He never came back. At least so far as anyone knew."

"So how did she end up with you?"

"I was down in Double A having my best season ever when my elbow went. It was August 20 of '72. I'll never forget the day. I was sixteen-and-two with a 2.32 ERA and a no hitter. The Yankees were in the cellar and my coach was telling me there be a good chance I'd be a September call-up. This was my final start before the trip to the Big Show. My life dream come true. Until I heard the elbow pop. My dreams were dead. I came straight back to Halifax. That's when I saw your mother sitting at a table in Woolworths. She was a wreck. Roy had left for college just after graduation. He told her he wasn't coming back. She was heartbroken. He loved football more than your mother and she knew it."

Isaiah closed his eyes for a moment. "She never told him," he said.

Odell stiffened. He could feel his heart starting to beat. "Told him what?"

"What I knew the moment I saw her. Her cheeks were flushed, her belly ever so slightly distended. Whatever I felt for her before I left Halifax I felt ten times when I took her hand in mine for the first time at that table. Roy was gone but I could protect her."

"You're saying?"

"Yes, Odell. I'm telling you I'm not your real father. Times were different. Your mother didn't want her child growing up a bastard in Halifax. And she wasn't gonna saddle Roy with a baby and ruin his life. Black and fatherless was not a way to grow up. Black was tough enough. I took advantage and convinced her to marry me. The whole world assumed you be mine."

Odell could feel the anger building. His hands were clenched. He needed to hit something. "Why now?"

"Part of my twelve-step program. I need to make my apologies. You can't apologize 'til you understand what you done to others and how you hurt them."

Odell didn't respond. He just sat staring into the darkness. His entire life was a lie.

"We rented an apartment and I found myself a job I hated. Selling textiles. My territory was long and wide as the mainland gets, from Sydney to Yarmouth and out to Campbellton. Always on the road. But I had your mother to come home to. After baseball, the only thing in the world I ever wanted. But she never got over him. I was an idiot to think she ever would. I started drinking. Her eyes never sparked at me. Never once. Not the way they had always sparkled at your father. She be all I ever wanted but she never wanted me."

Isaiah turned to face Odell. "I'm sorry for the way I treated you. It was never your fault. It's just that Roy was there every day behind your eyes. Growing. Watching me fail. You have his eyes, you know. And his defiance."

"Not accepted. I don't care what you did to me. I built a life despite you. So she didn't love you. Is that a crime? What did she ever do to you?"

"None of your business."

"It's all my business. You beat her into submission and then you beat me."

"You called me out on that twenty years ago. You didn't deserve it. I'm trying to apologize."

Odell caught a flash of light, the same light that preceded a profound insight about to hit him. It's what separated him from his peers, allowed him to close business deals with incredible resourcefulness and imagination. "I didn't deserve it. That's what you said." He waited a moment before continuing. "You're implying Mum deserved it. What did she ever do to you?"

"I don't want to talk about it."

"If not now, then when? Out with it."

Isaiah's head dropped and he whispered. "It's not for a son to know these things."

"I'm waiting," Odell said fiercely.

"She cheated on me."

Odell felt the pressure building behind his eyes, suddenly overpowering him. He was eight years old. They had just returned from a road trip to Toronto. The Blue Jays playing the Yankees. Father and son. Best weekend ever. Then Dad started drinking again. The beating that night wasn't bad enough to keep him home from school the next day. But by lunch he was feeling sick and took off. Dad had left that morning on another road trip, so he figured Mum could write him a note tomorrow for skipping out of school. His mother was usually out cleaning houses until three-thirty, so he let himself in the back door.

He went upstairs and lay down on his bed. He fell asleep until he heard the front door open. It was Dad. He could tell by the heavy footsteps climbing the stairs. What had happened to the road trip? Odell knew this was going to be trouble. The next thing he heard was the crack of a bat and his mother screaming. What was she doing home? Odell worked up the courage to get up and cross the hall. His parents' bedroom door was slightly open, just enough that he could peek through the crack. There was blood dripping off his mother's arms onto the bed and forming a trail that snaked to the floor. His father had his back to Odell, kneeling over another man, on his stomach on the hardwood floor, choking, bleeding. His father's belt was around his neck. Odell watched, mouth agape.

"Whore. That's what you are. That's what you always been."

"No, Isaiah. Don't," she cried.

"I can never trust you," he yelled.

"Noooooooooooo," her endless moan.

"Not a word to anyone ever," he said to Mum. "Not if you want to see tomorrow. I'll take care of Roy later." Mum didn't seem to be paying attention. She was sobbing and rocking back and forth and struggling to button up her housedress. She was getting nowhere. Next thing Odell remembered was running all the way back to school.

When he got home a few hours later, his father was sitting at the kitchen table, playing with a silver coin. Flipping it in the air. Odell knew this game from school. Heads or tails. The older boys played it. If you called it wrong, you got punched in the arm. Odell may have been three or four years younger but he was their size, so they never held back. Just another bruise as far as Odell was concerned. He approached cautiously.

"Call it," his father said.

"Heads."

"Come closer, son." It wasn't a request. More of a demand, though Dad seemed to be in one of his better moods. There were only two stubbies on the table. The coin spun high in the air and landed in his father's palm. He covered the palm over his left wrist. Odell was close enough to smell his father's shampoo. He must have just showered. Dad uncovered the top hand. A woman was sitting on a rock.

"Ever seen a coin like this, Odie?" His father handed him the coin to examine. It wasn't one of those shiny silver dollars with the goose on it that one of the rich kids played with every day in school.

"It be a very special American silver dollar. My daddy gave it to me just like his daddy gave it to him. It goes all the way back to 1864 when our ancestor fought in the Union Army. You know about that."

"Yeah. I have that set of tin soldiers that Mum got me for my birthday."

"Well, there was once a real war and our ancestor, the son of Elijah the slave, fought in it. The coin be passed down from father to son ever since."

His father tapped his index finger on the coin in Odell's hand. "You see how the lady is seated on one side? It's what makes the coin special. Her name is Liberty. She's all you can trust." He put the coin in Odell's hands. "I be giving it to you one day when you become a man, though you be almost big as one already. Like my father did."

Liberty was staring off into space. Odell wondered what she was thinking. She couldn't possibly know Odell, or what it was like in school, or what it was like living in this house. Why would she care? That was supposed to be Mum's job. If he could trust only Liberty, what did that mean?

"Where's Mum?"

"Sleeping."

Suddenly Odell felt sick to his stomach. "I don't want it," he yelled. "Never." He dropped the coin on the table.

■ ■ ■

At the top of the staircase Odell caught his breath. He felt queasy and his head was starting to hurt again but he had to know for sure. He slowly approached the door to his parents' bedroom.

"Mum," he whispered.

No answer.

He pushed the door open a little more. "Mum?" Louder this time.

He pushed the door open and stepped into the room. Mum was rolled into a ball on the corner of the bed, whimpering. His heart was pounding. Where was the body? Maybe he had dreamed the whole thing? Except for the footprints on the floor leading to the bathroom. He stepped into the smaller set. They fit. He slid his stocking feet along the floor until he reached the bathroom and stood there with his hand over the handle. He tried turning it, but it wouldn't move.

He hesitated, then heard the heavy footsteps coming up the stairs. He took off to his room and ran to his closet. The safe room. The only room in the house where life made any sense. He pushed his back up against the wall and pulled his knees up to his chest. Then he opened the box. He didn't need any light to feel around for the Union general. His favourite tin soldier. He reached in and pulled out a couple of lower rank Confederate soldiers. After a minute or two his eyes adjusted. In short order the entire battlefield was set. He knew what was about to happen because he controlled the outcome. Odell felt a growing sense of calm.

The war manoeuvres continued until he felt the grumbling in his stomach. A few minutes later he smelled the frying onions. He finally ventured out of the closet and back downstairs. Mum made dinner for the four of them and sat at the table without saying a word. Her eyes were blank. He and Sheneitha knew better than to speak before Dad said it was okay. They could never be sure when he was sauced until it was too late for Odell to get out of the way of a backhander. That night there was no drama at dinner. All he remembered was the clanking of cutlery on plates. He kept his head down and ate.

He tossed and turned in bed for hours until he heard the car door open in the driveway late that night. Odell got out of bed and peeked out the window. His father was loading a large package wrapped in blankets into the back of the station wagon and closed the lid quietly. Ever so slowly the car pulled out of the driveway and headed down the street with the headlights off.

The Woodie did not ever return. The next night a maritime thunderstorm hit. The wind blew hard, like it didn't care what it destroyed, and the rain poured down in sheets. Odell opened his bedroom window to hear the storm better. A car zigged and zagged slowly in the darkness until it finally pulled into the driveway. It was too dark to make out the driver when he stepped out into the rain. He wasn't moving. Just standing in the pitch black for minutes, getting drenched, listening to the booms that followed tiny flashes in the distance. The interval between lightning bolts and thunderclaps was getting shorter. Odell felt the hair raising on his head and jumped at the explosion like a gunshot, accompanied by a flash that illuminated the world, revealing Isaiah alone, holding a shovel high in the air. A tree across the street had been split in two. "Missed me, you fool," he shouted. Then Isaiah laughed hysterically. Then he bent over and cried.

Odell could see the bolt. Feel the heat of the explosion. Smell the burning wood, as if history was repeating thirty-six years later in the cemetery. Who was the fool? Who was the cheater who avoided punishments for his sins until tonight? The exploding light behind his eyes blinded him. He could feel Isaiah's arm reach for his shoulder. Odell pulled away, stood up from the bench, and staggered. He was holding his head, massaging the sockets, the tide of his pulse roaring behind his ears. Then the blackness descended.

■ ■ ■

Dawn was beginning to break when Odell lifted his head. No pain, but where the hell was he? And then the memories came rushing back. Dad, Sheneitha, the graveyard. He was lying in the grass but he was not alone. A body lay beside him, facing away. Inert.

He pulled himself up, jolted back to life. He reached for his father's forearm and hesitated. Odell caught himself holding his breath. Another blackout—another body. His fingers slowly traced a line up his father's shoulder and up to his neck searching for a pulse. It was strong. Thank God for small mercies. He stood up and walked around the body, then kneeled in the wet grass. His father showed no signs of violence. No blood, face undistorted and his breathing was unlaboured. Peaceful. Isaiah groaned slightly then pulled himself into a sitting position.

"Not proper leaving once you passed out so I figured I'd just lie down beside you," his father said. "I didn't want you getting robbed or nothing."

Odell now knew everything he had to know, everything he needed to know about his father.

"You okay?" Odell asked.

"Yup. I got one thing left to tell you."

"Keep it." Odell stood up and brushed himself off, then turned and left the cemetery and his father. Forever.

■ ■ ■

Isaiah took a seat in the dewy grass, back propped against Sheneitha's headstone. The sun was just beginning to rise. He didn't feel alone. There was another presence. Someone or some thing who was paying attention to his thoughts. Was it the higher power, as his sponsor referred to the god who still wasn't ready to take him for all his sins? More likely his daughter's spirit hovering right behind him.

You be with me here, Sheneitha? The voice in his head. *A few months ago, I decide to go to visit Dee. I knew Odell will never want me bein' there, but maybe she would. After all, we don't know nothing about each other. Maybe she be hearing the stories from Odell but I thought she might be happy to hear that I be changed for the better, now that I be sober and all.*

If I could make the breakthrough with her, who knows? My twelve-step sponsor has been pushing me for weeks. Now that I'm sober I need to go make my apologies. Sponsor be telling me you and Odell are carrying my baggage. I gotta loosen your loads. I suppose I should be saying sorry to you too, being my real daughter and all.

It didn't take much research to figure out they live in an apartment on the Upper East Side. I plan to visit Dee in the middle of the afternoon. I figure Odell will be at work. The bus let me off at the terminal in the late morning and I wander around Time Square marking time. I stop at one of them street vendors and pick up a Yankees cap. Brings back old memories. Good ones. Days I was pitching.

I feel like an idiot wearing gloves in the heat but the doctor's yammering about staying out of the sunlight. Sensitivity caused by all the drinking. About how the melanoma be killing me. It's that or the liver that'll get me. Soon I hope. Finally at around four o'clock I take the subway. It's a five-block walk to their corner. Except I get to their corner and I'm stuck in my head. Almost an hour, I'm pacing back and forth, rehearsing my lines. At one point I decide to forget it. This be just a half-cooked idea. Like when you boil a lobster and pull it out too soon. When you crack it open all you have is white goo and I'm afraid I'm about to go stepping in it. I try calling my sponsor. Three times. No answer. There's a bar at the corner and I pace outside for I don't know how long. I finally go in. I'm just gonna have one drink, or so I tell myself but I already know how this one's gonna end.

I don't know how much time's passed but it's some time after six-thirty when I finally leave the bar. I'm lingering outside the building, wondering how I get in. Then I hear an explosion. The power goes out everywhere. The guy at the front desk waits a coupla minutes, then leaves. I walk through the lobby. Fancier than the lobby of the best hotel in the Maritimes and I seen 'em all. I'm totally out of my league. I don't even know what floor they're on. There's no phone system working, so no way to buzz to get Dee's attention. There's a table in the lobby with a pile of Wall Street Journals that haven't been picked up. One of them says "Odell J Moore." A proud name. "Penthouse 1."

I arrive at the door, winded. It be a long climb up the staircase. It's part ways open. I hear a man's voice ... very loud. Aggressive. I can't make out what he's saying. I push the door open and wait. He has this big Southern *drawl. He's all talk and he sounds angry. This isn't what I be expecting when I come up stairs. The floor's a mess. They obviously be fighting.*

"Daddy, I'm pregnant" are the last words she says.

He starts raging. He yells at her that he won't abide by a black baby in his family. He's going to do something about it. I finally step around the hallway into the living room. He pushes her hard. She collapses and I hear glass shattering. She's lying on the floor and the blood be all around her. Everywhere. I didn't know what he was going to do to her next. My own blood's beginning to boil. The words are still ringing in my ears. "Black baby." As if it's a crime to have one. I stepped up for a black baby then had one of my own. That be you, Sheneitha.

Isaiah felt the strain in his lower back, shifted his knees sideways, and rested his left palm on the ground.

The rage I've worked so hard to control. Taking over. Making me do things I thought I'd never do again. I remember picking up Dee's phone and dialling 911. I hear a noise coming from the bedroom. Interrupting me. Someone's in there. It sounds like metal hitting metal. I recognize the sounds I haven't heard since you two be kids. Maybe I just want to get caught and be done with my life. I walk to the bedroom. The noise is coming from the closet. There he is sitting on the floor. Your brother. We're frozen in a time warp, reliving the nightmare. He thought I never knew where he was when he slipped into his closet to conduct the Civil War games. I always knew where he was.

This time I know what's going to happen. If I run, everyone gonna think it was him. I pull him up on his feet. He's in another world. Holding his head and covering his eyes. Then he sees the bodies. Wants to help clean up the mess. He's not behaving normal. I have to drag him out the door, put him on the elevator and I head for the staircase. I'm not thinking too straight but I just hope he walks out the front door like nothing's happened. As far as he's concerned, nothing has happened.

Isaiah stood up then bent over, dusting the grass off his pants. He felt a sudden searing pain across his back and a throbbing. The scars acting up once again. It didn't happen often, but this morning was particularly bad. He thought of his own father and the beatings. He breathed deeply as he had been taught and let the pain flow outwards. Leaving him to feel a serenity. The serenity that came from forgiveness. The serenity that came from finally doing the right things when you had to. His sponsor kept reminding him: it didn't matter how long it took as long as you finally acknowledged the higher power and took responsibility. Isaiah knew that time had arrived. He would take the responsibility. All of it. He owed it to himself. He owed it to Odell.

"It's closing night," he reminds the passing Maritime breeze. "Othello will smother Desdemona. Director keeps telling me 'Othello, do it like you mean it. Breathe the tragedy.' As if I need a lesson in life tragedy. The audience should hate me at the end. Yet they walk away each night feeling terrible for the two of us. Othello is the monster and the audience is always prepared to make some allowances for him. Maybe that be the greatest tragedy."

Isaiah left the cemetery and headed down to the harbour. The dark morning clouds were separating, allowing the sun to shine through the morning mist. A double rainbow had settled in against the black background. The higher power really was watching out this morning. The merchants were not yet out, and the storefronts would not be open for a couple of hours. He reached down to his waist to unbuckle the wide leather belt that he had been attached to for many years. Isaiah remembered discussions from a Bible class about how the ancient Jews used to perform a ceremony of throwing their sins into the water as an annual cleansing ritual. He stood and watched the weight of the metal buckle sink the leather belt. Gone forever. That wasn't enough for the ancient Jews. Beyond the cleansing they were obliged to perform acts of kindness to others.

Had there been a time when he loved his wife and his children, when he had been kind to them? He couldn't remember. There was so much he couldn't remember. So many memories he fabricated in order to make sense of his life. And then there was Roy. The final lie he carried—what to do about that? Odell didn't want to hear it this morning. Would going to jail for what was left of his pathetic life be an act of kindness to Odell?

The first step was to publicly confess. "Dear Lord, I atone. I am truly sorry," he said.

"For certain sins there can be no atonement." The voice came from behind. A man had approached and a couple followed behind him.

"You talking to me?"

"Isaiah Moore?"

"Yeah."

"I am Detective Crosby with the Halifax Police Department. The people with me are detectives from New York. We would like to bring you in to the station for questioning in connection with a murder that took place in New York last year."

"I be expecting you for months. Did my daughter-in-law finally figure it out? She saw me you know. Just before he grabbed her. Then he pushed her." Isaiah stopped for a moment. He could feel his heart beating faster, the words about to shoot out of his mouth. "He got what he deserved. I got no regrets."

"Are you confessing?" Crosby asked. "You know you have a right to counsel."

"Don't we have to formally Mirandize him?" Mac asked.

"We're in Canada. No disrespect, but our courts are more interested in substance than form."

"Yeah, but this has to stick in a U.S. court," Rachel said.

"I don't need no counsel. I just need to confess. I smashed him on the head and I strangled him with my belt. I'm going to hell anyway, just a question of how quickly I get there," Isaiah said. Best he make that journey on his own. "There's something else I need to talk to you about as well. An old missing person case."

Crosby put on the cuffs and loaded him into the rear of the police car. Mac and Rachel climbed back into a black Hyundai for the drive back to Halifax. Rachel drove for a couple of minutes then pulled off the road headed for a drive-through counter.

"See the big red sign?"

"You mean Tim Hortons?" Mac asked. "What about it?"

"Janet's brother is from Regina. He tells me that all Canadian cops live on Tim Hortons double doubles and chocolate glaze doughnuts. We've got to try them."

As they pulled away, Mac flipped back the brown plastic lid and took a sip. "So this is Canadian coffee?"

"Another mystery settled. Can you flip back my lid as well?"

Mac took a nibble of the chocolate glaze. "Not nearly as good as Ginnie's cupcake. By the way, great piece of detective work, partner."

"It was just sitting there for us in the file. The DNA analysis of the hair samples in the carpet. Almost all were matches to Moore. One hair had a three per cent correlation. Completely missed that at the first go-round. And then I was sitting with Kailey. Janet was brushing her hair and the light bulb went on.

"Something had been bothering me for months. Something I couldn't let go of. Three per cent had to mean something, but I didn't know what. Way higher than statistically random DNA, but not enough to be a brother or parent. I started doing some research. Turns out a three per cent match could come from a second cousin. Not very helpful. In a courtroom we could never convict anyone on that. But it also suggested we should be doing some research on other family relatives."

"So that explains all the Moore family research you were doing."

"It was complicated and I needed the feds' help. I found the obit on the sister, which referred to her parents. Moore's sister was dead, his half-brother was in jail, and his half-sister is married with three kids and living in Florida. That left the father or any assortment of cousins. The father would have been too close a DNA match so at first I was certain it couldn't be him."

"But you had him checked anyway."

"Wouldn't you if you were me?"

"I don't get it."

"Based on my own situation, Mac. If I was a man instead of a woman, the entire world would just assume that Kailey was my biological child. That was nagging in the back of my brain."

"Incredible." Mac took a bite of the doughnut. "Okay, I have to admit there is something to the legend of the coffee and doughnuts up here."

"Shut up and eat while I talk. Homeland Security was asked by our pals at the FBI to make a list of every Moore crossing any of our borders around the time of the murder. A little overzealous if you ask me, but it's what they do for a living. The list compiled by Immigration had thousands of names. But it was airports only. Worthless. I asked for something more comprehensive that only arrived a few days ago. On my second read-through I caught an Isaiah Moore crossing the border on a bus in and out of Plattsburgh, New York, in the two days around the murder."

"But Plattsburgh's gotta be what? At least six hours from the city?"

"Not much to go on, I admit. But what's a guy from Nova Scotia named Moore doing crossing the border on a Greyhound in Upstate New York? It was just a little too coincidental."

"Only if you're fixated on following a lead where the DNA evidence is telling you not to bother."

Rachel took a swig of the coffee and placed it back in the cup holder. "The final link in the chain was Isaiah's minor league statistics. He was a left-handed pitcher. I found an article on his arm injury. Same one that Tommy John had, but five years earlier. They still had not discovered the surgical cure. Still, it was all circumstantial and not enough to get a warrant for a DNA sampling from Isaiah. All we could do was go and talk to him. Thank goodness for your role in this, Mac."

Mac took the napkin and dabbed at his mouth. "Yeah, the tail on Odell was not a bad idea. I ordered it months ago, once he left the hospital. Sherman *might* have killed the senator, but I couldn't shake the feeling that Moore had done it and then hid the belt somewhere."

"The passionate killers want the souvenirs."

"I figured at some point he'd go and retrieve it but the trip to Halifax threw me for a loop. Lieutenant has a pal in the RCMP who made arrangements with the locals to keep an eye on him since he landed in Halifax."

"Not much to go on."

"Even less to get an approval from the department to fly us up here. I told Lieutenant I had a hunch. He already knew how uncertain you felt about Sherman as the perp."

Rachel glanced over at Mac. "So who's the one playing hunches and relying on intuition?"

"Just following the suspects to the evidence. Crosby's been following Moore since he landed."

"I'm sure he never expected to be spending the night staking out a cemetery."

"I asked the locals to hold back until we arrived. Our timing was spot on. I wonder what they discussed at the graveyard."

"Probably ghosts." Rachel laughed.

CHAPTER 39

Noon, Friday, August 25, 2017
Westchester County, New York

The silver Lexus coasted through downtown Ossining. Small-town America, overshadowed by one of its most famous prisons. Odell was riding shotgun. Michael had one hand on the steering wheel and another clenching his morning venti. He had flown in last night and his body clock was still on L.A. time.

They had been catching up on gossip, arguing about whether the Angels or Yankees were going to get to the World Series, and generally avoiding the reason for the road trip. Michael pulled into the parking lot at the rear of the hospital.

Odell reached into his pocket and pulled out a coin. "Before I get out of the car, I want to show you this. My father tried to give this to me when I was eight. He told me it was a family heirloom. Notice how Liberty is sitting? It's a Civil War era collectors' piece. He showed me the coin a few hours after he'd strangled my biological father. Told me I could never trust a woman. I suppressed the memory."

"Holy crap. So the man you thought was your father was really your stepfather."

"Technically my second cousin. I found out when I travelled to Nova Scotia to visit my sister's gravesite. Dee had insisted there was something in my past that was a key to unlocking whatever I'd been hiding from myself. But she had no idea that I was going to see my father."

Michael could not hold back his exasperation. "You thick-headed—"

Odell raised his hand and interrupted. "You don't have to tell me. I've learned a lesson about trusting my friends."

"That's why I flew in today."

"Let me finish, Cass. Neither of us could have imagined what Isaiah confessed to. Or the memories that flooded back. I felt like I was drowning. I returned home from Nova Scotia a complete wreck, feeling worse than before I left. For a week I would not get out of bed. That was when Dee insisted I go for help."

"You, who would never ask for the team doctor regardless of how badly you'd been beaten up?"

"You have no idea what a bully Dee can be." Odell smiled. "The therapist convinced me to share with Dee. To become her friend. We talked about my fears as a new father, my concern that the cycle of abuse would continue. Once I began to trust Dee, I began to see the differences in myself. The amnesia has never returned."

"So what triggered the amnesia in the first place? You were a very scary dude in Montreal all those years ago."

"Jackson Sherman's mother."

"Jackson Sherman? You're invoking the name of evil incarnate. And the demon who spawned him." Michael held up two fingers in the form of the cross. Then he laughed. "Did Sherman's mother come to New York and shake a voodoo doll at you?"

"Jackson's mother insisted on making me a gift. She must have thought she'd be currying favour to get me to support him for partnership. It was the same coin—1860. There she was, Liberty, just sitting there staring off into space. I started zoning out that day. It took a long time for us to figure that one out."

"Us?"

"Dr. Norman and me."

"So why the need to return? A final goodbye to the old man?"

"If it was up to me alone, I'd be done with him forever. But I still get that recurring dream of a strangled head. The doc thinks it's worth exploring with Isaiah."

"So that's why we're here at Sing Sing. But why the hospital wing?" Michael pulled the car into the lot at the rear of the hospital.

"They transferred him a while ago. His cancer is well advanced."

"You've come to solve one final mystery."

"I really appreciate your keeping me company for this one. I couldn't do it myself."

"Good luck, General."

■ ■ ■

Odell stood outside the doorway of the hospital room and took a deep breath. The heavy wooden door was closed and he reached for the door handle. It was frigid to the touch and he could feel the sweat of his palm cooling instantly against the metal. He slowly pushed it open. The curtains were drawn around the bed. The same hospital blue that had been around Dee's bed when Edward was born. Despite the joy in those first moments with Dee and the baby, nothing could erase the dread from those earlier days of vigil waiting for Dee to recover consciousness after the accident. Every time the doctors closed the curtains to examine her, he wondered when they were going to confess to the brain damage she must have suffered. A year later, she was behaving quite normally, though she still experienced the odd bout of dyslexia.

Isaiah lay on a bed in the far corner, hooked up to an IV and monitoring machine. His eyes were half open, rounder and fuller against his sagging cheeks, and he lay there shivering. There wasn't much of him left.

"A special visitor? Or am I already dead and the Maker wants me to make my apologies?" he said weakly. "Never expecting you again."

Odell bent over the foot of the bed and opened the blanket, spreading it across Isaiah's spindly legs. "Never planned to be here."

"It was the only way out of Sing Sing for me. I cheated a life sentence by dying quickly. Doctor says I maybe got a few days left. Cancer's just about finished dining on me. Not that they treated me bad inside. When you're old and sick they pretty much leave you alone, even in maximum." A trail of spittle dripped down his unshaved chin. Odell grabbed a tissue and dabbed at it gently. "My throat be really dry. Can you pass me the ice chips."

Odell reached for the plastic cup and passed it to Isaiah. "They feeding you okay?"

"They stopped a couple of weeks ago. No need to eat or drink. Body just shutting down. Could be like this for another three weeks. Or I could be gone tomorrow. All the same to me. What you doing here? Get to the point, boy, or you might miss your chance." Isaiah was probably right. There wasn't much left of him or his life force.

"I've been talking to a therapist for the past year. It's been helping."

"You sure don't want to turn out like me. Not with a kid."

"I'm still having nightmares. About the gurgling head. The man who's choking. The face is never clear. The doctor's advice was to come talk to you. You might know something that could help."

Isaiah's eyes closed. His breathing became more laboured. Maybe this was the end. Then his eyes opened. He sat up in the bed.

"I don't think you want to hear what I have to say." Isaiah's eyes had a new focus. He stroked his chin with his left hand. His energy had mysteriously reappeared. His voice had a sudden power. Strong, forceful. Almost desperate.

"I didn't come all the way out here to chicken out," Odell said. "Just spill it."

"It's about your biological father. My cousin."

"I already know that story. I saw you kill him. I'll never forgive you but I've learned in therapy to live with it."

"What happens and what we remember ain't always the same, Odell." Where was Isaiah going with this? How was he suddenly filled with this life wisdom? "You have one final chance to walk away. You didn't need to come today and you don't need to stay."

"I'm not weak like you were. Just spit it out and I will deal with it."

Isaiah drew a deep breath. "You walked into the bedroom after I knocked out Roy. Your real father. Smacked him pretty good in the back of the head. I was a pretty good hitter in my day. Your mother was shrieking. Begging for mercy. In my drunken rage I had my belt out and slipped it round his neck. He was beaten bad, but he wasn't dead. I had half a mind to kill him right there and be done with it. Then I see you standing in the doorway."

"Liar. You never saw me. You had your back to me. You just choked him until there was nothing left of him. I heard him choking to death." Odell's left hand was holding the bed frame, slowly squeezing it.

"That's what you remember, son, but that's not what happened. You don't want to know what happened."

"Go on. Then what?" Odell's grip tightened.

"You were never one to back away from me. From anyone. You asked your mother if she was okay. She didn't answer. I told you the man had tried to hurt her. He was a threat. We needed to eliminate the threat."

"First eliminate the threat, you said," Odell murmured.

"That I had to hit him to save your mother. You walked over."

"No!" Odell yelled. "I left the room." Odell jammed his eyes closed. He could hear the screech of the bed frame moving along the floor. His left arm was straining against the pressure.

"You walked over," Isaiah said. "You said…"

"'I need to protect Mum. Eliminate the threat.' You asked me to grab the belt and help you pull him away from the bed." Away from where he might still be able to hurt Mum if he woke up. "You took his legs and I took the belt and pulled." Odell could hear the choking, the tears, the screech of metal on linoleum. The pain in his arms and back hauling the body that was suddenly thrashing on the floor. He felt the pain in his arm. Past and present had merged. He had to pull harder to get him to the bathroom, then drop the body in the tub. "God have mercy on my soul." Odell began to sob, falling to his knees on the floor.

"You were just a child, son."

■ ■ ■

Odell had no idea how much time had passed when he felt a hand on his shoulder.

"Are you all right, sir?" the resident asked.

"I must have fainted. I'm fine." Odell slowly pulled himself to his feet. The resident was closing Isaiah's eyelids, turning off the monitor. "I'm sorry for your loss," she said.

"But just a few minutes ago he was perfectly fine. Lucid. Awake."

"We call it an end of life rally. Just before death the terminal patient experiences a final boost of energy and a euphoria. I'm glad you had the opportunity to spend time with him in that final light. Your father?"

Odell stood quietly for a couple of moments, then turned and left.

■ ■ ■

Michael watched Odell shuffling across the lot before Odell spotted the car, which Michael had been directed to park at the far end of the lot. His friend's gait was uncertain. Not the Odell who had walked in over an hour ago. His demeanour was that of an aged man, slouched, slow pace. A man going nowhere slowly. Odell slid in the passenger door. Collapsed on the seat as if he could no longer bear his own weight.

"Your face is one more reason why I am never going to visit the inside of a prison hospital. Or prison for that matter," Michael said. "You're pale as a ghost."

"He's dead."

"Isaiah?"

"I knew the cancer was advanced, but I had no idea he was in the hospice wing. I can't believe it's bothering me."

"Love him or hate him, he was the man who stood in for your father for all those years. I still remember a few stories you told about how he took you to ball games. Family is complicated. So are the feelings around them."

"You sound like Dr. Norman."

"Call me Dr. Cass." Michael smiled and reached his long arm around Odell's shoulder and gave it a squeeze. Odell seemed to appreciate the gesture. He smiled weakly.

"Did you get there in time to say goodbye?"

"You know that's not why I went. Thanks for doing this, though. I could not have endured this on my own and it wasn't something I wanted to put Dee through."

"Sometimes you just need a friend to share the good and the bad." That's why Michael had flown across the continent. A chance to be there for someone other than his daughter. A chance to continue rekindling an old friendship. But death? He was not prepared for that. What was the right thing to say right now? Maybe nothing.

"Good to have a..." Odell stopped dead in the middle of the sentence and began to cry. "What have I done, Cass? What have I done?" The tears were streaming down his cheeks. Michael withdrew his arm and turned in the driver seat to face Odell.

"Look at me, Odell." There was an edge of panic in Michael's voice. He was way out of his depth. This was nothing like Liz crying over being dumped and him having little idea how to pick up the pieces. Or maybe it was just like that in terms of the unexpected intensity of feelings. For a brief moment Michael wished he had a Dr. Norman in his life.

Odell was not responsive. He continued to sob. Michel swallowed hard. Then reached out toward Odell's chin. Just like he had with Liz. Like a caring father. Odell put up no resistance as he turned to face Michael. "What happened in there, Odell?"

"I killed a man, Cass. My father. When I was eight. How do I go on living with that?"

Whoa boy. Michael thought it. He thought it really loud, but fought to keep his mouth shut. Be a man Cass, he thought. Be a friend before being a lawyer. He sat for a moment trying not to think about the admission he'd just witnessed. The truth of it had to be overwhelming. Damning. He had to rise above the fear for his friend. He had to be a friend first. "There has to be a story to it that you need to tell me. Then Dee. Then your doctor. Then you have to keep on living. You have a wife and a child counting on you."

Odell reached out and rested his hand atop Michael's on the stick shift. "I do, don't I? And I have a great friend."

CHAPTER 40

August 2018
Berkshires

Michael Cassidy pressed the gas on the convertible, feeling the contours of the bending road beneath him. The sun warmed his back on an early Friday afternoon. At this time of year you really couldn't tell the difference in weather between the east and west coasts, but he did note the oppressive humidity in Hartford when he picked up his rental car. Just after pushing the ignition button, he ignored the Mercedes Drive-Genie, who offered to autopilot his vehicle from the airport to the destination. He still preferred manipulating a shift stick on the manual transmission, enjoying the acceleration as the car cornered the curves. Up in the Berkshires, an hour outside the city, there was little trace of anything urban, and the air was clear and dry. He pulled up the driveway to the summer getaway.

The boy was running around on the sprawling front lawn, kicking a soccer ball with Odell. There was a lot of yelling over the roar of the motor before it came to a halt. He hopped out of the car and jogged up to the front porch, where Dee was sipping an orange juice. Her mother was rocking slowly on the swinging couch beside a very attractive brunette, about Dee's age. The instincts kicked in as Michael took note. Sturdy, sexy, and hopefully smart. If so, he knew exactly what this all meant. Michael ran up the steps to give Dee a big hug. She was big as a house.

"Oh my stars," Michael exclaimed. "You're doing it again? Don't you two ever take a break?"

342

"You know as well as anyone, Michael. He promised me four and I've been holding him to it. The fertility drugs work better than any amulet. I'm only about five months, and when these little devils come out I'm done," she said rubbing her belly in circles. The staff at New York Presbyterian are getting sick of me with all these pregnancy checkups. They put me in a study for women carrying triplets."

"I beg to differ," Eleanor cut in from her seat on the swing. "The last few encounters have been considerably better than the first time you were in there."

"Let's not talk about that, Momma. Another lifetime."

"We need to keep talking about that, Dee, if only to remember how fortunate we all are."

Odell walked over and gave Michael a big bear hug. The toddler pulled on Michael's pant leg, raising his arms.

"Edward, mind your manners," Odell said sternly, then broke into a big smile. Michael picked Edward up and threw him in the air. The child giggled wildly.

"Endless energy," Odell sighed, "but growing up very nicely. I hear you're becoming the new kingmaker in Hollywood."

"A slight overstatement. It took me a couple of years to adjust after Wild Bill's stroke forced him to transfer all his clients to me. At first they were a little slow to come around, but the last six months have been dynamite. I'm getting all kinds of coverage in *Variety*. The journalists love my shtick."

"Now there's a very Hollywood term," Odell said. "But I don't notice any Texas drawl."

"The big Texan was Wild Bill's persona. Now they all go crazy for my beach bum act. Particularly after I've negotiated a lucrative deal. Bill taught me well."

Michael walked over to a small wooden table and poured himself a lemonade. "So you saw the light and got out of law!"

"For now, I'm just doing a little business consulting to some young tech entrepreneurs. The city is crawling with them."

"Who's the cutie sitting with Dee's mother?"

"What took you so long to ask?"

Dee came over and put her arm around Michael. "There's someone I want to introduce to you." She directed him toward the hanging swing.

"Hello, Mrs. Brabant. There's no question in my mind—you're becoming younger." Michael bent over and gave Eleanor a quick kiss on the cheek. His blue sports jacket was buttoned at the waist, and the grey T-shirt underneath clung to him, showing off his physique. A good choice for meeting a new prospect.

"Michael, you are truly wicked," Eleanor said with a slight grin. "But keep talking like that."

He turned to the brunette with a smile and began a closer appraisal. Dee broke the ice. "Michael, this is Juliana, one of my sorority sisters from Alabama. Juliana lives in Santa Monica. And she surfs! I thought you two should meet."

Juliana smiled, extending her hand to Michael.

Michael held on to it. Warm, soft and inviting, yet confident. This might turn out to be a very good weekend. He wasn't letting go of the hand so quickly and she wasn't resisting. Good start. "Do you all mind if the two of us take a tour of the lake?"

Juliana rose, with just a trace of a smile and walked down the staircase beside Michael.

"See ya," he yelled, raising the back of his arm with a wave. They walked the trail heading toward the lake.

Dee filled the vacated spot beside Eleanor on the swinging couch and put her arm around her.

"How are you doing today, Momma?"

"It's been three years. Some nights I still feel Edward's presence so strongly. He's with us watching and smiling. Oh, I know he had some issues with your marriage but I'm certain that over time he would have mellowed into being a grandpa. I know he wanted that more than anything."

"Odell still feels bad that he never got the chance to reconcile with Daddy," Dee said.

"He lived a life of devoted public service. Some people insisted on digging into his past in attempts to discredit his record but I only have to think back to his funeral and the words President Obama had to say about him and I'm comforted that my grandchildren are inheriting a legacy they can be proud of."

Late in the afternoon, Michael and Juliana returned holding hands. After Edward was put to bed, they all gathered together for dinner around the antique table in the kitchen.

Michael stood and raised his wineglass. "I'd like to take a moment and toast Jackson Sherman."

"Are you nuts, Michael?" Odell said. "He tried to ruin us."

Dee said, "True, but if you think about it, Odell, he's a major reason why our marriage has become so strong."

"Let me continue," Michael said. "Once he was indicted, and charged with the murder of the senator, the firm was mired in the muck of the investigation, and morale among the associates was slipping. TGO was on the front page of the newspapers for months and it was never good news. The partners were panicking about being raided by other firms. Wild Bill leaned in."

"They made Michael a partner immediately," Odell said, aiming the comment in Juliana's direction. "A few partners called me for a reference while I was on leave." Odell was smiling. Then his smile quickly disappeared. "Jackson really let me down. I trusted him completely. He was a brilliant lawyer but his ambition caused him to lose his judgment. What was he trying to accomplish? Stealing, invading our privacy, doctoring photos, tricking me into believing terrible things about you both."

"We weren't really friends, though, were we, Odell?" Michael said. "The crisis he inflicted on us brought us together, made us closer, forced us to be honest with one another."

"But not 'til I almost killed you in the waiting room."

"You what?" Dee said.

"Did I forget to tell you that story, Dee? I wasn't thinking straight," Odell replied.

"You weren't thinking at all," Eleanor said.

"I was poisoned by jealousy. I felt like a failure as a husband."

"But it all worked out for us," Dee said. "We're here together, aren't we?"

"Agreed, but the happy ending almost eluded us," Odell said. "I was such an idiot. I still can't believe how consumed I was by what Jackson was feeding me. That's a chapter of my life I'm not very proud to think about."

"Whatever happened to Jackson?" Eleanor asked.

"All I know is that he was released from jail when they arrested Odell's father," Michael said. "He'd been in the slammer for almost nine months. Even though he was innocent. No one at the firm seemed to care about that detail. He was toast at the firm and he knew it. They tell me they packed up his boxes a few days later and no one has any idea what became of him."

"I'm back in touch with Emily," Dee said. "She's married to a dentist in Buffalo. Two kids. Rumour has it Jackson's working for his cousin Earl in Louisiana. Nothing could have made Emily happier."

"I gave back the amulet to you over a year ago," Michael said. "Has it disappeared again?" All eyes at the table now focused on Dee's bare neckline.

Dee didn't hesitate for a moment. "News flash," she began. "Dee has returned the amulet to a resting spot in our safe deposit box. It has more than proved its potency for fertility.

"With a little help from modern science," Odell added. Everyone laughed.

"After the ultrasound, I told Odell I didn't want it anywhere near me anymore. I've done my share to propagate the Moore line. The amulet is now waiting for the first daughter-in-law of the next generation. A new family tradition."

■ ■ ■

After the last dish had been washed and put away in the cupboard, Odell was alone in the kitchen and turned out the lights. The guests had all gone upstairs to bed and Dee was probably waiting up for him. One final check of the lock on the back door then up to bed. A persistent scratching caught his attention. Three adult male coyotes were digging along the edge of the forest at the back of his yard. Probably out hunting for their families. He opened the back door, stepped onto the lawn, and clapped his hands. The animals picked up their heads suspiciously and slunk back into the forest.

There might be an overnight frost descending. The cold felt good. Painfully good. The moon was full in the sky and Polaris was shimmering. It was a night to celebrate life and to give thanks for the blessings he could finally appreciate. He was a father and a husband, feeling he had the chance to succeed at both. Ironic that one father had to die and a second had to pay the price, for him to find his peace.

Odell walked over to a spot, just off the back end of the property. The moon reflected brightly off something that the coyotes had left behind. He saw the remnants of a green garbage bag and reached down to retrieve the chewed-up metal and the remaining shreds of a cardboard box that he'd finally put out with the trash the other day. Perhaps he and Edward could come out here in the morning and give what was left of the tin soldiers a proper military funeral.

■ ■ ■

"October is such perfect time to visit Montreal." Dee practically sang the words toward the end of the seven-hour drive that took them through the Adirondacks. The multi-colour patchwork of leaves left her breathless.

"Look, Edward," she said to the four-year-old with the blond curls in the car seat immediately behind her. "Aren't the leaves just beautiful?"

"Yes, Momma, when're we gonna be there?"

"Just a couple more hours until we see Grammy Marisol." One of the triplets cooed from the car seat beside Edward's facing the back and the other two were facing backwards in their seats on the rear bench of the rented SUV. Behind them the rear of the car was filled to capacity with two double strollers, two portable playpens, a bag jammed with diapers, formula bottles, changing pads, wet-wipes, stuffed animals, and two large suitcases. "Good thing we're only going for the weekend," Odell joked.

Dee reached over and caressed Odell's hand that was resting on the stick shift. "You think your mother will recognize us?"

Odell smiled. "If we're lucky it will be a good day. The nurse at the home said it's better to see her first thing in the morning, so we'll check into the hotel when we arrive and visit tomorrow. Tonight we'll take the kids to the Old Port. Edward can run around and stretch and we can enjoy the ambiance."

"Yeah, a romantic night. Just me, you, a toddler, and three screaming babies." Dee laughed. "I love you," she whispered.

"Louder please."

■ ■ ■

The next morning the army of Moores piled into the visiting area on the main floor of the nursing home. It was much as Odell remembered it from his previous trip. A seven-storey modern redbrick exterior. The interior hallway had an artificial fireplace, with an electric fire cycling fake flame, four lily-white chairs facing it, and an open reception with two Filipino nurses stationed behind a desk in starched white uniforms. After signing in, the family made their way to the guest visiting room at the back of the hallway.

Marisol was sitting in a rocking chair with the largest smile imaginable painted on her face. This time she was dressed like Grammy. A long green pleated dress ran to her ankles and she wore a green and red plaid blouse. Her white hair was pinned in a bun and piled on her head. Someone must have helped with the makeup, which was light and effective. Her cheeks were lightly rouged to match the subtle lipstick.

"Can I touch your hair," Edward shouted out after she had given him a smacking kiss on the cheek.

"I have a gift for you, Edward," she said, reaching into her pocket and pulling out an oval wrapped in cheap painted tinfoil.

"A Kinder Surprise," he squealed. Edward stopped and looked up at Dee.

"Yes, you may go eat it now," she said softly. He ran to the table in the corner and wasted not a moment. The triplets were all asleep in the strollers.

"Thank you, children for making the trip," Marisol began. "I know it can't be easy moving all these troops, but I just had to meet the little darlings, before…"

"Now Mum," Odell interrupted. "I'm sure there's time for plenty of visits. You're still a young woman."

"Let's not kid ourselves, Odell. You don't think I'm unaware of how little time I have left before my memory turns off completely. If I get a half hour today, it's a good day. And I can't even begin to imagine how much this place is costing you."

Odell shushed her.

"Before I forget, there's a reason I needed to see you." Marisol reached for her necklace and pulled it over her head. The black polished stone with the carved rounded face of a woman twisted slowly back and forth. "This is the family amulet for Dee. I promised it to her and it's way overdue."

"Finally the real thing," Odell said. His voice rang with pride.

Dee stepped forward and slipped the necklace over her head. Then she gave Marisol a hug. "Momma Marisol, I understand what this means to the family and one of these children will be entrusted to pass it on. We're so thrilled to be able to have the grandbabies know you as much as they can. It's so important to me."

"Dee's the one who insisted we drive up here," Odell said.

"May I see one of the triplets?" Marisol asked. Her voice was tentative, as if she worried that Dee might say no. Dee walked over to one of the strollers and, with motherly attention, removed the sleeping infant. He protested ever so slightly and then put his mocha thumb in his mouth. She leaned over Marisol with the baby and placed him in her lap. "This one came out of me first," she said.

Odell stepped forward to stand beside his wife. He interlinked his arm with hers. "Mum," he announced, "his name is—" He felt the hard pinch on his arm before Dee could interrupt. "You call him Roy," Dee said gently, casting a glance over to Odell, that suggested he better keep his mouth shut.

"May I hold him?" Marisol asked. Her voice shook ever so slightly.

"Of course," Dee said, leaving her hand under the baby's head while Marisol lifted him, nestling his tiny head against her neck. She turned her head and breathed in the scent.

"He smells of coconut," she said with a laugh.

"I rub a little oil on their heads every night to keep the little ones soft," Dee said.

Marisol did not take her eyes off the baby. Her hand tenderly rubbed his back. "My precious. I love you, Roy," Marisol said. "I never stopped loving you." Her head tilted until her lips rested on the top of the baby's forehead. He fussed for a moment, then settled into Marisol's breast. "He's here with us you know," she whispered.

"He's here with us, Mum," Odell whispered. Marisol closed her eyes and rocked.

ACKNOWLEDGEMENTS

Thanks go to the following:

To Adam Lepofsky, whose inspiring life story has provided a framework on which I have constructed Odell's motivations and his success despite his life challenges.

To the people who were there with words of encouragement from the beginning of this journey: my wonderful friend Jeff Rayman, who served as first and ongoing reader of the manuscript from its days of inception, and who made a number of provocative suggestions along the way; Shelly Theriault, for her unflagging support; the late John Carter, who read the earliest draft and provided criticism when it was necessary; to my dog park friends, Earl, Rita, Mayor John, Dr. Jane, Martin, Rob, Joe, and Gordon, who patiently listened to me blather on about plot twists for the first couple of years—all before seven a.m.; Nessa Cooper, who also slogged through an early draft, encouraging me to continue, at a time when encouragement was more important to me than honesty. To her husband, film producer Robert Cooper, for the lessons concerning the importance of the "big reveal."

To Dr. Norman Straker, MD, DLFAPA, for his psychiatric insights. To Dr. Idara Edem, MD, MSc FRCSC, for sharing her considerable expertise in head trauma. Any errors in the medical descriptions in the text are strictly my own.

To my editor Jennifer Glossop, who was unrelenting with timeline and story line issues, who helped to turn me from a writer to a fiction author, who was continually there to point me in the right direction with the probing questions about my characters. To Marie Lynn Hammond, editor of *Breakdown*, who gave me sage advice to begin my journey as a fiction author. Little did I know how little I knew.

To Brian Burke for some timely anecdotes.

To the authors who unknowingly helped show me the way: Canadians Louise Penny and Linwood Barclay, as well as Ruth Ware and Paula Hawkins. Hopefully one day I will possess enough ability to pay it forward.

To my friend, mentor, and talented mystery author Robert Rotenberg, who provided the necessary moral support as well as some valuable direction to a struggling neophyte. To author Howard Shrier, for our discussions about the theory of writing and for teaching me how to fire a gun. It all began when I told him I preferred to murder lawyers than to work with them for a living.

To the team at Barlow Books, and in particular to Sarah Scott and Tracy Bordian, for all their faith in the project and assistance in getting this to market, and to Wendy Thomas for her useful and pointed suggestions. Wendy has been of great assistance in fleshing out the characters.

To my agent, Michael Levine, for talking up this novel with anyone in the city of Toronto who would listen, and with everyone else he encountered along the way. To my mother, Frances Bacal, who found an early draft of the first few chapters captivating, even when it was not.

To the ghost of William Shakespeare. I felt quite comforted to learn that the material for *Othello* was stolen from other previous works. It made me feel less guilty about what I've done here and will continue to do. My stories attempt to honour his legacy.

Finally and most important to my wife, Sharon, who insisted that I had a work of fiction in me and encouraged me every step of the way. Sharon pointed me in the direction of the Bard and picked me up in those moments of self-doubt, convinced this endeavour would be a success. She directed me with the artist's eye, along with continual reminders that the process is far more important than the result. That the joy of creating art is its own reward.